D0597054

13-4
16-1

JUSTICE

KAREN ROBARDS

JUSTICE

**Doubleday Large Print
Home Library Edition**

GALLERY BOOKS
New York • London • Toronto • Sydney

G

Gallery Books
A Division of Simon & Schuster, Inc.
1230 Avenue of the Americas
New York, NY 10020

For information address Gallery Books Subsidiary
Rights Department, 1230 Avenue of the Americas,
New York, NY 10020.

GALLERY BOOKS and colophon are trademarks of
Simon & Schuster, Inc.

Manufactured in the United States of America

ISBN 978-1-61129-814-7

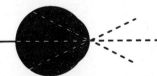

**This Large Print Book carries the
Seal of Approval of N.A.V.H.**

In memory of my beloved father,
Dr. Walter L. Johnson,
who passed away February 23, 2010

JUSTICE

CHAPTER ONE

"Will you marry me?"

Allison Howard's eyes widened. Her lips parted in surprise as she watched the tall, handsome, rich, kind, charming, absolutely wonderful man who'd spent the last week totally sweeping her off her feet drop down to one knee in front of her on the boat-house path. He held her hand and looked up at her with a rueful twinkle. Behind him, the Jefferson Memorial glowed like a Japanese lantern against the star-studded sky. Its reflection in the rippling black water of the Tidal Basin made the scene breathtakingly lovely.

Like something out of a movie. Like something out of a dream.

"I-I . . ." She, who was always so articulate, so precise with her words, was at a loss for them now. She could barely speak, barely think, barely breathe. Her heart pounded. Her throat closed up.

This is all happening so fast. Too fast?

She'd left on a business trip, met him on the plane. In the brief time they'd been together, he had become the most important person in her life. Once she would have said that falling for a man in a week wasn't even possible. Now she was so in love that she was ready to chuck everything—home, career, her whole hard-earned life—to be with him. If he asked her to, which he wouldn't, because Washington, D.C. was his home, too, and he was as proud of her career as he was successful in his.

"Look, I got you a ring."

The hand that wasn't holding hers delved in his jacket pocket. He was wearing a suit, expensive and perfectly tailored, with a white shirt and a fabulous silk tie with discreet symbols that told anyone who knew anything about that sort of thing just how fabulous it was. Unfortunately, she didn't yet know a lot about things like that, although she pretended she did. In this brave new world she was trying so hard to conquer, the world of wealth and power and privilege, she was still working to learn the language. And that tie was part of the language. Just like her short black cocktail dress was part of the language: in her case, Armani Privé. Although it had been purchased second- or third-hand at a consignment shop in Georgetown, no one knew but her. The dress was so understated that it screamed class, even if it was just a tad too tight around the hips and thighs. The sad truth was that at five-four and the one hundred forty pounds she had dieted down to—the bare minimum she was pretty sure she was ever going to achieve on her big-boned frame no matter how little she ate—she was never going to look totally elegant in clothes meant for a six-foot-tall, one-hundred-pound model. Just like her chubby-cheeked face was never going to be anything other than depressingly round.

He says I'm beautiful. Her pulse fluttered

at the memory. *Beautiful, sexy, the woman he's been waiting for all his life.*

"See?" He flipped open a jeweler's box, offered it to her like he hoped what was inside it would persuade her. The glow from the memorial channeled into a dazzling beam as it struck a diamond the size of a dime. Her breath caught. When he pulled the ring from its box and slid it on the fourth finger of her left hand, the precious metal cool and slick against her skin, her knees went weak.

At last, my love has come along.

The words of the Etta James song swelled in her mind. It was so perfect—he was so perfect—everything was so perfect. For the first time ever, her *life* was perfect. Her career—she was a lawyer, a thirty-one-year-old associate with the prestigious firm of Ellis Hayes—was thriving. Her finances were secure, to the point where she would never again have to lay awake at night sweating about having enough money. She'd been so lonely for so long, so certain that she wasn't the type of woman who would ever be half of a couple, so resigned to being single that she had never even realized how much she wanted more. And now—this. Her very own whirlwind romance. A marriage proposal. And to quiet her increasingly importunate biological clock, maybe, in a year or so, even a baby. Who'd have thought it?

Impossibly, incredibly, every dream she'd never even known she'd had was coming true.

How'd I ever get this lucky?

"Allie? You're making me nervous here."

She realized she hadn't said anything, had done nothing but stare dumbly at him, at the glittering diamond. His thumb caressed her fingers, nudged the ring. His smile was a little crooked now. His eyes searched her face. He looked like he thought she might actually be going to say no. This hint of vulnerability in him—she hadn't seen him vulnerable before—made her heart melt.

"Say something, damn it. Say yes."

She took a deep breath, striving to pull herself together enough so that she could actually speak. The thing was, she'd always been a little bit psychic. At least, that's what she'd told the girls in the group home where she'd spent her final two years in foster care, before she'd aged out of the system at the ripe old age of eighteen. They'd been tough girls, tougher than she'd been, bigger and meaner than she'd been, but the psychic stuff had scared them enough to make them leave her alone. Now, looking down at the ring that glittered on her finger like her own personal North Star, she knew it was true: she *was* a little bit psychic, at least about this. Because something inside her recognized this man, this moment, as the way things were meant to be.

He was her fate, her destiny.

"Allie?" He frowned up at her. The light from the memorial painted him in a golden glow, and she saw that his face had hardened, as if he was physically bracing now for rejection. His hand tightened on hers to the point where his grip almost hurt as he rose lithely to his feet. That broke the spell.

"Yes," she said. Then, giddy as his face changed, "Yes, yes, yes, yes, *yes*."

Grinning like an idiot, she threw herself into his arms. They closed around her, tight and strong, and hugged her to him. He was tall and solid, muscular from his running and workouts, fit and buff in a way she would never be, and she loved the feel of him. Loved the smell of him. Loved his dark good looks, his lopsided smile, his possessiveness where she was concerned. Surging upward, wrapping her arms around his neck, she raised her face for his kiss. As their lips met fireworks exploded behind her closed lids, and she knew she'd found her heart's home at last.

"When?" he asked when finally they had to surface to breathe.

"When what?" Her arms were still wrapped around his neck. Across the Tidal Basin, all around them really, the city glittered like a jewel. At night Washington was so beautiful, with darkness acting as a veil to hide the seamier parts and thousands of lights turning the streets into a fairyland. Closer at hand, the branches of the Japanese cherry trees that made the city a mecca for tourists in the spring dipped and swayed in the slight breeze that had briefly chased away the usual late July humidity. Insects sang in high-pitched chorus. The soft slap of oars and distant murmur of voices from tourists manning a quartet of paddle boats around the Tidal Basin reminded her that they weren't really alone, although the bend in the path that had taken them into the deserted area around the side of the memorial made it feel that way.

"When can we do the deed? Get married, I mean, not the other, although I think it goes without saying I certainly want to do that. As soon as possible, too."

They'd fallen into bed together that first night. The sex had been steamy, intense, unforgettable. Since then, except for the necessary work she'd had to do for her firm, and herself, they'd basically gotten out of bed only to fly home. He kept telling her how hot she was, how amazing she was. With him, she actually felt hot and amazing for the first time in her life. Having always thought of herself as chubby and plain—hell, she was chubby and plain, no way around that—she had been amazed at the transforming power of love. Because he said she was beautiful, she felt beautiful, and that, she discovered to her wonderment, made all the difference. Just imagining what they were going to do in bed later made her blood heat. Now, she marveled, that feeling was hers to keep. Drunk with joy, she smiled up at him.

"Whenever you want."

He grinned. "I was hoping you'd say that. How about—tomorrow in Vegas? I've got a private plane lined up to meet us at Dulles at midnight if you say yes. We'll get married at one of those cheesy wedding chapels, take twenty-four hours for a honeymoon, then get back here and work out all the juicy details of how we're going to spend the rest of our lives together. It'll be something to tell our kids one day. Besides, it'll be fun."

At the thought of the children they would have together something warm throbbed to life deep inside her. Then she frowned a little as the tiniest of serpents poked its flickering tongue into her budding Eden. It was Saturday night, and the timetable he was proposing had a serious flaw.

"I have to work Monday."

"So do I. So what? We'll call in sick. You can miss one day, can't you?"

His coaxing tone was irresistible. Besides, she *could* miss a day, she realized, without having to worry about the repercussions of not seeming totally gung-ho in her eighty-hours-is-a-normal-work-week firm. She had achieved financial independence. Impossible as it seemed, she didn't even really have to go to work anymore.

And that was a dazzling thought that she vowed to ponder more fully later.

"Vegas it is," she agreed happily. Then he laughed and kissed her and bundled her into a cab and rushed her off to her apartment in Logan Circle so that she could grab a few things, which meant, basically, retrieve her suitcase, which she hadn't even yet had time to unpack. Luckily she'd had her clothes cleaned at the hotel before leaving, and they were as well suited for Vegas as anything else she owned, so now she could just pick the suitcase up and hit the road again. On the way, at his urging, she made a quick call to her mother to tell her that she was off to Vegas to get married. Not that she actually had a mother, at least not one she was in contact with or knew how to get hold of, so the call was placed to a cell phone she knew wouldn't be answered, and she left a message while he listened with a lazy smile on his face. One day, when they'd been married awhile, she would confess to him that her mother was long out of the picture, if not dead, and the tale she'd spun for him of a mother and a sister in Baltimore had been a pretty story she'd made up to hide the ugly truth, but not now. She had always been ashamed of her lack of family, of growing up in foster care, and she was afraid that the truth would diminish her in his eyes.

That she couldn't take.

She had just finished up by leaving a real message for her boss at work when they reached her apartment, which was on Q Street. It was the entire bottom floor of one of the street's row houses, built in 1878 and currently painted mint green, with an elaborate facade and a much simpler interior, because keeping costs down while keeping up appearances had been paramount in the minds of the builder, who had constructed the linked residences in the then middle-class area nearly a century and a half earlier.

Opening the door, stepping into the air-conditioned darkness of her tiny foyer, Allison flipped on the light and typed in the security code to silence the tinny beeping that would turn into a siren if it wasn't pacified within the prescribed two minutes. She was immediately greeted by Clementine's questioning squeak as the cat swarmed in from the bedroom, where she presumably had been napping in her favorite spot, the middle of the bed. Clementine didn't meow like most cats. Instead she made a variety of sounds, including a drawn-out quasi squeak, because her voice box had been damaged by the wire loop someone had tried to hang her with before throwing her tiny, apparently presumed dead body into the Dumpster from which she had subsequently been rescued, weak but alive, wire still around her neck, by a kindhearted garbage man.

"Hi, baby." Allison scooped up the cat. There was nothing wrong with Clementine's purr, and she rattled away as she rubbed her head against Allison's cheek in obvious affection. Clementine's silky fur was long and black with a single white spot in the middle of her neck that had made Allison think of a Hostess cupcake the first time she had seen her, in a cage at the animal shelter where Allison had been doing her first stint of required pro bono work soon after having been hired by Ellis Hayes three years before. In fact, she'd nearly named the scrawny kitten Cupcake, but she'd figured it gave away too much about her own inner proclivities.

"Damn, I forgot about the cat." His voice held a hint of vexation, which made her frown at him.

Having closed and locked the front door and then stood silently watching as she'd typed in the security code, he now surveyed the two of them through narrowed eyes. He'd never met Clementine before, of course. This was his first time in Allison's apartment, in her real life, but he'd heard about the cat, probably way too much, since Clementine was practically Allison's only family and she talked about her a lot.

"This is Clementine. Clementine, this is Greg," Allison said by way of introduction, then passed her pet over to him. Clementine was nonnegotiable. Although if he said she had to choose . . .

"Love me, love my cat," she added, but her eyes practically begged him.

After meeting her gaze for the briefest of moments, he seemed prepared to, tucking Clementine into the crook of his arm, stroking her small head. Clementine's golden eyes looked mistrustful, which wasn't surprising, given the cat's history. Allison smiled in relief at the picture they made.

"I guess I just officially became a cat lover." His answering smile erased any last flicker of doubt his earlier tone had raised.

"She's a great cat. You'll see, once you get to know her."

"I'm sure I will," he said. "Better hurry. If the plane has to wait, it costs me—us—a small fortune. Besides, I want to take you to bed, and I promised myself that the next time I did you'd be my wife."

"I'm hurrying." Allison turned and headed for her bedroom, flipping on lights as she went. *His wife.* Just hearing the words made her heart beat faster. As did the thought of how they would celebrate their wedding afterward. She had, she'd discovered, a real aptitude for passion, although she hadn't had much chance to explore it before now. Fortunately, he had the patience and experience to teach her what to do with it. Her body quickened at the thought.

"There's bottled water in the fridge," she called over her shoulder, glad that she had something healthy, something he'd approve of.

Waving her tail and chirping, which was Clementine's way of making conversation, the cat was at Allison's side as she entered her bedroom. This time the chirps had an anxious quality to them, as if Clementine somehow knew that Allison was getting ready to leave again. Allison had left food and water out, and Paloma DeLong from Shelter House, the facility for delinquent teens where she had been doing her latest stint of pro bono work, had been checking in on Clementine in her absence. Surprisingly enough, because Allison didn't have many emotional attachments or interests outside of work, Paloma had become a friend, and the work Allison had been doing for Shelter House had become something of a mission for her. Or maybe it wasn't so surprising. The embattled girls there had touched a chord in her that must have been left over from her own rough teenage years. She understood them, felt the uncertainty and yearning and heartbreak behind their outward toughness, because she had lived it. Making a friend of Paloma had been an unexpected bonus. The only other time that Allison had gone out of town since Clementine had become a part of her life, she'd put Clementine in a kennel. Clementine had reacted so badly that the kennel had called and Allison had had to cut her trip short to rescue her. Anyway, she would put out more food and water before she left, and call Paloma in the morning and ask her if she would please keep checking on Clementine for another couple of days. Clementine would be fine, if not totally happy, until Allison returned.

Allison explained the whole thing to the cat as she changed, and Clementine, tail twitching unhappily, watched her from her perch in the middle of the bed.

"You know, we don't *have* to wait until we're married." Tone suggestive, Greg appeared in the doorway to give her a long, lustful look as she stood there in her black slacks and pale peach bra, ready to pull on the zebra-print top she loved because the vertical stripes were slimming. Still a little self-conscious about her less-than-tiny waist and slightly fleshy rib cage, she tugged the top on over her head before replying.

"Yes, we do." Resurfacing, she ran smoothing hands over her chin-length auburn hair. It was cut a little longer in front than in back in a layered style designed to slim her face, not that it seemed to work, particularly. "Now that you've put the idea in my head, I like the thought of waiting for my wedding night."

"Next time I start talking, remind me to shut up." With a wry smile, he headed toward her as she stepped into her black peep-toes, his eyes on the small, packed carry-on that waited near her feet. Her laptop case was perched on top of it. Her purse lay near Clementine on the bed. His glance took in all those things before returning to her.

"You all packed? That was quick."

"It was quick because I never unpacked," she confessed. "I had my clothes cleaned at the hotel before we left."

"Smart." He pulled her close. Allison slid her arms around his neck, in the process taking just a second to admire the sparkle of her new ring as it caught the light from the lamp beside her bed. Instead of kissing her, as she expected, he cupped her chin, tilting her face up to his, seeming to study it. She smiled into his eyes. His fingers moved caressingly along her jaw, warm as they stroked her skin. "Got your cell phone?"

"In my purse."

"Called everybody you need to call?"

"Everybody important."

"Fantastic," he said and returned her smile. His other hand slid up her back to curve around her nape.

Allison was just registering that there was something off about his expression, something wrong about the sudden, intent gleam in his eyes, when his fingers delved beneath her hair to settle on the back of her head, his hand firm and strong as it conformed to the shape of her skull, gripping rather than caressing her now. Just like the hand holding her chin was gripping it now. In a purposeful way, as if he meant to . . .

Something primeval inside her kicked into gear and sent a warning jolt of adrenaline surging through her veins. A cold, prickly sensation raced over the surface of her skin.

Together they screamed, *Danger.*

Her eyes widened. Her lips parted. Her pulse jumped. Instinctively she started to stiffen, to pull away from him.

"Wha . . . ?" she began, but before she could finish, before she could get out so much as the rest of the word *what,* as in *"what in the world are you doing?"* which is what she meant to ask him, before her brain could even finish directing her muscles to escape from his hold—it was too late.

His lips thinned. His eyes gleamed hard as glass. His hands tightened brutally, then made a short, sharp movement that twisted her neck violently to the left. There was a crack, loud as a brittle twig being snapped in two.

Her eyes still wide, her head at an unnatural angle now, her breathing cut off as her trachea crushed, blinded and deafened by the explosion of pure agony that rocketed toward her brain, Allison registered a jumble of thoughts, a thousand sensations, a lifetime of memories, a final burst of horror, in an instant.

Then she died.

CHAPTER TWO

From her position under the bed, Lucy Peel heard the snap of Allison's neck breaking without knowing what it was. Wedged in beside her, her best friend, Jaden Miller, grabbed hold of her hand. Already sweating, already tense, the fifteen-year-old girls were suddenly so petrified that they could barely breathe as they watched the shuffle of feet around the queen-sized bed and listened in vain for the resumption of the conversation that had just ended with that brittle crack.

Lucy looked at Jaden. *What the hell?* she mouthed.

Jaden gave a tiny, clueless shrug.

Their worst fear, besides discovery of course, was that the adults they were hiding from would decide to do the nasty on the mattress some three feet above their heads. That would just be gross, as they had communicated to each other in an eye-rolling exchange of glances when the guy had joined Miss Howard in her bedroom.

Now the girls lay facedown, their bodies pressed tight to the hardwood floor, trying not to inhale the amalgam of cat hair and dust and who knew what else floated around them as they waited in a state of silent anxiety for whatever would happen next. One sneeze, even a sniffle maybe, and they would be caught. Ten to one, the police would be called. Miss Howard would call them for sure—she was a lawyer who came in free to help out the Shelter House administrators. No way was she going to keep her mouth shut about two runaways who'd broken into her house and lived in it for four days. Especially since, besides eating everything they'd been able to find, they'd helped themselves to some cash they'd discovered in a kitchen drawer, pawned some jewelry and an iPod, and sold an old fur coat they'd found tucked away at the back of a closet, telling the consignment shop owner it had been left to Lucy by her recently deceased grandmother. All of that had netted approximately two hundred dollars, plus they'd grabbed eighty-seven dollars from the petty cash drawer at Shelter House when they'd decided to run, which Lucy was pretty sure put them in the felony category. They'd be arrested for sure, and then they'd be fed to the system one more time, only this time the chances for escape would be greatly reduced. It was unlikely they'd end up at Shelter House again, which was the only good thing about it. Shelter House was mostly for status offenders, like habitual truants, or the most minor of criminal transgressors. The key was that the female inmates, who ranged in age from fourteen to seventeen, had to have no stable home to return to once juvenile court spit them out. Lucy was in for shoplifting; Jaden, for being one of a gang of kids who'd stolen a car. For both, Shelter House had been a haven for about the first twelve hours. After that, after darkness had fallen, it had turned into a nightmare.

From which they had escaped. Five days ago. After spending a first scary night on the streets, Lucy, the more enterprising of the two, had gotten the bright idea of breaking into Miss Howard's house, which she'd known had been empty because they'd accompanied Mrs. DeLong on a visit to the cat, which Mrs. DeLong had stopped to check on when they'd gone to the clinic, where she had been taking both girls for court-ordered medical exams. Getting in had been simple: they'd broken one of the tiny, mullioned panes in a rear basement window, then Lucy had stuck her hand in to unlock the window itself. Jaden the bone-rack had managed to squeeze in between the security bars, wriggle through the window, and shut off the security code, which was ridiculously easy to remember, 4-3-2-1: Mrs. DeLong had asked Lucy to type it in before. They had subsequently found the spare house key amongst others on a ring that hung beside the back door, and they had been sleeping there, carefully waiting to enter at least an hour or so after dark, in case of nosy neighbors. Since Mrs. DeLong had said Miss Howard would be gone a week, they hadn't expected her back until Sunday. They had just come in from attending a free concert in Franklin Square to discover the suitcase in the bedroom. What it had meant had registered about the same time they'd heard the front door open. With no escape route available, they'd dived under the bed. Where they were now trapped.

Lucy was just thinking, *Maybe they'll go outside for something, and we can*—when something big fell, just smacked right down on the floor beside the bed, *crash*. The whole room rattled and shook. The floor jolted. The bed jumped, just like the startled girls beneath it. The edge of the floral bedspread fluttered up from all the movement; maybe four inches above the floor. Through the gap Lucy could see—Miss Howard. Miss Howard lying sprawled on her stomach on the floor. It was she who had fallen. The wind must have been knocked out of her, because she lay perfectly still, making no move whatsoever to get up.

Lucy's eyes widened in horror. Her heart started hammering in her chest.

Jaden gasped, an involuntary, quickly stifled inhalation that nevertheless made Lucy's stomach knot with fear. Not that the small sound mattered. Miss Howard had definitely seen them. Her eyes were wide open, and she was looking straight at them. As soon as she got her breath back, she'd be ordering them out from under the bed. Then the shit would hit the fan for real.

Lucy tensed, waiting for it. Jaden squeezed her hand so hard that Lucy would have yelped if she hadn't been stricken absolutely dumb.

Clementine the cat shot under the bed, saw them, and did her cat freak-out thing, where all her fur puffed out like she was being electrocuted. Changing course with a skitter of claws on hardwood, she headed for the wall at the head of the bed, where she crouched in the gloom beside the bed's left front leg, her yellow eyes glittering with alarm.

Miss Howard was so close that Lucy noticed for the first time that her eyes were blue. She was bone white, her lips were parted, and she had kind of a surprised expression on her face. Maybe that's why she wasn't moving: she was so astonished to discover Lucy and Jaden under her bed. Whatever, there was no way she didn't see them. She wasn't more than three feet away.

"Fat bitch," the man said. The words were distinct, although he was out of sight. There was hard contempt in his tone. Since as far as he knew Miss Howard was the only other person in the house, he had to be talking to her. A couple of minutes ago, they'd been so lovey-dovey it had been disgusting. Now he was openly disrespecting Miss Howard, a tough woman who Lucy wouldn't have thought was the type to take that kind of thing. But Miss Howard didn't protest, didn't move, didn't make a sound. Didn't so much as blink.

What's up with that?

Had he hit her? Was that why she was on the floor? Was she, like, maybe paralyzed with fear?

Lucy's insides began to tighten up.

The man's shoes, shiny black lace-ups with gray suit pants breaking across the instep, stepped into view, moved around for a moment, then disappeared again. Lucy could hear him walking away. Miss Howard still didn't move, still stared fixedly at them.

Maybe she didn't want to give them away?

But her eyes looked funny now. Kind of really blank and—glazed.

A scarlet thread—*blood, it was blood*—began to unspool from the corner of her mouth. Ropey with saliva, it stretched toward the floor. Lucy watched, transfixed.

She's dead.

The fact hit Lucy like a two-by-four.

He killed her.

Panic sent her pulse racing, made her heart buck and skitter like a spooked horse. She stared at Miss Howard, who stared unseeingly back.

Murdered. Murdered. Oh, Mother Mary, she just got murdered. Then, slowly, the rest of the equation occurred to her. *And we're stuck in here with the man who did it. We're witnesses. Oh, my God . . .*

The horror of it sent cold chills up her spine.

Beside her, she felt Jaden make a sudden, restive movement. The hand wrapped around hers squeezed so hard that it was enough to practically break her fingers. Mortally terrified that her more impulsive friend would scream or scramble out from under the bed or do something else that might bring Miss Howard's killer down upon them as soon as she figured out what Lucy now knew, Lucy whipped her head around to scowl at Jaden.

Shut up, she mouthed fiercely. *Don't you dare make a sound. Don't you dare move.*

Jaden stared back at her. Her expression was so deer-in-the-headlights terrified that Lucy was pretty sure Jaden got it. Jaden was kind of tall, maybe five-nine or so, but rail-thin, so thin that her brown eyes looked huge at the best of times and her bones seemed to poke through her sallow skin. Lucy privately thought she had anorexia, but Jaden denied it, and nobody else—none of the teachers, none of the counselors—ever seemed to pick up on it, so Lucy just left it alone. Jaden was all Goth, with short, spiky hair she'd dyed the deepest, deadest black, lots of dark eyeliner, black lipstick, and a silver stud piercing her right nostril. She wore black jeans and a black tee with a red rose pierced by a dagger in the center of it and black sneakers. Lucy wasn't Goth. She wasn't anything, really. She was a couple of inches shorter than Jaden and muscular enough to be athletic looking, even though the only sport she'd ever played had been kickball when she was in second grade. Her hair was carrot orange and frizzy curly, hideous really, which was why she always wore it scraped back into a ponytail. She had naturally very white skin, which was currently kind of dingy looking from self-tanner, eyebrows and eyelashes that were so pale that if she didn't use makeup (which she did, religiously) you couldn't even see them, and light blue eyes. Some people said she was pretty, but if she was honest it was usually boys trying to get into her pants, and she wasn't so stupid that she didn't know they said that to all the girls whose pants they wanted to get into. She wore black lace-up combat boots and ripped denim shorts and a pair of ratty tank tops, one black, one army green, which left a lot of skin on display and had to be at least part of the reason she was freezing. Another reason was the air-conditioning vent, which was blasting away under the bed. The third, and probably most important, reason was the dead body that had just dropped in front of her eyes.

We've got to get out of here, Jaden

mouthed at her, panic apparent in her face, which was when Lucy was for-sure positive Jaden knew Miss Howard was dead.

Don't move, Lucy said again, urgently. Then, *Shh.*

A squeaky sound—*screech, screech, screech*—sent every tiny hair on Lucy's body catapulting upright. Even as her head whipped around so that she could see out from under the bed again, she and Jaden surged closer together until they were practically on top of each other, taking up as little space as possible, trying to huddle in the very center of the floor beneath the shelter of the bed. God forbid any part of them should show.

If he finds us . . . Lucy went dizzy just thinking about it. He would kill them. It didn't take a genius to figure that out.

Lucy could feel Jaden trembling against her. Other than that, which Jaden clearly couldn't help, they both went as still as poor Miss Howard. The only difference was that Lucy could feel her own heart beating wildly, while Miss Howard's heart would never beat again.

Gorge rose in her throat. She thought

she might be going to vomit and swallowed hard to head it off.

Screech, screech. Screech, screech.

The guy pushed something into view. Something blue, with black plastic wheels that Lucy could see just the bottom few inches of beneath the bedspread. As it got closer she identified it: a garbage can, one of the big ones people in the neighborhood were supposed to lug out to the curb each week.

The garbage can stopped near the foot of the bed.

His shoes moved into her line of vision, walking around the garbage can, stopping. He stood between the bed and Miss Howard now, so close that Lucy could have reached out and touched his shoes. Instead, heart thudding, she pressed back against Jaden, who was trembling like crazy. Then all of a sudden she could see his hands. Blinking in surprise, she realized that he must have bent over. His hands were big, with short, thick fingers like sausage links, and strong looking. Holding her breath, she watched as they grabbed Miss Howard's unresisting hand, stripped the ginormous diamond ring from her finger. Miss Howard's hand hit the floor again with a thunk, and then his hands came into view once more, taking hold of Miss Howard's waist, sinking into the stripey shirt she was wearing and the flesh beneath like he was working to get a really good grip on her. There was a scar near his little finger on the hand closest to her, his right hand. It was silvery white and round, like maybe a small animal had bitten him there a long time ago. He had on a white dress shirt that just showed beneath the sleeves of his gray coat.

A suit. He's wearing a suit.

Grunting, muttering under his breath, he picked Miss Howard up.

It was horrible to watch. He picked her up by the waist, so that her head and hands and feet still dangled within view, limp as a rag doll's. Her hair flopped forward to conceal most of her face, but Lucy could still see one empty blue eye—and the long, ropey string of blood that continued to spill from her mouth to the floor. It elongated as he lifted her, until finally, at last, it broke.

Then Miss Howard was gone, completely disappeared from sight, except for the small puddle of blood and saliva where her mouth had been. A loud thump made both girls start. The garbage can shook, which Lucy took to mean that Miss Howard had been dumped inside.

He was disposing of the body. The garbage can would be perfect. Miss Howard, limp in the earliest stage of death, would be easy to stuff inside. Then he would use bleach to clean up the blood . . .

Oh, God, she had watched too much *CSI*. Only this wasn't TV. This was real. A real murder, a real murderer.

The clatter of plastic made her fairly certain he was closing the black plastic lid that came attached to the garbage can. Maybe now he would wheel it away and . . .

Mee-eee-eee-eee.

Clementine gave one of her pitiful, strangulated meows. It was loud enough to freeze the black shoes in their tracks, loud enough to send Lucy's horrified gaze shooting to the cat, loud enough to make Jaden bury her face in Lucy's shoulder with a shudder. Crouched on her belly, Clementine was staring out at where Miss Howard had been. Her fur was still all puffed up. Her eyes were wide and unblinking.

"What the . . . ?" The man broke off.

The black shoes turned toward the bed. Lucy could now see the highly polished toes, the crease in his pants. Watching, she felt as if time had somehow been suspended. The only logical place to look for the source of the sound was under the bed. Any second now he would bend down and lift the edge of the bedspread and . . .

The rest was too terrifying even to think about.

She held her breath. Her heart felt like it would slam its way out of her chest. Sweat poured over her in an icy wave.

Mee-eee-eee-eee.

Rigid with fear, Lucy awaited discovery. Jaden kicked at the cat, her black Converse sneaker soundlessly slashing the air. Hissing, Clementine shot out from under the bed.

"Damn cat." The man's tone made it clear he wasn't a cat lover. His shoes moved so that Lucy could see the sides, then the heels. He was turning away.

Lucy went weak with relief, letting her head drop so that her forehead rested on the floor. Beside her, Jaden closed her eyes.

The clatter of plastic made her think the black lid that came attached to the garbage can had been closed.

Screech. Screech.

He was rolling the garbage can away.

The next logical thing for him to do would be to come back and clean up the blood. The thought of having him so close again, of being just one bad turn of luck away from discovery, twisted Lucy's stomach into a pretzel.

Jaden nudged her. *Let's go,* she mouthed.

This time Lucy nodded, then put a cautionary finger to her lips: *Wait.*

They both listened to the screeching sound as it got further away. He was heading toward the back door, Lucy was all but positive, which was located in the laundry room. It opened onto a tiny yard, with a concrete path that led to a garage and an alley. He could bring a car there, maybe, and haul Miss Howard away. A distant clatter made Lucy think that the garbage can had just crossed over the raised threshold that separated the hall from the kitchen.

Now.

The word flashed between the two of them. They acted on it instantly, slithering out from under the bed, rising to a crouch, creeping on silent feet toward the bedroom door. Lucy's heart pounded so hard that she thought it might explode. Her breathing came fast and shallow. They could still hear the faint *screech* of the garbage can's wheels. As long as they could hear it, she thought, they were okay. The laundry room was off the kitchen, and from the sound of it he was almost there. They would have to go out the front. They didn't have much time.

Screech. Screech.

With Lucy in the lead, they slipped out into the hall and tiptoed down the red oriental runner. The hall was lit by a pair of candlestick lamps on a table. The warm yellow glow felt almost obscene under the circumstances. The kitchen was even brighter, a normal cheerful kitchen. They had to pass the entrance to the kitchen before they could get to the front door. If he looked around at just the wrong time . . .

Lucy shuddered. *If he catches us, we're dead.*

Clementine watched them come. She was crouched in the kitchen doorway. Her eyes looked as round and bright as an owl's. Her fur was puffed. Her tail swished.

Please be quiet, Lucy begged her silently. *Please.*

Scree—

The screeching stopped. Lucy and Jaden registered that with a single, horrified exchange of glances. The front door was within view. It was solid dark wood, no window, fitted with a couple of locks. They rushed it, fumbled with the locks, a dead bolt, a knob lock, turn one, turn both, trying to be quiet, trying to be quick, casting so many terrified glances over their shoulders that they could hardly watch their hands.

Footsteps in the kitchen, coming their way. Clementine jumped up and turned to look, tail raised stiff as a broomstick in the air. Batting Jaden's hands aside, Lucy frantically twisted the knob, praying they had both locks in the right position, as panic made her fingers shake, made her go weak in the knees.

Mee-eee-eee-eee.

"Who's there?" His voice was loud and sharp. Oh, God, he'd heard them. He was coming. Clementine skittered out of his way.

Heart in throat, Lucy wrenched the door open. She and Jaden practically shoved each other through it, then fled down the steps and into the hot, humid night.

As they raced away down the sidewalk, Lucy dared a quick glance over her shoulder.

Silhouetted by the light spilling out of the doorway they'd just escaped through, the man stood on the top step, staring after them. His face was shadowed, but she could see that he had thick, dark hair and a tall, muscular build.

"Oh my God, he's looking at us," Jaden gasped. Lucy saw that Jaden was looking back, too. Their eyes met in an instant of shared horror, then Lucy grabbed Jaden's hand and they ran for their lives.

CHAPTER THREE

Three weeks later . . .

"So you just—*gave* it to him?"

With all eyes in the packed courtroom on her as she stopped in front of the witness stand, Jessica Ford—no, Jessica Dean now: she kept forgetting that she was in the Secret Service's ad hoc version of the Witness Protection Program—could feel her palms starting to sweat.

"Y-yes." The witness looked at her with big blue eyes that were wide with apprehension.

"He didn't ask for it?"

"No. Not exactly. But . . ." Tiffany Higgs was twenty-four, a pretty, wispy blonde in a flowery summer dress who was every bit as delicately built as Jess's five-foot-two inch, undersized, newly (reluctantly) blond self. When Tiffany's voice trailed off, Jess's instinct was to urge her to continue. Then she hesitated. Hesitation was pretty generally held to be as dangerous for trial lawyers as it was for big game hunters—the prey, sensing fear, might well spring at you unexpectedly—but she had a goal she was working toward and Tiffany's answer was already enough to take her where she wanted to go.

Time to back off.

Resisting the urge to run her damp hands down the sides of the skirt of her bubblegum pink, picked-out-by-the-jury-consultant summer suit, Jess turned both hands palm out in a calculated gesture of confusion instead and concentrated on following the instructions she'd been given.

Which was to keep it nice. Jury-friendly. Nonthreatening. Forget attack dog. The impression she was striving to make while interrogating this witness was strictly Malti-poo.

"You're telling us that Mr. Phillips did *not*

ask for your phone number? You wrote it on a napkin and pressed it into his hand as he was leaving the bar on your own initiative?" Jess carefully kept her voice non-accusatory. It was imperative to keep the jury from sympathizing totally with Tiffany, the alleged victim in this rape trial of Robert John Phillips IV, who was sitting at that moment at the defense table trying to look like the innocent, falsely accused law student the defense team was portraying him as. Which, as a newly conscripted member of that team, Jess devoutly hoped was the truth.

Given that Phillips was the handsome, twenty-five-year-old only son of a wealthy, powerful,   also-present-in-the-courtroom U.S. senator, the stakes here were high for everyone concerned. The media was out in force—thank God cameras were not allowed in the courtroom!—and, on this twelfth day of what was projected to be a four-week-long trial, the prosecution team, which had rested its case the previous Friday, was clearly smelling blood in the water. Paul Olderman, the politically ambitious DA and lead prosecutor, was salivating at the thought of what a conviction could do to advance his career, and, in a happy co-incidence, derail the senator's, who was of the opposite political persuasion.

What the senator wanted, as Jess's bosses had made abundantly clear, was nothing less than a resounding acquittal for his son.

Fat chance. The problem was, Rob Phillips came across as overprivileged and obnoxious once he started talking, so much so that they had almost decided not to put him on the stand. *Looks 8, personality 1*, had been the verdict. Every indication was, the jury didn't like him. And to tell the truth, Jess didn't either. Not that her opinion actually mattered one way or the other. But the jury's did. In a he-said, she-said trial, which this one was shaping up to be, the defendant's likability was all important.

"Yes, ma'am." Tiffany raised Jess's Maltipoo and did her one better: she went for the full scared Yorkie. Her voice shook, her body shook, and she wiped a tear from the corner of one eye. A sideways glance told Jess that the gesture registered with the jury: the grandmotherly woman in the front row stopped her incessant knitting, her brows furrowing in sympathy. The portly school-bus driver on the far end of the second row pursed his lips and shook his head. At least six of the twelve good citizens seated just a couple of yards to her right looked noticeably moved by the witness's distress.

Crap.

Swallowing her chagrin at having been one-upped in the playing to the jury department, Jess tried to look both kindly disposed toward the witness and skeptical of her testimony at the same time.

No easy task. But she tried, because trying was her job. The defense team's position was that this was a vindictive, emotionally unstable young woman. Having had her Cinderella fantasies brutally dashed when the senator's son had slept with her and then made it clear that that had been all he'd wanted to do with her, she had set out to exact a ruinous revenge by falsely crying rape when the opportunity had presented itself, after which she hoped to win a million-dollar payday by means of a civil lawsuit.

As a scenario, and a defense, it was reasonable.

The problem was, Jess was increasingly having trouble buying it. Which meant she was having trouble selling it, although she was doing her best.

See, the thing was, the law was not about justice. It was not about truth. It was not about fairness, about right and wrong, about parity.

In the case of the elite D.C. law firm of Ellis Hayes Associates LLP, Jess's esteemed employer, it was about nailing your opponent's balls to the wall in return for your salary, which was embarrassingly large due to the obscene amount of money the firm was being paid *to win*. The firm's slogan? "Going to war when the outcome is life or death." The unstated corollary: and grinding your opponent's face into the dirt in the process.

Ergo, enter the gladiators.

Today, in courtroom 318 in Moultrie Courthouse in Washington, D.C., Jess was one of those gladiators. It was her first real foray into the stadium, as it were. She'd been on the job with Ellis Hayes for nearly four months and had been working the

Phillips trial exclusively for the past three weeks. But until jury consultant Christine Hubbard had decided that the jury had taken a dislike to hard-driving lead counsel Pearson Collins, Jess's had been a strictly supporting, research-based role. Pearse was a Rottweiler if she'd ever seen one, Christine said, using her own personal classification system, which had helped her win 308 out of 312 cases since it had come to her in a burst of what she could only describe as truly cosmic brilliance. It might sound foolish (and here she had glared at Jess, who had clearly failed to control her expression sufficiently when the system had been explained to her), but it worked. According to Christine, the largely working-class jury had turned hostile to Pearse from the moment he had started questioning Tiffany Higgs, which had been yesterday (Monday) morning at approximately 9:00 a.m. They thought he was too aggressive, too intimidating, too deep-voiced, too big. Christine's take on it was that when Pearse shot questions at Tiffany, what the jury saw was the equivalent of a bad-tempered Rottweiler threatening a shivering little Yorkie. As a result, their natural protective instincts were instantly aroused, and they instinctively sided with the Yorkie. The remedy had been arrived at in an emergency war session after court had adjourned the previous day: when the time came to question Tiffany again, the defense needed someone equally feminine, equally petite, equally inoffensive-looking, to do the job.

In other words, Jess. Hazel-eyed, square-jawed, even-featured Jess, who, with a disarming scattering of freckles dusting her small nose, was attractive in a girl-next-door kind of way that pushed no buttons. Jess, with her newly wavy, newly blond bob, tricked out in a nauseatingly pink suit that she protested, in vain, made her look like a bad caricature of Elle Woods in *Legally Blonde*. Only minus the whole adorably cute vibe.

Try accessorizing with a smile, Christine had snapped back as she had supervised the application of cotton-candy pink lipstick. *Otherwise, you just look like a hundred pounds of cranky. And juries don't like cranky.*

With all eyes now on her, Jess felt kind

of like a minor-league player unexpectedly called up to bat in the big leagues.

"Would it be fair to say that you gave Mr. Phillips the napkin with your number on it because you *wanted* him to call you?" Jess asked. The Cheerios she'd had for breakfast had coalesced into a churning mass in her stomach. At any moment she feared they were going to rebel. Losing her breakfast in front of the jury might have won her some sympathy points, but she'd really rather not go there.

"Yes, ma'am." Tiffany's voice wobbled. Even to Jess, she looked more like a scared teenager than the viciously scheming gold digger the defense needed her to be. *Why didn't I just say no when Cates—* her boss—*agreed to lend me to the defense team?* Then she answered herself: *Because working this trial is the opportunity of a lifetime, that's why.* Then her innate, much-despised streak of truthfulness forced her to add: *And because I really, really wanted to get away from Cates.* "I—he was nice to me. I thought he was nice. I didn't know he—"

Out of instinct, Jess jumped in before

Tiffany could add something that Jess was pretty sure would be detrimental to the client.

"There was also the fact that he was handing out fifty-dollar bills as tips all around that night, isn't that right?" Jess heard the sudden sharpness of her own tone with chagrin. Malti-poo, she reminded herself grimly, and tried her best to radiate sweetness and light while at the same time doing a decent job of interrogating the witness. "He gave you one of those fifty-dollar bills every time you brought him a drink that night, didn't he?"

And, oh yeah, let's not forget to smile.

Tiffany wet her lips as Jess stretched hers. "Yes, ma'am."

Turn that smile toward the jury. Let them see how unthreatening you are. Hey, the middle-aged woman in the yellow dress in the front row is smiling back. I think she l-i-i-kes you.

"And how many drinks did you bring him?"

"F-four."

"Two hundred dollars. Mr. Phillips gave you two hundred dollars for bringing him four drinks. No wonder you gave him your phone number." Too much snark, Jess realized as soon as the words left her mouth. The Cheerios gurgled threateningly.

"Objection!" Olderman, a no-nonsense, fifty-ish career prosecutor with an impressive won-lost record, leaped to his feet. He was average height, thin, dressed in an appropriately lawyer-ish dark gray suit, with a limp white shirt and a nondescript blue tie. "That was uncalled for. It tends to impugn my client's character."

"Overruled. But you might want to watch your tone, Ms. Dean." Judge Howard Schmidt looked at Jess reprovingly. Sixty-two, white-haired, carrying north of two hundred and fifty pounds on a five-eight frame, he resembled Santa Claus without the beard. The good news was, as everyone knew, Schmidt was prone to favoring women. The bad news was, Jess wasn't the only woman in the courtroom, far from it, so that only helped her as far as a match-up with Olderman was concerned.

"Sorry, Your Honor." Jess was determined not to let her Malti-poo slip again. "May I restate?"

The trouble was, she didn't believe in

Christine's idiotic system any more than she believed in Phillips's innocence.

And keeping up that damned Christine-ordered perpetual smile was starting to interfere with her concentration, to say nothing of the fact that it was making her cheeks feel as stiff as hardening concrete.

"Please do," the judge answered. "I didn't realize there was a question in there."

Jess tuned out the dryness of his tone and, with an apologetic glance at the jury, turned her achey/smiley face toward the witness.

"Did Mr. Phillips give you two hundred dollars for bringing him four drinks, Ms. Higgs?" Her tone was positively honeyed this time.

"Yes." Tiffany shot an anguished glance at the jury. "I didn't—it wasn't about the money. I—I liked him and . . ."

Break in quick, before the witness and the jury can connect.

"Two hundred dollars is a lot of money, though, isn't it? And you've already testified that you were short on your rent that month and had a number of other expenses you couldn't meet besides. Isn't that right?"

Tiffany's shoulders slumped in defeat. "Yes, ma'am."

Never mind that Jess was only twenty-eight herself, looked about eighteen, and was handling the witness as delicately as possible under the circumstances. Tiffany was making her look like a bully. Another sideways glance told Jess that those shaky "ma'am's" were playing well with the jury, which was broken down pretty evenly by race and gender but skewed fifties and older. She could see that many of them were thinking of their own daughters, or granddaughters, or nieces, or whoever, and she immediately vowed to ask no more yes-or-no questions to which a "ma'am" could be attached if she could avoid it.

And smile. Christine's voice seemed to echo in her head. Jess stretched her lips wide one more time.

"Mr. Phillips did subsequently call you, isn't that right? That same night? About what time was that?"

"I got off at two, so a little before that."

"What did he say?"

"He wanted to know if I wanted to go out with him, go to a party with him."

"And how did you answer?"

"I-I said yes."

"You said yes." Jess spun that out to maximum effect, looking significantly at the jury as she did so. There it was, straight from the horse's mouth, she willed her eyes to say above that fixed smile: Tiffany Higgs had said yes. Hopefully, the unspoken question that was left hanging was, what else had she said yes to that night? Jess watched the jury register it, felt a spurt of satisfaction, then let her attention swing back to the witness. "Where did he take you, Ms. Higgs?"

The courtroom went quiet in expectation. The grandmotherly juror's knitting continued to rest untouched in her lap. The third juror from the left in the rear—male, midsixties, retired pilot—quit the incessant rocking back and forth in his chair that had underlined most of the proceedings with a just-audible-enough-to-be-annoying squeak. The rustling in the courtroom pews stopped. Even the court reporter's fingers suspended over the keys.

There had been so much media coverage that everyone, it seemed, knew the prosecution's version of the story: Rob

Phillips had lured an unsuspecting Tiffany Higgs up to his apartment, where he had brutally attacked and raped her. Repeatedly. Over the course of a weekend that she claimed to have spent handcuffed to a bed. Only a fire in a neighboring apartment, which had brought firefighters in to evacuate the building, had saved her. The jury knew they were now getting to the steamy, salacious, sensational meat of it. Jess could feel the anticipation in the courtroom building, coursing like electricity through the air.

"He took me to his apartment." Tiffany's voice was so low that Jess had to strain to hear it. But asking her to repeat what she had just said might smack of badgering the witness, so she refrained.

"His apartment," Jess repeated distinctly instead.

"Yes, ma'am."

Crap. Another "ma'am."

"So you went with Mr. Phillips to his apartment at two a.m." Jess's tone made that in and of itself sound reprehensible. Before Tiffany could counter with another miserable-sounding "yes, ma'am," Jess hurried to add, "Would you say you went with him willingly? Or not?"

"W-willingly."

"Refresh my memory, if you would, Ms. Higgs: what floor is Mr. Phillips's apartment on?"

"The sixth."

"To reach his apartment, you and Mr. Phillips rode up in an elevator together, isn't that right? Do you recall how many others were in the elevator with you?"

"Three."

Jess felt a spurt of satisfaction. Tiffany's voice had gone way low again. Tiffany knew what was coming, and she feared it.

"Three." Jess nodded pleasantly. It was always good to agree with the witness when you could. Feeling virtuous because she was being so nice, and was even re-membering to keep her mouth stretched into that gotta-like-me smile, she cast a significant look at the jury. "We've already heard from those witnesses, but I want to make sure that there's no mistake, so I'm going to ask you, Ms. Higgs: what were you and Mr. Phillips doing as you rode up to his apartment in the elevator?"

Tiffany wet her lips. The look she shot Jess was resentful. "You know the answer. We were kissing."

"You were *kissing*." Jess rolled the word around on her tongue for the delectation of the jury, then felt vaguely dirty. And if that made her feel dirty, she hated to think what she was going to feel like when she took Tiffany through a blow-by-blow description of her version of what had happened in Rob Phillips's apartment that night. Maybe, if she was lucky, Pearse would take over before then. But then, she'd never been very lucky. "Correct me if I'm wrong, but hadn't you just met the man about two hours before?"

"Objection!" Olderman was once more on his feet. "How long she had known him is immaterial. Opposing counsel is again clearly trying to influence the jury's opinion of Ms. Higgs's character."

"Sustained." Judge Schmidt frowned at her. Jess tried to look innocent. "Watch yourself, Ms. Dean."

"Sorry, Your Honor." Jess took a deep breath and turned her attention back to Tiffany, who was visibly shrinking in her chair. "You stated that you and Mr. Phillips were kissing. Would you characterize your participation as willing or unwilling?"

The previous testimony on that point, plus the grainy security video that had been recovered, made it incontrovertible, or Jess wouldn't have asked the question. Never ask anything in court you don't already know the answer to: Law School 101.

"I was willing." Tiffany's eyes darted toward the prosecution table in obvious distress.

"According to the previous witnesses, you and Mr. Phillips were, in fact, 'making out' in the elevator." Jess managed to sound a little sorrowful at having to point this out, and mentally patted herself on the back for her tone.

Tiffany's head came up. She took a deep breath.

"That was when I still thought he was a nice guy." She looked toward the jury. Her eyes flashed. Her voice rose in sudden, unexpected defiance. "But he isn't! As soon as he got me inside his apartment he changed into a monster. He hurt me! He raped me! He said—I thought—he was going to kill me! It's the *truth*, so help me God."

Then, before Jess could even begin to counteract in any way, Tiffany dropped her head into her hands and burst into noisy tears.

CHAPTER FOUR

Jess felt the jury's sudden rush of sympathy for Tiffany slam into her like a gust of gale-force wind. The Cheerios clumped into a knot.

"Your Honor!" Olderman was on his feet, raising his voice in an effort to be heard over the sudden excited buzz from the gallery. "We request a recess to allow the witness time to compose herself. Your Honor!"

"The defense has no objection to giving Ms. Higgs time to compose herself, Your Honor," Jess said before Judge Schmidt could respond. The sounds emanating from beneath Tiffany's pale hands pressed to her even paler face were heart-rending. Enough so to make even Jess, who was busy steeling her heart by reminding herself that from the defense's perspective this emotional display was nothing more than a ploy designed to unfairly prejudice the jury, feel a nearly irresistible impulse to pat the weeping woman consolingly on the shoulder.

"This seems to me like a good time to take a lunch break," Judge Schmidt announced to the courtroom at large. "It's almost noon anyway. We'll reconvene at two."

Noise filled the courtroom as everybody sprang to life at once. The judge rose, as did the jury. The prosecution team converged on Tiffany. Jess retreated to the defense table.

"You call that a Malti-poo?" Christine greeted her under her breath, shaking her improbably red head so that the ends of her short, feathery 'do quivered. At forty-one, formidable in a black blazer, flowing skirt, and polka-dot bow-necked blouse that made her look just about as wide as she was tall (nearly six feet), Christine had coarse features, sallow skin, and small, snapping brown eyes. The combination should have made her unattractive, but it didn't, because her personality was forceful enough to overcome any physical flaws. She had a Ph.D. in psychology and a J.D. from Stanford Law and was arguably the preeminent jury consultant in the country. Which, of course, was why she was on Ellis Hayes's payroll: with a few notable exceptions, they only hired the best. Christine was already on her feet and gathering her belongings preparatory to going to lunch even as she glared at Jess. "Hell, you're as bad as Collins. Just smaller. And female."

Her bulk blocked her comments from being overheard by anyone else, for which Jess was thankful. Since Pearse had conscripted her onto the defense team, originally just temporarily, to help with background research because the member of his team who usually did that had been sent off on a quick business trip to follow a lead, and had then eloped and failed to return, she'd been working with Christine every day. She liked her, respected her, was learning a lot from her and appreciated her outspoken ways. Usually. At least when the caustic remarks

Christine was famous for weren't directed at her.

"I was gentle with her. I smiled," Jess protested in an aggrieved undertone.

"Some smile." Christine slid a yellow legal pad into her briefcase. "I've seen better smiles on barracudas. Hope you don't have any lunch plans, cause we've got some work to do."

Jess started to reply, then almost bit her tongue as a heavy arm dropped unexpectedly around her shoulders.

"How ya doin', sweetheart?" The defendant's father gave Jess a hard hug that had her fighting back a grimace. Though it might not have been working just at present on her, the three-term senator from Virginia was renowned for his charm. A blue-blooded charter member of the D.C. old boy network, he was a glad-hander, a kisser of babies, always clapping men on the back or hugging women, immensely popular with his constituents. Six feet tall, a little overweight, a little jowly at sixty-two, he was still a handsome man with regular features and a full head of dark hair (Grecian Formula, anyone?). He was also one of the leading contenders to be the next Republican nominee for president of the United States, or at least he had been before his son had been charged with rape. Appearing beside him, his wife, Vicky, nodded a greeting. A tall, thin, fifty-something blonde, Georgetown chic in a pale blue linen suit and pearls, she reached for her son's arm even as he, a younger, handsomer version of his father, came around the table to join them.

"I can't say I like the way this is going," the senator continued without waiting for Jess to reply. He was looking at Pearse.

"We've got to get the truth out of her." Mrs. Phillips, too, was looking at Pearse. "All that shaking and crying she's doing—she's making the jury feel sorry for her. Can't you get the judge to order her to stop that?"

"There's no doubt the witness's demeanor is having an effect on the jury, but I'd rather not make an issue of it." Pearse gave Mrs. Phillips his best reassuring smile.

He was on his feet, buttoning up the jacket of his perfectly tailored gray suit, which he wore with a white shirt and silver tie. Pearse was vain, as the best defense lawyers often were, gravitating to the profession because it called for much peacock-y strutting before a jury, and the ensemble had been chosen, Jess suspected, to play up the arresting light gray of his eyes. Six-three, forty-ish, with a leonine mane of raven hair and the burly build of a prize fighter, Pearse had a prominent nose, broad, high cheekbones, and a jaw so square it could have been stolen from Mt. Rushmore. Handsome wasn't the right word to describe him, although Jess supposed he was. Imposing was a better one. A Yale grad himself, he was the biggest of Ellis Hayes's big guns in the criminal defense division. "I'm hoping that when it counts, Ms. Higgs's emotionalism will work in our favor."

"It makes her look like the nutcase she is, Mama, don't you see? That's what we want. That's what Jessie here is trying to show." Rob smiled at Jess even as he spoke reassuringly to his mother. It was an effort to smile back: she hated the way he called her Jessie, which no one else ever did and no one had invited him to do. It was inappropriate under the circumstances. It was condescending. It was irritating, particularly since, given the fact that she was a very lowly member of the defense team and he was the client, correcting him wasn't in the cards. Add in the fact that he had somehow acquired her cell phone number and had called her on it twice, both times to ask her something he could have found out from anyone else, and it was also a little creepy. "It should be obvious to anyone from just watching her up there that she's got some major emotional problems. So that's good for us, huh?"

He, too, looked at Pearse, who made a noncommittal gesture by way of a reply.

"The woman's a liar." Mrs. Phillips's expression was fierce. "Can't they see that?"

"She's hanging herself up there. You just heard her admit we were making out in the elevator." Rob patted his mother's hand. "Jessie's got her on the run already." His eyes met Jess's. She realized that one of the things she found so off-putting about him was his smug assumption that she found him attractive. "You just keep hammering away at her, Jessie, and she'll fall apart, see if she doesn't."

She forced a smile in response and devoutly hoped he couldn't read what she was thinking: *I don't like you.*

He was tanned, with even features, gleaming white teeth, and dark brown hair kept short and well groomed for the trial. Handsome, well-educated, and rich—Rob Phillips shouldn't have been hard up for female company, so why, Jess kept asking herself in an effort to bolster her own personal belief in his innocence, would he need to resort to rape? She'd been in his orbit for weeks now, and he'd been nothing but friendly toward her. Overfriendly? That was, she supposed, a matter of opinion, based, objectively, on nothing more than those two phone calls and the way he called her Jessie. Still, above and beyond that, there was something about him that just simply made her radar go off.

Something about him that bothered her. Something that increasingly made her think, *I'm terrified Tiffany's telling the truth.*

It was a gut feeling that was inconvenient, unwelcome, unsettling. It also, she reminded herself grimly, had nothing to do with anything factual, or, indeed, anything at all. By law, Rob Phillips was entitled to the best defense money could buy.

And that was Ellis Hayes.

He smiled at her then, the slow smile of a man who thinks he's charming the woman he's targeting, and she couldn't help it: client or no client, she frowned and looked pointedly away.

Whatever the truth about his guilt or innocence, she was working hard to get Rob Phillips off the hook here. She didn't have to flirt with him, too.

"You're being too nice to the whore," Senator Phillips lowered his voice to say to Jess, his tone turning vicious. She felt her throat tighten, both at the word, which she hated to hear applied to any woman but found especially offensive in this particular context, and at the idea that this very important man who was paying the bill was less than pleased with her work. Fortunately, she didn't have to reply: he was already looking past her to Pearse. "With all due respect to Miss Dean here, I'd feel better about things if you were helming the ship, Pearse."

"I am helming the ship. Jess is just asking the questions," Pearse answered. "You know we agreed to follow Dr. Hubbard's strategy."

"You're paying me big bucks, Senator, and the reason you are is because I am damned good at my job," Christine said. "So I suggest you let me do what it is I do." She switched her gaze to Jess. "You're keeping the jury from going completely over to the prosecution's side, which is the important thing right now, while Ms. Higgs is up there shaking and crying on the stand. Later, when they have other witnesses up there, Pearse can do his thing."

They were all, including defense co-counsel Andrew Brisco—Columbia grad, mid-thirties, attractive if not precisely handsome, with shaggy auburn hair, blunt features, and rimless glasses that slightly magnified bright blue eyes—moving toward the door by that time. Andrew, who was five-ten and lean, looked small walking behind Pearse. Andrew was the physical evidence expert, but his role in the courtroom today was basically to serve as another set of eyes and ears, and an extra brain on which Pearse as lead counsel could rely.

"Interrogating the victim in a rape case is damned hard." Andrew's remark was obviously aimed at Senator Phillips. Jess was touched to realize that he was coming to her defense. She didn't know him at all well, as most of her interaction to date had been with Pearse and Christine. "You pretty much can't win no matter what you do. You just don't want to turn the jury off to your side of the story until you can give them the picture you want them to see."

No one replied to that, but Jess smiled gratefully at him as she pushed through the gate with the rest of the defense team. They fell in behind the straggling crowd of exiting spectators heading up the aisle.

Lunch would be waiting in the counsel room off to the left for the defense team. No need for any of them to so much as leave the floor unless they wanted to, which Jess wouldn't have even if Christine hadn't made it clear they were working through lunch: too much media outside, for one thing. Given her recent notoriety, the last thing she needed was an encounter with the media, especially when she'd been asked—no, ordered—to keep a low profile.

Which so far hadn't exactly worked out so well.

Two women came barreling down the aisle, pushing their way through the exiting horde, and Jess recognized Tiffany's mother and sister. The mother was short and heavy-set, with small eyes and a smaller mouth set in a round face topped by a slick cap of black hair. The sister was as blond and waiflike as Tiffany.

That's why what she said as she shouldered past Jess came as such a shock.

Looking Jess squarely in the eye as she shoved past, she muttered, "Bitch."

Head swiveling after the sister because she couldn't help herself, Jess saw that beyond her, in the well, Tiffany was just now stepping down from the witness stand. Olderman's hand curled around her elbow to steady her, and Sandra Johnson, the lone woman on the prosecution team, held her hand and talked softly to her. Then the mother and sister burst through the gate and fell on Tiffany with loud cries of sympathy. Jess jerked her eyes forward again, but not before she noticed that Sandra Johnson, who'd relinquished her position to Tiffany's family members, was smiling. And not because of the touching family tableau in front of her, either, Jess knew. She was smiling because, from her perspective, life was good. From Olderman on to Johnson and David Kister, also a veteran prosecutor, the vibe was quietly confident. They obviously felt the trial was going their way. Now their three-strong prosecution team plus Tiffany's family hovered solicitously around Tiffany, who was drooping in their midst like a wilted flower. Everything about the prosecutors, from the ink staining their fingers—courtesy of the cheap pens called for by government budget constraints—to their slightly seedy suits, made it clear: compared to the high-powered, big-moneyed defense, these were the low-rent guys. They were—or should have been—the underdogs. But they weren't, not with this trial, not today. Because, in the end, it was all up to the jury, and juries were unpredictable.

Which was why trying a case was more art than science, and why Christine's pronouncements were treated like they'd been handed down from Mt. Olympus, Malti-poos and all.

The bottom line was, teams with Christine on them overwhelmingly won. And Ellis Hayes was being paid to win.

"You're looking pale." Andrew gave Jess a wry smile as he slowed his step to walk

beside her. "At a guess, I'd say you're starting to feel a little vampirish right now."

"Vampirish?"

"That's what we get in the middle of
these big trials: vampirish. Because we're
up all night, and never see the light of day."

It was an effort, but Jess smiled. But he
was right, she realized. Outside, it was a
steamy late August day, drenched in sunlight, thick with the sweaty humidity of D.C.
in late summer, busy with the last gasp of
tourists straggling into the capital before
the nation's schools got back in session.
Since she'd been involved in this trial, Jess
had caught only fleeting glimpses of summer. Trapped in the artificially cool, fluorescent confines of various buildings until, at
something like eleven o'clock at night, she
was free to stagger home and fall exhausted
into bed before rising at dawn and doing it
all again the next day, she was indeed starting to feel like Persephone trapped in the
underworld.

Or vampirish, as Andrew had suggested.

But working hard—putting in the hours
required to get the job done to the best of
her ability—was what she did. It was the
only way she knew to climb the ladder.

She wasn't the smartest, wasn't the most attractive, wasn't the most politically connected young associate in the firm. Far from it, in fact. But what she could be, arguably, was the hardest working.

She was the only one of her colleagues that she knew of who hadn't come from an Ivy League college, a top-ten law school. Her alma mater was George Mason, a D.C. school that catered to part-time, working-class students. This position at Ellis Hayes was the chance of a lifetime for someone like her. She'd gotten it because she'd acquired some unlikely but highly useful connections. Having gotten it, she was prepared to do whatever it took to make it a success. To make herself a success.

The desire to succeed burned in her bones.

"Could I have a word with you, Pearse?" Senator Phillips asked as they reached the hall, and he and Pearse moved away together.

Jess followed Christine into the counsel room. Hayley Marciano, the fifth member of the defense team, was inside, already helping herself to the catered lunch that had been set out on the credenza.

"Oh, well, what could you do? You did the best you could." Carrying her plate toward the table as she spoke, Hayley greeted Jess with a shrug and a small, tight, faux smile. Jess was reminded that Hayley had been watching the proceedings on closed-circuit TV with the sound off—Christine was big on the importance of analyzing nonverbal cues from the witness as well as others in the courtroom—while taking notes to be dissected later, because the judge had refused to allow the proceedings to be taped. In her early thirties, tall, slender, and exotically lovely with faintly oriental features and sleek black hair pulled into a knot at her nape, dressed in the female lawyer's staple and Jess's own preferred garb of a black pantsuit, Hayley had volunteered for the job of questioning Tiffany when it had become obvious that Pearse's effort was not going over well with the jury. She had been smacked down by Christine, who'd pronounced her a Doberman. "Elegant," Christine had said. "Patrician. Cold as ice. Vicious in a fight. This jury won't take to her."

Hayley had taken the assessment badly. In consequence she had been more dismissive even than usual to Jess, whom, as she had made abundantly clear from the beginning, she considered beneath her Harvard-educated self. Now, with Hayley looking at her with more than a hint of smirky satisfaction, Jess concluded that her performance was making Hayley's day.

Ouch.

But she wasn't about to give Hayley the satisfaction of letting her know how much the knowledge bothered her.

"At least the judge hasn't banned me from the courtroom yet." Jess's tone was light, but Hayley's eyes widened angrily. In a firm like Ellis Hayes, gossip got around: even though Jess hadn't been working there when it had happened, she'd heard from numerous sources the tale of the judge who'd ordered Hayley removed from her courtroom for blatantly flirting with a male juror. Among those who worked with Hayley, the incident, including Hayley's subsequent dressing-down by the usually mild-mannered Pearse, had already become the stuff of legend.

"Like I said before, this is a sympathetic victim." Busy filling her plate, Christine intervened before Hayley could reply. "Isn't a lot anyone can do about that. We just got to work around it. We—"

The sound of the door opening served as an interruption, and they all glanced around as Pearse entered. As unflappable as they came, Pearse looked just as he always did, at least to Jess. But Andrew, who'd known him longer, grimaced. "Gave you hell, did he?"

"The senator tends to be very hands-on. He wanted to go over this afternoon's questions with me. Among other things."

"You tell him where he could stick it?" Christine rolled her eyes toward Pearse as he joined her at the buffet line.

"See, that's why I'm the head of this team: I don't tell the paying clients where they can stick it."

"He's smooth." Andrew's praise of Pearse was affectionately mocking.

"Unlike you." Hayley made a face at Andrew as he sat down. "We all know you couldn't be smooth if you tried."

"Someone get up on the wrong side of the bed this morning?" Andrew raised his eyebrows at her.

"Let's concentrate on the case, shall we?" Pearse intervened, giving the two of them quelling looks. "Hayley, you were watching the prosecution team. You notice any areas they seemed particularly sensitive to?"

"The elevator. The making out thing. They tensed up when that was alluded to. In my opinion, more should have been done to really hammer home the fact that Higgs was kissing Phillips willingly."

Recognizing that for the dig at her it undoubtedly was, Jess ignored the poison-dart look Hayley sent her way and sat down with her plate, which held half a turkey sandwich and a spoonful of salad, very little of which she expected to actually eat. Mindful of the Cheerios, which were still making their presence known, she thought it better to err on the side of caution when it came to putting anything else into her nervous stomach.

"This afternoon," Pearse promised.

"Somebody probably also needs to tell Rob Phillips's mother not to glare at Higgs the whole time Higgs is on the stand." Hayley's tone was strictly business now. "I'm fairly certain the jury's noticed. And Mrs. Phillips is not the most sympathetic character anyway."

"That would be you, Boss," Andrew said to Pearse, grinning. "You get to have all the fun."

"A couple of days from now, when the prosecution experts are trying to tear apart your forensics, then you'll be the one who's having fun," Pearse retorted. "Or not."

"They won't be trying. They'll be doing. People can cry, people can lie, but there's no arguing with good old physical evidence." Andrew grimaced gloomily as he stirred sugar into his tea. "Too bad almost none of it favors our side. Lucky I'm the best there is at making a molehill look like a mountain."

"I'll say," Hayley murmured with a wicked glint.

"You two aren't sleeping together, are you? 'Cause if you are, I'd like to be let in on it. I need some amusement in my life." Looking from Hayley to Andrew, Christine forked salad into her mouth.

"Of course not." Hayley and Andrew spoke in almost perfect unison, both on an identical note of repugnance, then exchanged wary, measuring glances.

"Focus, people. Focus. We've got a trial

to win here." Putting his plate on the table, Pearse sat down beside Andrew.

"And so far we're not getting the job done." Stabbing the air with another forkful of salad, Christine glared around the table. "This is a reasonable doubt jury. All we got to do is cast some reasonable doubt. How hard can that be?"

"Harder than you think," Andrew muttered, then took cover behind a hastily lifted sub sandwich as Christine's gaze swung around.

Jess was just taking a cautious nibble off the end of her turkey sandwich when Christine's glare stopped on her. The fork stabbed in her direction.

"First thing we got to do here is work on your Malti-poo. The jury doesn't like you, nothing else you say or do is gonna make a difference."

Good thing she hadn't planned on eating, because for Jess, after that, lunch turned into a drill session. By the time the break was almost over, Jess's anxiety level had ratcheted up to such a pitch that her mouth was dry and her hands were shaking. But this was a huge opportunity for her. She was determined to take it and run with it.

Or at the very least not totally blow it.

Please God.

Sick to her stomach: that's how Jess felt as she headed back into the courtroom. Girding herself for the afternoon session, she tried to control her nerves by taking a series of surreptitious, but deep and hopefully calming, breaths.

The net result of which was that she was light-headed from an overabundance of carbon dioxide, as well as anxious as she took her place at counsel table.

"All rise!" the bailiff called. Judge Schmidt took his seat, Tiffany returned to the witness stand, Jess tried for adorable and competent at the same time without, she felt, a whole lot of success with either, and it was *game on* again.

Only there was something different about Tiffany.

Jess didn't notice it at first. But as the testimony got more graphic—"If there was a struggle, how was it your underwear wasn't torn, Ms. Higgs?"—Tiffany began to breathe unevenly. Her hands gripped the chair as if she was afraid it was going to try to run away from her.

And she had yet to come out with a single "ma'am."

Even as she asked her next question, Jess lost her grip on her inner Malti-poo and frowned.

"Were you gagged, Ms. Higgs?"

"No."

"So you screamed, is that right?"

"No."

Although she had known the answer—Tiffany claimed that Rob's threats had made her too terrified to make a sound—Jess, playing to the jury, strove to look surprised. "You surely cried out for help in some fashion. After all, you were in his apartment for almost forty-eight hours, and there were other people in the building. You didn't scream, or at the very least yell out something like, *Help, help, call 911*?"

"No." Tiffany's truncated replies were starting to get to Jess. They just didn't feel right. But what could she do? She'd already thrown in a number of yes-and-no type questions just as a test. She couldn't stop and ask Tiffany point-blank if something was bothering her, which, in any case, wasn't her problem.

"The reason you didn't scream for help is because you didn't need help, isn't that right? And the reason you didn't need help is because the sex acts you were engaged in with Rob Phillips were absolutely consensual."

It was a flourish for the jury, meant to plant a certain image in their minds. The image the defense wanted them to have.

Tiffany's lips parted. They moved, but no sound emerged. Despite herself, Jess felt desperately sorry for the girl.

"Objection!" Olderman was on his feet.

"Overruled."

Jess took Judge Schmidt's weary-sounding answer as permission to continue in the same vein. "They were consensual sex acts, weren't they? Tiffany?"

Oops. Using Tiffany's first name out loud like that was a slip of the tongue. It was something opposing counsel rarely did, because it tended to humanize the witness for the jury, which was never a good idea. But it was too late to recall it now. All she could do was hope to gloss over her mistake. Jess expected Tiffany to gasp out some version of *No, that's not right, that's not how it was*, and got her riposte ready.

But to her complete amazement, the words that came out of Tiffany's mouth in strangled bursts of sound were, "Yes. Yes, you're right. Okay? It—everything was consensual. He—he—it was consensual."

Jess froze. Around her the courtroom went dead silent. Jess could practically feel the electric surge of energy as every eye and ear in the room focused on the young woman on the witness stand.

"Are you saying you were *not* raped by Rob Phillips?"

Tiffany met Jess's gaze. Her eyes were huge and anguished. Her fingers gripped the chair arms so tightly that her knuckles bulged. "Yes. I mean, no. No. I was not."

Then, for the second time that day, she burst into tears.

And all hell erupted in the courtroom.

CHAPTER FIVE

Jess was still in shock some eight hours later, when she left The Capital Grille, the chichi restaurant on Pennsylvania Avenue where Pearse had taken them all to celebrate, and headed for home. Slipping out a side door to avoid the media, a few members of which had gathered outside the restaurant hoping for more sound bites for their 11:00 p.m. newscasts, she glanced warily around as she went down the shallow flight of steps to the sidewalk. So close to the White House, there were a lot of people out and about, even at 9:20 p.m. Traffic was moving well, but the vehicles were practically bumper to bumper. One fender bender, and gridlock would ensue. On the sidewalk, shorts-clad tourists peering at maps competed for space with white-collar types in business suits, more festively clad vacationers intent on sampling the area's high-end restaurants and bars, and D.C.'s motley cast of permanent residents going about their business.

As soon as she left the steps behind, Jess was swallowed up by the moving crowd. She blended right in, and she was thankful to discover that no one seemed to be paying her the least bit of attention. Earlier, TV cameras had already captured them all—the whole defense team— leaving the courthouse together, which in her case was a big no-no. She had been instructed to keep away from the media at all costs. But she hadn't been able to help it: she'd been trapped, with no way to escape as the reporters had crowded around. While she had tried to unobtrusively shelter behind him, Pearse had given an interview right there on the courthouse steps, with a jubilant Rob Phillips and his beaming, triumphant parents standing beside him and the rest of the team gathered around. They all—all except Jess—had seemed eager to bask in the brilliance of the klieg lights, savoring the victory, savoring the moment.

The unspoken consensus among most of the celebrants had been, it just doesn't get any better than this.

Tiffany had recanted, right there on the witness stand. The judge had been aghast, the prosecution apoplectic, the defense over-the-moon ebullient. Pearse, Christine, and Andrew had been effusive in their praise of Jess's cross-examination, with Pearse singling out her "artful" use of Tiffany's first name for particular commendation. She hadn't corrected him, hadn't let on that it had been a total slip of the tongue, hadn't done anything to erase their apparent impression that she had known exactly what she'd been doing. Even Hayley had grudgingly said something to the effect of *What do you know, you actually got the job done,* accompanied by a sour smile. Senator Phillips, his wife, and son had whooped and hollered and hugged and kissed everyone within reach—Jess included, to her discomfort—before eventually heading off to National Airport, where a private jet had been summoned to whisk them away to a friend's summer home in Bar Harbor, where they meant to spend the next few days recuperating along the cool Maine coastline.

The trial had been over. Just like that. Directed verdict: not guilty. The defense had won.

Yay, team!

Rutherford Dunn, Ellis Hayes's octogenarian managing partner, had called to offer the defense team congratulations, which was rather like having Zeus call down from Mt. Olympus, and had spoken to Jess personally. *(Oh, the glory!).*

Pearse had practically floored her by offering her a permanent spot on his team.

And a large bonus check had been promised to each member of the defense by senior management, which was thrilled at the high-profile victory.

She should have been incandescent with excitement, Jess knew. For her, it was an important, career-making moment. Heading down 6th Street away from the little band of reporters gathered on the sidewalk in front of the restaurant, meaning to hail a cab at the first opportunity, she should have been walking on air. She should have been as aglow as the rows of windows in the historic buildings lining the street, which now gleamed brightly with golden reflections of the setting sun. Deep inside, she should have been feeling as warm and mellow as the truly gorgeous late summer evening, the first one she had actually experienced firsthand for quite a while.

But she wasn't.

Instead, she was anxious, worried, troubled. Depressed, even. Carefully cataloguing her feelings in an effort to account for her down mood, she concluded the list with an inner snort and a wry, *Typical me. Have to look for the fly in every ointment.*

The thing was, though, lucky always tended to happen to someone else. She wasn't that type of person: good fortune didn't just fall into her lap. Never had, never would. From the age of five, when her father and little sister had drowned before her eyes, more bad things had happened in her life than good ones. No way Tiffany should have folded like that. No way the trial should have been over, Rob Phillips vindicated, the defense coming up heroes. Her coming up a hero. Not so easily. Not just like that.

Maybe, she thought hopefully, *maybe I've changed. Maybe after twenty-eight years the tide has turned. Maybe I am that type of person now.*

Her mouth twisted. *And if you believe that, there's a Lotto ticket with your name on it for sale in that delicatessen right on the next corner.*

Jess knew already she wasn't going to pop in and fork over five dollars for it. Which meant, she acknowledged gloomily, that as much as she wanted to, she didn't believe. Her luck hadn't changed. The world hadn't suddenly turned all rosy and new.

Something's wrong.

The thought had been taking on form and substance in her mind since the first shock of Tiffany's confession had begun to fade. It had just coalesced into those two words when an enormous SUV, a black Chevy Suburban with tinted windows that kept her from getting a look at the driver, pulled over to the curb beside her. With her startle reflex now on near-permanent red alert, Jess jumped, nearly coming out of her Christine-selected, slightly too-large pink pumps as she cast a quick, nervous look toward it.

Which immediately turned to a fierce frown as the window lowered and she recognized the driver.

"Pink's definitely your color," drawled an all-too-familiar male voice, and through the open window her eyes locked with a pair of mocking blue ones that had just finished giving her a thorough once-over. He was as wicked handsome as ever—more proof that she just wasn't naturally lucky—with short, thick, light brown (dark blond? She could never make up her mind) hair, a lean, angular face that was deeply tanned from hours spent outdoors, and the kind of gorgeous baby blues that had once made her heart go pitter-pat every time they'd turned in her direction. His features weren't perfect: his nose was a little too thick, his lips a little too thin, and, at thirty-six, he had a few creases around his eyes and some deeper lines running from his nose to his mouth. All of which, of course, looked good on him. He was six feet two inches tall with the broad-shouldered, hard-sculpted build of the professional football player he had once been. He was Secret Service Agent Mark Ryan, among many other things eye candy extraordinaire, and she hated him. Especially when amusement at her twinkled in his eyes, like it was doing now. "So where're you hiding the Chihuahua?"

There was no mistaking what he was referring to. It burned her up that he had made the Elle Woods connection, too. Much as she would rather not acknowledge it, she and Mark had always thought alike. On some things, at least, although not necessarily the ones that mattered.

"What do you want?" Her tone was disagreeable. Even now, just looking at him made her heart beat faster, and the realization maddened her. She'd once thought this guy hung the moon. That he was the love of her life. Prince Charming to her Cinderella. As in so many other things, she'd been wrong.

"Thought you might like a ride home."

"Then you thought wrong." Baring her teeth at him—she couldn't really call the thing that stretched her mouth a smile—she walked on.

"Nice ass," he called after her, earning

that part of her anatomy interested glances from two male lawyer types and one bum picking through a sidewalk wastebasket that she happened to be passing just at that moment.

Jess barely missed a step, but inwardly she sizzled. Just as she was meant to, she knew. That comment had been intended to make her mad, to make her turn on him, to make her engage him in conversation.

Hah. She wasn't going to give him the satisfaction of seeing her rise to the bait. Her chin went up, her shoulders squared, and she took a quick, fortifying breath, but those instinctive physical responses were the only reactions he was going to get.

She simply kept walking.

Ignoring the bleating horns of inconvenienced drivers—a barricade for a road repair project was tying up a second lane, adding to the damage—the Suburban cruised along the curb just behind her. She was so acutely aware of it that she almost ran into a trio of elderly women headed in the opposite direction. And, even more embarrassing, a few strides later on, a tree, one of the planted-in-the-sidewalk variety with which the local movers and shakers hoped to beautify downtown.

Damn it.

"You know you want me."

The laughter in his voice made her fists clench. Thankfully one was curled around the strap of her shoulder bag and the other clutched the handle of her briefcase, so it was unlikely that he would notice. A few grins directed her way confirmed that their moving audience was still listening in.

"Go away," she snapped over her shoulder, earning interested stares from an even greater number of passersby as she kept walking.

"You just keep fighting this thing between us, baby. I'm still going to be right here when you give up."

The interested stares turned into a smattering of snickers. Jess felt her cheeks heat. It was all she could do not to flip him the bird. But she didn't and was rewarded for her forbearance by the sight of an empty cab nestled in among the traffic cruising toward her along Indiana Avenue, just about half a block from where it intersected with 6th Street, which was directly ahead of her. *Oh, joy!* Waving to catch the driver's attention, she took off for the corner.

And almost fell flat on her face as one of her cute little kitten heels caught in a crack in the sidewalk and she ran right out of her too-big left shoe. Stumbling forward, she barely managed to catch herself on another of those ornamental trees seconds before she would have landed on her knees on the pavement. A rolling wave of guffaws from the peanut gallery surrounding her was drowned out by the sudden, sharp blare of what sounded like dozens of car horns. Ahead of her, the cab sailed on through the intersection, blithely oblivious, lost forever.

Was that the way life worked or what? Her life, at least.

Regaining her balance with the help of the tree, Jess now felt like she was being watched by not only Mark but a cast of thousands as well, and she set her teeth.

"Do you need some help, miss?" The speaker was a nice old guy from someplace that wasn't D.C. A tourist, complete with map, in a brimmed hat and plaid shorts and sandals with socks. His alarmed-looking gray-haired wife clutched his arm.

"No, thanks. I'm fine." She smiled at them to prove it. They smiled back and moved on.

Thank goodness the crowd that had witnessed her discomfiture was moving on with them. It would be too much to hope that Mark had moved on as well. In fact, she was sure he hadn't. The giveaway was all those angry car horns blasting through the concrete canyon around her. And the intensifying smell of automobile exhaust, which, trapped in this airless corridor, was no doubt building up to near lethal levels as ticked-off drivers struggled to get around Mark's stopped car.

To get away from him, she needed her shoe.

Hopping on her one remaining shod foot, hanging onto the smooth gray trunk of the young tree for balance, she turned to look for it.

She found it instantly. The pink pump with its tiny kitten heel, chosen to keep her looking small and feminine for the jury, was moving toward her. Dangling nonchalantly from Mark's right hand.

"Lose something?" Wearing snug-fitting jeans and a muscle-hugging T-shirt instead of the dark suit that was his—and the Secret Service's—de facto uniform, he walked toward her with that cocky athlete's stride that had once had the power to make her pant. Secretly, of course. Certainly he'd never known it, and she wasn't about to let him in on the news at this late date.

"Give me my shoe." She held out her hand for it.

Grinning, he stopped in front of her, dropped into a crouch, and grasped her ankle, with, she knew even as she attempted to pull free, the intention of putting her shoe on for her. His hand was as big and warm and strong as she remembered it being, and he had no trouble hanging on despite her attempts to kick free of his grasp. His touch on her bare skin made her breath catch. She barely managed to repress a shiver. Jeez, she'd thought—hoped—prayed—she was over him. But if she wasn't, he was the last person on earth she ever wanted to find out about it.

"You're making a scene," he chided, looking up at her.

A sidelong glance into a few faces in the crowd streaming around them told her he was right, at least to the degree that a scene was being made, although she might have vehemently disagreed about who was the cause of it. Lips compressing, she quit fighting and let him maneuver her shoe onto her foot.

"Good as new." With her shoe now more or less firmly returned to duty, he slid a caressing hand up the back of her calf. Outraged, she kicked at him again even as swift arrows of remembered longing shot straight for her solar plexus, and he let go.

"You're welcome," he said as her eyes shot sparks at him. Then he stood up.

For a moment Jess found herself staring straight at his wide chest. His T-shirt was navy with a Coors logo, and its short sleeves and thin knit made his brawny arms and the hard definition of his pecs impossible to miss. Mad at herself for noticing, she quickly adjusted her gaze upward. Being almost a foot shorter, even in her delicate heels, was a disadvantage in the glare wars, as she had already learned, to her annoyance. So she did her best to banish hers.

"What part of 'go away' did you misunderstand?"

She tried for a falsely sweet smile instead but didn't get there. Probably because someone in the near-deafening traffic jam just beyond them chose that moment to yell at Mark, "You moron, move your damned car!"

Goaded by the sight of the gridlock that she somehow—foolishly, idiotically, knowing that it was not her fault—felt responsible for, galvanized by the not-so-distant sound of sirens that she had a terrible feeling were headed their way, she abandoned subtle sarcasm for concrete disapproval with a testy, "Would you get back in your car?"

Apparently unabashed by the chaos he had created, he smiled at her, his patented eye-crinkling, you're-somebody-special smile that used to make her bones melt and her toes curl and now made her regard him with active suspicion.

"Not unless you get in with me."

She snorted. "In your dreams."

"Jess. I want to talk to you. And you need a ride. Don't be an idiot."

"Yo! Numbnuts! Get your car the hell out of the way!" A roar from a frustrated commuter sent Jess's blood pressure skyrocketing and her gaze shooting sideways with alarm. Drivers were opening their doors, standing up in the street to look. Trouble was clearly on the way. Her stomach tightened with anxiety. Her pulse sped up. Mark, of course, didn't so much as bat an eyelash.

Typical Mark. Typical her.

"Are you really going to be this big of a jerk?" Temper sharpened her voice, snapped from her eyes.

"What do you think?" As always, he was imperturbably cool.

She knew the answer, and it annoyed the hell out of her: yes, he was. At least until he got what he wanted.

"Move that car, you SOB!" This enraged howl from an ignored commuter had all the savagery of a war cry, and Jess didn't even have to look—although she did, and was proven right—to divine the yelling guy was heading their way.

Her eyes, wide now with alarm, shot back to Mark.

"Would you please just go?"

"Not unless you come with me."

Okay, she didn't actively hate him, she decided with feverish haste and one eye on the puce-faced, burly guy threading his way toward them through the seething mass of stopped-up traffic. She wasn't even really all that mad at him anymore. Finding out that the gorgeous hunk of Secret Service agent she'd secretly lusted after for months seemed to have developed a thing for her shy, nondescript, less-than-hot self had clouded her judgment. When circumstances had flung them together, she had tumbled headlong into a blazingly intense love affair that she should have realized from the outset had been far too hot not to burn itself out. Or, rather, explode, which was basically what had happened as they'd gotten to know each other better. She hadn't been happy to learn that he'd slept with half the beautiful women in Washington, D.C., including Mary Jane Cates, her current boss. He hadn't liked discovering that she was slightly allergic to marriage and that low-keying her hard-earned career while she settled into domestic bliss with him was just not going to happen. No how, no way.

In other words, it had been a classic case of mutual disillusionment. Just because the breakup had been as hot as the affair didn't mean that she couldn't be civil now.

Just as long as she didn't have to be civil for long.

Honk. Honk.

"Let's go!" "What's the holdup?" "I called the cops!" "Whose car is that?"

The chorus of disapproval from the traffic jam was growing louder by the second. Glancing down the street in a tizzy of apprehension, Jess saw that at least a dozen people were now out of their cars looking around for the owner of the idling SUV. Puce-faced guy, who clearly knew, had almost reached the sidewalk, which would put him maybe twenty feet behind the Suburban. Jogging toward them now, he was shaking his fist at Mark and screaming, *"You think you're not gonna move that car, dickhead? Huh? Huh?"*

Jess's eyes widened. Her heart gave a leap.

"Mark—" She looked back at him in alarm.

Mark's eyes met hers. Without so much as a change of expression, he pulled his wallet out of his pocket, flipped it open, and held it up so that sunlight glinted on his badge. Puce-faced guy stopped, sputtering, in his tracks.

Jess's eyebrows snapped together disapprovingly. "I can't believe you'd use your badge like that."

"What, you want I should shoot him? Seems a little extreme."

Honk. Honk.

This she did not need. Time to go.

"Jackass," she called Mark bitterly.

A barely perceptible smile curved his lips. "Does that mean you're gonna get in the car now?"

"Come on." She capitulated with bad grace, marching past him toward where the Suburban was idling at the curb, relieved to see that the puce-faced guy was retreating back toward his car. Reaching the Suburban, feeling the laserlike heat of dozens of angry eyes, she tried calling out, "*Sorry!*" and waving penitently at the inconvenienced multitudes.

Her reward, as she hurried around the front of the SUV, was a thank-you chorus of irate honks, a fuming *you suck* look thrown over the puce-faced guy's shoulder, and a smattering of one-fingered salutes thrust high into the air from a number of drivers now disappearing back inside their vehicles.

Way to keep it classy, D.C.

Feeling about two inches tall, she opened the door and climbed into the passenger seat.

CHAPTER SIX

Mark got in beside her, put the Suburban in drive, and pulled away from the curb. Like champagne from a suddenly uncorked bottle, traffic was now free to flow, and flow it did, shooting forward in their wake and then spreading out to fill the available space.

"Where were you headed?" he asked.

"Home," she said, taking in a whiff of new car smell, and he nodded. A moment later, the Suburban made a left onto D Street and they were lost to the sight of their admirers as they disappeared into the steady stream of traffic.

Jess turned wary eyes on Mark. He flicked a glance at her but didn't speak. This whole situation would have been much easier to deal with if he hadn't still had the power to make her pulse speed up on sight, she decided.

Fool.

"If you've got something to say, say it." If there was a hostile edge to her voice, well, he deserved it. The last straw in their relationship—her walking into her new office some three months ago to find her new boss plastered all over him—was a vivid memory she didn't expect to forget anytime soon. Although she was trying. Sort of.

His lips thinned. "Remember that conversation we had a while back about you keeping a low profile?"

She should have figured that that was what this was about. Maybe her shoulders drooped a fraction. Maybe she was a tad disappointed. Maybe she'd hoped he'd popped into her life for the first time in three months to grovel a little. To ask her forgiveness. To beg her to take him back.

Not that she would have. She might be a fool, but she wasn't that big a fool. He might be as drop-dead gorgeous as ever, and she might still have the tiniest little bit of a soft spot for him tucked away somewhere deep inside her heart, but with her head she knew the two of them just weren't going to work out. A world-class hunk with a list of ex's as long as the Macy's Thanksgiving Day parade wasn't the man for her, as she had explained to him in the semicivil conversation they'd had after she had caught him with her boss, when, among other things, she had told him that they were over, and to please stay away from her. Which, until now, he had seemed perfectly willing to do.

"What about it?" Okay, she was still sounding hostile. And you know what? Hostile directed at Mark felt good, even after all this time. So maybe she was still madder at him than she'd thought.

"You don't seem to be very good at it." Where she was hostile, he was mild.

"Meaning?"

"For starters, you were on the six o'clock news tonight. Worldwide, I presume, since I caught it on CNN."

Glumly Jess remembered the TV cameras pointed at the defense team as they stood on the courthouse steps.

"I can't help what CNN chooses to put on the air."

"You can help putting yourself in the middle of what CNN chooses to put on the air."

"If you're talking about the news conference after the verdict, I was in the background. Nobody noticed me."

"Until Pearse Collins pulled you up beside him and introduced you to the press as the lawyer who'd been questioning Tiffany Higgs when she admitted no rape occurred."

It was all Jess could do not to squirm guiltily in her seat. "I couldn't help that either."

"You've already been all over TV. Tomorrow your face will be in half the newspapers in the country. You'll be getting calls from magazines wanting to do stories on the hotshot lady lawyer who won the Phillips case. Maybe the *National Enquirer* or one of the other tabloids will decide to do a feature. How long do you think it'll take any of them to figure out who Jessica Dean really is?"

Those ocean blue eyes flicked her way

again. There was the briefest of pauses. Since the obvious answer was *not long,* Jess didn't say anything. She even tried not to look as mutinous as she felt.

"You're putting yourself in danger, Jess." His voice was very quiet.

"I'm just doing my job, Mark."

"If that's the case, then changes are going to have to be made in your job." His tone had gone grim.

There it was, that assumption of authority, that presumption that he knew what was best for her, that drove her around the bend.

"You can't tell me what to do."

"On things like this, I can."

She stiffened. Her eyes narrowed. "Oh, no, you can't. You're out of my life, remember? As in, buh-bye."

He looked impatient. "Not anymore, I'm not. I've got orders to keep you out of harm's way. So keep pushing, and you'll find yourself locked away in a safe house somewhere so fast your head will spin."

"You can't do that."

He laughed.

"You better not."

"Right now I'm thinking it's probably a hell of a good idea. We should have pulled you out of circulation from the get-go."

"Is that you talking, or your puppet master?" His puppet master being the Secret Service director of Internal Affairs, Charlie Hasbrough, who'd taken on responsibility for her safety when she'd survived a concerted effort on the part of rogue government agents to kill her. Hasbrough had come up with her current incarnation of Jessica Dean, complete with blond hair, when she'd refused to leave D.C. and had, instead, stubbornly insisted on staying put, getting on with her life and taking the plum job she'd been offered with Ellis Hayes. She didn't know who her refusal to abandon her life and go into hiding in the hinterlands had irked more, Hasbrough or Mark. Or the whole shadowy netherworld of government-connected spooks who apparently spent multiple lifetimes lurking around keeping track of who was doing what to whom and thinking up ways to keep them from talking about it.

"Me."

She smirked. It wasn't something she generally did, but in this particular instance,

his refusal to give any outward indication
that her potshot about Hasbrough annoyed
him—which she knew it did—annoyed her
so much that she had to up the ante.

"You mean Hasbrough's not pulling your
strings anymore?"

"I mean I haven't heard from him about
this. Probably because he's on vacation,
and nobody else out of the millions who've
been following the Phillips trial has connected cocounsel Jessica Dean with Jessica Ford, the sole survivor of the car crash
that killed the former First Lady." He smiled
back at her, and although it wasn't a particularly nice smile, it didn't quite descend
to the level of a smirk. "Yet."

"Your point being . . . ?"

"The deal was that you were just going
to blend into the background, keep your
head down, and not attract attention if you
were left alone."

Along with keeping her mouth forever
shut, those were the terms on which she'd
been allowed to more or less resume her
old life. Mark, among others, had been in
favor of sending her somewhere far, far
away until the shock and questions swirling around the death of former First Lady

Annette Cooper had faded. Explanations other than accident seemed to delve deep into the realm of crackpot conspiracy theory territory, which was already starting to happen. With the capital and, to a lesser extent, the nation just starting to recover from the trauma of the resignation of President David Cooper in the wake of the tragedies that had befallen him, there was a concerted agreement on the part of those in the know—a small, tight-knit, high-ranking cabal of spooks whose identities Jess wasn't totally clear on, a few government officials, Jess and Mark, and a minuscule number of assorted others—that the truth must never get out.

In other words, no further rocking of the ship of state was going to be allowed, and woe betide anyone who made any more waves.

"Do you actually expect anyone to connect Jessica Dean with Jessica Ford? Jessica Ford is old news."

"Not now that she's just been on TV as the lawyer who got Tiffany Higgs to say she was lying when she accused Senator Phillips's idiot son of rape. Hell, it wasn't even four months ago that your picture was on every TV station and in every newspaper and magazine in the world, if you care to recall. I think somebody just might remember you." The sarcasm was unmistakable.

"I had dark hair then. And I wore glasses." Actually, she still did wear glasses, sometimes. Unlike the contacts she had in at the moment, they served as a barrier between her and the world when she needed one. She popped them on, and the world looked different. And saw her differently. They served as her own personal combination shield and invisibility cloak.

"Oh, wow, big change. That'll definitely fool 'em. No chance anyone will see through that." They stopped for a red light as he shot her a disgusted look. Then his gaze shifted to her hair, and some of the hardness around his mouth eased. "Oh, by the way and just for the record, baby, you make one red-hot, smokin' blonde."

That was so unexpected her brows twitched together. "What?"

"You heard me: of course, you were plenty hot as a brunette, too. You sure you don't want to marry me?"

The question hit her like a shaft to the

heart. Then indignation bubbled inside her. How dare he tease her? First he broke her heart, then he made jokes? He'd proposed as part of his hiding-in-the-hinterlands proposition—his exact words had been "How about if I go with you, and we make it a honeymoon?"—and despite her mild case of marriage phobia she'd been crazy enough in love with him that she had hovered on the brink of taking him up on it. Then she'd walked in on him and Mary Jane Cates, and she'd faced the unpalatable truth that her first instincts about him had been right on: the guy was an incorrigible player.

That kind of ongoing heartbreak in her life she did not need.

"Look, if that's all you have to say . . ."

Seething, she reached for the door handle. If she couldn't find a cab, she'd take the metro. Or she'd walk. Fifty blocks if necessary, in Christine's too-big shoes. Or no shoes at all. Anything that would get her away from him.

"Leonard Cowan's dead." The abrupt change in his tone stopped her cold. It was his Secret Service agent's voice, authoritative and clipped, with none of his usual distinctive Texas drawl left to it. She looked back at him, registered the hard set of his jaw, the purposeful glint in his eyes, and her anger was torpedoed by a sudden, sharp stab of fear. Her hand dropped nervelessly away from the door handle. She sank back in her seat with her eyes still glued to his face. The light changed to green, and the Suburban rolled on.

Mark might have been teasing before. He was dead serious now.

"Is that somebody I should know?" She might not have been able to immediately place the name, but she knew the answer, knew the context. It was there in Mark's face. The dead man was somehow connected to the terrible knowledge they shared.

The knowledge that she secretly feared was going to get them killed one day.

"Cowan was David Cooper's valet. He worked for him the whole time he was in office, and before, as far back as Texas. I—and probably a whole lot of other people—have to assume that he was privy to all the president's secrets. Probably knew pretty much everything that went on in Cooper's life. If you get my drift."

She did. Jess felt her stomach knot. "How did he die?"

"Suicide. Shot himself in the head. They found him just after dawn this morning, in his car in Rock Creek Park."

Jess felt a shiver rush down her spine, and she fought the urge to close her eyes. "I don't suppose you're telling me this because there's any chance it really was a suicide?"

"Anything's possible, but I wouldn't want to bet my life on it. Word is he had a drinking problem. My guess is somebody got tired of worrying he wouldn't keep his mouth shut."

Just like somebody might one day get tired of worrying that she and Mark wouldn't keep their mouths shut. All the pent-up anxiety that she'd almost managed to push from her daily consciousness over the past few months came rushing back.

"Oh, my God."

"Yeah."

Jess felt sick. Lately every time fear raised its ugly head she'd managed to push it away by telling herself that the danger was past, that the world had marched on, that no one was interested in hurting her—or Mark.

Now the terrible certainty that this thing would never be behind them exploded like an IED in her brain. Their secret, shared knowledge that the former First Lady had been murdered was something they could never escape.

"They're going to kill us, too, sooner or later, aren't they?" Folding her arms across her chest, barely repressing a shiver, she spoke very quietly.

"I got friends in high places. They tell me the answer's no."

Jess made a skeptical sound. "And you believe them?"

"As long as they believe we're not going to talk, they're better off not killing us. Any kind of suspicious death of the sole survivor of Mrs. Cooper's car crash would raise a lot of questions nobody wants to see raised. And if they take you out, they have to take me out, because I sure as hell wouldn't keep my mouth shut and they know that, too. Then there's your family, who they probably suspect know more than they should. And my guys at work, who don't know everything but know something. Enough to make them uncomfortable. And—well, any number of people could know just a little bit too much. So we're talking about eliminating a good number of people, which is always a chancy thing. As long as they think we continue to pose no threat to them, I believe they'll let us be. Keep the status quo intact and all that."

"How sure are you of that?"

His mouth quirked a little. "About as sure as I am of a lot of things. Fairly sure."

"Great."

"Which brings us back to the little matter of you on CNN. Not smart."

"You know what? I don't really need you to tell me that."

"Looks like you need somebody, so I'm going to say it one more time: what you want to do is remain quietly anonymous at least if you won't let us get you out of here, which I still think would be the smartest thing you could do, at least for a while."

"I'm not going to run and hide. Anyway, we both know there's nowhere on earth I could go that your friends couldn't eventually find me."

He couldn't argue with that, because he

knew it was true as well as she did. When he—or the powers-that-be above him— had originally suggested she leave the capital, it had been to remove her from the reach of inquisitive reporters. Not to protect her from the Alphabet Soup gang, as she called the CIA, FBI, DEA, SSA, and all the other initial heavy government agencies who had her in their sights.

Instead of arguing the inarguable, he said, "Anonymous means you keep out of the public eye, just to be clear."

"I'm trying, okay? What happened at the end of that trial was totally unexpected."

His answering grunt she took as his acceptance of the truth of what she was telling him. A moment later he added, "Congratulations, by the way. On the win. That's a big one."

She looked at him a shade mistrustfully. He hadn't been exactly supportive of her career to date. What he'd wanted her to be, as he'd made clear in those few lost days when they'd been madly in lust and she'd been actually trembling on the brink of saying yes to him, was a part-time lawyer and his full-time wife.

"Thanks."

"I was betting he'd be found guilty, my-self."

Jess almost blurted out *so was I*, but she thought better of it. Best to keep her view of what had happened to herself until she'd had time to think it over. Then Mark stopped at a traffic light, and she looked away from him long enough to notice their surroundings. It was full dusk now, with stars just beginning to twinkle in the purple sky and only the thinnest line of fluorescent orange on the horizon to mark where the sun had been. The trees here were tall and round with foliage and growing out of postage-stamp-sized yards. The people on the sidewalks were a wholesome mix of mostly family types and college kids. Streetlights cast long shadows over the hustle and bustle that was Washington Circle. She took a deep breath, both relieved and a little sorry to realize she was almost home.

"You want to grab a coffee or something?" Mark asked as the light changed and he drove on. He knew where she lived as well as she did, knew they were almost there. Pearl's Coffee Shop was right around the corner, and stopping for coffee and maybe a meal at Pearl's had been something they'd done, when they'd been together. Just remembering hurt, and the pain made her angry at him all over again.

"With you? No."

He gave her a glinting look. "You ever hear of forgive and forget?"

She laughed.

"Jess—"

"Just take me home, would you please?"

His jaw tightened, but he didn't reply, which suited her just fine. She looked away again. Talking to him, seeing him, having him so close, was making her ache inside. The fact was both appalling and infuriating. She should have been over him by now. It was just that . . .

Don't be an idiot. Face the fact that it was just a fling and move on.

She took a deep breath, stared out the window. Her apartment was in Foggy Bottom, not far from where she'd gone to law school. Of course, as a law student she never would have been able to afford the spacious, two-bedroom, third-floor apartment she now shared with her sister Grace,

but it was good to live in a familiar neighborhood. She knew every inch of it, from
the university to Kennedy Center to Pearl's,
where breakfast was three dollars and
the soup was to die for, to the less savory
fringes that bled into downtown. When it
was dark like this, it wasn't hard to imagine that the colorful nineteenth-century
town houses that lined the streets were
still home to the area's earliest residents:
the poor Irish, Germans, and African Amer-
icans who'd once worked the surrounding
factories. In fact, with the deepening shadows disguising many modernizing details,
it was as though time had stood still. Mist
from the Potomac, just starting to creep
westward as night fell, could have been
the factory smoke that had once lain over
everything and given the low-lying district
its name.

Jess was just registering with a faint,
wry smile the bicycle shorts and miniskirts
and baggy jeans worn by a gang of kids
rushing toward the metro stop—there went
the whole nineteenth-century vibe right
there—when someone emerging from the
depths caught her eye.

A slender young woman whose long,

straight blond hair hung halfway to her waist, wearing a floaty-skirted sundress that didn't quite reach her knees, popped into view, leaping nimbly up the stairs that led down to the metro. Her head was down, and her hair and skirt billowed behind her. As she reached the top, she looked around, then darted across the sidewalk toward the newspaper stand on the corner. A man stepped out of the shadows near the large brown column that marked the entrance to the metro to stride purposefully after her. Catching up a heartbeat later, he grabbed her arm. She jumped as her head swivelled around toward him, then she seemed to try to pull away. He shook his head and she stopped struggling and stood still, looking up at him. There was something about her posture, and that of the man—he was a tall, well-built man with dark hair in a dark suit—that set off alarm bells in Jess's head.

Especially since Jess was almost positive the young woman was none other than Tiffany Higgs.

Tiffany was walking away with him now. His hand still gripped her arm. She looked—afraid.

Something's wrong . . .

"Stop." Her tone was so urgent that Mark stood on the brakes. As the car jerked to a halt, Jess pushed open the door and scrambled out.

CHAPTER SEVEN

By the time Jess's feet hit the sidewalk, she'd lost sight of her quarry. They'd disappeared behind the newsstand. Driven by a sense of urgency that she couldn't quite explain, she hurried toward the newsstand herself, desperate to catch a glimpse of them. The misgivings that had assailed her earlier—had Tiffany's recantation been somehow coerced or forced?—filled her with unease. Granted, she hadn't been close enough to see the expression on the young woman's face, hadn't even been close enough to be absolutely, one hundred percent certain that it *was* Tiffany. But somewhere deep inside she was convinced that it was, and she felt that what she had just witnessed was Tiffany in trouble.

Felt it so strongly that when she ran right out of one of her pumps—and when had she started to run?—she kicked off the other one and left them both behind. Barefoot, she dodged around knots of pedestrians, deaf to their chatter, so focused on the darkness on the other side of the newsstand that she barely felt the grit or the heat of the pavement beneath her soles or noticed the curious glances she was attracting.

"Hey, want a newspaper?" A wizened old man working the booth waved the *Post* at her as she sprinted past. She didn't even bother to shake her head in reply. Bursting past the side of the stand, she stopped dead, looking all around: a lot of concrete, sidewalk, curbs, streets. A three-way intersection, brightened by a streetlight and tinged an eerie green from the glowing top orb of a stoplight. Multiple storefronts, in front of her, to her right, and, across the street, to her left. Some lighted, some not.

Filled tables outside, in front of a busy café. People walking, lots of people, singly, in pairs, in knots, on this sidewalk and the one across the street and the one catty-corner, at the top of the intersection. Cars cruising past with their headlights on now because it was dark. A bicycle rack with two bikes chained to the bars. A row of knee-high shrubbery. A wastebasket, big, wire mesh, chained to the light pole. The sounds of stop-and-go traffic, people talking and laughing, muffled music probably leaking from somebody's iPod. The smell of popcorn—a kid nearby was scarfing it.

No fluttering sundress no matter which way she looked. No slender blonde being frog-marched away by a tall, dark-haired guy in a dark suit.

In other words, no Tiffany.

Where are they?

"Tiffany?" Jess called. Then, her voice growing stronger, she tried again. *"Tiffany?"*

No answer except for more curious looks.

Unmoving except for her turning head, Jess gave up on calling and instead did her best to see into the closest of the lighted storefronts, hoping to discover Tiffany inside. Catching a glimmer of blond hair through the plate-glass window that fronted the Library Bar, she hurried toward it. The inside of the bar was only a little brighter than the shadowy expanse of sidewalk she was crossing. Just a few barely glowing overhead lights provided illumination for the bar's interior. The artful dimness prevented her from seeing anything besides the color of the woman's hair. A moment later Jess came close enough to discern that the blonde inside was plump and wearing jeans. Definitely not Tiffany.

Stymied, she stopped some twenty feet short of the bar's deep red door and once again looked anxiously around.

"Tiffany?" she called.

Where could they have gone?

When a hand clamped around her own arm, Jess jumped a foot in the air.

"What the hell are you doing?"

It was Mark. Of course it was Mark. Even as her heart had begun its instinctive leap into her throat she'd realized it was him. He'd parked the SUV and followed her. Since she didn't hear any honking horns, she assumed he'd found a halfway legal spot. Or at least one that didn't impede the flow of traffic.

"Jeez, you scared me to death." Her voice was breathless from her run and recent fright. "I think I saw Tiffany Higgs. Here. With a man."

His brow knit. "What, so you just thought you'd hop out of the car and run right on over to say hello?"

Shrugging an impatient shoulder at him, she pulled free of his grip and returned to scanning the area. The stoplight was red now, tinting everything within its orbit with a hellish glow. There were people everywhere, lots of people, of practically every size and shape and description. None of them was Tiffany.

"She looked like she was in trouble. This man came up behind her and grabbed her arm and wouldn't let go. She seemed scared of him. He was wearing a dark suit."

"You ever think you might be developing an unhealthy phobia about men in dark suits?"

Despite the dryness of his tone, that was so absolutely spot-on that she turned narrowing eyes on him. Damn Mark anyway, he knew her too well.

"That doesn't mean I'm wrong about what I saw."

"You're not paranoid if they're really after you, hmm?"

"That's right." She frowned as the traffic that had been waiting at the light surged forward. "Could they have gotten into a car? If they'd headed back toward the metro I'm sure I would have seen them."

"Maybe. But the point is, why do you care?"

"I told you, she looked like she was in trouble."

"You're not even sure it was her."

He had her there. "I'm almost sure." Honesty compelled her to add, "As sure as it's possible to be without seeing her up close."

His mouth twisted. "Whatever, she's gone now. And if you can't find her, there's nothing we can do. Let's go, I'm parked illegally." Clamping a hand around her wrist, he started walking back the way they had come, pulling her with him. Typical highhanded Mark. "All things being equal, I'd rather not get towed."

"So if the tow truck shows up, flash your badge."

Yanking her wrist free, she nonetheless kept pace with him, although she didn't stop looking around. The alarm she'd felt upon catching sight of Tiffany—and she really was all but positive it was Tiffany—was still there, vibrating across her nerve endings like a shiver of unease, a disconcerting feeling that she couldn't quite shake. It was possible that Tiffany had disappeared inside another of the nearby buildings, but searching all of the mix of bars and shops and private residences that lined the triangular conjunction of streets was clearly too big a task to undertake with any degree of thoroughness. Besides, the more she thought about it, the more unlikely it seemed that Tiffany and her companion could have reached any of them before Jess had rounded the newsstand and spotted them. It was, therefore, far likelier that they had gotten into a car. And if that was the case, they were long gone.

All of a sudden Mark stopped.

"Tell me that's not your shoe."

Stopping too, Jess followed his gaze to discover one of her pumps lying on its side on the pavement. People were sidestepping around it. Casting a condemning glance at her bare feet, which it was obvious he had just noticed, he moved to scoop the shoe up, clearly not needing to hear her answer to know the truth.

"Channeling Cinderella today?" He turned back to her, shoe in hand. Like the rest of her, her feet were small, and her shoe looked absurdly feminine dangling from his long fingers.

"They're too big," Jess explained. "Christine—the jury consultant—picked them out. To go with this awful suit."

"What's awful about it? Like I said, you look good in pink." He started humming the theme to *The Pink Panther.*

It took her a moment to recognize it. Then she made a face at him. He grinned, and for a moment, as their eyes met, her heart gave a weird little flutter. God, she was crazy about him. No, *had been* crazy about him. Past tense, although her body couldn't seem to get with the program. That he should be so staggeringly handsome just wasn't fair; it was what had gotten her in trouble the first time, when, as special agent in charge of the First Lady's Secret Service security detail, he'd started accompanying Annette Cooper to the law office where Jess, fresh out of law school, had worked. She'd fallen hard at first sight. He hadn't known she'd been alive until he'd had to start saving her life. Now, jerking her eyes away from his face in an effort to combat the attraction that was proving as hard to kill as crabgrass, she started walking again, determinedly not looking at him even when he fell in beside her. A couple of steps further on they came across her other shoe. Mark picked it up, too, then handed them both to her. She stopped to put them on. He stopped beside her, but at least this time he showed no disposition to help.

"Tell me something: if that *was* Tiffany Higgs," he said as she stepped into her shoes, "and you *had* caught up to her and the guy she was with, what were you going to say to her?" His voice took on a sardonic edge. "Beware of men in suits?"

"Ha ha."

"You can't imagine she wants to talk to you. I doubt you're her favorite person in the world right now. I hear the DA's thinking about filing charges against her, for one thing. Maybe you might want to leave her alone for the foreseeable future."

"She looked like she was in trouble. I was going to ask her if she needed help."

His mouth tightened. "You're not responsible for everybody in the whole wide world, you know."

She flashed a look at him and started walking again in the direction they'd been heading, where, presumably, they would find the Suburban. They'd had that discussion before, once upon a time, and she wasn't going there now. Bottom line was, how she interacted with the world was no longer any of Mark Ryan's business. And that, she assured herself, was just the way she wanted it.

"Tiffany had no reason to recant," she told him as he caught up to her. "The prosecution was in a good position to win. They knew it. She must have known it. So why, just like that, did she admit that the sex was consensual?"

"Because it was the truth?"

Jess snorted.

"I take it you don't think so?"

"I think if it was the truth and she was going to admit it, she would have done so a heck of a lot earlier. Like, before the trial. Having gone so far, why give up when she did, the way she did? She must have known Olderman and the rest of the prosecution would blow a gasket. She must have known she was going to get in trouble."

"Maybe you scared her."

Jess snorted again.

"Good point." He went silent for a moment, thinking it over. "You think somebody got to her."

It wasn't a question. Jess nodded.

"So welcome to the real world. It happens all the time. Rich guys have been buying wronged women's silence since the earth began. In this case, the only thing to do is be glad it worked out for you."

Jess knew he was right, but she still worried. Tiffany's demeanor at the end of the trial, coupled with what she had seen tonight, did not add up to avarice appeased, in her opinion. What it added up to was fear. Besides, if all Tiffany had wanted was money, winning the case would have opened the door to a huge payout via civil lawsuit.

"Maybe she wasn't bought off," Jess said slowly. "Maybe she was threatened."

"Let it go." Mark's tone was abrupt. "She

has her own lawyers, her own people to look after her. This is not your problem."

"That's your solution to everything, isn't it? Just let it go."

"At least I don't go around wearing myself to a frazzle trying to clean up everybody else's messes."

"No, you don't, do you? You just shrug your shoulders and walk away and leave them to wallow in it—unless it's Taylor, when you threaten to ship her off to boarding school."

Taylor was his fifeen-year-old daughter. She mostly lived with Mark's ex-wife, but Mark, who adored her without having a clue how to deal with her, got her on weekends and some holidays. Jess liked Taylor, Taylor liked Jess. Even after she and Mark had broken up, she and Taylor had kept in sporadic touch. And thanks to Facebook, Taylor and Maddie, Jess's youngest sister, were fast friends.

"Heard about that, did you?"

"Oh, yeah."

"How?"

"Jungle drums. I also heard that your daughter's not talking to you now."

"Hey, I caught her boyfriend climbing in

through her bedroom window at two a.m. Damn right I threatened to ship her off to boarding school. And it wasn't an idle threat, either. One more incident like that, and I'll do it."

"You think threatening her is the answer?"

"It's better than having her wind up like Maddie."

Jess sucked in air. Her voice sharpened dangerously. "Are you talking about my sister?"

"No. No." Mark backtracked quickly, looking harassed. "I love Maddie. You know I do. She's beautiful. Bright. A sweetheart in every way. She's also eighteen years old and pregnant."

The fact that everything he said was true in no way mitigated Jess's wrath. The straight-A student who'd just missed being valedictorian of her high school class, which had graduated in June, was indeed seven months pregnant and, having broken up with her baby's father around the same time Jess had broken up with Mark, determinedly bent on single motherhood. With her head, Jess could understand why having Taylor follow in Maddie's footsteps might be Mark's worst nightmare. But with her heart, although she might not agree with all of Maddie's choices, she was still prepared to defend her little sister to the death.

"Hey, pregnant happens." Jess's voice was brittle.

"I know it does. Which is why I'm talking boarding school, if that's what it takes to get Taylor away from that boy she's seeing."

"You don't like him?"

"He's after one thing."

"Recognized the trait right off, did you?"

"Damn it, what you saw with MJ—it was just a kiss, okay? A damned kiss. She kissed me and—okay, I kissed her back. I admit it. But that's all it was. One kiss. Nothing more."

At this reminder of what they'd once shared, Jess felt like someone was hacking at her heart with a dull knife.

"You know what? At this point, I really don't care."

"You don't believe me, do you?"

"Whether I do or not is immaterial."

"What do you mean, it's immaterial? It's material. It's why we broke up."

"I refuse to have this conversation."

"Too bad, because we're having it."

"No, you're having it. Without me. Because I refuse to participate."

"You know what I think? I think you latched onto that kiss because it let you off the hook. You're so damn afraid you're going to get hurt that you won't let yourself love anybody outside your damned family."

Jess stopped dead. "I think I'll walk home."

"Oh, for God's sake—" Mark broke off as he met her eyes. If how she felt was any indication, they blazed like twin howitzers at him. "Fine. You want to walk? Walk. Knock yourself out."

Jess turned on her heel and stalked away from him, feeling his eyes boring into her back with every step she took. Her apartment was only about five blocks away, on F street. It was a trip she made nearly every day without incident. She could certainly manage it one more time without Mark as an escort. He was out of her life, and she meant to keep it that way.

It wasn't until she reached the intersection of 23rd and H streets that she realized she'd forgotten all about Tiffany. Not that there was anything she could do at this point, and not that Tiffany was her problem, anyway.

She could almost hear Mark saying it, which made her mad all over again.

It was full dark now, but streetlights glowed on every corner and lots of people crowded the sidewalks. Traffic streamed continually past, so it wasn't like she was alone on some moonlit moor or something. D.C. was many things, but eerie it wasn't. Although she owned a car, usually the hassle and cost of finding parking made driving within the city not worth it, so she was accustomed to taking the metro just about anywhere she wanted to go. But she had to admit, tonight felt different. Maybe because of Mark, maybe because of the trial, maybe because she couldn't get Tiffany and the man she'd disappeared with out of her head, she felt on edge. Anxious, even. Ready to jump at every too-loud sound. Spooked by anyone who brushed too close. Wary of shadows, suspicious of sideways glances, uncomfortable with the proximity of strangers.

She had never before noticed just how long five blocks could be.

"You're so damn afraid you're going to get hurt . . ."

What bullshit, she told herself stoutly, even as a little voice inside her head whispered, *You don't really think he slept with Cates while you were together, do you?*

Maybe she didn't, now that the blinding pain of discovering him kissing Cates had receded. But he had slept with Cates before. He'd admitted it. He'd also admitted to sleeping with his va-va-va-voom neighbor Lynn Bowling, who'd shown up with a box of doughnuts and obvious hopes for more than a shared breakfast early one Sunday morning while Jess had been staying over at his house. Also with his ex-wife on several occasions postdivorce, and, well, the list was long and she wasn't going there. If he'd already been kissing Cates when things had still been hot and heavy between them, what were the chances that he'd give up the tomcattish habits and gorgeous partners of a lifetime to stay faithful to ordinary little her if she married him?

Jess was many things, but stupid wasn't one of them. Looking at him and Cates entwined in Cates's office, she'd known the answer in an instantaneous flash of bitter realization: slim and none.

So she'd gone ahead and cut her losses.

The pain was still there, as she'd discovered tonight, but most of the time she had it under control, and it was definitely lessening as time passed. The key was to keep on keeping away from Mark.

Which as far as she was concerned wasn't going to be a problem. She refused to even so much as think about him again.

With that laudable goal in mind, she turned her focus to other matters. Happier matters. Like Pearse's totally awesome offer to become a permanent part of his team. Like possible uses for the mouthwateringly large bonus she'd been promised. Like—why Tiffany had recanted. And what could have been going on with her and the guy who had hustled her away from the metro stop. Remembering Tiffany's body language, Jess felt another little frisson of disquiet.

Fear looked like nothing else.

"*. . . not your problem.*" Mark's words. Mark's voice.

Arggh.

The further she got from the metro stop,

the fewer people were on the sidewalk and the lighter the vehicular traffic. The specter of a cadre of murderous spooks on her trail started to feel like an all-too-real possibility. Maybe—just maybe—she'd been too quick to walk away from Mark.

Too late now.

Streetlights came further apart, making long stretches in the middle of each block absolutely dark—dark enough to have her jumping like she'd been shot when a cat meowed at her suddenly from one of the tiny, fenced yards. By the time she was half a block away from her apartment, there was a couple ahead of her—far ahead, at the edge of the fuzzy white circle of light cast by the streetlight on the corner—and that was all. Her building, which was in the middle of the block, had only the tiny stars and sliver of moon floating high overhead to illuminate it, along with the occasional flash of passing headlights. There were undoubtedly people at home in the lineup of attached houses that crowded together shoulder to shoulder like a row of high-kicking Rockettes, but all she had as concrete evidence was the occasional light radiating through closed curtains.

The couple ahead turned the corner and moments later disappeared from sight. The street was dark and silent except for the distant hum of traffic. All at once she felt horribly alone. And vulnerable.

Is someone watching me?

The back of her neck prickled. She glanced compulsively around: not a soul in sight. The parked cars crouching in a hump-backed line between her and the street were dark and *empty*, which, she reminded herself, was the important part. Just like the street was empty. Empty meant no one was there. It meant no one was lying in the gutter getting ready to spring out. It meant no one was behind her, sneaking after her through the dead of night. *Of course* no one was doing that. Who was she expecting, Jason Voorhees? Freddy Krueger?

May-be.

Okay, the truth was embarrassing. She was glad she didn't have to admit it to anyone but herself. But the trade-off to being a size-challenged woman in a crime-ridden city was living with a niggling sense of insecurity that mainly manifested itself when she found herself alone. In the dark. On foot. On a deserted street. Like now.

To combat it, she slowed her breathing and quickened her step. And pushed the thought of Leonard Cowan's suspicious suicide from her mind.

What are the chances . . . ?

A car passed, and then another, both as welcome as rain after a drought, both catching her in their headlights, both disappearing with no more than a quick swish of tires and a red glow of taillights. For one of the few times in her life, Jess found herself wishing for heavy traffic just so she'd know there were other living beings in the vicinity. Instead, after that, she got no traffic at all. Except for the breeze sighing past the buildings and the muffled rumble of activity that was happening somewhere else, there was not even a sound other than the quick tapping of her own heels on the pavement.

Almost home, she told herself.

Slow breaths. Quick steps.

She could see her apartment now, three dark windows on the top floor of a three-story, colonial-blue row house. Apparently

Grace, who liked the nightlife, wasn't yet home. The other windows in the building were dark as well. Was no one at home in any of the other apartments?

A few more minutes, and she would be safe inside. She reached for her keys . . . and made a terrible discovery.

I left my purse and briefcase in Mark's car. I don't have my keys. Or my phone. Or—anything.

Horror stopped her cold. For a moment, as she absorbed the absence of her belongings and exactly what that meant, she stood frozen on the sidewalk in front of her building and simply stared at her dark windows wide-eyed.

What to do?

Her building was the middle one of three attached houses. Its small front yard was dominated by a thirty-foot-tall magnolia with creamy blossoms that gave off the faintest of citrusy scents. The broad, shiny leaves rustled like paper being shuffled as she stood there frowning blankly past the dense foliage. Inky shadows even darker than the night itself stretched between the tree and the building, and between the building and its twin next door. Luckily, she didn't have to pass through that abyss of blackness to reach her front door. The sidewalk was moonlit, the pavement glowing faintly silver through the gloom. The door itself was solid paneled oak, as old as the building, and painted a deep red that looked charcoal at night. To her, in that moment, it promised sanctuary.

Except she couldn't get in.

And there was no point in heading for the front door without her keys.

Reality hit: she was locked out. Stuck out on the street. Jess's pulse kicked it up a notch.

I can wait outside until Grace gets home—assuming she does get home tonight, which she might not—or I can go bang on a neighbor's door until someone lets me in. Then I can use their phone and call Mom. Or Maddie. Or Sarah. (Her third sister, who was married with two little boys and currently living in her own house on Clay Street, was the only one who was almost certain to be home at that hour. The rest of the gang had varied and unpredictable social lives.)

Or I can call a cab, or . . .

But she instantly dismissed the next

name that popped into her head: Mark. She wasn't calling Mark.

Whoever she decided to call, banging on a neighbor's door and asking to use the phone was clearly a better option than waiting in the street for Grace to show or not.

I hate the dark.

Her heart thumped as around her shadows shifted and swayed. The back of her neck crawled. Once again she had the sensation of being watched. She glanced nervously in every direction. There was no one in sight, anywhere. But the night felt alive.

So move already.

Doing her best to ignore the rampaging imagination that had her pulse racing and her heart thudding, Jess turned on her heel and headed toward the nearest neighbor with lights, which was two doors back the way she had come. She hadn't taken more than three steps when out of the corner of her eye she caught a blur of movement.

What? . . .

Instinctively she looked in that direction. Her breathing suspended and her eyes went wide as the blur resolved itself into something—*someone*—rushing at her from the dark behind the magnolia.

"Ah!" Her cry was high-pitched and shrill as she stumbled a little, then started to run toward the house with the lights. It was a man, a solid black figure as featureless as a shadow, she registered in those first horrific seconds as she fled and he gave chase. Then he was upon her, grabbing her jacket, hauling her backward, catching her around the waist.

"Shut up!" It was a rough-voiced growl, uttered as a big, gloved hand clamped down hard over her mouth, cutting off the scream she hadn't even realized was ripping from her throat. Terrified, she tried to whirl, tried to punch, tried to fight him off, but he was too strong for her, too quick for her. Snatching her clear up off her feet, he clamped her back to his front and bore her kicking and struggling into the grass, toward the deadly shadows beneath the tree.

CHAPTER EIGHT

Fighting for her life, Jess discovered that her mind remained curiously detached.

Who? . . .

No one she knew, Jess was sure.

A stranger. A brutal, violent stranger.

The hand over her mouth blocked her nose as well. It was suffocating her. She couldn't breathe. She could barely think.

A random attack? Or . . .

Heart jumping with terror, Jess mentally reeled with the realization that whoever her attacker was, she was in deadly danger. Rape, murder—every horrible fate that was the stuff of her worst nightmares was happening, *now*.

Leonard Cowan's suspicious death. Could this be more of the same?

Her blood turned to ice.

Trying to jerk free of that smothering hand, kicking and twisting like a contortionist without any appreciable result, she grabbed at his uppermost arm—it was hard and muscular—with both hands. He was wearing a long-sleeved knit shirt, she registered as she tore at it, and then at the gloved hand that clamped onto her face. His grip didn't loosen. He carried her ruthlessly, not caring that she couldn't breathe, that he was hurting her. His indifference to her pain ratcheted her burgeoning panic up to a whole new level. This was no mugging, no attempted robbery, no random street crime, she was convinced.

He's going to kill me.

In her mind, it became a hideous certainty. Her stomach turned inside out. Cold sweat drenched her. Adrenaline kicked in, rushing like speed through her veins. Reacting with the kind of fierce self-defense that a small person in the land of larger ones learns early on, she bit down viciously on one of his thick fingers, chomping through leather and flesh with all her might, going for bone.

"Bitch!"

Cursing, he jerked his hand away, which was what she had hoped for. She screamed, not the siren scream she wanted but a pitifully thin sound because she had almost no air left. Filling her lungs, she screamed again, a full-on screech this time that exploded from her lungs with the urgency of an escaping animal. It shrilled for no more than a couple of seconds before his fist slammed hard into her side, truncating the sound with brutal force.

The pain was unbelievable, as sharp and stunning as a knife through the ribs. The wind was knocked out of her; she was momentarily paralyzed. The blow, combined with lack of air, made her light-headed. She couldn't think, couldn't breathe. His arm around her waist compressed her bruised rib cage like a vice. His hand clapped tight over her face again, only now it was curved in such a way that she couldn't bite him.

Help! Help! But her cries were all in her head. She had no air for so much as a moan. Not that her screams had done any good anyway: no one had come. No one had peered through a curtain, or opened a door to glance out. She doubted anyone in any of the nearby buildings was busy dialing 911.

Either no one had heard, or, curse of the big city, no one wanted to get involved.

I have to fight.

By sheer force of will she did, sucking in what air she could, forcing her quivering limbs to move, punching and kicking and writhing to be free, battling for her life with everything she had. He maintained his grip in the teeth of her efforts, but at least she was making him work for it. His breathing came hard and fast. Against her back, she could feel his chest heave. His muscular body emanated heat. He smelled; she registered that he smelled. Sucking in, with every desperate flaring of her nostrils, the scent of body odor inadequately masked by some kind of sickly sweet cologne, Jess felt a surge of nausea. She heard a frenzied drumming in her ears and realized that it was the frantic pounding of the blood in her veins.

I need air.

Thrusting both hands back toward his face despite her weakness, despite the pain it caused her, she clawed for his eyes. He was wearing a silky-feeling ski-type mask, which impeded her efforts, and she, a nail-biter, didn't have much in the way of claws to begin with, so she couldn't do enough damage to help herself. She tried something else.

"Fuck!" He jerked his head back as she gave up on the clawing in favor of slamming her fist hammer-like into his nose. The solid thunk as she connected was satisfying but didn't so much as loosen his grip. They were almost even with the tree now, and she feared that the darkness behind it was his goal. Or maybe he was bent on carrying her into the night-cloaked passage between the buildings.

I'm running out of time.

Fueled by abject fear, she struggled with panicked strength. *No luck.* Then, in a flash of cunning, she took deliberate, focused aim and drove the sharp heel of her pump into his right knee.

"Shit!" His leg jerked back, but still he didn't let go.

He's wearing long pants, some kind of heavy cloth. Too thick to . . .

Instead he violently shook her from side to side, like a vicious dog with a kitten in its teeth.

Her shoes flew off, but her head swam so much that she barely even noticed. Overhead, the stars suddenly seemed further away, the moon dimmer and more distant. Although the night was hot, she felt cold all over. Her ribs ached. Her arms and legs tingled. Gorge rose in her throat. Without sufficient air, her struggles grew weaker. Kicking, punching, writhing, clawing—she did it all, and none of it helped.

I don't want to die.

I can't lose consciousness. If I do, I'm done.

Despite the fight she was giving him, already they were being swallowed up by the Stygian shadow of the magnolia. Another few steps, and no passerby would be able to see them even if one happened by and looked their way. She would be at his mercy. Limbs flailing, eyes darting everywhere as she sought for help, for a weapon, for anything that could save her, she summoned her resources one more time and kicked backward high and furiously, heels slamming into his thighs, aiming with blind inaccuracy for his crotch.

Thud, thud, thud, thud. His thigh muscles were meaty, dense. The impact hurt her heels.

His hand left her mouth. The sudden rush of air was so unexpected that her chest heaved and she sucked in a great, thankful breath instead of screaming. Then he punched her hard in the side of the head, snapping her teeth together and rattling her brain against her skull.

The pain was so sudden and intense, Jess almost blacked out. Her body went limp. She saw stars. Her head lolled back against his shoulder. Only sheer force of will kept her even semiconscious.

I can't give up.

She didn't have the strength to fight anymore. He lugged her, unresisting, behind the tree. Now she could see the window wells that curved in front of the basement apartments, see the glint of the leaded glass panes that were as dark as slabs of onyx, see the black velvet carpet of carefully tended grass.

Fresh terror washed over her in a freezing wave.

It's going to happen here. She didn't know how she knew it, but she did.

Summoning her last reserves of strength and will, she girded herself to fight for her life.

Headlights cut through the night. Headlights of a car coming down the street toward them. Despair was pierced by a forlorn stab of hope.

Oh, please . . .

Bright beams illuminated the empty sidewalk where she had been walking just moments before. They flashed over the grass, swept toward the tree. Galvanized, Jess fought with a burst of renewed strength to win free even as her captor lunged with her the rest of the way into absolute darkness, where no one in a passing car could possibly have seen them even if they'd been trying, even if they'd known where to look, which, of course, wasn't going to be the case.

The car sped up. She could hear it coming, see the headlights cutting through the branches as it hurtled forward, sense the disturbance in the air. Her captor went still, tense, waiting for it to pass. His hold on her tightened so much that it was painful. Unbreakable.

Please please please . . .

A tremor coursed through her. The throbbing engine was scarcely louder than the pulsing of her blood in her ears. The car was moving fast, speeding toward the intersection at the far end of the block. In a moment it would be gone, taking her last best chance of survival with it.

Weak now, she struggled desperately still, kicking at the branches nearest her, managing to shake the tree.

Maybe the driver will see . . .

The hand over her mouth crushed down viciously, smashing her lips, digging into her cheeks, hurting her jaw. Her breathing completely cut off now. Her heart felt like it would pound through her chest.

Brakes squealed, a door opened, feet hit the pavement.

"Federal agent! Freeze!" It was a roar.

Mark.

His voice was the most wonderful sound she had ever heard.

Relief turned her bones to jelly. Her

muscles sagged with the knowledge that she was saved, that she wasn't going to die tonight after all. *Thank you, G . . .* was just bubbling into her head when she felt herself flying through the air as her captor flung her violently and without warning to the ground. She hit with bone-jarring force. Her head snapped back to crack against the stone ledge surrounding one of the window wells. Pain knifed through her skull. Light exploded behind her eye sockets.

Then there was nothing except an utter, all-enveloping blackness.

". . . attacked. Maybe three minutes ago. Get some people out here. Yeah, I'm . . ."

Mark. She came to to the sound of his voice. Recognition brought a comforting feeling of security with it. Basking in it, Jess lost the thread of what he was saying as she simply listened to him speaking urgently into the ether above her head. The burgeoning terror that had started to surge through her veins upon her return to consciousness subsided.

Seconds later she cracked her eyes open just enough to see him crouched beside her. He was no more than a dark shape looming over her, a large hand threading carefully through the hair at the back of her head, a grim voice. But he was there, and she was safe.

He hit a spot on her skull that made her wince.

"Ow!"

Their eyes collided.

She took a deep breath. *Being able to breathe feels wonderful.* "A man . . . attacked me." Her voice was ragged.

Mark withdrew his hand from her hair and she latched onto his warm, strong fingers like she was afraid he'd leave her if she didn't.

". . . last seen running toward G Street Northwest between 21st and 22nd. Possibly armed." His fingers locked with hers. With his other hand Mark held his cell phone. *Of course.* He talked into it with the clipped, controlled voice he used when he was on the job. "And send an ambulance, *now.*"

"I don't need one." Jess started to shake her head, but the pain that shot through it made her stop and close her eyes again. She felt shaky. Cold. Not quite all there.

The hard ground against the back of her skull *hurt*.

"Look at me." Mark had finished his call, she realized as she obediently opened her eyes again. Woozy and faintly nauseous, she was glad to let him call the shots. Nonetheless she recognized that this feeling of meek acceptance that he knew what was best for her was not normal, not for her.

He stroked her cheek, brushed her hair back from her face, leaned in close. So close that she thought he meant to kiss her. His warm breath feathered her lips, which parted instinctively in anticipation. Then a blue glow bathed her face. Using his phone as a flashlight, he peered into her eyes.

"One pupil's bigger than the other. You're getting checked out."

The disappointment that flooded her had nothing to do with the state of her eyes. She had *wanted* him to kiss her.

To combat her sudden upsurge of weakness where he was concerned, she gritted out a reply she knew would annoy him. "Guess what, pretty boy: you're not the boss of me."

His grip on her hand eased. "Mature as ever, I see. Good to know you're not at death's door." He thrust his phone back in his pocket.

Where was her attacker?

The thought brought a surge of renewed terror with it, and she forgot everything else. Her gaze darted all around. She would have shot to her feet instantly if she'd been able, and booked it out of there. But she wasn't, she discovered when she made a first abortive attempt.

"Stay still," he ordered.

She obeyed, simply because at that moment doing anything else was impossible.

Her head hurt like it had just been whacked with a hammer, which, in essence, she supposed it had. Her ribs ached with every breath.

But what if he comes back?

She said it aloud.

"Are you kidding? Baby, I promise you, you're safe as houses with me."

She knew it was true. Perversely, that didn't feel a whole lot better. The last thing in the world she wanted to do was get sucked into counting on Mark again. Jess depended on Jess, and that was the way she meant to keep it. It took every bit of strength and willpower she could muster to let go of his hand and sit up under her own steam.

But she did it.

The world spun. She couldn't help it: she made a pitiful little sound that was very nearly a moan.

"What the hell's the matter with you?" There was an alarmed, scolding note to his voice. "You know enough not to move until EMS gets here."

"Yeah, well."

Her head swam so sickeningly that if Mark's shoulder hadn't been close enough to rest her forehead against, she would have had to lie back down.

"Damn it, Jess." His arm came around her, steadying her. "There's a knot the size of a ping-pong ball on the back of your head. You were out cold when I got to you. The last thing you need to be doing is moving around." When she didn't reply, he added grimly, "Are you hurt anywhere else?"

She started to shake her head before the pain that shot through it made her think better of it. Tell Mark about the pain in her ribs and he'd be ripping off her jacket to check her out. She knew him.

"That's it, I think." Her voice had a thready quality now. She really shouldn't have moved, he was right about that, but at the thought of how exposed she had been, just lying there in the dark, fear had tightened her throat, churned in her stomach. And they were still exposed, the two of them. Her attacker could be anywhere. Without lifting her head she tried to look in every possible direction at once. Even moving her eyes hurt, she discovered. "Is he gone? Are you sure?"

The arm around her tightened. "I'm sure. He threw you down and ran like hell. I never even got a shot off. And I wasn't about to leave you, so the bastard got away. For now."

She latched onto the part she found most comforting. "You have your gun?"

"Of course I have my gun. I'm a federal agent, for God's sake."

Okay, she definitely felt better. But she didn't say it aloud. What she did say was, "We have to catch him."

"I've got people on the scramble looking for him right now. Did you recognize him?"

"No."

"Any chance you can describe him?"

"Six feet, muscular. Smelled of cologne. A deep voice, no real accent. That's all I got. He was wearing a ski mask, and a long-sleeved T-shirt and long pants. All black or some other dark color. How hard could it be to find somebody dressed like that in this heat?"

Heat or no, at the memory she shivered.

"That jives with what I saw. That's the description I called in. Jesus, you took ten years off my life tonight. One minute you're standing on the sidewalk in front of your apartment. Safe enough, I thought. My phone rings, I answer it, then I look back and you're gone. *Poof!* I drive down the street, and some piece of shit's dragging you behind a tree."

She narrowed her eyes. "Were you *following* me?"

"Of course I was following you. You didn't really think I was going to let you walk home by yourself, did you? Anyway, you left your stuff in my car." He looked around impatiently while she leaned against his shoulder and concentrated on getting her brain fully functional again. "What the hell's taking that damned ambulance so long?"

Good question. Mark's gun or no, the fear that her attacker was out there somewhere in the dark made the hairs prickle to life on the back of Jess's neck. Not that she really thought any harm could come to her while Mark was with her, and clearly Mark would not have put away his gun if he'd anticipated trouble, but if the guy was armed and chose to come back, he could shoot them both from a distance, maybe. Or if there was someone else around meaning to mop up the mess . . . Cold chills chased down her spine as possibility after hideous possibility occurred to her.

We need to move.

Cautiously she lifted her head from Mark's shoulder. The resulting stab of pain made her wince. A wave of dizziness hit her. She fought against collapsing against Mark again, instead taking careful breaths as she slowly sat up. Her ribs hurt, but it was more of a dull ache now that made her think they were bruised rather than broken.

"What the hell are you doing?"

"I'm not waiting out here like this for a

stupid ambulance to show up. If the guy comes back, we're sitting ducks."

"You think I'd let somebody get to you?"

"Not if you could help it. But you never know, they might get to you first. Anyway, I'd rather be safe than sorry."

The grass felt cool and prickly beneath her legs. She realized that she was just noticing, which told her how out of it she had been. Now she also registered the hard strength of Mark's arm around her, the sultry scent of the magnolia, the rattling hum of a nearby central air-conditioning unit. Her skirt had ridden up almost to the tops of her thighs, leaving her legs bare. They looked slim and pale amidst so much darkness. Her eyes had adjusted to the night enough now to allow her to make out Mark's features fairly well. His jaw was hard and set and his mouth was thin, which was never a good sign.

He was worried, too.

"Fine," he said.

Then he stood up, scooping her up in his arms, catching her completely by surprise. He lifted her easily: he was strong, she was light.

"Hey, I can walk," she protested despite

the fact that the world suddenly seemed to be doing a slow spin around them. In his arms was the last place she wanted to be. They felt too much like home.

"Just for the record, you are a royal pain in my ass." His tone had an edge to it. His expression was anything but loverlike.

"Oh, thank you very much. You can just put me down anywhere along here."

"You talk too much."

"Screw you."

"Maybe later. If you ask me nicely."

She eyed him with what venom she could muster but didn't say anything more. Quarreling with Mark took too much energy, and she didn't have any to waste. Anyway, the way she was feeling now, in any war of words she wasn't going to win. Putting her arms around his neck was tantamount to giving up, but she did it, albeit with poor grace.

Doing her best to ignore the pounding in her head, fighting off the dizziness that made the world seem to shift in and out of focus, she tried to concentrate on finding answers.

"You think this had something to do with what happened to Leonard Cowan?"

He slanted a look at her. "The thought had occurred."

The memory of Tiffany Higgs being accosted outside the metro popped into her head.

"Or maybe it's somehow connected to the Phillips case."

"Maybe."

Various other scenarios started revolving through her mind.

"I did some pro bono work for the domestic violence shelter in Anacostia before I got pulled into this case." The possibilities started coming fast and thick. "Some of those men were pretty violent. And before that I helped Cates win an acquittal for an accused embezzler. There were a lot of unhappy plaintiffs on that one. Then there's one of Grace's ex-boyfriends—I had to file a restraining order to keep him away from her. Maybe he still hates me, although I think I would have known if it was him. Or—"

"Wait a minute. Jesus, just how many enemies have you collected over the last few months, anyway?"

That earned him a frown. It might well have become a full-blown scowl, but twitching her eyebrows together hurt, so she stopped.

"The thing is, I don't think this was just a random attack. He didn't try to rob me. Didn't demand money or anything. He just grabbed me and . . ." She broke off as a shudder racked her. This tremor was too obvious for Mark to miss. His arms tightened around her and his mouth went hard by way of a response. Well, he had always had a protective streak a mile wide.

It was one of the things she had loved about him. Most of the time, anyway. When he hasn't been crossing the line into overprotective, and that overprotectiveness hasn't been driving her nuts.

"Could have been an attempted sex crime." There was no inflection at all in his voice. Which, if you knew Mark, spoke volumes.

"Maybe." Jess thought that over. It was possible, although that hadn't been the vibe she had gotten from her attacker. But then again, maybe murder had been the *second* thing on his agenda.

Mark had left the Suburban in the middle of the street with the motor running and the driver's door hanging open, she saw as they neared the curb. She could hear the muted throb of the engine. The soft glow of the interior light lit up the night like a lantern. It was both comforting and scary. If someone lurked in the dark with a gun, she and Mark made perfect targets.

"Where'd he come from, anyway? I watched you walk down the sidewalk, and I'm willing to swear there wasn't anybody anywhere around you."

"He was already at my building. Behind the tree. I think he was waiting for me." It was all she could do to keep her voice steady. Lightning memories of the attack kept flashing through her mind like quick cuts from a movie. Deliberately closing her mind to the images, she fought to keep her breathing steady and get her heart rate under control.

It's over. I'm safe now. A beat later, that was followed by, *Thank God for Mark.*

"From now on, you don't even think about going anywhere alone."

There he went, being all dictatorial again, which, since it gave her something to think about besides the attack, was actually kind of a relief. Jess would have called him on it, but she figured it was a waste of her breath. Number one, that was just Mark being Mark. Number two, since she was no longer with Mark, his attitude wasn't her problem. She concentrated instead on keeping an eye on their surroundings as he walked around to the passenger's side door with her. It took a little juggling, but he managed to get it open without dropping her and deposited her in the seat.

"Forget the ambulance. They're too damned slow. We'll go down to the clinic on Virginia instead." He was still leaning over her. His eyes darkened as they moved over her face. "You're going to have a bruise." His fingers brushed her temple, their touch gentle. "Right here."

"He punched me." Her hands were trembling, so she clenched them before he noticed, too. And her ribs ached every time she tried to take a deep breath. Although she still wasn't about to tell him that. The last thing she needed was to have him fussing more over her. Having him there and concerned already felt too good, too right.

Mark's face hardened. Without another word, he pulled her seat belt around her, clicked it shut, closed her door, walked around the front of the car, got behind the wheel, and put the Suburban into drive. They were almost to the stoplight when a cop car came careening around the corner, lights going crazy, siren blaring.

"They're playing our song," Mark said, and flashed his lights.

CHAPTER NINE

The ambulance arrived almost on the heels
of the cop car. Turning Jess over to the
paramedics, Mark talked to the uniforms
and to the occupants of an unmarked car
that rolled up while she was being exam-
ined. Discovering that her injuries basically
consisted of a couple of bruises and a
bump on the back of her head, the paramedics were unimpressed. D.C. was a city
in which crime was rampant, murders occurred hourly, and the convoluted freeway
system spawned grisly accidents by the
dozens. For these rescue workers, blood
and gore were a staple of daily life. It was

clear that in their opinion what she had suffered was little more than a boo-boo that was hardly worth their time.

After shining a penlight in her eyes, having her track an upheld index finger, and checking her vitals, they gave her a couple of Advil and an ice pack and left. The cops took a cursory statement from her and shoved off, too. Their stated intention was to patrol the area, hunting for the UNSUB. Without, Jess thought, much real expectation of apprehending anyone.

Jess put more faith in the occupants of the unmarked car. A single glance at them had been enough to tell her that they were some of Mark's alphabet soup buddies, and she suspected him of calling in favors on her behalf. Not that she really wanted to know the details. To date, she'd had about as much involvement with the shadowy world he slid in and out of as she ever wanted to in her life.

"So where to?" Mark asked as the cop car pulled away. They were in the Suburban again, which was double-parked near the streetlight, and she was busy holding the ice bag to her head. A quartet of gawkers, all of whom seemed to be neighborhood residents with their dogs in tow, had gathered on the corner to watch the excitement. As Mark put the Suburban in gear and pulled off, they started to drift away.

"My apartment." She was surprised he'd asked.

Mark turned left, heading, Jess presumed, around the block to her apartment. She figured he was opposed to making his usual illegal U-turn given that the patrol car was still within sight.

"Just so we're clear, I'm spending the night." He said it as if he expected her to argue. Good call.

She sat up straighter. "I don't think so."

"You weren't listening, were you? My job is to keep you safe. And for the sake of argument, let's say you're right and you weren't attacked at random. If the guy had a motive, like, say, it's now open season on everybody who knows anything about Annette Cooper's death, then you can bet your bottom dollar he'll be back."

Jess experienced a sinking sensation in the pit of her stomach as she faced the horrible truth: Mark was right. A shiver snaked down her spine, and she had to fight a tendency to let her eyes dart fearfully in every direction. Which would be useless. If one thing was more certain than anything else, it was that she wasn't going to spot her attacker just standing there in somebody's yard waving at her. Whoever he was, whatever his motive had been, he was long gone, at least for tonight.

She said as much.

"You willing to bet your life on that?"

"I don't want you to spend the night. You're *not* spending the night. Anyway, I won't be alone. Grace'll be home." *Sometime,* she added silently. *Or not.*

"No, she won't. She called and said she's spending the night out."

After a surprised moment in which she simply blinked at him, Jess remembered that while she had walked home he'd had her cell phone. Since Grace, who was one hundred percent sister-loyal although she had once liked Mark a lot, wouldn't have called him in a blue million years, she realized what must have happened.

She glared at him in outrage. "You answered my phone."

"I thought it might be important."

"You fished my phone out of my purse and answered it."

"It was actually in a side pocket. No fishing involved."

"What about the fact that it's *my* phone—mine, not yours—are you missing?" Then something even more surprising hit her. "Grace actually talked to you?"

"You say that like I'm Public Enemy Number One. We had a very nice chat. She said you'd missed me."

"She did not!"

He grinned a little. "All right. She called me a liar and a scumbag, among other things. That was after I explained you'd left your phone with me and I was in the process of returning it to you. Finally she calmed down enough to give me the message. Actually, it was talking to her that made me take my eyes off you long enough for that bastard to grab you."

"I can't believe she gave you a message to give to me. Hate to burst your bubble, but you are definitely not on her list of favorite people."

"I got that. She probably wouldn't have if she hadn't been going into a nightclub with her date. I got the impression she expected to lose the connection momentarily."

It took Jess a moment to regroup. "I don't care whether Grace is going to be home or not. You can forget spending the night in my apartment. Not gonna happen. We broke up, remember?"

"Baby, if you think there's anything personal about this—" Before he could finish, his phone rang. As he fished it out and answered, their eyes clashed.

"Hang on a minute," he said into the phone, then covered the mouthpiece, his eyes still on hers. "You're not spending the night alone and that's the end of it. I can come to your place with you, or you can come to mine with me. Your call."

Actually, neither worked for her, as she started to make very clear. But she knew Mark, knew she wasn't getting rid of him short of calling the police, and she really wasn't up for the fruitless argument that was getting ready to ensue if she persisted. Also, the idea of sitting sleepless in her empty apartment until dawn broke and she could legitimately go to work was starting to hold less and less appeal the more she realized that that was exactly what she would be doing. Whether she

liked it or not, the attack had left her feeling frightened and vulnerable. It was going
to take a while for her to get over it.

"I'll stay at my mother's." Her tone was
almost sulky. "So I won't be alone, okay?"

He acknowledged that with a curt nod,
then turned his attention back to the phone.
"Sorry. Go ahead."

Jess looked out the window as he turned
right instead of left at the next intersection
and headed north, toward where her
mother lived with Maddie in an aging neighborhood that they called the BBB (Big Bad
Boonies), because it was so far on the outskirts that D.C. had given up and spilled
over into Maryland.

"I'm not surprised." Mark's tone was grim
as, a moment later, he replied to whoever
was on the other end of his phone call.
"Yeah. I have no idea. It's out on WALES,
right?" He listened again, said, "Keep me
posted, would you?" and disconnected.

"Wales?" Jess asked as he tucked his
phone into his pocket again.

"Washington Area Law Enforcement
System."

"They didn't find him," Jess surmised.

"Nope."

"They're not going to, are they?"

"At a guess, I'd say no."

Jess's shoulders slumped a little. Not that the answer wasn't exactly what she'd expected. The ice pack had frozen her scalp solid and was starting to feel clammy, so she gave up on it, dropping the thing into the footwell.

"You don't think whoever attacked me will show up out here, do you?"

"If he'd wanted an audience, he wouldn't have been lurking in the dark waiting to catch you alone."

"But I got away. Maybe he's desperate now."

"Maybe. But it would still be easier to wait and catch you alone. Your mom's house is a zoo."

"Good point." Jess felt relieved. The last thing she wanted to do was endanger her family. But she didn't want Mark playing bodyguard either, and even if she managed to get rid of him, she was (face it) too scared to spend the rest of the night alone. Which left her mother's by default. And as Mark had said, the place tended to be a zoo, with people coming in and out all the time and no telling who was there at any given moment. No killer in his right mind would come after her there.

It was just after 11:00 p.m. now, and traffic in this mainly residential area was light to nonexistent. Unlike New York, the city that never slept, D.C. was the city that went to bed early, because all the resident workaholics had to get up at the crack of dawn for jobs or school or whatever. Only street people, teenagers taking advantage of the final days before school started to get up to no good, and a few solid citizens giving their dogs the last-call-before-bed walk were out and about.

"I hear you got offered a promotion."

Considering the fact that Pearse had only invited her to become a permanent member of his team about six hours earlier, Jess looked at him in surprise.

"How'd you hear that?"

He smiled a little wryly. "Hey, I got sources. You going to accept?"

"Yes." Although Jess hadn't consciously decided before the answer left her lips, she realized that somewhere inside she'd made the decision as soon as she'd been asked. "Are you going to tell me who your source is? Because I'd love to know."

"No. Anyway, you don't know her." The quick gleam that accompanied that told Jess she was being teased. She refused to rise to the bait. "Working for Collins, you realize you're going to be going flat-out, twenty-four-seven."

The subtext was, henceforth there would be little time in her life for anything except work. Like a social life. Like love, marriage, men. Like him, although he was already out of the picture, of course. Amend that to someone like him.

She faced the truth of it, embraced it, even. After the debacle that had been their relationship, men were the last thing she wanted any part of anyway. In her experience, they weren't worth the pain they caused.

"Yes."

"Still hell-bent on being little Miss Over-achiever, aren't you?"

She bristled. "Do you have any idea how patronizing that is?"

"What? That isn't patronizing. That, from someone who's seen how you oper-ate close-up, is a simple observation. And for what it's worth, here's some advice to go with it: don't work yourself into an early grave trying to take care of everyone else."

"And what does that mean, precisely?"

"You know what it means. I know Maddie's tuition got paid. I know your mother leased a building so she could open a real day-care facility instead of keeping children in her house. I've heard about Grace's brand-new consignment shop."

"So?"

"C'mon, Jess, this is me you're talking to, remember?"

"Not . . . your . . . business. Any of it."

"You're right. It isn't. How's the headache?"

Lips firming, Jess didn't answer. Instead she looked pointedly out the window. Not that there was much to see. Narrow, two-story frame houses crowded together on either side of the street. White was the aluminum siding color of choice, although there were a few tan and gray ones thrown in for good measure. Most, like her mother's, had black shingle roofs, small porches out front, and a generally run-down air. Even in the dark they looked tired. It was a neighborhood where people struggled, lived paycheck to paycheck, and worried about whether they were going to be able to make next month's mortgage or rent payment.

She felt fortunate that she was now earning enough to make her family's lives a little easier. And why shouldn't she? She was the oldest sister, and she'd always felt responsible for the rest of them. For her mother, too, who had married three times (so far) and unfortunately always seemed to be attracted to the wrong sort of man. They were a unit, she and her mother, Sarah, Grace, and Maddie. They always had been. Whatever happened, good or bad, they stuck together. In a screaming, hair-pulling fight, sometimes, but still, together through thick and thin.

The Suburban turned onto Laundry Street, where, looking down the way, she discovered her mother's house was one of the few with the downstairs lights still on. Jess said coldly, "You can just drop me off in front of the house."

"What, you don't want me to come in?"

"No."

"Don't you think you might be getting a little carried away with this whole 'I hate my ex' thing?"

"No. Anyway, I never said I hated you. I don't hate you. I am *over* you, which is something entirely different." She was pardonably proud of the conviction in her voice. "You not coming in has nothing to do with that."

"So what does it have to do with?"

"I don't feel like explaining why you're with me, okay? If you come in, Mom will know something's up. I'll end up telling her what happened—or you will—and she'll worry. She'll tell Grace not to go out at night. She'll send Maddie over to live with us, because she thinks there's safety in numbers. For all I know, next time Sarah's marriage hits a bad patch, she'll send Sarah to live with me, complete with kids. None of which would help, and all of which would drive me completely around the bend."

"Let me get this straight: you're not planning on telling your mother what just happened?"

"No."

"What about Grace?"

"What about her?"

"She lives in the same apartment you do. Maybe she should know that you were just violently attacked in your mutual front yard."

Jess hadn't thought about that. If by some chance the attacker hadn't been specifically targeting her, Grace could be at risk, too.

"So I'll tell Grace." Knowing that telling Grace was the same as telling her mother, which was the same as telling the whole gang because that was just the way her family worked, she temporized. "Enough to keep her safe."

"Isn't your mother going to wonder why you're showing up on her doorstep wanting to spend the night?"

Good question. Before Jess could think of an answer that had any chance of satisfying her mother, she felt her foot brush against something freezing cold and damp. Glancing down into the footwell in surprise, she realized she had another problem.

"I lost my shoes." The memory of how they had come to fly off her feet made her heart quicken all over again. *You could have died tonight.* "They must still be out there in the yard."

"So add showing up barefoot to the list of things you get to explain to your mother."

"She won't notice." As long as Jess could get inside the house without being spotted, that was, because it was her invariable practice to kick her shoes off as soon as she was inside the door.

"What about the bruises you're bound to have by tomorrow? She'll notice that."

Jess could feel the tenderness just above her right temple, the soreness of her ribs: Mark was right about the bruises, she was sure.

"I'll cover them with makeup. Believe me, Mom has plenty in the bathroom, and if it's bad I'll have to do it anyway to go into work." She sighed as more difficulties occurred to her. "The bigger problem is, how am I going to go to work tomorrow without any shoes? Or clothes? Oh, well, I guess I'll just have to get up early and run over to my apartment and get dressed there."

"I'd be surprised that you're planning to go into work tomorrow after just escaping being murdered by the skin of your teeth, except, oh, wait, I know you."

Jess opened her mouth to wither him with a few well-chosen words, but the sight of a red minivan pulling over to the curb and then slamming to a halt in front of her mother's house and, a split second later, Maddie all but leaping from the passenger side door to the sidewalk distracted her. Five-foot-six-inch Maddie was as slender as ever except for her round tummy, which, at seven months along, looked like a beachball stuck up under her tank top and droopy cutoff sweats. Her long blond braids bounced with the force of her exit. She was clutching what looked like a pillow, and even in the dark and from a distance it was clear she was spitting mad.

"Forget it! Just forget it!" Maddie whirled to scream at whoever had dropped her off. It didn't require genius to guess the driver's identity: Brice Wollinski, Maddie's twenty-year-old car mechanic ex-fiancé and the father of her baby, Jess was all but certain, who, over the last few months, had earned at least a big capital L-O-S on the word loser. This was looking like capital E, and then he'd just have R to go before the whole family turned on him en masse and tore him limb from limb on Maddie's behalf.

"Stop. I'm getting out," Jess told Mark,

her eyes on her sister. There was just enough illumination, from the moon and the light spilling out from her mother's windows and a distant streetlight, to allow her to see the bright gleam of tears coursing down Maddie's cheeks.

Mark braked as the minivan took off with a squeal of tires, leaving Maddie behind. Jess was just pushing the door open when Maddie screamed, "Asshole!" at the top of her lungs, then hurled the pillow after the departing van.

CHAPTER TEN

Give me Black Ops assassins anytime.
That was Mark's first rueful thought as Jess jumped out of the Suburban to rush toward her furious sister, and he realized that the next item on the night's already jam-packed agenda was going to be pure domestic drama. Mired in a world of women as he always seemed to be, it was nothing new, but still it was something he preferred to avoid if he could.
No such luck.
Keeping one eye on Jess, who was focused on her pillow-tossing sister, Mark pulled the Suburban over to the curb, which

was not a problem out here on the rag-
gedy fringe of the city. Not that he was in
any hurry to rejoin Jess. In fact, he welcomed a moment or two alone to regain
some perspective. The idea that Jess
could have died tonight was making him
nuts. And the fact that it was making him
nuts confirmed something for him. No matter how hard he had tried, no matter what
he had told himself to the contrary, the
woman still had a stranglehold on his heart.

A few scant weeks after meeting her,
he'd found himself proposing to her. The
speed with which he'd fallen in love had
been totally contrary to his nature. After the
breakup of his marriage years before, his
MO had been to play the field and keep it
light. Finding out that his then-wife had
been sleeping with a fellow agent had cured
him of the marriage bug forever. Or, at least,
that's what he'd thought until he had en-
countered Jess.

Their relationship had been forged in
danger. He knew from his military experience that things can get intense pretty
quickly when your life is on the line, and so
it had proved with him and Jess. As special agent in charge of First Lady Annette

Cooper's security detail, he had rushed to the scene of the car crash that had killed Mrs. Cooper, her driver, and the Secret Service agent who had accompanied her that night. He'd been the one who'd found the fourth occupant of the burned-out car, the lone survivor who'd owed her life to the fact that she'd been thrown clear. That survivor was Jess, and from the moment he'd discovered her lying dazed and broken on the dark hillside the car had tumbled down, he'd thrown in his lot with hers, making it his mission to keep her safe from the rogue operatives who were determined to finish the job they had started and kill her, too.

They'd come within a heartbeat of dying half a dozen times. In the fraught process of staying alive, they'd fallen head over heels in love. The speed with which it had happened, the intensity of it, had caused him to panic a little, he saw now. Hearing himself propose marriage, which he'd had no idea he'd meant to do until the words left his mouth, had ramped that panic way up. So what had he done? How had he coped? Almost immediately found a way to fuck the relationship up.

When MJ Cates, an old girlfriend, who,

as fate would have it, had turned out to be Jess's boss, had surprised him by coming on to him while he'd been waiting to take Jess to lunch, he'd reacted just as he would have pre-Jess, letting MJ kiss him, kissing her back. Done that when he had known Jess was there in the same building, on the same floor. On her way to meet him, yet. Had he done it on purpose? He wasn't much for psychology, didn't spend a lot of time delving into his own motives, but looking back now with the useless benefit of hindsight, he almost had to say yes.

He'd known Jess. He'd known she wasn't going to tolerate finding the man she loved kissing another woman.

He'd been right. After that, there had been no going back. No apologies accepted. No second chances handed out. Truth was, he'd almost been relieved when she'd told him it was over, had almost been relieved to have been kicked out of her life.

Until he'd tried to go back to the way his life had been before he'd met her, had tried to live his life without her in it, and had found that nothing had felt right.

He'd buried himself in work, too stubborn to face the possibility that maybe, just maybe, he'd made the mother of all mistakes. But as the weeks had passed, he'd found himself missing her more, not less. The hole he'd torn in the fabric of his existence had just seemed to keep getting bigger, more ragged. The hottest, brightest summer day had felt a little cold, a little gray.

Without Jess.

He'd still been getting his head around the implications of that when he'd gotten the call from a buddy at the FBI about Leonard Cowan's suicide.

Supposed suicide.

Because he wasn't buying it. Not so easily. Not yet.

Burned out in the aftermath of Mrs. Cooper's death, Mark had left the White House security detail to work for the Secret Service's investigative branch. That afternoon he'd walked out on a scheduled interrogation of a suspected money launderer to go in search of Jess. He'd found her in court, had waited until she had come out.

He'd lied, though. As of this moment, he wasn't under any kind of official orders to keep her safe. He'd come for her on his own initiative, because the one thing he knew for sure was that he wasn't going to let her get killed. Hasbrough would almost certainly issue such an order once he learned what had happened, but Mark hadn't been about to wait.

"Your job is to handle the survivor." That's the way it had come down in the beginning, and that's the way it had to stay, world without end. Because he was the only government operative he could be sure didn't have a secret agenda. His sole purpose was to protect Jess.

Although he had downplayed it to Jess, a cleanup operation on the order of what he suspected had happened to Leonard Cowan was his default explanation for the attack on her, which luckily, he had been on hand to thwart. If that was the answer, then she was in deadly danger still. Once activated, those guys never gave up, and they never forgot. The best he could hope for was that having temporarily failed they would decide to lay low for awhile.

Nobody came after me.

There was that, so maybe he was wrong. Maybe the attack on Jess wasn't a follow-up to what had happened to Cowan after all. Maybe it was random, just D.C. being

D.C. Or maybe it was something else. Because if they came after Jess, they must know they had to take him out, too.

The only intelligent thing to do would be to take him out first. Unless, of course, another fed on the kill team had an aversion to eliminating one of his own kind. Still, it would be dangerous to the point of foolhardiness to kill her and leave him alive.

Although if they knew the two of them had been an item, knew she had dumped him, they might assume he wouldn't care.

Stupid assumption.

Frowning, Mark stared into the darkness beyond the windshield, weighing the possibilities.

"Maddie." The fear in Jess's voice was enough to make him refocus in a hurry. He saw Maddie folding toward the sidewalk as if her knees had turned to water, and he was out of the car in a flash. Alarm jangled his nerves, which was kind of funny, because his nerves never got jangled on his own behalf. Bullets flying past, knives slashing toward him, bombs blowing everything in his vicinity to smithereens— any kind of physical danger just tended to make him go colder and calmer.

But women in distress got to him every time.

He heard Maddie's sobs almost as soon as he was on the ground, and he slowed his steps accordingly: his worst fear, that something had happened to her, that she'd been shot or stabbed in another attack maybe, was immediately assuaged. As the father of a daughter who changed moods more often than she changed her clothes (and that was damned often), he recognized furious weeping when he heard it. He had the same reaction to it that he always did: he wanted no part of it. But sometimes there was no help for it and you just had to deal.

Fortunately, right now Jess was the designated dealer-in-chief.

She leaned over her sister, who was kneeling on the pavement with her face buried in her hands. Maddie was a pretty girl, big blue eyes, fine features, a hint of Jess's square jaw, but Mark was unsettled by the juxtaposition of long schoolgirl braids and the same kind of funky teen clothing and flip-flops Taylor might wear with a swollen-with-child belly.

Probably because he kept thinking that

if a girl as smart as Maddie could get herself into a fix like that, what chance did he have of keeping his own way less academically inclined, already rebellious and defiant daughter on the straight and narrow?

Pure dumb luck might not be enough, and the thought scared him cold.

"He didn't even *care*," Maddie wailed. "I can't even count on him for *that*. What a fucking asshole."

Mark didn't hear Jess's reply, mainly because, in reconnoitering the area for possible danger, he spotted the pillow Maddie had thrown and used the need to retrieve it as a way to take himself out of the hot zone. Then he backtracked to the Suburban to fetch Jess's purse and briefcase, which she would surely want. By the time he returned with the pillow tucked under his arm and Jess's bags slung over his shoulder, Maddie was talking and crying at the same time and Jess was helping Maddie to her feet. Maddie was some four inches taller and, just at present, no telling how many pounds heavier than bird-boned Jess. Jess had just suffered through the severe physical and psychological trauma of a would-be murderous attack, but nobody would have guessed it watching the two of them. Jess was every inch the protector. She wrapped her arm around Maddie's waist and the younger sister leaned on the elder, resting her head against Jess's, soaking up sympathy and support as they headed up the short concrete walkway that led to the porch. Watching, Mark's lips compressed.

As far as he was concerned, it was Jess who needed the sympathy and support, not the other way around. But try convincing her of that.

Jess took care of her sisters, took care of her mother, took care of everybody. It was one of the things that made him crazy and had made him crazy about her at the same time. One of the things that had made him think, once upon a time, *This one's a keeper.* Of course, that was before he'd discovered her less-attractive traits, like distrust and jealousy and paranoia and temper, which latter quality had been on eye-opening display as she'd blasted him with her opinion of his character before casting him, as she had supposed at the time, permanently out of her life.

Not that that was going to be possible. Even if she apparently hadn't figured it out yet, the stone-cold truth was that the dangerous knowledge they shared about Annette Cooper's murder meant that they were forever linked.

It was kind of like having a child together. Because of Taylor, he was permanently connected to his social-climbing, money-grubbing, blame-laying, divorcing-for-the-third-time ex-wife, too.

He didn't necessarily have to like it. But there was absolutely nothing he could do to change it.

"It was so *embarrassing*." Maddie sounded both furious and anguished. "There were all these couples and *me*. Just me, all alone. At our first Lamaze class. Brice swore he'd show up and so I told them all he was coming, and the whole class waited on him. And he didn't come until something like five minutes before the end. And he didn't even apologize. He didn't *care*."

Jess said, "If you want, I'll track him down and cut off his balls for you."

Mark heard that because he'd just fallen in behind the two of them, not too close, as they reached the steps. He was pretty sure she was being facetious. Still, knowing how fierce Jess could be in defense of her family, his own *cojones* shrank just a little in automatic reaction. That kid had no idea of the kind of trouble he was courting if he kept messing with Maddie.

Maddie sniffled as she and Jess negotiated the quartet of concrete steps that led to the small covered porch. "He's the father of my child. Or I'd say yes."

"Maybe later, then."

"He says he's not ready for a baby. Well, guess what, me neither. But I'm having one, ready or not," Maddie continued bitterly. She was no longer crying, which had to count as a good sign.

"Brice is immature."

Mark knew Jess was being careful about what she said, not wanting to trash the kid until she was sure he and Maddie weren't going to manage to make it up. Of course, Maddie and the entire family were going to be connected to her baby daddy forever, like it or not, in another one of those fate-mandated permanent connections. Not that any of them seemed to have grasped that yet.

"Well, time to grow up." This time Maddie's bitterness was pronounced.

Mark realized he must have made some small sound or otherwise done something to remind Jess of his presence, because she glanced around then, her eyes meeting his behind Maddie's back as he climbed the stairs in their wake. He had been admiring her ass. It was, as he'd told her, a nice one, even if he had said it to piss her off, and the way the snug pink skirt clung as she moved reflexively drew his gaze. Fortunately, he'd stopped before she'd turned to look at him. No way had she caught him at it. But still, even through the shadowy darkness, there was no mistaking the glare she gave him. From it, Mark got the distinct impression that he was unwanted. Innocently, he pointed to the pillow. Well, somebody had had to fetch it.

"We'll get you through this." Jess's tone was soothing as she replied to something else Maddie said. Her eyes met Mark's again, unwelcoming as before. He smiled at her. In return, if looks could have killed, he would have died on the spot.

"I just—I want my baby to have a father." Maddie's forlorn confession redirected

Jess's attention and unexpectedly touched Mark. "A *real* father."

"We never had one and we turned out fine." Jess's tone was bracing. "Believe me, men are overrated."

It was a double-sided message, with one particularly well-honed edge meant for him.

"But we always wanted one. At least, I did."

That was apparently unanswerable, because Jess said nothing in reply. Having crested the stairs, Mark discreetly hung back while Jess and Maddie, still arm-in-arm, crossed the porch. With the curtains open, he could see inside the living room. He was familiar with it—yellow walls, floral couch with its back to the window, a wooden rocking chair and a blue plush recliner, all facing the fireplace and the plasma TV that was mounted above it—and so he paid no attention except for a quick glance to ascertain that the room was empty. The large window spilled light out over the porch, illuminating the white-painted garden swing that hung from the ceiling and the dusty fern that huddled in a plant stand in the far corner.

He and Jess had spent a number of late spring evenings just sitting there in that swing talking and watching the world go by. That, of course, had been when they'd still been talking, and the memory might have made him nostalgic if he'd let it.

Not that he meant to. Like Jess had said, their relationship was over, and for now he was prepared to leave it at that. The last thing he needed was a new marriage, to say nothing of a new wife. He must have had rocks in his head to have even considered it.

But if somebody got to Jess, it was going to be over his dead body.

All of a sudden the porch felt way too exposed.

By that time Maddie and Jess had reached the front door. Maddie had her key out. As she inserted it into the lock, Jess held back to give her room, and not incidentally to glare at him as he stepped up behind her, positioning himself between her and the street.

Jess whispered, "Probably this would be a good time for you to go away."

He whispered back, "Thanks, Mark, for saving my life."

"*Shh*. Would you please leave?"

"Nope. And unless you can come up with a better explanation for why you're with me, I'd suggest you start acting like you like me again."

Her eyes glinted at him. "When pigs—"

"Mark!" The door opened, and either because of that, or because his presence on the small porch, coupled with the whispering going on between him and Jess, was impossible to miss any longer, Maddie turned at that moment and saw him. Since she was now awash in the light from the entry hall, he was able to see that her first reaction on finding him there was pleasure. That was good: he had a real soft spot for Maddie. Then clearly she remembered that he'd supposedly done her sister wrong. Her brows snapped together and her expression darkened as her eyes swung from him to Jess. "Nobody told me you'd gotten back together with Attila the Hun."

"We're not back together," Jess replied. From the Attila the Hun reference, which Taylor had used on Facebook—as in, Attila the Hun's going ape-shit over nothing as usual—Mark was reminded that Maddie was now Taylor's good friend. He sighed inwardly. His daughter stayed with him most weekends, and being a single father to a young woman who seemed determined to grow up fast was a challenge he hadn't anticipated. Boarding school had only been a threat, although it was a threat he wasn't kidding about if the situation with the boyfriend continued to deteriorate. Grounding his daughter had been his immediate reaction for a transgression that had made him want to alternately shake her and tear out his hair in fear for her. Thus he was now Attila the Hun. Well, he could deal.

"Good to see you too, Maddie." His voice was dry.

The sound of another vehicle coming fast down the street toward them made his shoulder blades tighten. After a quick, assessing glance at the oncoming headlights, Mark used his superior size to herd both ladies inside, then stepped in after them. From the muffled sound of laughter and voices that greeted them, Mark realized that there were a number of other people somewhere in the house, which wasn't a surprise. Judy Ford Turner Whalen,

Jess's gregarious, three-times-married-and-currently-widowed mother, was a people person. Being alone didn't suit her, and so she very rarely was. Which was why her house should be a fairly safe place for Jess to hang out until he could assess the magnitude of the threat. With an expression that told him she wasn't happy about his presence, Jess watched in silence as he closed the door.

Turning around, he smiled at her. A little mockingly, although not so much so that Maddie would necessarily pick up on it.

See, the thing was, Jess was fresh out of options. What was she going to do, tell him to get lost? If she did, all he had to do was tell her mother about the attack on her and the danger she might still be in, and Judy would be begging him to stick to her daughter for life.

Which he and Jess both knew. And acknowledged via a lightning exchange of clashing glances.

Outside, the passing vehicle didn't even slow down. Mark tracked its progress through the living room window, and then through the narrow glass panes on either side of the front door.

Dismissing the visions of drive-by shootings, Molotov cocktails, and the like that had been dancing in his brain, Mark handed Maddie the pillow she had thrown.

"Thanks." She clutched it to her chest.

Unburdening himself of Jess's bags, he handed them over next.

"Thank you."

"You're welcome."

Jess gave him a false smile. "Well, I appreciate the ride, but . . ."

Before she could finish her fated-to-fail attempt to get rid of him, a voice from the direction of the kitchen called, "Maddie? Is that you? Who's that you're talking to?"

Judy.

"Jess," Maddie called back. She was already making a beeline toward the kitchen. Mark noticed she made no mention of him. Jess glared meaningfully at him, looking as if she hoped that by sheer force of will she could force him back out the door. Physically, she didn't stand a chance, or he had little doubt she'd try.

"How was your class?" Judy's question to Maddie floated out to the hall. Maddie responded with something Mark didn't quite catch, although the overall tone was pure growl.

"If I were you, I'd say my air-conditioning went out." Mark's advice was given in a confidential aside to Jess as he moved to follow Maddie. Jess's eyes shot daggers by way of a reply. Skirting her, Mark headed toward the kitchen. It had been a while since he'd seen his once future mother-in-law, and he had no idea what kind of reception to expect. He discovered he was kind of looking forward to finding out. An only child himself, he'd missed Jess's big, boisterous family.

"When it comes to having babies, you can forget your classes. The only thing that helps is drugs." Judy's advice was underlined by the scraping sound of a chair being pushed back. A babble of observations from her guests on the trials and tribulations of childbirth broke off abruptly as Mark entered the kitchen in Maddie's wake. A little surprised at the sudden dead silence that greeted him, Mark scanned the group of middle-aged and older women sitting around the kitchen table. They looked back at him with a mixed bag of expressions that ranged from consternation to wariness to what he was fairly certain was out-and-out fear. His first thought was that they hadn't been expecting a man to appear in their midst and were concerned because they felt they weren't looking their best. His second was . . . he didn't know, but he was intrigued. Two of the women were waving their hands in an effort to dissipate a thin cloud of whitish smoke. One stern-faced lady had iron gray hair that hung straight to the middle of her ears. Another, thin, with a lived-in kind of face, had a salt-and-pepper crew cut. The rest were various shades of blond. They were casually dressed, in T-shirts or short-sleeved blouses, or, in the case of the lady with the crew cut, in a pink terry robe that zipped up the front.

"Uh, by the way, Mark's here," Maddie said.

"Mark." Judy sounded, and looked, delighted to see him. Smiling broadly, she hurried toward him. Pleasingly plump, or, as she liked to put it, generously curved, fifty-two-year-old Judy wore jeans and a pale blue T-shirt with some kind of saying in French printed on it: *Voulez-vous couchez avec moi ce soir*? Mark translated and smiled. *Would you like to go to bed with me tonight*? That pretty much summed up Judy. About Maddie's height, which meant she was inches taller than Jess, with short platinum blond hair that flipped up in little wisps around her ears and nape, Judy had blue eyes, regular features, plump cheeks, and a round chin. Lots of makeup—tonight's eye shadow was electric blue—and a minimum of wrinkles made her look younger than her age. She was an attractive woman, and she knew it. She was also naturally flirtatious, with a deep appreciation for men.

The opposite of her oldest daughter, in fact.

Reaching him, she enfolded him in a hug. Mark hugged her back with genuine affection.

"Never tell me you two are getting back together?" Letting him go, she addressed the question as much to someone behind him as to him. Mark didn't have to look around to know Jess was there.

"Working on it," he answered before Jess could, receiving a sharp jab in the ribs from Jess's elbow in payback as she passed him. She'd lost the purse and the other bag, and he could only assume she'd set them down somewhere.

"Oh, honey, I saw you on TV today." Judy hugged Jess, then stood back to run her eyes over her. "In your pretty pink suit. You looked so nice. You know how much I like you blond. And you won!" Then she looked a little closer at her daughter and frowned. "What in the world did you do to your face?"

"I ran into a door." Jess got away with her brief reply because the other women all started talking at once. Looking at her, Mark saw that the place on her temple where that bastard had punched her was puffy and starting to turn purple. If most of it hadn't been covered by her hair, the door excuse wouldn't have flown. He had little doubt that she had other bruises as well.

Mark was suddenly consumed by a wholly primitive urge to kill. His hands curled into fists at his sides. Realizing, he consciously relaxed them.

Judy's friends were chiming in with the TV talk.

"I saw you, too." "I was at work, and it came on during lunch." "I told 'em you're my neighbor's daughter." "First time I ever knew anybody who was on TV who wasn't getting arrested." "You're a real celebrity now."

Jess smiled by way of a reply. Judy chose that moment to introduce him.

"This is Diane, Lennie, Pat, Dee-Dee, Betsy," she said, waving a be-ringed hand at each in turn. "My book group. This is Jess's Mark."

Jess looked sour at the description, but she didn't dispute it. Which didn't signify anything except a desire not to argue with her mother in front of visitors, Mark knew.

"Pleased to meet you." Slightly mystified by the looks he was still getting from the assembled ladies, Mark tried putting them at ease with a smile.

They smiled back, but the impression they gave was of nervous hens eyeing a fox.

Maddie, over by the refrigerator pouring herself a glass of milk, grinned maliciously at him. Okay, clearly there was something going on here that he was missing. Then the smoke must have wafted his way at last, because the smell hit him, registered, and suddenly he understood: Judy and her friends had been smoking weed. His mind boggled. The shock of it widened his eyes. The ladies around the table stared back at him, looking guilty.

"I didn't know you had company," Jess said apologetically to her mother and hooked her hand around Mark's elbow. Since she never would have done that except under conditions of extreme duress, he realized that Jess was aware of the situation, too. "We'll get out of your way. You don't mind if I stay the night, do you? Uh, my air conditioner broke."

"Of course you can spend the night. You can always spend the night. This is your home." Judy frowned as Jess drew Mark out of the kitchen. "But what about Grace?"

"I think she was planning to stay overnight with a friend," Jess replied. With a last wave at the flustered ladies, she towed Mark around the corner and out of sight.

"Isn't he the Secret Service agent?" Despite Jess's determined efforts, Mark was still close enough to hear the hushed question. "Do you think he noticed anything?"

Whichever woman had spoken sounded worried. Well, given what the ladies were up to, it wasn't any wonder.

"Don't worry, he's cool," Maddie answered, then added darkly, "sometimes."

"I'm sure he didn't even realize." Judy's tone was reassuring. "You know how thick men are."

"He's real cute," said one. "And he's got a good job. Your Jess better hold on to that one."

Upon hearing that, Jess shot him a look that would have made a lesser man cringe. He threw up both hands in disavowal.

Then a babble of talk broke out that Jess and Mark were, probably fortunately, now too far away to decipher. They were back in the hall by that time, and Jess was towing him determinedly toward the door.

"Your mother and her friends are smoking weed in the kitchen." If he sounded slightly bemused, it was because he was.

"If you have a problem with what you saw, all I can say is it's your own fault for not leaving when I tried to get you to go the first time," she told him in a severe undertone. "Dee-Dee's getting chemo. It makes her sick, and pot's the only thing that helps. When she gets a treatment, all her friends from the book club get together and they do a sleepover. Well, actually, they sit up all night talking and whatever, but still. I guess tonight was Mom's turn to host." She stopped in front of the door to skewer him with a look. "Believe me, none of them would be here if they'd known I was going to show up with you."

"Hey, I'm a Secret Service agent, not a cop. It's nothing to do with me."

"Go." She unlocked the door, then turned back to him with her hand resting on the knob. "I appreciate everything you've done tonight, but I'll be fine now."

Despite her brave front, she was pale and wide-eyed and bruised and so vulnerable looking that she made his gut twist. Without the least bit of premeditation, his hands cupped her shoulders and he bent his head to press his lips to her soft, eminently kissable mouth.

Her lips parted beneath his. He felt their heat, the moist warmth of the inside of her mouth, like an electric jolt. She kissed him back, her mouth unexpectedly as hot and hungry as his, and for a sizzling moment the chemistry between them superheated the air.

"Jess!" A voice above their heads broke them apart, made them both look up at the

same time. Still slightly stunned by the unexpected impact of that barely underway
kiss, it took Mark a second to process who
he was seeing. Sarah stood at the top of
the stairs that rose at the side of the hall,
resplendent in purple pajamas and a head
full of pink sponge curlers. At twenty-five,
the sister who was next to Jess in age was
a slightly slimmer copy of their mother, although she lacked Judy's effervescent
spirit and generally went lighter on the
makeup. Tonight she was wearing none at
all, and from the oily sheen on her skin
where the light hit it he deduced she had
covered her face with some sort of beauty-
enhancing potion. Probably she slept in it.

Sometimes knowing too much about
women was a bad thing.

Jess had slipped out of his hands. God,
he shouldn't have kissed her. At least not
until he got a few things sorted out in his
mind. Truth was, he didn't know what he
wanted where she was concerned. All he
was one hundred percent sure of was that
he wasn't about to let her die.

"What are *you* doing here?" both sisters
demanded of each other.

"Ron and I had a fight and he left. So I

left, too." Sarah's chuckle had a forlorn quality. "Maybe when he gets home and sees I'm gone, it'll make him think twice."

"Oh, Sarah. Where are the boys?"

"At camp until Saturday." Sarah's eyes narrowed as she peered myopically down at them. Mark remembered that without contacts, which she clearly wasn't wearing at the moment, she was as blind as Jess. "Is that *Mark* you were kissing?"

"Hey, Sarah," he offered, cursing inwardly as instant color bloomed in Jess's cheeks.

"Yes, and no, we're not back together. He gave me a ride over because my air conditioner broke. And he's leaving." Jess looked at him then, a hard look that told him that as far as she was concerned, nothing had changed. Then she pulled open the door. A wave of steamy heat rolled in. Outside, the street was dark and quiet. A nice, peaceful summer night, at least from all outward appearances. He could see the black hulk of the Suburban waiting at the curb. "Good*night*, Mark."

With the house full to bursting with women, the chance that a killer would come after Jess during the night was as close to zero as it was possible to get, he judged. He could safely leave her. With that in mind, he allowed her to bully him out the door.

"I can't believe you did that," she whispered as he passed her, and he knew she was referring to that blistering kiss. *Not* something he wanted to discuss at the moment, especially with Sarah nearby.

"Stay inside," was his reply as he stepped out onto the porch. "You hear? Just in case."

"I'm not *stupid*," she sniffed and shut the door on him.

A wry smile played about his lips. Scanning the shadowy yards, sidewalk, and street with reflexive professionalism and finding nothing out of the ordinary as he went, Mark walked to the Suburban and got in. Then he pulled his phone out of his pocket and punched in a familiar number.

Hasbrough answered on the first ring.

"We need to talk," Mark said. "Something's happened. Jess needs protection."

CHAPTER ELEVEN

"You want some of this?" Lucy offered a piece of the chocolate doughnut she was eating to Jaden, who shook her head. It was just after midnight, technically the dawn of a new day, and Miss Howard's Quik-Stop preferred customer card, a tiny laminated version of which had been attached to her key ring, entitled her to a free cup of coffee and doughnut daily. They'd been making use of it ever since they had learned of it, during their second day of hiding out, when they'd gone into a Quik-Stop in Anacostia and the clerk had pointed it out to them and explained the benefits.

Lucy didn't know when the entitlement ran out, if it ever did, but for now it was a lifesaver. They'd gone to Anacostia because Lucy had once had a friend there and she had hoped they could crash at her place. But when they'd gotten there, they'd found out the friend was long gone and the place, which had been in foreclosure according to the For Sale sign out front, had become a kind of flophouse. They'd hung around, staying out of the way, sleeping on the floor. The Grand Plan was to head for California, a place where Lucy had always dreamed of living, but there were a couple of problems with that. One was that two bus tickets to L.A. cost hundreds more than they had, and the other was that they had no ID. Lucy had picked up some copies of *Street Sense*, the homeless person's version of craigslist that was available for free in newspaper form at soup kitchens and the like around the city, and had tried selling them for a quarter each. Jaden tried applying for a job at the nearest McDonald's but had made the mistake of telling the curious manager that the reason she'd had no permanent address or phone number or ID was that she had seen a murder committed and had been hiding out. The manager had called the cops, and Jaden had barely made it out of there ahead of their arrival. Consequently, Lucy and Jaden had fled Anacostia, and Lucy had made Jaden swear not to talk about what they had seen to anybody else.

"I'm sick of doughnuts." Jaden sipped the coffee as they pushed out through the heavy glass door. Anxious and stressed, she was in full starvation mode. The way she had been eating lately, the coffee was probably going to be her big meal for the day. Just in case, Lucy had loaded it with lots of creamer and sugar, because those came free wwith the coffee and Jaden needed all the calories she could get. The only positive thing she could say about Jaden's lack of appetite was that it was easy on the budget. Their little stash of money was almost gone now, depleted by trying to survive on the streets for the last three weeks. Lucy didn't know what they would do when it ran out. After the McDonald's disaster, applying for a regular job was out, and selling *Street Sense* wasn't exactly bringing in the bucks. They would come up with something, though. Maybe sell their blood. The blood banks paid for that, didn't they? Or maybe—well, something.

"You didn't even eat your hamburger yesterday." Burger King had been running a special, two hamburgers for a dollar, and Lucy had succumbed to hunger and handed over a buck around 3:00 p.m. the previous day. Except for the single bite Jaden had taken out of hers, Lucy had ended up eating both. The sad thing was, by midnight, when she'd nagged Jaden into going out to get their daily doughnut and coffee, she'd been starving again.

"I hate hamburgers." Jaden's shoulders hunched as she looked nervously all around. Lucy knew how she felt.

The lights surrounding the Quik-Stop spooked them both. The white glow was harsh and way too revealing. Being so glaringly visible made Lucy's skin crawl. Knowing Miss Howard's killer was out there somewhere was terrifying. The thing was, he could have been anyone from a mob hit man like in *The Sopranos* to a guy Miss Howard had met online in one of those dating horror story kind of deals. Since he had seen them, figuring out who he was and then turning him into the cops seemed

like the best way to make sure she and
Jaden stayed alive. But since she didn't see
any way to uncover his identity, and cops
spelled bad news for her and Jaden anyway, that probably wasn't going to happen.
Which left them with the alternative they'd
been left with by default: hide until they
could get enough money together to leave
the city.

"You want some of this coffee?" Jaden
offered.

"No."

Keeping close together, she and Jaden
hurried across the parking lot toward the
relative safety of the darkness enshroud-
ing the apartment buildings across the
street. Having run as far and as fast as their
funds would allow, they were now in College Park, Maryland, living on the fringes of
the University of Maryland campus. Lucy's
thought was that they would be a lot harder
to spot in a campus town filled with teenagers, many of whom didn't look any older
than themselves, and maybe they could
score a couple of fake ID's and use them to
get jobs. The problem was, it was August,
and the fall semester hadn't started yet.
There weren't that many college students

to get lost among. And the people who sold fake IDs seemed to be staying away until the college students came back.

"Cop." Jaden grabbed Lucy's arm as a patrol car nosed into the convenience store parking lot. Coffee sloshed out of the cup to splash down on the pavement, barely missing their feet. Jaden jumped back but didn't let go, her tight grip a sure indication of how close to the edge she was coming. They were both nervous wrecks, but Jaden showed it more. Lucy tended to keep what she was feeling inside.

"Chill." Despite her soft-spoken order to Jaden, Lucy's pulse quickened. Her stomach clenched. Trying to make it look like she wasn't looking, she tracked the cop car's progress toward the front of the store. There was a lot of glare from the outside lights that reflected off the windshield, so she couldn't really see the cop behind the wheel as the car stopped next to the curb in front of the door they'd just exited. It was a man, she saw enough to know that. He was by himself—didn't they usually travel in pairs?—and he seemed to be looking their way. The length of time he just sat there like that made Lucy jittery as hell.

Was he giving them a long once-over, or what? Then he moved, and she thought he was looking in the direction of the guy filling up at the gas pumps. One thing she knew: he wasn't looking at them anymore. He was facing the wrong way.

Relieved, Lucy muttered, "He's not interested in us. He's just here for the free doughnuts."

Jaden giggled, the sound high-pitched and nervous. Lucy was glad she'd made her friend laugh. It lightened the atmosphere, if only for the moment. Supremely conscious of the cop behind them, the girls kept walking, looking both ways, heading across the busy four-lane road. Lucy's shoulders were tight. Hungry as she was, the doughnut hung forgotten in her hand. She couldn't help it: despite the brave front she put on for Jaden, she quaked inside. At any second, she half-expected the car's siren to go off, the cop to call after them to stop. All the cop had to do was demand to see some ID, and they were done. Once he found out they didn't have any, he would order them into the back of his car, and when they couldn't give him a home address to take them to, he'd take them to the police station instead. Once there, it wouldn't take the cops long to figure out that they had escaped from a detention facility. She knew how the system worked: she and Jaden were wanted. One bad turn of luck, and they were goners.

Luckily, they were low priority. No all points bulletins would have been issued or anything. They would only be discovered if they got picked up for something else or some nosy cop got suspicious for some reason and decided to check them out.

"Maybe we ought to just tell them." Jaden's eyes darted her way. It was a sly, sideways look, meant to test her friend's reaction.

"We already called 911." Which they had, from an as-hard-to-find-as-a-public-toilet pay phone, just as soon as they'd gotten far enough away from Miss Howard's apartment to stop running. The dispatcher had taken their information and promised to send a car to check it out. Lucy, who'd made the call, had hung up when the woman had asked for their names. How the whole thing had worked out they had no way of knowing. Jaden had wanted to circle back around by Miss Howard's apartment to see what had been going on, but Lucy had been adamant: they couldn't ever go back there. She'd watched enough TV to know that that was one major way people got caught: they returned to the scene of the crime. "And you remember how that whole McDonald's thing worked out."

"Yeah, but, you know, I meant, like, maybe turn ourselves in."

They stopped on the concrete island in the middle of the road to let traffic on the other side go by. The whoosh of the cars speeding past was loud enough to make Lucy raise her voice a little when she answered.

"We escaped from Shelter House. We took their cash. We broke into Miss Howard's apartment. We stole some of her stuff." If there was an impatient undertone to her reply, it was because she'd said all this before. "If we go to the cops about what we saw, what do you think is going to happen to us? We're going to get locked up again, that's what, and we probably won't get out until we're eighteen. If we're lucky. If we're not lucky, maybe they'll even say we did it. I mean, we broke into her house. How do they know we didn't kill her?"

"I know, I know." Jaden sounded wretched. "But what if the killer finds us? I mean, I get nightmares that he's out there hunting us."

The thing was, they *were* being hunted. Lucy knew it, sensed it physically like the pull of unseen eyes you could nevertheless feel staring. Just thinking about it made her heart pound. Constant fear kept her looking over her shoulder no matter where they went. Her stomach stayed in a perpetual knot. Miss Howard's killer—no way was he just going to forget about them. But she couldn't see any way he could find them. How could he? They weren't even in D.C. anymore. He'd seen them, yes. But two girls in an area that was home to millions of girls, millions of people, had to be almost impossible to search for with any success.

She shared none of this with Jaden. Jaden was already just about at the end of her endurance.

"He's not going to find us." Lucy's voice held several degrees more conviction than she felt. But she really was pretty sure of it. She hoped. "All we have to do is lay low."

"For how long?"

Traffic finally thinned out enough for them to run across the remaining westbound lanes. Lucy's answer was a little breathless because she was talking while they ran.

"I don't know. A while longer. We'll manage, okay? Once we score some ID it'll get easier. We—"

A siren went off behind them just as they made it to the sidewalk. Startled, Lucy cast a quick, scared glance over her shoulder. The cop car was pulling out of the convenience store parking lot, lights flashing, siren screaming. It was headed their way, but it couldn't be coming after them— could it?

Beside her, Jaden dropped the coffee. The Styrofoam cup hit the pavement with a soft *thunk*. Hot liquid splashed Lucy's feet. She jumped back but nevertheless managed to keep the cop car in view. She couldn't be certain, because the windshield, with its reflections and everything, distorted things, but she was pretty sure the cop was looking straight at them. Swallowing hard, heart knocking in her chest, she forced herself to turn away.

"Don't run," she ordered Jaden through gritted teeth, hooking a hand around her friend's elbow and heading down the side-walk at a walk, like she was innocent as could be, propelling Jaden along with her so that she was walking again, too. "That's the worst thing we can do."

From the corner of her eye she watched the car, which was on the move again, ease into the westbound lanes, then nose over into the lane that was nearest to the sidewalk where they stood.

Maybe he *was* coming after them. Just the thought of it made Lucy's heart pound like crazy. She felt herself break out in a cold sweat.

The light from the convenience store parking lot backlit the driver. He was a big man, with thick dark hair . . .

She realized that Jaden was looking back over her shoulder, too.

"How do we know it's not *him*?" Jaden's voice was hoarse with fear.

Then Jaden broke and ran, jerking her arm free, tearing off across the strip of scraggly grass that separated the sidewalk from the dark parking lot behind them, bolt-ing toward the gap between the buildings where they'd come through on the way to the store. Beyond that was the maze of the apartment complex, and another street, and, not too far away, the campus itself and the cheap room where they were holed up.

After one wild-eyed glance at the cop car, which was now pulling up beside her with its stroboscopic lights flashing red all over her and its siren shrieking a warning, Lucy did the only thing left to her.

Doughnut falling from her suddenly nerveless fingers, she ran, too.

CHAPTER TWELVE

Dawn was just lighting up the sky the next morning when Jess hurried down Laundry Street's sidewalk on her way to the metro station. Today of all days she absolutely refused to be late. It was the first day of her new job, and to say she was thrilled to her toes about it was an understatement. In her heart, she knew she could take no credit for Tiffany's meltdown on the stand, but the opportunity it had opened up for her was a dream come true. She meant to seize the day, and the job, with both hands.

The air was already thick and steamy, but not as thick and steamy as it would be later. Pink streaks swirling through the lavender sky to the east heralded the arrival of the sun. Its neon orange upper curve rode the horizon. At about fifteen minutes before 6:00 a.m., the rest of the sky was deep purple. Which was better than black, just like the old blue Taurus rolling down the street was better than no car at all, and the kid riding his bicycle toward, presumably, the university was better than having no one else outside at all.

But not a whole lot better. Being alone didn't feel good. Probably the attack last night had been random. But having to deal with fear on a day like this brought home the whole fly-in-the-ointment quality of her life: on the one hand, a promotion she could only have dreamt about; on the other hand, a would-be murderous attack, a lingering concern over what had become of Tiffany, and Mark's reentry into her life. He had kissed her. And for a weak instant there she had kissed him back. Not, as God was her witness, that it would happen again. From here on out, her focus was going to be on making the most of the chance her new job represented. Mark might have made himself the center of her existence once; she wasn't about to let him even begin to get in the way of her career again.

Booking it toward the first corner, her purse slung over her shoulder, her brief-case and a plastic grocery sack containing the despised pink suit in her hand, Jess felt a prickle at the back of her neck. The weight of unseen eyes, she thought with a shiver, and shot a quick glance behind her. The good news was, if the guy from last night was anywhere around, he probably wouldn't recognize her. She was wearing a blue, spaghetti-strapped, smock-topped sundress from Maddie's pre-pregnancy days. It was loose and almost ankle-length on her, and she'd coupled it with a pair of too-big flip-flops. Her hair was twisted up into a haphazard bun. She'd dabbed some foundation on the fist-sized bruise on her temple, and in the uncertain light she was pretty sure it was nearly invisible. Without her usual contact solution, she'd tucked her contacts away in her purse and fallen back on the sturdy black glasses she kept as a backup. In other words, she looked almost nothing like the woman who'd been attacked the previous night.

Which didn't keep her from being jumpy as all get-out.

She was nearly at the corner when someone unexpectedly stepped out of the shadowy gap between two parked cars. In that first startled instant she registered that he was big, a man, and coming her way.

Gasping, her heart giving a giant thud, she jumped back even as he stepped onto the sidewalk and the light hit him: Mark.

"Want a ride?" he asked.

"Good God, you scared the crap out of me!" Having clearly not gotten the message that it was a false alarm, her heart pounded as if she'd been running a race.

"Sorry."

She might have thought he was genuinely penitent if the twist to his lips hadn't told her he was suppressing a smile. Her eyes met his. The memory of that brief, blazing kiss hung in the air between them. Jess's lips compressed in sheer self-defense even as she shook her head.

"I'll take the metro, thanks." She started walking away.

"Jess." He fell into step beside her. "We both know I'm not going away. If you want,

I can get back in the car and just cruise along in the street beside you while you tramp down the sidewalk, but that's just stupid."

Meeting his gaze, Jess gave it up. Truth was, she was glad to see him. At least his presence meant she wouldn't have to jump at every swaying shadow between here and her apartment. After that, hopefully, it would be full daylight, and the streets would lose their power to terrify.

"Fine."

Now that she was looking for it, she spotted his Suburban on the other side of the street, nestled among a long line of other vehicles. With a quick glance left and right, she headed across the street toward it. He followed and got in without coming around to open the door for her, the subtlety of which she appreciated as she walked around to the passenger side and climbed in on her own. Opening the door for her was something he would have done if they'd been in a relationship. Something he had done, before. Now he didn't.

Wise man, she thought. But her heart gave a little pang.

"Thanks for the ride." Surprised at how relieved she felt to no longer be on the street, she pulled on her seat belt as he started the engine. Hot air began blowing out of the air conditioner vent, and she repositioned it away from her. "How long have you been out here waiting for me?"

It couldn't have been too long, because he was freshly shaved, showered, and dressed in one of the ubiquitous dark suits that, with a white shirt and dark tie, was the universal fed uniform. The maddening thing was, he looked supergood in it. Tough and handsome. Typical Mark.

She immediately felt both scruffy and cross.

"Little while." They passed the kid on the bicycle, cruised on through Friendship Heights. A few more vehicles were on the streets, a few more people were moving about. A new day had dawned. In which, as his presence made clear, in addition to everything else she had going on, she had to worry about being killed. It was starting to feel like the story of her life. Which didn't make it any more fun.

"You're babysitting me, aren't you?

What, do you think whoever attacked me last night is going to try again?"

"Since I have no idea who attacked you last night, I don't know. Think of me as an insurance policy."

"I don't want to think of you as an insurance policy. I don't want to think of you at all. If I have to have a babysitter, I want somebody else." If she was being unreasonable, she didn't care. Being with Mark again was making her . . . tense. Yeah, that was the word. It was playing with her emotions. Especially in light of that thrice-damned kiss.

"You want somebody else, huh? Baby, answer me this: who else can you trust?"

That was so true it momentarily shut her up. Dried up every protest that had been hovering on the tip of her tongue. The fact of the matter was, there was no one else. If the attack last night had been some shadowy government agency's attempt to silence her permanently, Mark was the only fed she could be absolutely sure wasn't in on it. The only law enforcement type she could be absolutely sure wasn't in on it. Even a safe house wasn't safe if your minders were the ones who wanted to do you in.

"What you're saying is, I'm stuck with you, right?"

"That about sums it up."

Running beneath her very real annoyance was a deep, dark, secret little thrill that that was so. Acknowledging its existence aggravated her so much that she was goaded into directly addressing the elephant in the room.

"You kissed me last night."

"You're right. I did."

"Why?"

He shrugged. "Habit?"

"Don't do it again."

"I kind of got the impression you liked it."

"Then you kind of got the wrong impression."

"Kid yourself if you want." He slanted a look at her. His voice went soft. "You can't kid me. You kissed me back."

Just because that was true didn't make it palatable. Jess saw red and grabbed for the door handle. They were slowing for an intersection, and she'd had enough.

"To hell with this. I don't need the hassle."

The door was locked, which infuriated her more. As the Suburban came to a stop, she yanked at the handle in frustration. "Let me out. I'm taking the metro."

"Jess, wait. Stop. Calm down. I apologize for the kiss, all right? It just . . . happened. I won't do it again, I promise." The Suburban was once again moving, rolling in its turn through the intersection. "From here on out, our relationship is strictly professional."

She shot him a narrow-eyed look.

"I swear," he said. "No more personal stuff. You know you can trust me. To keep my word, and to keep you safe."

The funny thing was, she did know that. Which didn't mean she had to like the situation. Being with Mark was not good for her peace of mind.

"This sucks," she burst out.

"You're not the only one suffering here, you know. I got maybe four hours of sleep."

"Oh, stop. You're breaking my heart."

"You know, I'd forgotten how crabby you always were first thing in the morning."

"Bite me."

He laughed.

"You find out anything pertinent about Leonard Cowan's death yet?"

"Nope."

"Crap."

They rode in silence for a moment.

"So how's the head?" Mark asked.

Jess shrugged. "Advil helps."

Actually, her ribs were what had bothered her most during the night, because she'd kept rolling onto her bruised side. But now that she was upright and stoked with pain reliever, it wasn't too bad. The creeping, ever-present fear was much worse, but she wasn't going to think about that. Not now, not while it was daylight and Mark was with her, in any case. She might have been through with him romantically, but she had to admit that his presence had an upside: she was a lot less likely to wind up dead.

"Did you—did they find anything that might lead to that guy, last night?" She meant the man who had attacked her.

He understood. "No. I picked up your shoes."

With a jerk of his head, he indicated the backseat. Glancing around, Jess saw the pink heels she'd lost last night. Remembering how she'd lost them made her go cold all over.

Please God let it just have been a random attack. So it can be over and forgotten and I can get on with my life.

"You went by my apartment? When?"

"After I left your mother's. I wanted to go over everything for myself. There wasn't anything. The grass was too thick for any footprints. No surveillance cameras anywhere in the area. We had people go door to door checking for anybody who might have seen or heard anything, and there'll be more of that today, but we got nothing last night and my guess is we won't today."

Jess shook her head. "There wasn't anyone around."

He nodded. "Hasbrough doesn't think it was any kind of covert ops thing, and I'm inclined to agree."

"Why?"

"Nobody tried to kill me."

A beat passed while she processed that. "Oh, great, so you're the canary in the mine now?"

"If I was coming after you, I'd kill me first. Anybody with any sense would."

Jess hadn't even realized they'd reached Foggy Bottom until he turned onto her street. The line of painted brick row houses looked stolidly respectable in the now pink-tinted light. Anybody looking at them would automatically think, *Nice neighborhood: nothing bad's gonna happen here.* As they approached her building, details like the black shutters against the colonial blue walls and the wrought-iron window boxes bursting with colorful flowers beckoned. The magnolia tree with its creamy white blos-soms oozed Southern charm in her front yard. Its long shadow was the gossamer gray of smoke now, not menacing at all. The deep red front door radiated welcome.

Looking it over, Jess unexpectedly felt her stomach clench. The last thing she wanted to do, she discovered, was head up that sidewalk again.

Thank God Mark's here.

"You okay?" Mark must have seen in her face something of what she was feeling, because he frowned at her as he parked the car.

Jesus, the lease runs for another ten months.

"Of course I'm okay. Why wouldn't I be?"

Bravado on the hoof, Jess grabbed her shoes from the back, then slid out the door before he could even turn off the engine. Seconds later, he did, and got out, too. Keys in hand, flip-flops slapping the pavement determinedly, she was already on her way to the front door when he caught up.

Like she didn't need him at all.

"What you want to do is get a security light installed. Right out front here. That way there wouldn't be anyplace for anyone to hide."

"I'll take it up with the owner. Oh, and the historic commission. And the other tenants." Sarcasm was a good way to mask the edginess she was trying to hide. As she inserted her key into the lock, her gaze slid sideways to the shadowy alley behind the magnolia. The curved stone window well on which she had hit her head gleamed pale against the dark jade of the carpet of manicured grass.

I almost died there.

Jess couldn't help it. She shivered.

"You don't have to worry. Whoever he was, he won't get to you again." Hard certainty was in Mark's voice.

She realized he'd seen her shudder. "I'm not worried."

By way of a reply, his hand dropped onto her nearly bare shoulder in a gesture that was both protective and clear proof he knew perfectly well how uneasy she was. It felt big and warm and so achingly familiar that it made her stomach tighten. Giving him a hands-off look over her shoulder, she shrugged it off.

As she stepped into the hallway a rush of cold air greeted her. Glancing nervously around was an instinctive reaction: of course no one was there. But the gloomy corners and echoing silence made her more than ever glad of Mark's presence, not that she had the slightest intention of letting him know it. The small chandelier meant to add elegance as well as light to the space had two of its six candle-shaped bulbs out, which meant the hall was even gloomier than usual. The walls were creamy white, the floor age-darkened hardwood. Each floor held two apartments divided by the center hall. This downstairs hall also contained the mailboxes for all six apartments, in a big brass rectangle set into the wall, and, at the rear, a staircase that zig-zagged upward.

Her mailbox was 6B, the very last one. Jess automatically collected the mail—bills and junk—then headed toward the stair-case. There was an elevator, but it was ancient and balky and so slow that it was just easier to take the stairs.

Mark was right behind her. Once they reached her apartment and she unlocked the door—no sign of a break-in, she was relieved to note—he followed her inside, then proceeded to walk through the place, turning on lights as he went.

Ignoring him, she headed straight for her bedroom. The front door opened into a small square entryway, which opened into a large open space that had been fur-nished as a living room/dining room com-bination. Courtesy of Grace, who liked to decorate, the walls were lavender, the up-holstery beige, with a fluffy rug under the Plexiglas coffee table and hardwood floors and touches of apple green and black to liven things up. A short, beige-painted hall led past the kitchen, half bath and laundry room to the two side-by-side bedrooms, each with its own en suite bathroom, at the back. Grace's was deep purple. Jess's was, at her insistence, untouched, which meant it was creamy white. Grace's door was open; her bedroom was presumably empty. Jess poked her head in just to make certain—sure enough, no Grace— then went into hers and closed the door behind her. Firmly.

When she emerged again some half an hour later, showered and dressed in her fall-back workday ensemble of a black pantsuit with a white V-neck tee, feet in her favorite power pumps, which gave her at least three additional inches of height, contacts firmly in place, bruise hidden under layers of cover stick and powder, she felt significantly better. Refreshed, reenergized, and ready to tackle all manner of problems.

The first of which was Mark.

He was in the kitchen. She knew that even before she saw him, because the smell hit her as she was coming down the hall: coffee.

Reaching the kitchen's open doorway, she paused briefly to take in the scene: white cabinets, white appliances, black and white tile floor. Apple green walls, again courtesy of Grace. A small glass-topped table in the center, surrounded by four black-painted bistro type chairs. Mark sat in one of those chairs, his jacket off, his tie loosened, his sleeves rolled up. His shoulders in the crisp white shirt were broad enough to dwarf the chair, and he would have looked like he'd come right out of one of those upscale coffee commercials if it hadn't been for the shoulder holster complete with gun strapped to his left side. The usually unflattering overhead light was not unflattering to him. It picked up gold strands in his thick hair, and, while it did indeed accentuate the tiny lines around his eyes and the deeper grooves bracketing his mouth, they just made him look more ruggedly masculine, in, of course, a really hot kind of way. As she acknowledged that, her mouth turned down at the corners: as she knew from experience, that same light played up the hollows under her eyes, making her look like she hadn't slept for days, and washed her out so that her naturally fair skin looked as pale as the undead's.

Her nose had not lied: Mark was tucking into a plate of scrambled eggs and toast, with a cup of coffee and a glass of orange juice within easy reach. An identical meal sat across from him.

Jess was struck by a pang of remembrance so sharp that it felt like an arrow to the heart.

Talk about déjà vu all over again. How many times had he made her breakfast in her kitchen, or his, before . . . ?

He looked up and saw her, gestured at the second plate. "Hungry?"

She folded her arms over her chest and scowled at him. "You know, I was perfectly happy with you out of my life."

He placed a hand over his heart. "If I believed that, I'd be wounded."

"By all means, consider yourself wounded."

"Come on, Jess. Even ambition-crazed lawyers have to eat."

"I don't have time for this."

But there the food was, and, admittedly, wasting it would be foolish. She gave up, sat down, and picked up her fork.

"You look good." His eyes slid over her as she swallowed some eggs, then bit into a piece of toast. "But I got to admit, I miss the glasses."

She felt another of those heart pangs. He'd always insisted he liked her in her glasses, which were big and thick-lensed and made her feel about as attractive as a mole.

"Do you mind if we don't talk? I really only have a few minutes. I need to be at work by seven thirty."

"Half an hour before the big shots get in."

"How do you know? Oh, that's right, you have sources, don't you?"

"You're pressed for time, remember? Eat, don't talk."

She ate because she was hungry and because Mark, for all his failings, knew just how she liked her eggs. It was unfair, really, when she'd worked so hard to get over him.

They polished off their meal in a near silence that Jess refused to even think about terming companionable. Spending time like this with Mark was such a mistake, but under the circumstances she didn't seem to have any other choice. She ate in record time, then whisked her dishes into the dishwasher and went away to brush her teeth. Then, to the sound of the

dishwasher doing its thing, which meant
he must have put his own dishes in and
turned it on, she retraced her steps and
found him with jacket and tie restored,
waiting for her by the door.

"Tick-tock." He greeted her with an eye-
crinkling half smile that she refused to be
charmed by and opened the door for her.
Lips firm and head held high, she sailed
past him, clattering down the stairs with
him at her heels. It was full daylight now,
she saw as she emerged from the building.
The street was filling up with vehicles, and
the sidewalk sported a reassuring number
of people hurrying to get where they needed
to be. What was the saying about there being safety in numbers? Add, and daylight,
too. She could absolutely safely take the
metro now. Walking down the front steps,
she glanced at Mark over her shoulder.

"Aren't you supposed to be at work at
eight? If you drop me off, you'll be late." He
worked at the Secret Service headquar-
ters, which, given the usual crush of early
morning traffic, was probably a good hour's
drive away from Ellis Hayes.

"I'm not worried."

Because of breakfast, she was already

later than she'd meant to be. With a shrug, she headed toward the Suburban. If he wasn't worried, why, then, neither would she be. Her type A self was over getting worked up about his perpetually laid-back attitude. Right now, the only person she needed to worry about getting to work on time was herself.

"Well, I am, so could we hurry?"

He didn't reply. In fact, he was no longer right behind her, she discovered as she glanced back. He was staring down at something on the sidewalk: a scattered newspaper that she'd walked right past in her determination not to look at the area behind the magnolia again. Apparently someone, the delivery person or a fellow tenant, had dropped it.

"Shit." Mark picked up a section.

Jess frowned, looking to see what had prompted his reaction, and, to her horror, got a glimpse of her own face staring back at her.

CHAPTER THIRTEEN

"Phillips's Lawyer Is Death Car Survivor" the headline screamed. Two pictures of her accompanied the story. One had been taken on the courthouse steps yesterday. The other showed her with her natural dark brown hair and, yes, her glasses, the way she had looked when Annette Cooper had died. Before she'd gone all blond and girly.

"Shit," Mark said again. He'd been skimming the story. Now he looked up at her. "So much for keeping a low profile."

"So maybe I'm better off being high profile. If your buddies are trying to kill me, maybe they'll think twice if they think it'll hit all the papers and make a big stink and maybe make someone start digging into Annette Cooper's death again. Or if they aren't trying to kill me, maybe it'll make them think twice about trying in the first place."

"You know, in a weird kind of way that almost made sense."

Jess gave him a withering look. "I'm getting tired of this. I want my life back." Snatching the paper out of his hand, she tucked it under her arm to read later and started toward the street. "I've got to go to work. Are you going to give me a ride or not?"

Once in the Suburban, Jess read the story while Mark drove. It was in the Features section, first page but below the fold. Apparently her celebrity had dimmed since the last time she'd been in the paper. In any case, she was relieved to note that she was no longer front-page news.

The story was basically a "what is she doing now"? kind of piece, rehashing her role as the sole survivor in the car crash that had killed the First Lady and marveling that she had gone on in such a short period of time to put her life back together, complete with new look and new name, and had then been a key component of the team that had won what everyone agreed was an unlikely acquittal for Rob Phillips in the sensational rape trial that had just concluded.

The worst part was they called her "The Survivor" again, and once more recounted in excruciating detail the drowning deaths of her father and her younger sister Courtney when she, Jess, was only five. None of her other sisters—Sarah, Grace, or Maddie, all children of her mother's second marriage, while she and Courtney had been products of the first—had been present that day. Grace and Maddie had not even been born at the time her divorced father had taken his two young daughters for the weekend. They'd ended up at the beach, and the girls had had a wonderful time playing in the surf until three-year-old Courtney had been swept away. Their father had died in a futile attempt to save her. Jess had seen the whole thing but had been helpless to prevent it. The trauma had stayed with her a long time. If she was honest, she had to admit it was with her still.

"You okay?" Mark, who knew the story

and had clearly read enough to know that it was included in the paper's account, gave her an assessing look as she glanced up after finishing.

Jess schooled her expression. The last thing she wanted was for him to see her pain.

"Yes, of course. Why wouldn't I be?"

That hung in the air between them for a moment. Although both knew the answer for the lie it was, each let it go unchallenged.

"There's something you should know." His words were abrupt.

"What?" She glanced at him without really seeing him. Every defense mechanism she possessed was busy trying to shove assorted hideous images from her past out of her mind.

"I'm going to be working as a consultant for Ellis Hayes for the next couple of weeks. The Service agreed to lend me to them. So you'll be seeing me around."

That refocused her attention in a hurry. *"What?"*

"You heard me."

"You're doing this because of me!"

"Just for the record, everything I do is not about you."

"No."

"There's no 'no'. It's a done deal."

"Like hell it is! I don't want you anywhere near Ellis Hayes. I'm building a career there. The last thing I need is you showing up at work following me around. In fact, I won't have it."

"There's nothing you can do about it." There was cool finality in his tone. "And believe me, I've got better things to do than follow you around. Like I said, I'm going to be acting as a consultant. They pay large for that, and I can use the money. Taylor's got college coming up in a couple of years."

"Bullshit. Don't you dare bring Taylor into this. Anyway, consultant on what? And for whom? Who do you even know there? Oh, besides Mary Jane Cates, I mean."

"I'm consulting on a murder case. And you know what? You need to work on that jealous streak of yours. It's big, and nasty, and about a mile wide."

Jess got mad.

"That's it. This is not happening. You are not coming into my workplace and disrupting my career. If some of your *buddies* are out there trying to kill me, you'll just have to find some other way to handle it." A furious glance around told her that they were on Massachusetts Avenue about two blocks from Ellis Hayes. There were maybe ninety thousand lawyers in D.C., and from the looks of the people hurrying along the sidewalk, about half of them were on their way to work in these few blocks near the U.S. Capitol. The bustle of dark suits and briefcases reminded her of a swarm of frantic ants.

"Here's the deal," Mark said. "You're going to be seeing me at work. You want to make a big deal out of it, then it'll be a big deal and the powers that be are probably going to notice that you're bringing a shitton of baggage with you. You don't, it won't. The consultant thing is real. Okay, I'm going to be keeping an eye on you, too. It doesn't have to be a problem. You go to lunch or something with friends, do something like that, that's fine. You should be perfectly safe, and I don't have to come. The bottom line is, you don't do things alone. You don't work late alone, you don't wander around the city alone, you let me know when you're ready to leave for the night and I make sure you get home safely. If there's something you need to do that ordinarily you'd do alone, you take me with you. How hard is that?"

"And what if I say too damned hard?"

He simply looked at her, but it didn't matter. She could read the answer in his eyes as plainly as if he'd said it aloud: *too damned bad*.

"I'll let you out here." He pulled over in front of the building, braking in front of the line of parked cars already staking out the prime real estate along this side of the street. "Unless you want to drive around into the parking garage with me. We can ride up the elevator together. Cozy."

Jess grabbed her possessions and slid out. "Fine, but you keep your distance. Nobody is to know that your being here has anything to do with me. While I'm at work, we have nothing to say to each other," she told him fiercely and slammed the door. Marching between the line of parked cars, she barely made it to the sidewalk before horns started blaring.

Consultant, my ass. Although Mark's connections at Ellis Hayes must have been at a much higher level than she'd suspected if they were letting him come on board simply to babysit her. So maybe he *was* consulting on a murder case. Even so, she knew perfectly well that his primary purpose was to keep an eye on her.

The sidewalk was hot, crowded, noisy, and, with the sun now peeping over the tops of the boxy concrete-and-steel buildings that lined Massachusetts Avenue, bright as your average sunny August morning. The thought that a killer could lurk among the multitudes brushing past her occurred to Jess but she shrugged off the resultant uneasy tingle. Thoroughly riled, she refused to be afraid any longer. She was going to carry on with her life. If someone was out there who wanted to try to kill her, by God, they could hit her with their best shot.

That defiant mood took her inside the building and across the well-polished marble floor, and it had her frowning impatiently at the pair of uniformed security guards manning the main entrance checkpoint as they scanned her badge. Then she turned that frown into a full-blown scowl at the one-way mirror behind the checkpoint, where she knew the security higher-ups were watching as she was made to wait while a hand search of her purse and briefcase was conducted. Given the elite nature of Ellis Hayes's clientele, security was necessarily tight, but Jess wasn't in the mood for excess, and she had no doubt it showed. Finally allowed to pass, she traipsed through the truly impressive lobby along with the steady stream of other just-arriving workers and reached the marble-walled hallway that housed the elevator banks just in time to catch an elevator. Crowding in, she stared stonily at the brass door, which was shiny enough to act as a virtual mirror. The good news was, as far as she could tell none of her injuries showed. The bad news was, with her pale blond hair waving almost down to her shoulders and her glasses nowhere in evidence, looking at herself was like looking at a stranger. So she quit looking, and to her annoyance found herself thinking about Mark instead. The truce between them might have been uneasy, but at least it was a truce. Despite all the complications inherent in having him back in her life, she found she was glad about that.

Her cubicle was on three, in the middle
of a large room that served as a workplace
home to the most junior lawyers, para-
legals, and support staff. Those who were
stuck in it called it the cesspool, and just
then the name felt particularly apt. She
didn't even have four walls to call her own:
the mint green space that she optimistically
thought of as an office was open to all com-
ers on one side. It had been nearly a month
since she'd actually worked on this floor,
and she realized she hadn't missed it. The
bright overhead lighting, the steady hum of
conversation and ringing of phones and
rattle of chair wheels and file carts being
pushed along the marble floors that ampli-
fied every sound, the smell of too-strong
coffee, brought it all back: the stress, the
competition, the need to stand out. This
floor was the firm's in-house version of
Fight Club, from whence only a few would
emerge bloody but victorious to scale the
heights toward the ultimate goal: a shot,
one day, if you were very, very good, and
very, very lucky, at a coveted partnership.

Be still my heart.

At seven fifty, forty minutes before Ellis
Hayes's official workday starting time of

8:30, the room was at least three-quarters full. It was a grim reminder that she wasn't the only ambitious young lawyer around.

I should never have stopped for breakfast.

Responding to greetings with an abstracted wave, shedding her jacket, she settled in in front of the desktop computer that was provided at every workstation, then called up her notes from the Phillips case. First item on the agenda: find Tiffany Higgs's phone number, then call just to make sure she had made it home safely last night.

If everything was all right, Tiffany would probably curse her out. If such a fragile-looking girl was given to cursing people out, that is. Remembering the sister, Jess decided that Tiffany was probably tougher than she looked, and she resigned herself to getting an earful.

Still, she couldn't just let it go. Not after what she'd seen last night. Not after that stunning turnaround in the courtroom. Not after she herself had been attacked.

Now that the trial was over, what Tiffany did was none of Jess's business. In fact, contacting her was probably against all kinds of rules. Tiffany had not been their client, or even their witness, after all.

Tiffany's contact information popped up on the screen.

It was early, maybe too early to call, but . . .

"So, you in or out?" The deep voice behind her made her jump. Whirling in her chair, Jess gaped guiltily up at Pearse, who stood blocking the opening to her cubicle. He was looking as dapper as she'd come to expect, his black hair waving back from his freshly shaved face, dressed like the high-priced lawyer he was in an expensive navy suit, blue shirt, and blue-and-silver patterned tie. As big as he was, he cast a large shadow that fell across her and the workspace behind her. It was as if a mountain had moved in front of the sun.

"W-what?" It was almost a stutter. Jesus, her heart was beating like she'd been caught stealing or something. She only hoped that he couldn't see past her to what was on her computer screen. No way to be sure, of course, but her gut told her he wouldn't want her to have anything else to do with Tiffany. Case closed and all that.

"The job I offered you yesterday. Remember? I'd like to give you more time to consider, but I can't. The reason I hire people is because I need them, and the position's been effectively vacant now for over three weeks. Work's piling up. I need your answer: yes or no?"

Talk about a no-brainer. Every associate in this room would kill to get such an offer. It was the chance of a lifetime. Everything she had been working toward since she'd first started law school. The big time.

"Yes." She was proud of how cool she sounded, when what she really wanted to do was jump up and down and punch the air with her fist and yell *Yippee.*

"Good." Pearse stepped forward, held out his hand. Jess stood up and took it. Professionalism personified, that was her, and never mind the excitement bubbling up inside her. Like the rest of him, Pearse's hand was big. Thick-fingered and broad-palmed. She gave it a firm shake. "Welcome aboard. Get your stuff and come on up to Six. I'll tell Lenore to be on the lookout for you, and she'll help you get settled in. Team meeting at 8:30 sharp, conference room 6A, so you want to hustle."

"Okay. Thanks." Jess felt rising bubbles

of excitement. She was on her way, climbing the ladder, thrilled to leave the cesspool behind. Then she remembered something, and at least a few of those bubbles popped. Pearse was already striding for the elevators, his long legs eating up the distance. *Crap.* She had to catch him.

"Uh, wait up."

She still didn't quite feel comfortable calling him Pearse like the rest of his team did, but Mr. Collins didn't seem right either. Her new position was going to take some getting used to, she realized.

He turned to wait for her, frowning as he watched her hurrying toward him. Jess swallowed hard.

I really, really don't want to lose this chance.

She stopped in front of him, clasping her hands in front of her in a nervous gesture she was totally unaware of. "There's something I need to tell you."

Pearse's brows went up. He dwarfed her physically, and his expression was more impatient than encouraging. They were standing at the end of her row of cubicles, near the hall that was home to the elevator bank. The nearest cubicle was empty, but there was plenty of coming and going from the elevators and the break room, with its coffee and doughnuts and the copying machine, so any real privacy was out the window. Anyway, it didn't matter. No matter how much she might have wished it had been otherwise, this was something she wasn't going to be able to hide.

So be it.

Jess squared her shoulders. Her hands fell to her sides, where they would have clenched if she hadn't caught her fingers closing and deliberately relaxed them.

"My name isn't Jessica Dean, it's Jessica Ford." Despite her brave stance, tension made her chest feel tight. "My picture is in the *Post* this morning because I was in the car with Annette Cooper when she was killed, and I survived the crash. That means the media have an interest in me, and—"

His frown cleared. "You think I offer people jobs without checking them out? I know all that."

Jess would have gaped at him if she hadn't caught herself in time. "You do?"

He nodded. "What I'm interested in is the quality of your work. I've been impressed by it. So do you want the job or not?"

"Oh. Yes. Absolutely."

"See you at 8:30, then."

He turned on his heel and was gone.

Jess practically sagged with relief.

The warm little niggle of pure good feeling she was experiencing lasted about halfway back to her cubicle, when she saw Cates heading her way. Jess would have indulged in a fond hope that the woman's current path was just coincidence, but unfortunately Cates's eyes were fixed on her.

Jess's steps slowed. An arrestingly attractive thirty-six-year-old divorcée, Cates was tall and thin and elegant, with honey-blond hair twisted into a loose upsweep, steel blue eyes, a long, narrow nose, and a full mouth, the proportions of which Jess suspected had been enhanced by artificial means. Today she wore beige heels, a beige knit skirt, and a white silk shell with a ton of jewelry. As always, she looked wonderful.

Jess always felt small and insignificant and frumpy in her company. Which was one more thing she held against her.

It was all Jess could do to keep a neutral expression as Cates approached, but
she tried. The last encounter of any substance she'd had with Cates was when
she'd backed out of her boss's office after
finding her in Mark's arms, the files she'd
been on her way to deliver hanging forgotten in her hands. Mark had had his back
turned, but Cates had seen her over Mark's
shoulder the moment she had entered, not
that seeing her had had any effect that
Jess had noticed on the length or enthusi-
asm of their embrace.

"I hear you're leaving us," Cates said
when Jess was close enough. Her tone
was cool but professional. Her eyes raked
Jess. Cates was notorious for hating it
when the young female lawyers under her
supervision did well and got promoted.
Add in the fact that Jess had been involved
for a while with a man Cates wanted, and
Jess didn't think she was being paranoid
to think that she detected an extra dollop
of animosity in Cates's expression now.

"That's right." Knowing that Cates was
no longer her boss went a long way toward easing the hard knot that had been
lodged deep in her chest ever since that

never-to-be-forgotten day Jess had seen her with Mark. She and Cates had never spoken of what Jess had seen—Jess at first had been too stunned, and then too proud—but that moment hung in the air between them whenever they crossed paths.

"Be sure to clean everything out of your space before you leave. Someone else will be in there, probably as soon as tomorrow."

"Yes, I will."

"Good luck." Cates gave her another of those raking glances, then turned to leave.

"Tell me something." The words were out before Jess could stop them.

Cates turned back to look at her. "Yes?"

"The day I walked in when you were kissing Mark Ryan. Did you initiate that?" Jess's gaze held steady on the cold blue eyes.

They widened, as if Cates was surprised that Jess had the nerve to confront her so directly. Then they narrowed, then Cates smiled.

"Did he tell you that?" Her smile grew broader. "That's right, you two were sort of an item then, weren't you? If he told you I initiated what happened that morning, then I'm certainly not going to contradict him. Of course, that's what he would say, though, isn't it?"

Jess's throat was suddenly dry. "Was that kiss the extent of it? Or was there more to it that I didn't see?"

Cates looked her up and down. "That's my business. And Mark's." Then she walked away, cool and confident as always.

Jess was left without an answer. But that wasn't exactly true, she realized as she gathered up her few belongings. Something in Cates's manner made her think Mark had been telling the truth.

She'd suspected it for some time, really. That was the unwelcome knowledge Jess faced as she rode the elevator up to the sixth floor, murmuring what she hoped were appropriate responses to the casual greetings and occasional congratulations that were thrown her way by assorted colleagues as she went. After the initial shock had faded, she realized she had leaned toward believing Mark's version of events.

Still, she'd let the breakup stand. Had been determined to put him out of her life.

Why? Because the sense of betrayal had been bone-deep and shattering.

Had she overreacted?

"You're so damn afraid you're going to get hurt that you won't let yourself love anybody outside your damned family."

God, was it true? Was she really that much of a screwed-up mess?

The elevator pinged, and she was fresh out of time for soul-searching. She wasn't the only person to get off on six, but everyone else seemed to know where they were going and be in a rush to get there. Although she'd been on this floor numerous times during the month she'd helped with the Phillips case, it had been on a dash-in, dash-out basis, without a chance to really get her bearings or be on the receiving end of any introductions. A glance at her watch told her it was already 8:24—she needed to hurry. Nervous anticipation tightened her stomach. As much as she'd ever wanted anything, she wanted this new job to go well. She'd thought finding Lenore might be difficult, but it wasn't. Going right, the hall containing the elevators led

into a large open space complete with onyx
marble floors, lots of expensive-looking
dark wood furniture, a wall of windows with
a killer view of the building across the
street, and, in front of the windows, an impressive desk, which she remembered
from the times she'd darted past it running
to do something for Christine. Behind that
desk a woman talked on the phone. Forty-
ish maybe, she had medium brown hair
cut chic and short, regular features, fair
skin, and, Jess saw when the woman
looked up, bright blue eyes. She was wearing a burgundy sweater set, probably because the air-conditioning on this floor was
just this side of frigid. The nameplate on
her desk read Lenore Beekman.

Bingo.

She greeted Jess with a gesture and a
warm smile as Jess stopped in front of her
desk.

"Mr. Collins will be there tomorrow at
nine," she chirped into the phone, then said
good-bye and hung up, directing her attention to Jess. "I'm sorry to keep you waiting.
You must be Jessica Dean."

"Um, Jessica Ford, actually." Jess had

already decided that the newspaper article made the whole pretend-to-be-somebody-else thing a waste of time. She was going back to her real identity, and screw the consequences.

Besides, everybody who was interested clearly already knew who she was. Someone had even gone so far as to try to kill her.

So, to badly mangle Shakespeare, a Jessica Ford by any other name was in just as much danger, so what was the point of the subterfuge?

"Oh? I must have gotten it wrong." Lenore got to her feet. She was wearing gray pants with her twin set, Jess saw as she came out from behind the desk, and was of medium height and lush, hourglass proportions. "I'm Lenore Beekman"—she gestured at the nameplate on her desk—"as you've probably guessed. Just call me Lenore. And I'll call you Jess, if I may?" Jess nodded. "We're all on first names, up here. Pearse told me you'd be coming. Follow me, and I'll show you where to go." Talking non-stop, she headed off to the left, turning down a long hall punctuated with a line of closed doors. Jess noted a doorplate reading conference room 6A at the top of the hall. Now at least she knew where she needed to be. "You'll like this office. It's a nice big one, with a good view. The previous occupant left on a business trip, fell in love with someone she met, got married right out of the blue, and resigned to go on an extended honeymoon." She sighed. "So romantic. We all like to think that kind of thing can happen to us, but—"

"Lenore! Could you come here a minute?" It was Pearse's voice, calling from somewhere out of sight. "I need you."

"I'll be right there," she called back. Shaking her head, she said to Jess, "He really is helpless, that man. At least with the little things. Two doors down on the right is the one you want. The nameplate says Allison Howard. We'll get you one made up, probably by next week. Just make yourself at home, it's all yours now."

"Lenore!"

"I'm coming." With a quick, apologetic smile at Jess, she turned and hurried in the direction of Pearse's voice. Jess was left to find her way alone. Which wasn't difficult. As Lenore had said, a brass plate bearing the name Allison Howard etched in big block letters screwed into the door made it impossible to miss.

With only enough time left to drop her stuff in her new office and hotfoot it to the conference room, Jess opened the door and rushed inside, only to stop dead just over the threshold.

Her initial impression was of a spacious room with all the usual office accouterments: bookshelves, credenza, big desk in the middle, some chairs. Two floor-to-ceiling windows separated by about eight feet of wall space, outfitted with wide vertical blinds that were only partly open, making the space seem gloomy at first glance. Dark, patterned carpet. Richly paneled walls.

The whole thing reeked of success. Expensive success.

This is mine? was the thrilled thought that was just running through her head when she spotted a woman standing next to the window behind the desk and stopped in her tracks, confusion and embarrassment combining as she realized she somehow must have entered the wrong office by mistake.

The woman stood with her back to the door, looking out the window. She was a little on the thick-set side, with short, shaggy auburn hair, dressed in black pants and a black-and-white striped top.

"Oh, I'm sorry," Jess said as the woman, apparently a little slow to realize she had been intruded upon, finally glanced around.

Jess had barely gotten the apology out before the woman vanished.

CHAPTER FOURTEEN

Jess was still in shock as she sat all by herself on one side of the big oval table in conference room 6A some fifteen minutes later. It was a corner room, sunny and bright, with the blinds opened to a dazzling view of busy Massachusetts Avenue. The assembled group consisted of Pearse, herself, Hayley, and Andrew, and the space was almost ridiculously large for the four of them. The luxuriousness of the conference room thrilled her. The knowledge that she was now part of this elite group thrilled her more. Having announced at the beginning of the meeting that Jess was now a permanent member of their team, an announcement that appeared to come as a surprise to no one, although Hayley looked somewhat less than wowed by it, Pearse was still on his feet talking. Jess did her best to pay rapt attention as he scribbled things on a dry erase board. He was going over things that needed to be done, prioritizing schedules that had been blown to smithereens by the premature conclusion of the Phillips trial, giving out assignments that would keep them going forward until, as he put it, "we harpoon another whale." As attentive as she was trying to be, though, Jess found that she wasn't able to keep totally focused on what Pearse was saying, and she inwardly cursed the distraction.

She couldn't get her mind around the fact that a woman had disappeared in front of her eyes. *Poof*, just like that. Gone.

Right after it had happened, Jess had rushed behind the desk to make sure the woman hadn't had some kind of an attack and collapsed. Then she'd touched the blinds, the glass, and even looked out the window to make sure everything was solid and the woman hadn't somehow silently fallen out to her death on the sidewalk below. Then she'd done a quick visual and physical search of the office. Conclusion: there simply wasn't anywhere to hide.

Either the woman had been there and vanished, or Jess's eyes were playing tricks on her and she had never been there at all.

Could what she had seen been some kind of trick of the light? A weird shadow? A hallucination conjured up by her now once again severely aching head? She'd banged it pretty hard last night, after all.

A knock on the conference room door pulled her back to the present. She was just in time to watch as the door opened and Mark walked into the room.

Jess blinked in surprise. Her gaze stuck to him like fuzz to Velcro. He didn't afford her any more than the same passing glance he gave the others, which told her that he'd known she would be present in that room. It would have been nice if he'd given her a heads-up that he was going to be there, too.

". . . have a consultant working with us on this one." Wearing a broad smile, Pearse offered his hand as Mark joined him in the front of the room. "Ryan."

"Collins."

They shook hands. Pearse turned to the rest of them.

"People, this is Special Agent Mark Ryan. He's the Secret Service liaison who's been going over the Whitney tapes for us. Since we're getting close to trial, he'll be here on the premises acting as a consultant for us for the next few weeks. The information he's uncovered may just be enough to keep our client from being indicted for murder." Pearse looked at Hayley. "Meet Hayley Marciano." Mark came around the side of the table to shake hands with her. Jess noted sourly that Hayley eyed Mark with the happy surprise of a bird who'd unexpectedly stumbled across a fat, juicy worm. "Andrew Brisco." Andrew looked a whole lot less thrilled than Hayley as he and Mark shook hands. "And Jessica Ford. But I think you know Jess."

"We've met," Mark confirmed. Jess recovered enough presence of mind to offer him a tight smile as they shook hands.

"Ford?" Andrew frowned at Jess. "What'd you do, get married last night? Yesterday your last name was Dean."

"Obviously you haven't read the paper this morning." Hayley produced the section containing the feature on Jess from somewhere beneath the table—Jess presumed her briefcase—and slid it over to Andrew. It was folded so that the two side-by-side pictures of Jess were uppermost. Hayley glanced at Jess as Andrew took the paper. "Nice makeover, by the way," she added under her breath with a not-so-subtle smirk. Then she looked at Mark, employing the full power of her thick-lashed, coffee-colored eyes. With her seal-black hair slicked back in a long ponytail and a sea-foam silk blouse to play up their color, her eyes looked amazing. Hell, all of her looked amazing. "I was impressed that you were able to lift all that information through the background noise on that tape. Our guys couldn't come up with anything."

"Better equipment." Sounding becomingly modest, Mark smiled at her. Jess kept her face carefully neutral, but she didn't have to be a mind reader to pick up on Hayley's reaction to that smile: Jess had been there herself.

Her reaction to Hayley's reaction reminded her of just why she was better off without Mark in her life.

"Okay, everybody knows what they're supposed to do." Pearse's brisk announcement signaled the breakup of the meeting. "Jess, you're to assist Ryan for the morning. He'll fill you in on the details."

Mark looked at Jess.

"I'll meet you in the lobby at ten," he said. "In front of the revolving door. Does that suit?"

Jess nodded. What else could she do? Mark's appearance was a curveball she hadn't expected, and she was terrified that having him in the office would affect Pearse's opinion of her ability to handle the job. The very last thing she wanted to do was protest, and thus make Mark's presence seem personal. Anything like that would simply draw more attention to that which she hoped to conceal.

"Great. Don't forget that the party at Mr. Dunn's on Friday is formal. Andrew, that means a tux. A black one. With a white shirt and black tie. Nothing funky, not like last time." Pearse shot Andrew a warning look. Andrew grinned. "Meeting's adjourned. Get to work, people. You want to keep your jobs, we got hours to bill here." Pearse turned to Mark, beginning a low-voiced conversation that he clearly meant to be private.

"I hate those damned parties," Andrew muttered as he, Hayley, and Jess headed down the hall together. Jess had already learned from the nameplates on the doors that his office was next door to hers and Hayley's was next door to his. Pearse's was the first office in line, which, from the space allotted to it, appeared to be the size of all three of theirs put together and then some. Proving once again that rank had its privileges.

"I like them." Hayley wasn't bothering to flirt with Andrew. Her tone was flat.

"Another instance in which we're clearly incompatible. Gee, I was beginning to think we'd exhausted them all."

"If you hate Mr. Dunn's parties so much, don't go."

"I wouldn't, except, oh, I don't know, they're mandatory."

"Mandatory?" Jess piped up. This party was something else she'd known nothing about. If they'd talked about it early in the meeting, she'd missed it.

"The whole firm is expected to put in an appearance," Andrew explained. "That means everybody."

"Even where you were before, you should have received an invitation." Hayley's tone left no doubt in Jess's mind about what Hayley thought about the third floor, aka where Jess was before. Contempt iced every syllable.

Jess rallied. She'd already learned that showing weakness to Hayley was kind of like dripping blood in front of a shark.

"I've been busy," she said with a shrug.

"We're always busy. Deal or die." With that bit of encouragement, Hayley lifted a hand and walked off.

"Hayley tends to get a little competitive. Don't let it throw you." Andrew's grimace was faintly apologetic.

Jess went for a light note. "Her bark is worse than her bite, hmm?"

"Nah, I think her bite is definitely worse. Woman's in it to win it. In fact, when I saw your face this morning, I half expected to hear she'd pulled a Tonya Harding on you. Take out the rival and all that."

"My face?" Jess had been hoping nobody had noticed. But apparently foundation, powder, and artfully arranged hair could only hide so much.

"You look like somebody played Whac-A-Mole with the side of your head."

Jess sighed and went for a version of the truth. After all, Andrew, not being her mother or Mark, would hardly mount his own round-the-clock protection operation. "I got mugged last night."

"Mugged?"

"In front of my apartment. Man grabbed me, punched me in the head, then got scared off by the timely arrival of a friend. I was hoping the bruise wasn't all that noticeable. Nobody else has mentioned it."

"I would cop to being the tactless one, but the truth is, the rest of the gang is just completely self-centered."

That made Jess smile. Then she changed the subject. "So tell me about this party. When and where?"

"Friday. It's a schmooze-fest with the major clients. Everybody meets here at the office at eight, and Mr. Dunn has us driven out to his place by limousine. There's a fleet of them, as you can imagine. First class all the way, baby." Andrew grinned at her. "Boring as all hell, but first class. Kind of like the swankiest funeral you ever saw. We do it three times a year, end of April, August, and December. December is the big one. Wait till you see it. Christmas and New Year's rolled into one." They reached his office, and he said, "That's it, off to the salt mines," and went inside with a wave.

Which left Jess alone. Given that four different groups—two other criminal defense teams, Christine's operation, plus a small army of support staff—occupied the sixth floor, there was constant activity. Right at that moment was no exception. People scurried hither and yon, coming toward her, going past her, flitting around corners. A young woman with an armload of files shouldered her way into Christine's sanctuary, which was at the far end of the hall. Interns—you could spot them by their youth and dress—raced from office to office. A uniformed security guard trundled a dolly loaded with sealed boxes toward the freight elevator. An expensively dressed couple with the tentative expression of new clients walked toward her, reading nameplates as they came. Jess was surrounded, but, stopping in front of her new office with her hand on the knob, she felt totally isolated. She realized she was not quite okay with the idea of walking inside. Apparently vanishing women had that effect on her.

Go figure.

With that bracing thought, she pushed the door open and went for it. Even with the room better lit than it had been before, due to the changed position of the sun and more light filtering in through the half-closed blinds, she reached immediately for the light switch and flipped it on. The overhead fluorescent flickered once, twice. Then the office was suddenly brighter than the Beltway at noon.

Her eyes shot to the window behind the desk. No one was there. The space in front of the window was absolutely empty. There was, however, a potted ficus tree just on the other side of the window, bushy and green, its top reaching higher than Jess's head.

How did I not notice that before?

Frowning, Jess moved around the desk toward it, toward the window, taking in everything from the pristine expanse of well-vacuumed carpet to the texture of the half-closed vertical blinds. Reaching the window, still looking warily around, she groped for the beaded chain that operated the blinds, found it, and pulled the blinds all the way open with a rattle loud and unexpected enough to make her breath catch. More light flooded in. Across the street, blue-tinged office buildings shimmered in the heat like a row of melting ice cubes. The street below was clogged with traffic, the sidewalk with pedestrians: all perfectly normal. Transferring her attention back inside, Jess looked down at the carpet, a plush pine green with beige diamonds and no hint of footprints. She looked around at the polished paneled walls on either side of the window: no fingerprints. She looked at the blinds, which were beige like the carpet diamonds, with each slat the approximate width of her hand. She looked at the plant that stood almost in the corner, a live plant, well-watered and dusted, in a big, blue-and-white ceramic pot.

There was nothing whatsoever to indicate that anyone had been standing in front of the window earlier.

Was it possible that in the uncertain light

she had somehow mistaken the plant for a woman?

It was the only explanation.

A woman in black slacks and a striped top? With shaggy auburn hair? Who looked around at me?

Remembering, Jess felt her heart start to beat faster. The woman she had seen had looked so *real*. True, she'd suffered a blow to her head, but what blow to the head does *that*?

Get over it. Get it together.

"Knock, knock." The cheerful voice, accompanied by a light rap on the open door, made Jess jump.

"I'm sorry, I didn't mean to startle you." Lenore advanced into the room carrying a large cardboard box, which was stuffed with files. "Pearse asked me to give these to you. They're the case files Allison was working on. He's hoping you can pick right up where she left off on these. Also, on her pro bono work. The details and a schedule are in the box. If you have any questions, just come ask me. Oh, and there's a meeting with a client, Mrs. Shively, at three, in Pearse's office. He wants you to sit in on it." Lenore's voice dropped conspiratorially. "You've heard of Camilla Shively? The stripper—oh, pardon me, exotic dancer, Pearse doesn't like us to call her a stripper—who married the billionaire who died of an insulin overdose six months ago?"

Jess nodded. She had, indeed, heard of Camilla the Thrilla. Who hadn't? The story had been tabloid fodder for months.

"Pearse got the inside word that she's about to be indicted for murder. He wants to have you in there with him when he breaks the news to her. Another woman, you know."

Jess felt excitement lick through her veins. The case of Camilla the Thrilla was tabloid fodder worldwide. And now she was going to be a part of it.

Lenore's voice lowered still more, until it was scarcely louder than a whisper. "Pearse doesn't like to be alone with her, because she, well, she's very touchy-feely with men. And very . . ." Lenore broke off, shaking her head. "When you meet her, you'll see."

"Three in Pearse's office," Jess corroborated. At least she was getting more comfortable using her new boss's first name. Probably because so much was being thrown at her at once, she was quickly getting over sweating the small stuff. If this was sink or swim, she was damned if she was going to sink.

"I have a doctor's appointment, or I'd do it," Lenore confided. "And Mrs. Shively *hates* Hayley." She changed the subject without taking a breath. "Pearse wants a brief on possible defense angles on the Lyman case. All the details are in the file"— she patted the side of the box—"before you leave today. Everything else can wait until tomorrow."

"Brief on the Lyman case." Since she'd never heard of it, Jess was hoping the answers she needed would be in the file. "To Pearse before I leave."

"That's right." With a big smile, Lenore headed for the door.

"Um, I hear that there's a party at Mr. Dunn's on Friday night. Am I expected to go?"

With her hand on the knob, Lenore looked around at her, nodding vigorously. "We all go. It's actually a lot of fun. No dates required, so don't worry about that.

A lot of us go stag. A lot of politicians show up. So do a lot of clients. The idea is for all of us to meet the clients, you know, create goodwill, build the business, et cetera. Mr. Dunn has the most fabulous mansion, and he really pulls out all the stops. You need to wear a long gown. Nothing too wild. Mr. Dunn's pretty conservative. At Christmas, Andrew showed up in a red-and-green plaid suit with a red shirt and a bolo tie with jingle bells on the end. I thought Mr. Dunn was going to fire him on the spot."

Remembering Pearse's homily to Andrew about the importance of a black tux, Jess smiled. A series of chimes had Lenore pulling a cell phone out of her pocket. Glancing down at it, she said, "Oh, my goodness, emergency. I have to run."

Then Lenore was out the door, closing it behind her.

Jess looked at the closed door in some dismay. She hadn't been on the job an hour, and already she was feeling swamped— and unnerved. A quick, involuntary glance at the window behind her reassured her: nothing there but the plant.

If she'd been thinking properly, and if

she'd been able to get a word in edgewise, she might have mentioned the disappearing woman to Lenore.

Yeah, and have her think you're a nut.

Okay, there was that.

It was the plant, Jess told herself firmly. *Of course it was. Coupled with the thump on the head.*

With a glance at her watch, she realized she didn't have time for such mental dithering. If she was going to meet Mark in the lobby at ten, she had to get a move on. She was dying to dive into Allison's files, but at the moment there wasn't time. Sitting down at her new desk—her wonderfully big mahogany desk with the multitude of brass-handled drawers and the deep cubbyhole for her knees—she rolled back and forth in her cushy leather chair once or twice, allowed herself a moment to marvel, then powered up her computer, pulled up Tiffany's information again, and called Tiffany's cell.

And tried not to look over her shoulder more than once or twice.

After four rings, voice mail picked up. No surprise: if Tiffany screened her calls, the chances of her answering this number had to be about nil.

"Hi, you've reached Tiffany. I'm busy right now, but I'll call you back as soon as I can."

Jess had already decided what to say. She figured if she told the truth—*I saw you last night, and I'm just checking to make sure you're alive and well*—she'd never hear a thing.

"You dropped something yesterday. I picked it up, and I'd like to give it back to you. Please call me as soon as you can." Jess gave her name and phone numbers, office and cell, and hung up. It was a lie, but the important thing, for Jess's peace of mind, was that Tiffany was physically able to call back.

She couldn't rid herself of her conviction that Tiffany was somehow in trouble.

Jess spent the last few minutes of her available time eagerly flipping through the files Lenore had left, but when she headed down to the lobby she left her blinds open wide and the overhead light on, and to heck with the company policy on conserving energy whenever possible. No way was she coming back into a gloomy office. Too much scope for the imagination that way.

It had to have been the plant.

Whatever, she wasn't going to think about it anymore. She wasn't going to think about the fact that someone had tried to kill her last night. She wasn't going to think about Tiffany. She wasn't going to think about Leonard Cowan's suicide.

She was going to dismiss the knot of dread that seemed to have taken up permanent residence in her stomach, and get out there and do her job.

Looking sexy enough in his suit and tie to make a nonagenarian think impure thoughts, Mark waited near the revolving door. Two of the young women security guards searching purses and bags not far away were eyeing him with scarcely veiled interest. As a result, the look Jess gave him by way of a greeting was less than friendly. The Suburban was already parked out front, she discovered as she preceded him out the revolving door into the baking heat of the noisy street.

A beep told her he'd unlocked it. She got in.

"You know, you could have given me a

heads-up before you showed up at the meeting this morning," Jess said when they were underway.

"If I'd given you a heads-up, what would you have said?"

Jess didn't even have to think about it. "No way in hell."

"There you go. See, I saved us a futile argument."

Jess didn't reply, but the look she shot him expressed everything she wasn't going to waste her time putting into words. After a moment, in a carefully calm voice, she asked, "Where are we going?"

"The Criminal Justice Center. For the Whitney case. What, you didn't know?"

"Since I was just brought in on the case today, no, I didn't. Maybe you can fill me in."

"Being a lawyer, because lawyers are the only people he's allowed to meet with, you're going to get me in to talk to Dustin Yamaguchi. That's his voice in the background of the 911 tape where Roger Whitney's business partner's wife is reporting finding her husband's body. There's a lot of static, but once that gets cleared away he's there."

"And that matters because . . . ?"

"Dustin Yamaguchi is a contract killer. A pro. If he was still at the scene talking in the background while Mrs. Keeler was hysterically reporting the discovery of her murdered husband, then Whitney didn't hire him. Mrs. Keeler did. Otherwise, she'd have been found dead alongside her husband."

"That makes sense." The logic of it smoothed some of the sharp edges off Jess's morning. "I take it we're defending Mr. Whitney on a charge of murdering his partner, Mr. Keeler?"

If it hadn't been Mark, she wouldn't have asked. She would have just kept her mouth shut until the facts became clear.

"Now you're getting up to speed."

"Like I said, first day. I've never heard of Mr. Whitney or Mr. Keeler. My question is, how have you?"

"Ellis Hayes came to us for help analyzing the 911 tape a couple of weeks ago. Since then, I've made it a point to get familiar with the case."

"Why?"

"Part of the job."

Knowing that Mark certainly had a full load of high-level investigations that dwarfed the Whitney/Keeler murder in importance, Jess digested that blatant piece of stone-walling in silence, then looked at him con-sideringly. "I take it Pearse knows you're babysitting me?"

Mark slid her a glance. "I don't think the word 'babysitting' was ever used. But, yes, he knows the Secret Service has you under its official protection. And I'm part of that."

"Who told him?"

Mark shrugged. Jess's lips thinned. She knew Mark well enough to know that was as much as she was going to get.

"Does he know why?"

His lips curved into a half smile. "If he knew why, somebody'd have to kill him."

"Funny."

"He knows enough not to ask."

"So now I know why he stuck me with you for the day. But why are we going to see this Yami-whatever guy? Why isn't Pearse, for example?"

"I know Yamaguchi. You might say we're old friends. That's one of the reasons they brought me in to listen to the tape. He'll trust me when I tell him prosecutors have got him by the balls and his best bet is to take the deal that's shortly going to be offered to him. And like I said, I need you, Ms. Lawyer, to get me in."

"You know a professional killer?" Jess looked at him, aghast.

"I know a lot of people."

Jess decided she didn't really want to hear the details. One thing she'd well and truly learned over the course of the last few months was that too much knowledge could be a very bad thing. Besides, Mark probably wouldn't tell her anyway.

"So you really are consulting for Ellis Hayes."

"Did you doubt it?"

"Absolutely."

"You've got some real trust issues, you know that? How about I make you a deal: you politely, pleasantly put up with me until we find out how Leonard Cowan died and who attacked you last night, and then I get the hell out of your life again and everything goes forward just like none of this ever happened. What do you say?"

Like she really had a choice. "Fine."

"Good. So, you want to know what's going to go down once we get to the jail or not?"

"Yes."

By the time he had finished filling her in, Mark was pulling into the underground parking garage that adjoined the Criminal Justice Center.

"But as the defense we have a legal obligation to tell the prosecutor's office that we've isolated and identified what's-his-name's voice on that tape," Jess protested as he parked. "For one thing, it's part of discovery. If we don't, the case can be thrown out. It might open up grounds for a Brady motion. It—"

"You don't have to tell them *today*," Mark interrupted as they both got out of the car. "Yamaguchi was just picked up early this morning. They have evidence that he was the triggerman, that he was paid. According to Collins's sources, they're sending over an assistant DA to offer Yamaguchi a chance to cut a deal if he'll tell them who hired him. Yamaguchi makes the deal, fingers Mrs. Keeler instead of, as they expect, Mr. Whitney. On the strength of Yamaguchi's testimony, Mrs. Keeler gets charged with her husband's murder. Your Mr. Whitney is off the hook without ever going to trial. That makes it a slam dunk for Ellis Hayes."

"What happens when the prosecutors hear Yama-guy's voice on the tape for themselves and realize they don't have to cut him a deal because they can prove he's the triggerman and Mrs. Keeler hired him?"

"Once the deal's made, it's made. The DA can't go back on it without jeopardizing the whole case."

That was true. It was also diabolical, and probably at least borderline unethical. It was, however, undoubtedly in their client Mr. Whitney's best interest. And doing what was in their client's best interest was why Ellis Hayes got the big bucks—and the glowing reputation as the firm to call when the proverbial shit hit the proverbial fan.

"Truth and honor," Jess bitterly quoted a key phrase from the lawyer's oath.

"Plus a couple of dollars will buy you a cup of coffee. Maybe. Unless you're at Starbucks. By the way, I'm your assistant, if anybody asks," Mark said in her ear as they entered the basement door of the vast, windowless, redbrick structure. "And the name of the guy you're going to be asking for is Dustin Yamaguchi." He spelled it for good measure, and Jess carefully repeated it. They went through the usual security without a hitch, then along a hall to a long, dingy rectangle of a chamber with all the charm of a dentist's waiting room. There were easily a dozen lawyers already there, sitting, reading the paper, looking over files, playing games on their iPhones, whatever, as they waited to be taken back to talk to their clients. Jess went to the sliding glass window to ask to speak to Mr. Yamaguchi, show her credentials, and sign the register. The woman clerk on the other side of the window barely looked up. Jess retreated to sit beside Mark on one of the uncomfortable molded plastic chairs that lined the walls until, some fifteen minutes later, her name was called.

Mark followed her as a uniformed corrections officer led them into a visiting room. It was a long space designed for the simultaneous use of perhaps two dozen inmates and their lawyers, who were separated from one another by a wall of thick Plexiglas. The room was further divided into three-sided booths, which provided little in the way of real privacy but offered two more of the molded plastic chairs and a laminated counter on which to rest briefcases or papers. The partitions on either side were tan laminate, the floor was speckled terrazzo, the back wall was puke green concrete, and the smell was institutional. About half the booths were already occupied. The steady rise and fall of a number of hushed conversations was broken only by the scraping of the chairs across the floor and the occasional tramp of feet as somebody entered or left.

When another uniformed guard escorted a muscular, black-haired, faintly Asian-looking man in an orange jail jumpsuit toward them, Jess realized he had to be Yamaguchi even before he sat down.

Hard-looking black eyes met hers through the Plexiglas. He was close enough that Jess could make out faint acne scars on his lean cheeks and see that the whites of his eyes were bloodshot. He had a thin, mean mouth, a swarthy complexion, and forearms as thick and hard-looking as baseball bats.

Jess was already battling a shiver of distaste as she picked up the black plastic phone that was the only means of communication from her side of the booth to his. On his side, Yamaguchi followed suit.

"Dustin Yamaguchi?" Jess began briskly. It was protocol, a means of confirming ID.

"I got a lady lawyer now?" Yamaguchi's eyes moved over her in a way that made Jess glad that she was not, in fact, his lawyer. "Good deal."

Mark took the phone out of her hand before she could introduce herself, as she had intended to do next.

"Morning, Gooch," he said into it. "Remember me?"

CHAPTER FIFTEEN

Until that moment Yamaguchi had been busy eyeing Jess, paying no attention whatsoever to the man lounging at her side. Now he met Mark's gaze and his brows twitched together. Glancing at Mark, Jess saw that his face had hardened until it was all jutting planes and sharp angles. His eyes had turned to steel. This was a side of him she had glimpsed only rarely, and it reminded her that underneath the handsome, laid-back exterior was a man she had seen kill.

"Well, if it isn't Agent Ryan. Why aren't you off catching bad guys?"

"Most of 'em are so dumb they're already caught. Like you. But today you're luckier than the rest of the dumbasses, because I'm about to hook you up with the deal of the century."

"Do tell."

By the time they left, Yamaguchi had agreed to think over the deal Mark had, with Jess's help on the legal details, presented to him. When he was approached by prosecutors, as he would be that afternoon, he could take the deal they offered him, admit that he had indeed been hired to kill Tim Keeler, and then finger Kathleen Keeler as the person who had hired him. In return for his testimony against Kathleen Keeler, the death penalty would be taken off the table and he would be given a sentence of twenty years to life, which would make him eligible for parole in about seven years. If he did not agree, he would wind up taking the fall as Kathleen Keeler, who would be offered a similar deal by prosecutors, testified against him, and his voice, which had been isolated on the 911 call, was used to seal the deal.

"Or I could take my chances with a jury," Yamaguchi suggested, watching Mark through the glass. "I hear there's a real strong case against that Whitney guy, especially if a smart lawyer wanted to argue that the tape you're talking about was doctored to make it sound like my voice is on there when it isn't. I might even walk."

"You might," Mark agreed.

Jess stepped in. "Speaking as your temporary lawyer, I feel I should advise you that if you ever want to see the light of day again, you'll take the deal we've described when it's offered. As soon as it's offered. You're lucky the prosecutors want to nail the person who hired you more than they want you."

"What can I say? I'm a lucky kind of guy."

To Jess that didn't sound all that promising, but Mark seemed well satisfied with it.

"He'll take the deal," he said as they left.

"How do you know?"

"He's a psychopath, but he isn't stupid."

They were back in the Suburban pulling out of the parking garage when Jess's cell phone rang. She frowned at the number, which was unfamiliar, but answered.

"Jessica Ford."

"Oh, um, hi." The female voice sounded hesitant. "This is Paloma DeLong from Shelter House. Lenore Beekman gave me this number. I understand that you're going to be taking Allison Howard's place as our legal advisor?"

"Yes." According to the files Jess had thumbed through, Shelter House was where Allison Howard had been doing her firm-mandated pro bono work. (Ellis Hayes believed its lawyers should give back to the community. Or, to put it more accurately, should be seen to be giving back to the community.) Which meant that Shelter House was where Jess was going to be doing her firm-mandated pro bono work, at least for the foreseeable future. "How can I help you?"

"We've just been served with a lawsuit. Two of our girls, um, ran away, and one of their families is apparently suing us for negligence for letting it happen. I've got the papers right here, but I don't know what to do."

"Are you at Shelter House now?" Jess glanced at the dashboard clock. It was 11:47. If she hurried, maybe she could deal with this now, on what was supposed to be her lunch hour, and then get back and make a good start on the brief Pearse wanted before her meeting with him and Mrs. Shively at three. "I can come by and look at them for you."

"I'm just on my way out the door. I'll be back at three, and then I'll be here until somewhere around eight."

Jess suppressed a sigh. "I'll try to make it around seven thirty, then."

"Thank you." The woman hung up.

Mark looked a question at her.

"I have to be somewhere around seven thirty tonight. Since you're babysitting, I assume you're chauffeuring as well?"

"Wither thou goest . . ."

"Good. I'm goest-ing to Shelter House about six forty-five. It's a residential facility for troubled teen girls, I'm volunteering to do their legal work, and they've just been served with a lawsuit." Jess was mentally organizing her schedule. Since there was nothing else she could do at this moment except possibly bicker with Mark, now would probably be a good time to see about getting a dress to wear to Mr. Dunn's party. Given her connections, acquiring one should be a relatively quick and pain-

less procedure, even for a woman as or-
ganically opposed to shopping as she
was. Trusting Mark to get her safely back
to the office without the need for any input
from her, she called Grace.

"I need a long dress," she said to her sister without preamble when Grace answered
with the name of her very high-end consignment shop, Past Perfect, which was
located in the hallowed precincts of Georgetown. "For Friday night. Do you have anything?"

"You need a *gown*?" Grace sounded as
if the request was mildly mind-boggling,
which Jess supposed, coming from her, it
probably was. "Where are you going?"

"Ellis Hayes's managing partner is having a party. Apparently it's this huge deal.
I have to go, and I have to have a *gown*.
Do you have anything? Can you get anything?"

"Hmm." There was very little her sister
loved more than the idea of dressing Jess
up. This hadn't changed since high school,
when Grace had first decided her older sister had been in dire need of fashion assistance. It was the challenge, Grace told her
every time Jess let her do it, that fascinated

her, the artistry of turning a (sorry, sister) sow's ear into a silk purse. Or Skipper into Barbie. "I actually do. There's a hot pink Marchesa . . ."

"Not pink," Jess objected, casting an evil look at Mark, who was starting to smile.

"What do you want, black?" Grace responded tartly. "Of course you do. I keep telling you, black is *not* your color."

"Black's professional," Jess said. "I want to look professional. It's a party, it's a long dress, but I want to look professional."

"You need color. Warm tones." Grace's voice held the impatience of someone who had said the same thing many times before.

"Nothing bright," Jess insisted. "Or slinky. Think conservative. Tasteful." Remembering some of the outfits Grace had put together for her before, she frowned admonishingly at her absent sister. "No strapless, no backless, minimal skin. Think something a female Supreme Court justice would wear to, say, the White House."

"Think something somebody's grandma would wear, you mean," Grace retorted. "Is our air conditioner still broken?"

"What?" It took Jess a moment to remember the lie she'd told their mother, which apparently Judy had passed on to Grace. "Oh. No."

"I take it you didn't tell Mom about the mugger in our front yard? Because she didn't mention it when I talked to her."

Jess had texted a warning to Grace from their mother's house before going to bed the previous night, just in case Grace's date hadn't worked out and she'd decided to go home. Grace had texted back asking if Jess was okay, Jess had said she was, and that had been the end of that. She'd hoped.

"What do you think?"

That so clearly didn't require an answer that Grace moved on. "I hear Mark's back in the picture."

Jess slanted a look at the man in question. From his expression, she was pretty sure he could hear a good part of Grace's side of the conversation as well as her own.

"Kinda-sorta."

"Oh, yeah?" Grace said. "Just so you know, I called him a low-life bastard when he answered your phone last night. Among other things."

"That's okay," Jess assured her.

"He's right there, isn't he?" Knowing her sister well, Grace had clearly picked up on something in Jess's voice. "We'll talk about this later. Oh, um, if I didn't come home tonight, would you be all right?"

"Is he cute?" Jess's voice was dry. She, too, knew her sister well.

"Divine. But if you need me to keep you safe from muggers or whatever, I'm there."

"Oh, what are you going to do? Slam 'em with your kung fu?" Grace had been taking martial arts lessons for the last few weeks. Jess suspected the mystery man was someone she'd met in the class.

"Two women with 911 on speed-dial are better than one."

Jess laughed. "True. But I don't need you. I promise, I'm perfectly safe."

"You've got Mark, huh? Okay, then, I probably won't be home. I'll see what I can do about the dress. Steer clear of muggers."

"I will," Jess said. "Thanks." Then she hung up.

"Nice to know your sisters love me." A faint smile curved Mark's lips.

"My sisters are on my side."

"Your mom's on mine."

"I wouldn't get excited. She's got a real weakness for hot guys."

He sent her a wickedly teasing glance. "Did you just say something nice to me?"

Jess felt a flush of heat. How had that slipped out?

"Just so you know, what my mom thinks and what I think are not necessarily the same thing."

"You think I'm hot. Come on, Jess, admit it."

Rescue came as she glanced out the window and registered where they were. "You're driving past the building! Pull over."

"I'm taking you to lunch. At Rafferty's, around the corner."

"I don't have time."

"It's lunchtime, I'm hungry, and you're stuck with me, remember? Don't worry, this place is quick."

Rafferty's was a busy storefront café with lots of windows looking out onto New Jersey Avenue. It was less than a block from Ellis Hayes, so Jess didn't know why she was unprepared to find the place full of familiar faces when they walked in.

"It's Death and Taxes," she murmured to Mark in surprise as she spotted two young women lawyers she knew from Ellis Hayes seated side by side at the counter. One was blond, the other was a redhead, and both were gorgeous. Then she did a double take as her gaze swept past them to snag on a grim-faced, fifty-something brunette in a powder blue blazer sitting at a table for two in the corner with a lean, bald-as-an-egg old man in a lawyerly gray suit. "And, oh my God, the Queen of Torts! And she's with Mr. Dunn."

Jess said that last with as much awe as she might have had she announced the other woman had been with God.

"You realize I have no idea what you're talking about." Clearly unimpressed, Mark was looking around for a table. Fortunately, a hostess was coming toward them, menus in hand, presumably to help them find a seat. As the smell of grilling meat and some kind of tomato-based sauce and fresh bread wafted beneath her nostrils, Jess realized to her own surprise that she was hungry, too. Since the noise made it impossible to be heard at any distance, Mark held up two fingers to the hostess, who nodded.

"Death works in the estate division and

Taxes works in the tax division. They're both on four, they're best friends, and word in the building is they spend their nights trolling the bars for rich men so they can retire and spend the rest of their days producing little rich babies." They were following the hostess by that time. She was leading them through the center of the restaurant toward an available table somewhere. Mark was so close behind Jess that they were practically touching, and Jess was looking up at him over her shoulder as she talked. "The Queen of Torts is what we call Mary McGarvey. Her group's on seven. They've won so many cases that the partners just bought her a Bentley to show their appreciation. And then there's—"

"Jess!"

At the sound of her name, Jess glanced around in surprise. Andrew waved at her from a table by the window. Sitting with him were Hayley, Pearse, and Lenore.

"Well, lookee there," Mark muttered behind her. Lifting her hand in an answering wave, Jess assumed he was seeing the same thing she was.

"Come join us," Andrew called. Pearse beckoned to them, and Lenore beamed and scooted closer to Pearse as if to make room. Only Hayley looked less than pleased. Or at least she looked less than pleased until she looked past Jess and saw Mark. Then her expression changed to one of conflicted interest.

"Time to do some schmoozing," Mark murmured in her ear, his hand light on the side of her waist as he steered her toward the table. Overcoming her initial flicker of instinctive shyness, Jess mentally put up her chin, pasted on a smile, and took the seat that was offered her.

Lunch was, as Mark had promised, fast, but surprisingly enjoyable. They talked, and laughed, and ate, and even Pearse perked up when Mr. Dunn, who was tall and stoop-shouldered with unexpectedly kind blue eyes, stopped by their table on his way out of the restaurant to congratulate them again on winning the Phillips case. Jess actually shook hands with the great man, since it was the first time she had met him in person. By the time the meal was over, she realized she was beginning to feel like part of the team.

The afternoon passed in a blur of work. She pulled out Allison's appointment cal-

endar, transferred the things she was supposed to cover to her own calendar, and
noted in passing that today's date had a
big red ink star drawn on it with the words
Shelter House and a time of 12:30 written
inside it. Allison had obviously considered
the appointment important. But as it was
already after 12:30, it was too late now to
even try to do anything about it, so Jess
put it out of her mind and got down to work.
The brief Pearse wanted required a ton of
research, and Jess was feverishly pouring
through precedent-setting cases that might
apply when three o' clock rolled around.
Hotfooting it to Pearse's office, she reached
his side scant seconds before one of the
women from the secretarial pool, recruited
to take Lenore's place for the afternoon,
escorted Mrs. Shively back.

Mrs. Shively—Camilla to Pearse—was
around thirty, outrageously blond, outrageously beautiful, and outrageously
stacked. Her lips were scarlet, her eyes
outlined in kohl, her lashes false. Her triple-
Ds (Jess was guessing here) were barely
contained by a flimsy white blouse that was
unbuttoned to the point where her lacy
black bra showed with every move she

made, which was probably the point. Her skirt was a teeny-tiny black ace bandage that barely reached the tops of her thighs, and if she was wearing anything beneath, it didn't show.

When Pearse stood up to greet her, she cast herself into his arms and started weeping copious tears all over him. Not having had time to sit down, Jess watched wide-eyed for a moment before she remembered that she was there to protect Pearse from Mrs. Shively's touchy-feely tendencies. Spotting a box of tissues on Pearse's desk, obviously kept for just this type of emergency, Jess pulled a couple free.

"Would you like a tissue, Mrs. Shively?" she asked politely, holding the tissues out.

Mrs. Shively stiffened. Her head came up. As she frowned at Jess and the introductions were made, Pearse was able to get her into a seat, press the tissues into her hand, and retreat behind the safety of his desk. After Pearse broke the bad news, Mrs. Shively spent the rest of her appointment sobbing repeatedly as she protested her complete and utter innocence and insisted that she had loved "horny ole Frank" with all her heart and soul. As a sidebar, she kept crossing and uncrossing her legs. For Jess, who was seated slightly behind Pearse, this provided way too much confirmation that, indeed, nothing came between their client and her skirt.

When they were finished at last, Pearse walked her to the elevator with Jess, his faithful shadow, in tow. While Mrs. Shively bade him farewell by kissing his cheek and giving him a big, full-body-contact hug, Jess pressed the down button.

Pearse's eyes rolled in Jess's direction when he was released. Stepping into the breach, she stuck out her hand.

"It was so nice to meet you, Mrs. Shively."

"You too, hon." As Mrs. Shively shook Jess's hand, the elevator arrived. The relief on Pearse's face when the elevator door closed on their still teary-eyed client was palpable.

"If she has to go before a jury, God help us," Pearse said to Jess as they both turned away to head for their respective offices. "If we're not able to tone her down, the prosecution won't have to say a word."

But that was a problem for another day, and Jess promptly put it out of her head as she settled in and got back to work. She checked her messages: nothing from Tiffany. Quickly she placed calls to Tiffany's home number, where voice mail picked up, and to her cell once more, with the same result. Then she resumed wrestling with the brief. Her concentration was slightly affected by the occasional unpleasant sensation that someone was watching her from behind, and the subsequent need to whip her head around just to reassure herself that nothing more unsettling than the ficus was there. The sensation was creepy enough that, by the time she was pounding out the last few words of the brief, she was vowing to have maintenance remove the plant first thing in the morning.

Because the shadow she thought she kept catching out of the corner of her eye had to be something to do with the way the light hit the damned plant.

CHAPTER SIXTEEN

Jess's cell phone rang just as she was e-mailing the finished brief to Pearse.

"You ready to go? I've got the Suburban double-parked out front."

It was Mark. A glance at her watch told her the time was already six forty-five. She groaned.

"I'm on my way."

Grabbing her belongings, pulling on her jacket, she rushed for the door. Pausing to turn out the light only because she felt she had to, she glanced involuntarily at the corner behind the desk. Even in the sudden gloom, the plant still looked like a plant.

Of course, the disappearing woman had not been real, she told herself as she rode down the elevator and hurried out of the building, so she was going to put her permanently out of mind. What *was* real was the huge backlog of work Allison had left behind that Jess needed to power through to get caught up. The sheer amount of it should have been daunting, but Jess found that she was actually looking forward to digging into it. Besides being a way to prove her worth to Pearse and anyone else who was interested, it was something she was good at. In this very exacting small sphere, she could make a difference.

Jess was so tired, so frazzled, so drained by her day so far that she barely spoke except to give Mark the address once she was ensconced in the Suburban. Having forgotten to take any Advil since the two she had popped at lunch, she was now paying the price. Her head pounded and her side hurt worse. Shaking two of the small tablets out of the bottle in her purse, she swallowed them without water, casting Mark a sideways glance that dared him to comment as she did so.

"I have coffee." Sending a half smile her way, he tapped the lid of a Styrofoam cup he'd wedged in the cup holder. With one of the pills lodged in her throat, Jess accepted the de facto offer without a word and took a grateful sip. The coffee was fresh, hot, and strong. She guessed he had bought it at the cantina in the lobby as he'd gone to fetch the car. Without much more than a grunt of thanks, she drank about half of it, then left him to finish the rest.

Luckily, Mark didn't require conversation. With Jess resting bonelessly in her seat waiting for the Advil and coffee to take effect, they listened to the radio and the occasional voice of the GPS giving directions until they reached Shelter House.

The city was divided into quadrants, and Southwest was the quadrant no one wanted to be in. That some people had no choice just seemed to tick them off. Street gangs patrolled the blocks, and turf wars over whose block was whose were common. Hookers and drug dealers routinely worked the corners. Cars left on the street for more than five minutes risked being stripped of everything from their tires to their seats, and never mind about anything in the nature of CD or DVD systems, which usually didn't make it past the one-minute mark. Housing ranged from flat-fronted brick tenements to abandoned, boarded-up, single-family homes that provided a haven for roving meth labs. Graffiti was everywhere, and so was trash. Eruptions of gunfire were as common here as fire-crackers on the Fourth of July. Drive-by shootings were an everyday occurrence. The area took perverse pride in reporting more murders per capita than anyplace else in the nation. If D.C. was the murder capital of the country, Southwest was the murder capital of D.C.

It came as no surprise, then, to find that Shelter House looked like a bunker. A long, two-story cinder-block building the color of mustard, it sat almost on the side-walk and sprawled out over half a block. The windows were bricked up and painted over. The front door looked to be solid steel. A vacant lot directly to the left of the building held a single metal picnic table, bolted down to a slab of concrete. The lot was surrounded by two layers of chain link fencing topped by loops of razor wire. The outer layer of fence had big No Trespassing signs affixed to it. Another solid steel door opened from the side of the building directly into the lot. That scraggly, dusty rectangle of grass had to have been what the young residents used as a yard.

Shelter House, indeed.

"Grab my police tag out of the glove compartment. It might buy us a few extra minutes."

As he parked in front of the building, Mark was looking at the pack of toughs on the corner, who were already eyeing the Suburban like vultures spotting fresh carrion. The usual street characters—the wino shuffling past with his hand wrapped tight around the neck of a bottle in a brown paper bag, a homeless woman pushing her few belongings in a shopping cart, a couple of brothers who looked like they were on their way to swell the ranks of the gang on the corner—he ignored.

"You're not police," Jess protested even as she found the long white tag with its DCPD symbol and handed it over.

"Yeah, but we get a police parking tag. It's easier." He hung the tag from the rearview mirror. "If we're lucky, they won't want to mess with the cops. Sit tight, I'll come around for you."

The implication that she couldn't walk twenty feet without his protection didn't set well with Jess. In consequence, she got out, grimacing at the pain in her side and her head, which had not yet significantly decreased. She trudged a couple of feet along the sidewalk through the thick humidity before Mark caught up with her. Their ranks having just been increased by the two newcomers, the youths on the corner seemed emboldened. They looked her over, made some catcalls, and one of them even made a move in her direction until Mark shot him and his buddies a look that stopped them cold. The would-be aggressor melted back into the group, and the catcalls ceased. Meanwhile, with a single glinting glance that rebuked her for not having done as he'd said, Mark hustled her to the door, placing himself between her and the youths as she stopped in front of the entrance. He was in his Federal Agent mode, his body language authoritative, his face tough and aggressive. Clearly the message that he was not a man to be messed with had gotten across, because they weren't bothered as she rang the button and waited. Identifying herself to the disembodied voice that finally answered, Jess was buzzed in.

The place was surprisingly quiet for an institution that housed some eighty—Jess had checked—teenage girls. With the all-female household she'd grown up in for a template, Jess would have expected her ears to be bombarded with sound: talking, laughing, arguing, something. Instead, there was a palpable hush. The smell of some strong cleaning agent—Pine-Sol?—hit her the moment she walked through the door. Jess wrinkled her nose in silent protest. Inside, the place looked as much like a bunker as it had from the outside. The room she entered was stark with fluorescent lighting, its gray linoleum floor and beige walls unremittingly dingy. Bulletin boards thick with layers of papers in a host of colors broke up the walls. A metal desk staffed by a bored-looking receptionist sat in front of another metal door. Jess barely had time to notice that the receptionist was young and had dreadlocks before the door behind her opened and a woman came out to greet them.

She was around Jess's own height, but her stockier build and the swirling bun perched like a doughnut on top of her head made her appear taller. In possibly her midfifties, she had black hair, dark eyes, swarthy skin, and small, pinched features. Her only makeup appeared to be vivid red lipstick. Her short-sleeved black dress was midcalf length, and she wore it with mid-heeled black pumps.

She held out her hand. "Ms. Ford? I'm Paloma DeLong."

"Please, call me Jess. And this is Mark Ryan."

She didn't specify that Mark was Special Agent Mark Ryan, because the explanation that would entail would be long and involved and had nothing to do with her purpose in visiting Shelter House. Better to let the woman assume what she would, which was probably that Mark was with Ellis Hayes, too. Which, temporarily, Jess supposed he was.

"And I'm Paloma. When will Allison be back in town, do you know?"

Jess shook her head. "I don't really know. I understand she's on her honeymoon."

"I heard that, too. What a surprise! I'm so happy for her, of course, but I'm a little disappointed that she didn't let me know in time to cancel today's luncheon. It was more than awkward not to have our guest of honor show up, as I'm sure you can imagine."

Jess remembered the red star Allison had drawn on her calendar.

"She was supposed to be your guest of honor?"

Paloma nodded. "We were presenting her with our Volunteer of the Year award. She seemed to be thrilled when I told her about it, and we had our board of directors and everybody come, and then she just didn't show up. When I frantically called Ellis Hayes to see where she was, they told me what had happened, and of course I can understand that eloping like that could make anyone forgetful, but I just wish she had called."

"I'm so sorry," Jess said.

"Well, it certainly isn't your fault. I'm just glad you're here. But I am concerned about Clementine."

"Clementine?"

Paloma nodded. "Her cat. When Allison originally left, she said she would be away on a business trip and asked me to come by her apartment to feed Clementine while she was gone. She was supposed to get back a week later, on Sunday night, so the last time I stopped by was that Sunday morning, when I left the key on her kitchen table. I just assumed she was back. But when she missed today's luncheon and I called in and Lenore said she had run off to get married and was on her honeymoon, and that you would be replacing her because she'd resigned, I wondered who was watching the cat." She took Jess and Mark back into her office as she spoke. It was basically a smaller version of the reception room except for what was on the bulletin boards, which seemed to be covered with photographs by the dozens instead of flyers and notices.

"I don't know anything about her cat," Jess said apologetically as she and Mark followed Paloma to her desk.

"Well, I'm sure she made arrangements for her. Probably another friend, or a kennel. Only she said Clementine was really funny about kennels." Walking behind her desk, shrugging as if to dismiss the subject, Paloma opened a drawer and pulled out a sheaf of papers, which she handed over to Jess.

"This is courtesy of Jaden's brother, apparently. His name is Jax Johnson. I mean, he claims he's her brother, but I don't have any way of knowing for sure." Paloma clasped her hands together in a gesture that betrayed her anxiety as Jess looked the papers over. They were all standing, with Paloma behind her desk and Jess and Mark in front of it. "He called us wanting to speak to her about four days after she went missing. We had to tell him what had happened. Well, I guess we didn't, but it wasn't a secret. We were trying to find Jaden and Lucy, and we thought he might be able to help. Since then, he's been calling two and three times a day, pestering everybody, demanding that we find Jaden. He's become such a nuisance that we stopped taking his calls. So I guess this is the result."

The suit, filed against Shelter House and Child Protective Services, appeared to contain a number of irregularities, Jess saw, although the central charge—negligence in allowing the minor child remanded to Shelter House's custody to escape—seemed on the surface of it to have at least some small degree of merit.

"He's her brother?" Mark asked while Jess flipped through the papers. "Where's he been? Where are the parents?"

Paloma shrugged. "The parents are out of the picture. Mother's a junkie, currently in jail. Father's dead. I verified that there actually is a brother. He's about twenty-three, but we'd never heard anything from him until this. He's never called before, or visited Jaden while she's been with us."

Looking up, Jess said, "Unless the brother is her legal guardian, he has no standing to file a suit of this nature. Do you know who her legal guardian is?"

"She's a ward of the District of Columbia."

"Has the brother asked you for money? Tried to shake you down in any way?"

Paloma shook her head. "He says he wants to know where his sister is. I keep telling him we have no idea. That we are doing our best to find her. We've notified the police. We've notified the social service groups in the area—homeless shelters, soup kitchens, that kind of thing. We've put out flyers. There's really nothing else we can do until the girls—Jaden ran away with another girl, Lucy Peel—resurface. And they will. They'll do something, they'll get picked up, they'll be back in the system sooner or later. They all come back into the system, I can vouch for it."

The woman sounded, and looked, as if she was resigned to the cycle.

Jess glanced around. "This is a lockdown facility, isn't it? How did they get out?"

"A delivery man left a door open."

Leaving a door open where a pair of troubled girls could use it to escape could also argue negligence. Not that it really mattered. Getting the suit dismissed would be easy enough—first, because successfully suing a government agency was almost impossible, and, second, because the purported brother did not have standing. The larger question, though, was what had become of the girls. As pro bono counsel for Shelter House, Jess had to ask herself whether finding escaped residents was part of the deal. Who knew? Jess decided that it was a gray area, and also decided to follow her heart, which urged her to do what she could.

"Have you tried calling . . . what are their names?"

"Jaden. And Lucy."

"Have you tried calling Jaden and Lucy on their cell phones? Or tracking them down through Facebook, something like that?"

Paloma gave her a wry smile. "We can't call them on their cell phones, because the first thing we do when they get here is confiscate those." She pointed toward a large plastic bin tucked away in a corner, which Jess could see was full of neatly labeled manila envelopes, all of which, from the bulge in them, presumably contained cell phones. "No, I haven't tried Facebook. I guess I could do that. Well, truthfully, I could have my assistant Teresa, who is not here right now, do that. I'm not really familiar with Facebook. That dates me, I know."

"If you want to give me their cell phones, I'll check their call history and see if I can turn up friends, family, someone they might have been in contact with before, some-

one who might know where they are now,"
Jess said.

"Can you do that? I had no idea such a
thing was even possible. When the police
came to take the report, they didn't say a
thing about looking at the girls' cell phones,
so they must not know it either. Or else
they're too busy. Probably too busy. But in
any case, I thank you." Bestowing a quick
smile on Jess, she turned to rummage
through the bin. "Finding them would be
the best thing that could happen. Jaden's
brother would be satisfied, and then maybe
all this"—her tone made it obvious she
meant the lawsuit—"would go away."

"Don't worry about the lawsuit. I'll take
care of it."

"That is such a relief to hear."

"Do you have a picture of them?" Mark
asked.

"I had flyers made up with their pictures
on them. Though I think we've run out."
Paloma straightened, two manila envelopes in her hand. She gave them to Jess.
"Our staff has put them up everywhere. I
can get more, of course. We still have the
pictures from their IDs, which is what we
used, but I don't know where Teresa's put

them right off the top of my head." Moving out from behind her desk, she pointed to a photo tacked near the bottom of one of the bulletin boards. "But if you just want to see what the girls look like, here they are right here."

Mark joined her in front of the picture. Tucking the envelopes under her arm, Jess walked over to look at it as well. It showed maybe eight teenage girls, plus adults she assumed were chaperones, standing on the steps of the U.S. Capitol Building.

"So they aren't on twenty-four-hour lockdown," Mark said.

"No, of course not. We take them out for approved events. Doctor appointments, church, the occasional movie, or concert. As long as they're well supervised. Here they're on a field trip. It was taken just last month. This is Jaden." Paloma pointed to a tall, thin, girl with spiky black hair. "And this is Lucy."

With her frizzy red hair, Lucy looked like a funky teenage version of Little Orphan Annie. Okay, a funky teenage version of Little Orphan Annie with a sulky stare instead of a beaming smile.

Both of them—all of them—looked like

typical teenage girls, not juvenile offenders who deserved to be locked away.

**They could be Maddie's friends. Or
Taylor's.**

Jess was just thinking that when one of
the three adults in the picture caught her
gaze. She did a double take, her eyes wid-
ening as she stared in growing shock at
the image.

It was of a woman who was standing at
the back of the group. She wore a yellow
summer jacket with a jumble of bright orange beads around her throat. Most of her
body was hidden because she was behind
the others, but Jess could see that she
was a little thick-set and not particularly
pretty. She was blunt-featured, with blue
eyes and shaggy auburn hair.

Looking at her, Jess felt as if the room
had just decompressed and all the air had
suddenly been sucked out of her lungs.

**That's the woman in my office. The
one who vanished.**

"Who is that?" she asked, her finger mi-
raculously steady as she pointed at the
tiny pictured figure, and hoped her voice
didn't sound as croaky to the others as it
did to her own ears.

"Why, that's Allison. Allison Howard." Paloma looked at her curiously. "Don't you know her?"

Jess shook her head. "We've never met."

But Jess was almost positive she'd seen Allison before.

CHAPTER SEVENTEEN

"What the hell happened in there? You went white as a sheet."

Mark's hand clasped her elbow as he steered her back down the sidewalk toward the Suburban, which thankfully seemed to be in one piece. The gang on the corner had left. The usual suspects were on the sidewalks, but singly or in pairs, which made them seem not as threatening.

Jess said nothing until they were both back inside the Suburban and it was turning left two blocks away, on Lamont. It wasn't that she was deliberately ignoring Mark. It was simply that she was still processing the possibilities. And, okay, admit it, also because she was still in something very closely resembling shock.

She finally answered his latest sharp *"Jess?"* with "I think I saw Allison Howard in my office this morning."

"So?"

"Then she vanished."

"What?"

"When I walked in this morning, Allison Howard was standing there behind my desk—her desk—kind of looking out the window. I said something like, oh, sorry, thinking I had disturbed her, and she looked at me over her shoulder. Then she vanished. As in, disappeared. You know, no longer there. Gone. Just like that."

"What?"

"See, this is why I don't tell you things. You're too damned slow on the uptake."

"I'm slow on the uptake?" Mark shot her a disgusted look. "You just told me you saw a woman vanish. That takes a little processing."

"So process."

"You ever think that maybe Allison Howard was actually in your office this morning? Maybe she stopped by to pick up some things, or to visit somebody, or, well, who knows? That's entirely possible. What isn't possible is that she vanished. Just like that. Think about it."

"I have been thinking about it. Believe me, I've been thinking about it all day. I even tried to convince myself that what I thought was a vanishing woman was a plant that *didn't* vanish."

"What?"

"Never mind." Jess stared unseeingly at the blazing orange sun that was just beginning to sink below the horizon. "If that really was Allison Howard in my office this morning, then how did she disappear? I was standing in the doorway. The only other way out is to fall out the window, which she didn't, because I checked."

"You checked."

"Yes, I checked. Of course, I didn't know who the woman was until I saw that picture just now in Shelter House. Now I know it was Allison Howard. She looked just like her picture, except she was wearing black pants and a black-and-white kind of animal-print striped top. She was standing there in my—her—our office, she looked at me, and then she vanished."

"You realize that if she wasn't really in your office and you didn't just somehow miss her exit, what you saw was probably a trick of the light. Or a reflection, or a shadow, or something like that."

Jess shifted sideways in her seat and leaned earnestly forward so that the seatbelt strap pulled tight against her shoulder.

"That's what I thought at first. I mean, what other explanation could there be? I thought I imagined that a woman was standing in front of the window in my office. I thought by some kind of trick of the light or something the big plant that's in the corner had somehow fooled my eye. But what are the chances that a woman I just conjured up out of nothing would look like Allison Howard, whom at that point I had never even seen?"

Mark didn't reply for a moment. Then, very calmly (for her benefit, she knew, because getting very calm was what he did when she started to get agitated) he said, "There's got to be a reasonable explanation."

"Like what?"

"Maybe there's a picture of Allison Howard somewhere around Ellis Hayes. Maybe you saw it. If so, it's not such a stretch to think you'd imagine her in the office you're taking over from her."

"I saw it and don't remember." She was skeptical.

"Maybe it registered on you subliminally."

Now it was Jess's turn to be quiet as she thought about it.

"I guess that's possible." She felt a niggle of relief.

"She's not dead, is she? Didn't I just hear you say she got married unexpectedly and quit?"

"She's on her honeymoon." Jess took the first deep breath she'd been able to manage since seeing Allison Howard's picture.

"So we're not talking a ghost here."

"No, I guess not." Jess shifted positions again and let her head drop back against the cushioned seat. She was bone tired and her head still hurt, although at least the pain in her side had subsided to a manageable degree. Mark's observation made sense, but still she felt uneasy. As an explanation, it wasn't entirely satisfying. Still, it was the only explanation she had.

She turned her head to look at him.

"You're obnoxious and bossy and way too full of yourself, among your many other faults—but sometimes you do make me feel better."

He smiled a little wryly. "I aim to please."

"When do you think we'll hear something about Leonard Cowan's death?"

They stopped at an intersection and he looked over at her. "In a hurry to get rid of me, are you?"

"Yes." Even as she said it, she realized it was true—and also not true. She liked having Mark in her life. But it was dangerous to get too used to his presence. Where he was concerned, if she wasn't careful, she could soon find herself as needy and vulnerable as ever she had been.

"A few more days. Maybe a week. The investigation's on the down-low, but we've got the top forensic pathologists in the country working on it."

"Wouldn't Hasbrough know if somebody had ordered Cowan killed? Or me attacked?"

"Hasbrough has no such knowledge. I'd stake my life on it. If the Secret Service wasn't serious about keeping you safe, they wouldn't have assigned me to watch over you, nor would they be putting the resources that they are into Cowan's death." His face tightened, and he glanced at her. "If this is about what happened to Annette Cooper, it's coming from somebody deep undercover. Somebody—some faction—completely off the grid."

"Which we both know is perfectly possible."

"Yeah, it is." His expression lightened. Through the deepening gloom, she saw his eyes twinkle at her. "Look at it this way: as long as I'm alive, you've got nothing to worry about."

"Great." They were on Connecticut now, and the lights from the shops and restaurants lining the street dappled the interior of the car.

"Okay, enough about us possibly dying young. You've got the same choice tonight you did last night: your mother's house, your apartment, my house: which one's it going to be?"

Jess groaned. "None of the above?"

"You wish."

If she went to her mother's two nights in

a row, questions would be asked. If too many questions were asked, Grace would, under pressure, spill the mugger story beans, and her mother would deploy all her considerable resources in an effort to keep her oldest daughter safe. So that forced her mother's house out. Mark's house, which was located in Dale City, was simply too far away when she had to be at work so early in the morning. Besides, it was in Mark's house that they had lived for the few weeks they'd been a couple. The memories would, she feared, be overwhelming, especially since they were, even in a strictly nonromantic way, together again.

"If I pick my apartment, I take it you're planning to spend the night?"

"Yep."

"How can you spend the night at my apartment? You don't have any clothes or anything for tomorrow."

"Now, there's where you're wrong. Anticipating this very problem, I packed a bag when I went home last night."

"So you could stay in my apartment."

"So I could stay wherever you chose to stay. Except your mother's. If you want to go there, and if the house is as full as it was last night, I'll sleep in the car out front."

Jess looked at him with sudden suspicion. "You didn't do that last night."

"Yes, I did. I went home, packed a bag, and came back. This car's perfect to sleep in—plenty of room. I got up early, took a shower, and got dressed at the Y around the corner. Then I got back in time to watch you go marching down the street by dawn's early light."

Touched in spite of herself at the thought of the discomfort and trouble he'd gone to on her behalf, Jess frowned at him in pure self-defense.

"I pick my apartment."

"Your apartment it is. Good thing Grace won't be there. Unless you're better at making up lies than I think you are, you and I would have had to share a bed."

"Not happening."

"I was just sayin'. If Grace was there."

"You could have slept on the couch. We could have said your air conditioner was broken."

"That only works once. And I probably will sleep on the couch. The key is for me to be the closest to the door."

Jess felt a cold little prickle of fear between her shoulder blades. "Do you really think someone might break in?"

"I doubt it. If they'd wanted to do that, they would have done it the first time. Think about it: Cowan commits suicide, you're the victim of a happens-every-day-in-D.C. street mugging. If this is a Black Ops cleanup operation, they're trying to make the deaths look random."

Jess tried to push the gruesome thought out of her head. "So you really don't need to spend the night."

He grinned. "But, see, there's always the possibility that I'm wrong. And I don't know about you, but I'd rather not take that chance."

Thinking about it, Jess discovered that he was right. The idea of sleeping all by herself in her apartment after the events of last night and today gave her the willies. Visions of murderous attacks and vanishing women did not a good night's sleep make. And, face it, a butcher knife under the pillow was no substitute for a big, buff, and trained-in-all-the-deadly-arts Secret Service agent sleeping on the couch.

"I should get a gun," she said.

He laughed. "For a gun to be effective, you have to be willing to shoot it. You have to know how to shoot it. You have to be reasonably accurate at shooting it. None of which applies to you."

"It could. I could get a gun, and learn." The idea was so appealing that it was already taking root and sending up shoots. Really, she didn't know why she hadn't thought of it before. She was getting damned tired of having to be protected whenever things in her life went south. It was time she learned to protect herself.

"Jesus, I know that look. Baby, you don't want a gun. You'll wind up shooting yourself. Or Grace. Or one of her boyfriends. Or me. Or—"

"There you go, being all patronizing again. I'm an intelligent, competent person. I can learn to operate a gun."

"You don't *operate* a gun. You fire it."

"Whatever."

"You need a permit."

"I can get a permit."

Jess got the impression that Mark swallowed a groan that he was too crafty to let her hear.

"Definitely something to think about," he said diplomatically.

Jess's lips twisted. She knew when she was being fobbed off. Luckily, she didn't require Mark's permission for anything she wanted to do, including this. With that in mind, she made no attempt to keep him from changing the subject, which he did a moment later by asking, "So where do you want to eat?"

Jess saw that they had reached Foggy Bottom. The streetlights were on, the sidewalks were packed, and flowers and greenery and good smells and happy sounds were abundant. The contrast with the Southwest quadrant they had just left couldn't have been more marked.

"You can't be hungry."

"Sure I can. It's after nine o'clock. Way past my suppertime." He shot her a look. "We could go to Pearl's. I have this hankering for their pulled pork sandwich. I haven't had one in a while."

Since they'd broken up, Jess imagined. Just like she hadn't had her favorite wonton chicken soup since they'd broken up, either. Because she hadn't been to Pearl's since they'd broken up. Because it was their place, the place the two of them had gravitated to as the default hangout for meals. The thought of eating there tonight, with him, made her chest feel tight.

That was their together place, and the very worst thing she could do was let herself forget that they were no longer, in that sense, together. Which she was beginning to see would be alarmingly easy to do.

"You're going to have to make do with pizza. I'm tired, I have a headache, and I want to take a bath and go to bed."

At the shortness of her tone, he shot her a quick, unfathomable look.

But "Pizza it is," was all he said, and he made the call for a delivery. A few minutes later he was easing the Suburban into a parking spot near her apartment.

With Mark behind her, Jess was able to get inside without more than an instinctive shiver as she passed the magnolia. Once in her apartment, Mark did the now standard walk through while she shed her jacket and shoes and checked the answering machine for messages. Her mother, Maddie, Sarah, some guy for Grace, some other guy for Grace: in other words, messages as usual. Nothing from Tiffany. Nothing on her cell phone, either. Either Tiffany didn't care what she had dropped, or she was simply not calling back. Jess then got out the cell phones Paloma had given her, only to discover that neither of them was charged. Fortunately, the power cords were in the envelopes as well. Jess connected them to a wall outlet in the kitchen as Mark stopped in the doorway to see what she was doing.

A knock heralded the arrival of pizza.

They ended up on either end of the couch with the pizza on the coffee table in front of them, watching TV as they ate. His shoulder holster, complete with gun, rested on the end table at his elbow. With his coat and tie off and his shirtsleeves rolled up, Mark looked totally relaxed, totally at home—and so handsome that Jess did her best not to look at him. Instead she watched the TV—she couldn't have recalled what program it was if her life depended on it—and finished off her piece of pizza without tasting it at all. The word *companionable* came to mind again when she sought for one to describe how sharing a pizza with Mark like this felt, but she dismissed it instantly. She didn't want to feel companionable, or comfortable, or at home in his presence, because inevitably, when he was gone, she would lose all those things. And that scared her.

In this one facet of her life, she feared she was too much like her mother, who had a weakness for gorgeous, sexy guys who were the human equivalent of catnip to other women and who, when they inevitably strayed, left her mother heartbroken in their wake.

Judy had never learned. But Jess had.

Loving a man like Mark was simply too great a risk. What had once been between them, what could blaze between them again if she wasn't careful, was a big love, a grand love, the kind of love that could cause her soul to sing and her body to burn. When it crashed, as most love inevitably did, would the resultant pain be worth it?

She didn't even have to ponder to know the answer: no.

One thing she'd learned about herself over the years was that her heart was tender. She wanted to be very, very careful about the man to whom she gave the power to break it. Her mother might cheerfully survive the constant romantic train wrecks. Jess could not.

When she and Mark had broken up, she had wanted to die. She had wanted to crawl into bed and curl up under the covers and sleep for days. She had wanted to cry until she'd had no more tears left.

What she had done instead was get up and get on with it. Leaned on her family. Thrown herself heart and soul into work.

She'd put the pieces back together. But she was determined never to put herself in a position to feel pain like that again.

Which meant that no matter how good it might feel to have Mark back in her life, she wasn't about to let him back in her heart.

Mark, who seemed intent on devouring the rest of the contents of the pizza box, barely grunted when she finished her single piece and left the room, only to return a few minutes later with a pillow and some sheets and a quilt, which she dropped unceremoniously in a pile on the end of the couch she had just vacated. He could make up his bed himself.

"I'm going to bed," she announced.

Absorbed in the TV, he gave her an abstracted wave.

Jess retreated. Half an hour later, after luxuriating in the hottest bath she could stand, she popped two more Advil and went to bed. As exhausted as she was, she expected to fall asleep the instant her head hit the pillow. But she didn't. She wanted to toss and turn, but tossing and turning was difficult because her side was sore. Instead she shifted positions gingerly, kicking off covers, pulling them back on, listening to the muffled thrum of the shower as Mark apparently decided to take one in Grace's bathroom before going to sleep. After listening to him pad back down the hall, and straining her ears to catch the subtle creaks that meant he was settling into the couch for the night, she dozed off, only to wake up again with a start. A glance at the bedside clock revealed that it was 3: 09 a.m. She had, she realized as she lay there blinking into the dark, been dreaming about Allison Howard.

Vanishing.

Oh, God. Jess pulled a pillow over her head and tried to think of something else. After a while, when it became obvious that sleep wasn't going to happen, she gave up. What she needed was something to drink. Like a glass of wine. Or a shot of vodka. Something strong. Something sleep inducing.

Since unfortunately the only thing in the apartment with alcohol in it was strong mouthwash, she was going to settle for milk.

Fumbling for the glasses she kept in the drawer of her bedside table, Jess put them on and headed for the kitchen. The apartment was dark, but not so dark that she couldn't see where she was going. Moonlight filtered in through the curtains, the night-light in the hall emitted a soft blue glow, and light from the landing outside glimmered golden under the door. Anyway, the kitchen was close, and she knew where she was going.

Practically tiptoeing, listening to the even rasp of Mark's breathing that fell just short of snoring, she made it into the kitchen. Retrieving a clean glass from the dishwasher, she set it down on the counter and quietly pulled open the refrigerator. The sound was minimal. The white glow of the interior light seemed as bright as the sun.

Jess got the carton out, filled her glass, and put the carton back. Closing the refrigerator door, she was relieved by the restoration of near darkness. Taking a sip of the cold milk, with only the smallest regret that it *was* only milk, she turned to head back to her bedroom when the glow of the recharging phones caught her eye.

They were resting on the counter at the far end of the kitchen, next to the microwave.

I'm up. I might as well check them out.

Changing course, she set her glass down on the counter and picked up the nearest phone. It was hot pink, some brand she couldn't make out in the darkness. Flipping it open, she saw immediately that it was recharged and ready to go. A push of a button told her that it held seven new messages.

Jess was just getting ready to listen to them when the kitchen light came on, startling her so much that she gasped and whirled. In the process, her elbow caught the glass. It crashed to the floor and shattered, showering her feet with an explosion of cold milk and glass.

"What the . . . ?" It was Mark, of course, who stood in the doorway staring at her.

Stumbling back, Jess registered that he was wearing only boxers and looking as hot as only Mark could look, when he barked, *"Don't move."*

But the warning came too late as Jess's foot came down hard on a dagger-like shard of glass.

CHAPTER EIGHTEEN

"Ow!" Her face twisted with pain.

"Damn it, I said *don't move*."

"You scared me to death!"

Having fallen back against the counter, she shot him an accusing look even as she lifted her foot to check the damage. What she saw made her wince. A sliver of glass about half as long as her little finger stuck out of the ball of her foot just below her second toe. Blood welled around it. She was going to have to pull it out, and she was just bracing herself to do it when Mark, barefoot and maneuvering carefully to avoid both the glass and the spilled milk, reached her.

"Here, let me see." Scooping her up in his arms, Mark stepped back out of the mess with her, then deposited her on the counter a safe distance away. The smooth white Corian felt cold and alien against the backs of her bare thighs, giving her a moment of acute self-awareness in which she registered that the lavender sleep shirt she was wearing was *all* she was wearing, and it had ridden up to dangerous heights.

With Mark wrapping his hand around her ankle and lifting her wounded foot so that he could inspect it, there wasn't a whole lot she could do on the order of yanking her hem down. A quick glance reassured her that she was at least minimally decent. All that was on display were her slim bare legs.

He touched the ball of her foot with a gentle thumb.

"Yow. Be careful."

"What the hell were you doing in the kitchen in the middle of the night anyway?"

"I couldn't sleep. I got some milk."

He rolled his eyes. "You ever hear of turning on the light first? Then maybe I wouldn't have had to get up to check what all the stealthy activity going on in the kitchen was."

"Are you blaming *me*?"

Blood ran across her foot to drip toward the floor now. Just looking at the piece of glass sticking out of her flesh surrounded by all that welling blood made her feel a little light-headed. Wrapping her hands around the smooth edge of the counter for stability, she leaned back against the cabinets behind her and closed her eyes.

"Hold tight."

That was all the warning she got before the grip on her ankle tightened and the glass was yanked out of her foot.

"Ow!" She jackknifed upright. Her eyes flashed open. Her glasses slid down her nose, reminding her that she was wearing them, that her hair was twisted up for sleep, that she had on no makeup except for a little ChapStick. In other words, a sex kitten she wasn't, which was all to the good. Given that the half-naked guy in her kitchen was Mark, she did not want to go there. Pushing her glasses firmly back into place, she looked down at the blood now flowing from the slit in the bottom of her foot, then up at Mark. He was already putting the bloody shard on the counter. Feeling as limp as a soggy noodle, she leaned back against the cabinets again and watched as he grabbed some paper towels from the holder, then pressed them to the bottom of her foot.

"That hurt," she added belatedly.

"I'm sorry." Cradling her foot in one hand, he stanched the blood as best he could, then lifted the wad of paper towels away to inspect the damage, then stanched some more.

"Just so we're clear, this is all *your* fault. If you hadn't startled me, I wouldn't have knocked over the glass." Her breathing was normalizing now, and some of the wooziness was starting to fade.

"Fine. I take full responsibility, okay?"

That took the wind out of her sails. "You know perfectly well it wasn't your fault."

"Yeah, I know. Does it still hurt?"

Jess almost said no out of habit, but then she opted for honesty. "A little."

His mouth thinned. "You're lucky it's not too deep. Do you still have that first-aid kit in your bathroom?"

"Yes."

Looping more paper towels around her foot in rough approximation of a bandage, he said, "Let's go."

He scooped her up again, which didn't surprise her because that was how Mark operated, taking advantage of her lack of size to cart her around pretty much at will. She curled an arm around his neck as he carried her down the dark hall toward her bedroom, then she found herself disturbed by how automatic the action seemed. She was feeling recovered enough by this time to notice again that he was naked except for his boxers, and all those firm muscles covered in warm flesh felt just exactly the way she remembered them.

Sexy as hell.

He smelled sexy, too. Warmly masculine, with the merest hint of Grace's gardenia-scented soap.

Completely against her will, Jess felt her heartbeat quicken.

"Hit the light, would you?" he asked, and she realized that they had gone through her dark bedroom to the bathroom beyond. Her hand brushed the cool tile wall as she did as he requested. The resultant brilliant illumination gave the phrase "blinded by the light" a whole new meaning, but she welcomed the brightness as an antidote to her sudden acute awareness of him. Or at least, she thought it might serve as an antidote until he sat her down on the vanity's wide counter and she looked up at him.

He met her gaze, his eyes very blue in the unforgiving light. His hair was ruffled with sleep, and stubble darkened his jaw. The magenta boxers he wore rendered him minimally decent, but they left way too much of him bare for her peace of mind. Broad, well-muscled shoulders loomed above her, and if she refused to look at them she could instead let her eyes rest on a wide chest with a thick wedge of light brown hair, or sculpted arms, or a truly impressive six-pack punctuated by his belly button and, just an inch or so lower down, bisected by the boxer's waistband. Lower than that she refused to allow her eyes to wander, although she knew without needing to look what was there. Lean hips, long, powerful legs, well-shaped feet.

I want him.

The thought came out of nowhere. Jess set her teeth. But there was nothing she

could do about her pulse, which was going crazy, or her body, which was starting
to heat.

He turned on the faucet, then pulled the
paper towel swaddling off her foot.

"Put your foot under the water."

Scooting around, glad of the distraction,
she did as he told her, thrusting her foot
beneath the rush of cool water shooting
into the sink while he opened the medicine
cabinet. Tugging at her shirt again, Jess
got a good look at herself in the mirror on
the open cabinet door while he rummaged
around inside. Her glasses were big and
black, their coke-bottle lenses slightly
magnifying her eyes, and they dominated
her small face. Her hair was falling down
from the twist she had pinned it into so
that wavy blond tendrils caressed her
cheeks and neck and all but covered the
bruise on her temple. Her mouth was pale
and soft from the ChapStick. The hollow of
her neck and her delicate collarbone were
just visible above the neck of her sleep
shirt, which was loose fitting and comfortable and that was about it.

The blond hair helped, she supposed,
but the sad truth was, *smokin' hot* wasn't

the first descriptive phrase that came to mind when she looked at her reflection. Try kinda cute, sorta wholesome, and more than a little bit nerdy.

Ouch. Facing the fact that he was the beauty in the room hurt more than her foot.

"Does it feel like there's any glass still in there?" Mark shut the cabinet door with a snap, turned off the water, and picked up her foot again. Luckily, the bleeding seemed to have slowed to an ooze.

"No. Ow. You know, I can do this myself."

That *"Ow"* had come as he'd upended a bottle of hydrogen peroxide over the cut. They both watched white foam bubble up.

"You just want me to go clean up the mess you made in the kitchen."

Jess would have smiled if she hadn't been battling a severe reaction to so much half-naked masculinity. "Seriously. I can. If you'll get out of here, I will."

"You know how to do a butterfly bandage?"

"No."

"Then sit there and let me do it."

He patted her foot dry with the discarded paper towels as he spoke. Left with nothing to say, Jess watched, wincing a little, as he dabbed antibiotic ointment on the cut, then pulled the edges together by deft use of a pair of Band-Aids. His hands looked big and dark against her pale foot, but his touch was gentle. Leaning back against the cool hardness of the white tile wall, she absorbed the concentration in his expression, the play of muscles in his arms and chest as he moved, the smooth tan of his skin.

And her stupid, stupid heart beat faster yet.

"How does that feel?" He looked up, caught her staring. His eyes took on a gleam that she recognized with alarm. The problem was, Mark knew her too well. She glanced hastily down at her foot.

"F-fine. Better."

"You're going to be limping tomorrow."

"I know. Damn it."

Determined to be done with this, Jess swung her legs around in preparation for scooting off the counter. The problem inherent with that became evident only after she had done it: the movement brought her way too close to Mark. Her arm and shoulder butted right up against his warm, bare chest, her hand, which was gripping the edge of the counter, came in contact with his boxers, and her legs and dangling feet brushed his legs. All this unwanted sensory stimulation burst on her without warning. As she registered the soft tickle of his chest hair against her arm, the smooth texture of his boxers against her knuckles, the hard strength of his legs against her calf and foot, her body tightened deep inside in a way she remembered all too well.

Oh, no.

"I think it's the glasses." Mark's tone was thoughtful as with his index finger he pushed her glasses, which had once again slipped down her nose a little, back into place. She could feel his gaze on her face.

"What's the glasses?" Barely daring to glance up at him for fear of what he might read in her eyes, Jess stealthily inched away from him along the counter. Once she'd put enough distance between them, she would slide down and run—no, hop, which she feared might lose something in the execution—away.

"That do it for me."

It took Jess an instant to process that. Then, caught by surprise, she looked sharply up at him.

"Tell me you're not coming on to me."

His expression turned equal parts rueful and amused. God, he looked good standing there. Damn genetic predispositions anyway.

"I guess that depends on what would happen if I am."

Her heart knocked against her ribs.

"I don't have time for this." Her tone was astringent, her eyes hard, but she didn't slide off the counter. She'd even quit inching away. "Enough. I have to go to bed now so I can get up and go to work in the morning."

This time he smiled right into her eyes.

"Going to bed works for me," he said agreeably, and without any more warning than that leaned over and kissed her.

It started out as a gentle kiss, soft and testing, but then he parted her lips and licked into her mouth and she went up in flames. After a single deep, shuddering breath that served as the last dying gasp of her resistance, her hands clenched around the edges of the counter, her head relaxed into the big hand that came up to cradle the back of her head, and her mouth molded to his. She kissed him back like she was starving for him, which, she realized deep inside, she was. Wrapping her arms around his neck, meeting his tongue with hers, she responded to the heat and hunger of his mouth with a blazing passion of her own. He kissed her like he was dying for the taste of her mouth, hot deep kisses that made her go all light-headed and weak-kneed and shivery inside. When he moved, shifting positions so that he was standing in front of her, his hip bones nudging her knees, she opened her legs to let him get closer still. Then she went dizzy at the feel of the hard contours of his hips against the soft insides of her thighs. His hands closed on her bottom—which, she noted dazedly, was still covered by her nightshirt, probably because she was sitting on the hem of it—and pulled her against him. Shivering, she felt the hard urgency of him brushing her nakedness, with only the crisp cotton of his boxers between them. She nestled more firmly against him, and the resultant searing heat made her bones seem to melt.

"Ah, God," he said, lifting his mouth from hers. Jess only became aware that her eyes had been closed when they blinked open to take in the hot glitter in his and the deep flush that had risen to stain his cheekbones. His face looked taut and hard, his mouth sensuous, and her blood turned to steam just from looking at him. An electric tension arced between them, and suddenly she was breathless. When she realized that he was tugging at her nightshirt, pulling it out from under her, she had one stark moment of clarity in which she knew she was going to regret this, knew she was going to be sorry—and then she helped him, lifting her arms so the garment could come off. When whisking her nightshirt over her head knocked her glasses askew, she took them off and laid them on the counter, out of harm's way, with unsteady hands. When she turned back, he was slightly blurry, which was good because what the tiny part of her mind that was still functioning wanted to do was pretend this was only a dream, one of the hundreds of sexual fantasies she'd had starring herself and Mark since she had first laid eyes on him all those months ago. What was happening wasn't real, she wasn't this stupid, she couldn't make this big a mistake again: that's what she tried to tell herself, only she couldn't.

Because Mark was right there in front of her, solid and strong against her and hard with wanting her and absolutely real. She was real. The dark, pulsing thrill that was building inside her was real.

God, I want this.

That was the sad and simple truth: she burned for Mark. Burned for sex with Mark.

He was looking at her body, a long, lingering look, taking in her small, high breasts with their dainty pink nipples and her tiny waist and her slim hips as if he couldn't get enough of looking at her, and from the set of his mouth and the heaviness of his lids she knew that he was as turned on as she was.

"Son of a bitch."

Jess blinked in surprise, but his hand gently touching her side answered the question before she had a chance to ask it: he was reacting to the bruise on her rib cage.

"I'll live," she told him. But the sudden

huskiness of her voice carried a separate message, too.

His eyes came up to meet hers. They were bright with desire, aflame with wanting her.

In response, her body quaked and clenched and she felt a dazzling rush of heat.

"You know what else does it for me?" His voice was thick now. His eyes holding hers, he fondled her breasts, his hands warm and possessive.

Jess shook her head. "What?" She could barely get the word out. He cupped a breast, then bent his head until his mouth hovered just a warm breath above her nipple, which was already pebble-hard from his ministrations.

"Your pretty tits. Your sweet . . ." He broke off as he drew her nipple into his mouth, but his hand sliding between her legs gave her an explicit demonstration of what he meant. Jess closed her eyes and clutched his shoulders and cried out as he touched her where she yearned to be touched, the way she yearned to be touched.

The thrill of it was indescribable. It made her pant. It made her wet.

"Oh."

"Tell me how much you like it."

She felt heat flood her cheeks. Trembling, knowing he was watching her, she kept her eyes closed as he did it again. But telling him was exciting, too.

"I like it—a lot. *Oh.*"

The thing was, he knew what turned her on. He had her squirming, and gasping, and arching her back for him, and kissing his mouth when it wasn't busy elsewhere, and planting little urgent kisses along his bristly jawline and neck and across the broad expanse of his shoulder when it was. She was helpless with desire, totally his, totally responsive as he sucked and delved and played. Then, when he replaced his fingers with himself and came inside her, huge and hard and hot, she cried out at the pleasure of it even as his mouth closed over hers and stopped the sound with his kiss.

What they were doing felt so good, so incredibly, satisfyingly right, that she was lost to it, abandoning all inhibition in the throes of the fierce, primal lust that had her wrapping her legs around his waist and digging her nails into his back and responding to each urgent thrust with hungry movements of her own.

She let him take her like that, naked on her bathroom counter, his mouth everywhere, his hands everywhere, his body possessing hers completely, and reveled in every erotic thing they did together. Her body clutched and burned and throbbed and spiraled ever higher, ever tighter, as she gave him back kiss for kiss and caress for caress.

In the end, when he had her absolutely mindless with ecstasy, when he rocked into her with fierce, deep thrusts that drove her over the edge, she came with a fiery urgency that made her body convulse around him and skyrockets burst in a series of brilliant explosions against her closed lids.

"Mark, Mark, Mark, *oh, Mark.*"

"Jess." He groaned her name, came deep and hard inside her one last time, and found his own release.

Nirvana lasted about a minute. Okay, maybe two. Then reality hit, her eyes came open, and the situation became horribly clear.

Wrapped in his arms, she was clinging to Mark as if he'd been a tree and she'd been a monkey and there had been a hurricane, and they were sweaty and sated and still joined together and . . .

He was looking at her.

CHAPTER NINETEEN

"You're beautiful," Mark said, and he smiled that slow, sexy smile that God must have expressly designed to make strong women melt.

She narrowed her eyes at him.

"You're squashing me." She pushed at his shoulders, wriggled to be free. "Let me up."

Panic was already building inside her, and her tone bordered on sharp.

What have I done?

Because she could feel it all starting to come back, the magic, the bedazzlement, the infatuated high-school-girl-like devotion she'd felt for him before, when she'd been totally under his spell. The kind of *I'm so in love* feeling that could break her heart.

Been there, done that, not ever making myself that vulnerable again.

She fought to beat the panic back.

"O-kay."

Uncoupling was awkward. Bright fluorescent light bathing two naked people who'd just had great sex, one of whom was sitting on a bathroom counter with her feet dangling some inches off the floor feeling ticked off at herself while the other one watched her like a hawk zeroing in on a mouse, did not for a graceful dismount make. She slid off the counter, discovering in the process that bare flesh didn't slide all that well. She landed on both feet, winced, then shifted her full weight to her uninjured foot. Since being naked was not conducive to dignity and her nightshirt was on the floor out of reach, she pulled a fluffy blue towel from the rack and wrapped it around herself.

She retrieved her glasses, but her nightshirt was too far away. She would have had to go around him to get to it, and she really wanted to get this over with.

Putting her glasses on, she said, "I'm going to bed now. Good-night."

Limping, she escaped into the bedroom. Her dresser was against the wall opposite the bed. Pulling open a drawer, she extracted another nightshirt and turned around to find him standing in the doorway between her bathroom and bedroom. He was wearing his boxers, thank God. The bathroom light was still on behind him, making his face impossible to read.

"I take it that wasn't make-up sex." His voice was dry.

She finally looked him in the face. "No."

"Want to tell me what the hell it was, then?"

Her chin came up. "Just sex."

"Is that right?"

"You have a problem with that?"

"You don't do 'just sex.'"

Her lips compressed. "Maybe I'm taking a page out of your book. Maybe I just chalked up notch number two thousand seven hundred and three on my bedpost."

"That's bullshit and you know it."

"Look, do we have to talk this thing to death? I'm tired, and I'd like to go to bed."

"Alone." One shoulder leaned against

the jamb as he folded his arms over his chest and seemed to study her.

"Yes."

"I'm going to say it one more time, and this is the last time I'm ever going to say it: I did not sleep with Mary Jane Cates. Or with anyone else while we were together. What happened was, she kissed me, and I kissed her back. But that's all."

This would have been a lot easier if she'd pretended she absolutely did not believe him. But it also wouldn't have been fair.

Reluctantly she said, "I asked her about that yesterday."

"You *asked* her? What did you ask her?"

"Whether she initiated that kiss I saw. And whether that kiss was all there was."

"What did she say?" He sounded slightly fascinated now.

"She said that's what you *would* say if you were trying to convince me."

"Goddamn it." He straightened away from the doorjamb, and she thought he was going to come toward her.

"Wait." Jess held up a hand to hold him off. "You know what? Now that I've cooled off some, now that I've had time to think about it, now that I've talked to Cates, I believe you. Well, enough to give you the benefit of the doubt. There, I said it. But even if I do, that doesn't change a thing."

"You want to explain that to me?" There was a dangerous note to his voice now.

"I don't want to be in a relationship. Not with you, not with anybody. For one thing, I don't have time for one in my life right now. You said it yourself: my job is very demanding and I mean to work hard at it. And—and we're basically incompatible, you and I."

"I thought we just demonstrated that we are very compatible."

"There's more to a relationship than sex, Mark."

He stared at her for a moment. "You have got to be kidding me. Fine. At least now we're down to the truth. You don't want to be in a relationship. Baby, I'm hearing you loud and clear this time." He moved then, heading toward the bedroom door. "You get horny again, I'll be on the couch."

Her temper started to ignite. "You know, I don't think I want you on my couch. I think I want you to leave."

"Tough shit," he said, then added, "catch"

as he tossed something at her. Her night-shirt, she realized as her fingers closed around it.

For a moment she simply stood there, listening as he stalked away and threw himself down on the couch. She was experiencing a whole kaleidoscope of emotions, of which anger and regret were the most recognizable. Mark was being a jackass, she told herself. But then the part of her that was always inconveniently, scrupulously honest faced the truth: *maybe you're being a jackass, too.*

If she was, she couldn't help it. Some women might have been able to forgive an illicit kiss. She could not. She'd made her choice, and even through the pain it was causing her, she knew it was the only one she could live with. This relatively small pain would be nothing compared to the huge, shattering agony that allowing herself to love him with all her heart could lead to. She might have a fatal tendency to be attracted to dangerously good-looking men, but that didn't mean she had to give in to it. Like someone with a genetic tendency toward alcoholism, she could ward off disaster by refusing to walk that path.

She might be her mother's daughter, but she didn't have to relive her mother's life.

He was pissed. Mark finally acknowledged it at about 5:00 a.m. when he gave up trying to sleep and got up, got dressed, put on a pot of coffee, and got to work instead. Being kicked to the curb twice by a woman he was crazy about was not an experience he enjoyed, he discovered. Especially when he knew damned well—well, he thought he knew—that she was in love with him. Granted, he'd made a major mistake kissing MJ, but one mistake shouldn't have been enough to destroy a relationship as special as his and Jess's had been. It had been a *kiss* (okay, a hot, salacious kiss), not an affair, which he had since explained, repented, and promised not to repeat. Not a deal breaker, or at least it shouldn't have been. Except for the fact that Jess was emotionally fucked up, of course.

He kept telling himself, *A woman who's as emotionally fucked up as that is a woman I don't need in my life.* Problem was, he hadn't quite convinced himself yet.

The worst thing about it was, it was an

own goal. He'd done it to himself. The whole sorry-ass debacle was his fault entirely. Including tonight's blazing-hot encounter.

When he'd heard those noises in the kitchen, he should have just stayed on the damned couch.

What made it all the more frustrating was that he couldn't just cut his losses and walk away. Pissed or not, he was stuck with her, stuck on this way-too-personal protective duty, until he, or the deep-cover Service investigators assigned to the case, or the D.C. Police Department, whoever got there first, figured out who had attacked her. Not being a glutton for punishment, he would otherwise take her latest kiss-off as the blessing in disguise it undoubtedly was and move on. Plenty of very pretty fish in the sea, and all that. But for now, he was locked into being an on-loan consultant for Ellis Hayes with the primary mission of keeping Jess alive while the Secret Service busted a gut trying to figure out if some clandestine cov-ops hit squad had her in its sights. Hasbrough had pulled some strings to get him inside her law firm. Mark had asked for the assignment, he'd gotten it—of course he had, who better than him, who not only knew the truth but was in the crosshairs right along with Jess?—and now he had his own first-floor office at Ellis Hayes. Said office was right down the hall from the office of the head of security, Ed Lally, a former FBI agent whom he knew and who kept congratulating him on his move up to corporate America with its big-time salaries and commensurate perks.

If Lally said "Ka-ching" to him one more time when they passed in the hall, Mark was afraid he was going to lose it.

Although maybe corporate America was something he ought to be thinking about. When Annette Cooper had gotten killed on his watch, it had pretty much put paid to his Secret Service career as he had known it. He was still on the payroll, still doing a damned good job in the Service's investigative arm, but he was starting to recognize that his heart was no longer in it. Working the White House security detail had been an adrenaline rush, a high-wire act where one misstep could prove fatal. Investigating crimes was a worthy endeavor, but it lacked thrill.

Just putting in his time until he qualified

for a government pension might not work for him.

The government wasn't paying him enough to spend the next twenty-some-odd years riding a desk, bored to tears.

He had his daughter to think of, too. In the next few years, besides college expenses, which he hadn't been kidding about, Taylor was going to be wanting a car, and maybe some more trips like the school-sponsored excursion to Italy she was hoping to be able to go on next summer, and possibly grad school, and for sure, one day, a wedding for which he would be expected to pay.

He was a highly trained operative with an impressive set of skills. So maybe he ought to start seriously considering looking for a private-sector job that appreciated those skills, a job with a big-time salary and a boatload of perks. Maybe it was time to get out and cash in. Maybe he should go for Lally's *ka-ching*.

Since an injury had forced him out of pro football at the age of twenty-two, he'd been working for the government in one capacity or another. But when he'd cast in his lot with Jess, when he'd stepped in to protect her instead of looking the other way while she was killed, he had made enemies of some of the world's most dangerous people.

If Jess had a target on her back, he did, too.

There was no going back for either of them.

Finding himself on the wrong side of the government he'd sworn to serve and protect was a new experience. He didn't like it, but he was starting to get the hang of it. New game, new rules.

Feeling like he'd just been used for sex was a new experience, too, and another one he didn't like. Usually the woman he was with was the one angling for commitment. Usually he was the one wanting fun with no strings.

Payback's a bitch, as they say.

His thoughts didn't please him. His mood verged on savage as he checked his e-mail via his iPhone and discovered that the information he'd been waiting for had been sent overnight. In the absence of footprints, fingerprints, any kind of physical evidence at the scene that might have been used to identify the bastard who'd attacked Jess, he'd reached out to the digital age's best friend: security cameras.

The only one on Jess's street was up by the bus stop. It hadn't captured anything of interest. But by searching in concentric circles from her building out, and gradually broadening the area of the search, they'd found something. A camera at a drugstore four blocks away had captured someone tossing a bundle into a Dumpster some five minutes after the attack. The image itself wasn't all that useful: the shot only included a sliver of the man's face, his right hand, and maybe a third of his forearm. But the technicians the Secret Service employed were the best in the business. If anybody could get anything from a picture like that, they could.

Better still, they had searched for the bundle in the dump where the refuse from that particular Dumpster had been taken. The message on his phone was: *found it.* The accompanying picture showed a black turtleneck, black balaclava-type ski mask, and a pair of black leather gloves laid carefully out on top of a plastic grocery bag. He had no doubt that what he was seeing held DNA evidence galore.

Looking at it, Mark sent a mental message to the unknown assailant: *You're mine, asshole.*

Then he called Randy Rothenberg, his contact in the forensic pathologist's office.

"Are you nuts, Ryan? It's six thirty in the morning," was how Rothenberg answered the phone.

"What can I say? The Service never sleeps. I need to know what you've got on the Cowan case."

The sound of a yawn came over the phone. "We're still doing toxicology tests."

"I don't give a damn about toxicology tests. I know you've had time to get a pretty good feel for cause of death. Did Cowan shoot himself or not?"

"At this time, anything I could tell you would be preliminary."

"So give me preliminary."

"The residue on his right hand says yes. The trajectory of the bullet through the skull is more problematic. The angle doesn't seem quite natural, but we're still running it through the computer, going through various scenarios, that kind of thing, to see if we can work it out."

"What's your best guess?"

"I'm a scientist. I don't do best guesses."

"Remember when we were in Mexico, and I got your sorry ass out of jail?"

"You're never going to let me live that down, are you? All right, you want my best informed judgment at this preliminary stage of the investigation. No, I don't think he shot himself. But until all the tests are complete, I can't be sure."

"Shit."

When Mark disconnected, he was feeling grim.

He and Jess might be over. Hell, he might even be glad they were over. But that was personal. As a professional, he was going to stick to her like a tick on a dog until he could be sure that, when he walked away, she would be safe.

When he'd gotten the call about Leonard Cowan, his first stop had been Rock Creek Park. Cowan's car had still been parked in the overlook where it had been found. Since it had been getting on toward noon, the heat had been oppressive. The smell of putrid meat, the death smell which over the years he had learned to instantly recognize, had hit him even before he had ducked under the yellow crime scene tape roping off the area. Uniforms and a couple of plainclothes detectives had still been on the scene, and a police photographer had been taking pictures, although the body had been removed. Flies had swarmed in a buzzing black cloud above the roof of the blue car. At first he'd thought the driver's side window had been tinted black. Then he'd gotten close enough to realize that the glass had been coated with blood.

"Cause of death?" he'd asked, flashing his badge at the detective who'd approached him.

"Gunshot wound to the head."

A gunshot wound precise enough so that there hadn't even been any splatter on the windshield. A professional hit, had been his thought then, and it was his thought now.

If his suspicions were correct, he was all that stood between that kind of death and Jess.

Which meant, bottom line, that he wasn't going anywhere. No way, no how.

"What do we do now?" Jaden stared in horror at the flyer taped to the wall of the metro station.

"Get out of here," Lucy whispered urgently, because that was obviously the first thing they needed to do.

MISSING was written across the top of the flyer in big, bold black letters. Beneath it were side-by-side photos of herself and Jaden with their names and other information below the pictures. Lucy recognized them: they were the ones that had been shot for their ID photos when they'd first been taken to Shelter House, which meant they were nice and current and all that.

Skinny, black-haired Goths like Jaden might have been pretty common on the streets of the city, but her own frizzy red hair stuck out like a blowtorch on a dark night.

Fear made Lucy sick to her stomach.

"If he's seen these, he knows who we are. He knows our names." The words burst out of Lucy's mouth seconds after the realization hit her brain. The knowledge petrified her. She heard Jaden suck in air. Her friend's face went white as death. Her eyes looked like two big black holes in the middle of it.

Lucy didn't have to explain who "he" was. Both of them knew: Miss Howard's killer.

"Do you think he has?" Jaden's voice was unsteady.

"I don't know." Lucy swallowed. "Come on. Keep your head down."

Heart pounding, rigid with tension, feeling as if every eye in the busy metro station had been on them, Lucy linked her arm with Jaden's and held her to a hopefully casual-looking walk as they headed for the escalator. It was still real early in the morning—6:42 a.m. according to the big digital clock above the train schedules—but this was the heart of the city and there were a lot of people around. Lucy would have thought that was a good thing if her and Jaden's faces hadn't been taped up all over the walls.

As it was, she expected somebody to grab them at any minute.

"I want to go home," Jaden whispered as they rode to the street. Her mouth quivered. Her eyes as they met Lucy's were shiny with tears.

"Yeah, I know."

But they both knew that wasn't happening. Home wasn't there anymore, not for either of them. Jaden's mom, having had four different fathers for her four children, three of whom were currently in the system, was in jail on drug charges. Lucy's mom had taken off when Lucy was five, leaving her with her grandmother. The grandmother had died three years ago, putting Lucy in foster care. Both their dads were missing in action. Lucy didn't even know who hers was. Her mom's hair was dark brown, so every time she saw an old guy with red hair she checked him out. What she wanted to ask was: *am I your kid?*

"I don't feel good," Jaden muttered. She looked almost skeletal in the gray early morning light, Lucy thought, like a character out of that movie *The Nightmare Before Christmas.*

"You want to sit down or something?" There was a park across the street with benches in front of it, so that was possible, but Jaden shook her head, which was probably a good thing. Besides the fact that they needed to get off the streets, there were mountains of dark clouds piling up overhead. The air was heavy, thick. Even as Lucy glanced up, a rumble of thunder warned of a storm to come.

Mother Mary, she wanted to be some-place safe more than she had ever wanted anything in her life.

They'd been on the run all night, first to elude the police chase that had resulted when they'd bolted away from that cop, then dodging through the streets and al-leys as they'd tried to get out of College Park altogether. With sixty-two dollars and forty-nine cents left between them, there hadn't been many places they could have gone. Finally they'd chanced the metro, feeling like they'd wanted to jump out of their skins until they'd been were safely on the train. They'd ridden aimlessly for a while until Jaden had had the bright idea of going to see if one of her past stepdads would take them in. Lucy hadn't thought it had been the best idea ever, because the ex-stepdad might turn them in, or some-body might come looking for them there, but she hadn't had anything better to offer and, anyway, she'd been too tired to ar-gue. So they had gotten off at Farragut North, and now they were walking along M Street to the ex-stepdad's apartment a couple of blocks over. Not that Jaden had talked to him in like five years, but she said it didn't matter: he would take them in if he was there.

Lucy thought that was a pretty big "if," but she didn't say so. Her alternative plan was to crash in one of the tunnels that ran beneath the city, where colonies of the homeless camped. Their long-term plan was still California Dreamin', but it required both ID's and cash, neither of which they had. After a sleepless night, they were both so exhausted that they were almost punch-drunk, plus hungry, and dirty, and a hundred other bad things as well. Jaden kept getting dizzy, which made her stagger like she was drunk. Lucy was worried about her, but she was worried about herself, too.

At least the furnace room in the basement of the apartment building across the street from the Quik-Stop in College Park, where'd they'd holed up for most of the last week, had been a place to crash.

Now finding a place to hide was urgent. No telling how many of those flyers were out there, or where they were. Anybody could have seen them. Anybody—just some random person they passed by—could recognize them and call the cops.

Maybe they should go to the cops. They'd be in a world of trouble and probably be separated and locked up until they were twenty-one at least, but at least they'd be alive. If Miss Howard's killer caught up with them, they'd be dead.

Maybe he wasn't even still looking for them. Maybe he'd just run away, putting as many miles between himself and the murder scene as possible. Maybe . . .

A familiar neon sign caught her eye.

"Look." It was a Quik-Stop, on the corner across the street. Lucy's stomach growled at the sight of it. She supposed it was conditioned now, like Pavlov's dog.

Jaden's mouth drooped at the corners. "I can't eat anything."

"Well, I can."

Jaden's step was slow as Lucy pulled her across the crosswalk. Lucy left Jaden outside, leaning wearily against the red-brick wall as she went in to claim their daily coffee-and-doughnut ration. The one she picked out was chocolate-covered, with cream filling, because she figured it had the most calories. Just looking at it made her mouth water. The smell was so good that she could practically taste it. Saliva pooled in her mouth. Not even realizing that she was licking her lips every time she looked at it, she set it down carefully on one of the little squares of waxed paper the store provided as she filled a Styrofoam cup with coffee. She loaded the coffee with sugar and creamer.

When she came back out of the store, carefully carrying her prizes, Jaden was gone.

It was just after 7:00 a.m. when Jess emerged from her bedroom. She had showered, being careful not to get her injured foot wet so as not to disturb the bandage Mark had rigged up. She'd also taken another dose of Advil, put in her contacts, and dressed in a charcoal gray pantsuit with a black tee. She wasn't in the best of moods, which, given the events of the previous night, wasn't really a surprise. Her feeling of general grumpiness, however, was something she was determined to hide, because it might have made it seem as if her bad mood had somehow been related to Mark. Which it wasn't, because he had no power to influence her moods, because the two of them were over, last night's unfortunate aberration notwithstanding. Just like they had been over before.

Only this time she meant to make it stick.

No further drama required. She walked— well, limped—toward her kitchen as if last night had never happened. When his blue eyes flicked in her direction, she did not scowl at Mark, who was sitting on her couch fully dressed except for his jacket, with his cell phone in his hand as he apparently checked his e-mail. She merely glanced at him with untroubled serenity and went into the kitchen to grab a cup of coffee, which she would have thanked him for making except she knew him: he needed his coffee in the morning, too. So it was not like he had made it especially for her. It was simply Mark taking care of Mark, which was how she wanted it to be.

As if to underline that, today he hadn't done anything about breakfast. But he had cleaned up the glass and spilled milk from the night before, so she owed him a thank-you for that, which she would deliver, with dignity, later. As she poured herself a cup of coffee, visions of what the mess had led to assaulted her, and her body tightened and tingled in reflexive response. Determinedly she fought the unwelcome memories off.

Spotting the cell phones she'd left on the counter provided a welcome distraction. Coffee in hand, she picked the hot pink one up, flipped it open, and pushed the Play Message button.

Then she listened, one by one, to seven messages. The first thing she learned was that the phone was Lucy's, and most of the messages were from a kennel where she had apparently worked just before she had found herself at Shelter House. Four in a row, they were all demands to know where she was and when she would be in to work. The fifth message was from the manager, firing her. The sixth message was from a girl named Amanda. Amanda wanted to know if Lucy wanted to hang out.

It was the seventh message that made Jess catch her breath.

"Hi, Mom, it's Allison. I'm getting married! Can you believe it? His name is Greg and we're eloping to Las Vegas tonight. I'll

call you in a couple of days with the details, okay? Talk to you later. Bye."

Jess stared at the phone in surprise.
The message was only a little over three
weeks old. The name that came up on the
caller ID was Allison Howard.

CHAPTER TWENTY

"Mark."

Mark was on his feet when Jess hurried out of the kitchen, her eyes bright with excitement, a cell phone in each hand. After one comprehensive glance that took in her entire, unharmed person, he turned expressionless. Instead of answering, he merely lifted his eyebrows at her. Okay, clearly he was still feeling a little hostile toward her. At the moment she had more important matters on her mind.

"Allison Howard called Lucy." She waved the pink phone. "Listen to this."

She played the message for him.

He looked unimpressed. "Sounds to me like she called a wrong number. Or did you miss that whole 'Hi, Mom' thing?"

Jess blinked at him, taken aback. She hadn't thought of that.

"A wrong number? Yes, I guess it could be. But what are the chances of *that*? That Allison Howard would call a wrong number, and that number would happen to belong to runaway teenager Lucy Peel's cell phone."

"I've got no idea. But that's the simplest explanation, and usually the simplest explanation is the right one." He picked his jacket up from the back of the couch. Today's suit was navy pinstripe, the shirt white and the tie red. With his jaw set and his mouth grim, he looked every inch the on-duty fed. Of course, the shoulder holster helped, too.

"It just seems so unlikely . . ."

"Unless your missing teenager is doing a Benjamin Button number and aging backward, a wrong number is what it has to be, because it's not possible that she's your vanishing woman's mom." He shrugged into his jacket.

"You're being deliberately dismissive of this, aren't you?"

"And why would I do that?"

"Because you're still mad at me about the whole no-relationship thing."

"Believe me, the idea of you and me in a relationship leaves me cold. I've already moved on."

"So why won't you admit that this is important?"

"Important how? Face it, Jess, your imagination's running wild again." Her purse and laptop case were on the floor beside the coffee table, where she had dropped them the previous night. He picked those up, too, and handed them to her. "You ready to go?"

Even as she accepted the items, Jess divined his meaning and looked at him indignantly. "What do you mean, my imagination's running wild again? Are you by any ill-advised chance alluding to my seeing Allison Howard in my office yesterday morning?"

"Seeing her vanish, you mean?" He was shepherding her out the door as he spoke. "Baby, that's only the latest, greatest example."

Heading down the stairs, Jess bristled. "Maybe if you had a little more imagination, you'd see that the kind of coincidence that has Allison Howard mistakenly calling Lucy Peel's cell phone is what's not possible."

"If you can come up with an explanation besides a wrong number for your vanishing woman calling a teenage girl 'Mom,' I'm all ears."

Jess pushed out of the door and headed across the stoop and down the sidewalk, thinking furiously all the while. Lightning flashed overhead, and she glanced up to find that the sky was ominously dark and low. The smell of rain was in the air, which was hot and sticky even so early in the morning. The Suburban was parked conveniently close, thank God.

"Can't think of one, can you?" He beeped the doors open.

"I'm working on it." She was all the way in the Suburban and the door had slammed shut behind her before it occurred to her that he'd walked around to open it for her. The unsettling ramifications of that had her narrowing her eyes at him as he got in beside her. "And what part of 'we're not a couple any more' did you miss?"

Starting the car and pulling away from

the curb, he looked at her like she'd lost her mind. "What the hell are you talking about now?"

"You opened the door for me."

A quick flash of consciousness crossed his face. He knew what she meant, she could tell.

"Well, gosh, golly gee, let me apologize for that. But before you let your imagination run totally away with you again, I want to point out that I came around to your side of the car and opened the door just to make sure there wasn't anybody hiding over there out of my sight waiting to try to kill you."

"You didn't open the door for me yesterday."

"Probably because we were in a crowded section of the city where there would be all kinds of witnesses to notice somebody crouching on the far side of the car with a weapon waiting to kill you."

Silence reigned as Jess digested that.

"Oh," she said.

"Try to get your mind around the fact that I'm just doing my job here." His profile could have been carved out of granite. His hands gripped the wheel with a little more tension than usual. Looking at those bronzed, long-fingered hands, Jess had a flashback to the way they had touched her last night. Her body quickened, her breath caught, and heat flooded her veins. Glancing instantly away, Jess gave herself a mental kick. *Over and done with, remember?* Big fat drops of rain plopped down on the windshield, creating a welcome distraction. A moment later, the world beyond the windshield blurred as rain began to fall in earnest. Mark turned the lights on, the windshield wipers on. The wipers' gentle swish, coupled with the darkness and the roar of the rain, made the inside of the Suburban feel like a world unto itself.

A world in which she and Mark were trapped together forever with no possibility of escape.

"I'm getting tired of this," she burst out. "I need this to be over. I want my life back."

"Believe me, you and me both."

They exchanged not another word the rest of the way in to Ellis Hayes.

The good news was, there was no sign of Allison Howard or anyone else when Jess walked into her office. Flipping on the light, crossing to open the blinds, looking around a second time just to make sure she was alone—she absolutely was—Jess felt tension leaving her muscles. Tension she hadn't even realized had been there until all of a sudden it wasn't anymore.

Maybe Mark was right. Maybe I did see Allison's picture somewhere around here.

Whatever, she didn't see Allison today, and that was what mattered.

Jess began her morning with a quick check of her own phone messages—no Tiffany—and a perusal of Lucy's and Jaden's call histories to see if there was anything that jumped out at her as to where the girls might have gone. Nothing did. Likewise, their text messages yielded nothing. She called Tiffany, got her voice mail, left another message. Then it was off to the morning meeting—a regular feature of office life when they weren't working flat-out in imminent preparation for a trial, Jess learned. At present the team was in various stages of preparation for a staggering number of cases, most of which wouldn't come to trial either because some circumstance, such as Yamaguchi's fingering of someone other than their client, prevented it, or because of a plea bargain. Mark put in a brief appearance at the meeting, during which the status and strategy of the Whitney case was discussed, then left again. While he was there, he sat several seats away from Jess and paid her no particular attention. Which, to her own annoyance, Jess found annoying. Especially when Hayley kept eyeing him like he was sex on a stick.

Once back in her office, even in the midst of diving into Allison's files, Jess found herself eyeing Lucy's phone again. Allison's cell phone number was right there in front of her. If she had questions about why Allison had called Lucy, why not go straight to Allison and ask?

She called Allison. The call went straight through to voice mail. Jess left a message explaining who she was, informing Allison that Lucy Peel had run away from Shelter House and they were trying to find her, and asking that Allison call back. Then she sent Allison a text, just in case the memory was full or something, just to be sure her message was getting through.

With no answer forthcoming from that quarter, she placed a quick call to Paloma and told her about the message from Allison on Lucy's cell phone.

"All I can think of is that it must have been a wrong number," Paloma told her, unconsciously echoing Mark. "Maybe Allison's mother's phone number is similar to Lucy's. Or maybe Allison just pressed the wrong automatic dial button on her phone."

"Why would Lucy's number even be in Allison's phone?"

"The girls were allowed to take their phones with them on field trips. That way, if someone got separated, it was easy to contact them. Allison had just gone with a group to tour the Capitol. Lucy and Jaden were part of the group, so Allison probably entered their phone numbers in her phone then."

"That's possible." Even likely, Jess considered. After all, what other explanation could there have been? None that immediately jumped out at her, certainly.

"Have you found anything on their phones that might help us find them?" Paloma asked.

"Not yet," Jess said. "But I'm not very far into it. I'll let you know. And I'll let you know about the lawsuit."

Paloma thanked her, which ended the call.

While the matter was still uppermost in her mind, Jess quickly filed a motion to dismiss Jax Johnson's lawsuit as frivolous, e-mailing it to the appropriate court.

All the while Jess was working, Allison's calendar, with the big red star marking the award luncheon she had missed, was right there on the corner of her desk.

Jess didn't know Allison. But Jess did know that if she had had an engagement that was important enough to mark with a big red star, she wouldn't have forgotten about it. Granted, some things in this world were more important than others, and a honeymoon just might have been enough to make someone cancel a luncheon being given in her honor, but not without letting someone know. Not without giving someone a call.

Looking at Allison's caseload, being impressed with the caliber of Allison's work as she went through the files, Jess learned that Allison had taken her job seriously. She'd been meticulous, detail-oriented, the opposite of sloppy. The type to cross every legal t and dot every legal i.

Forgetting about the awards luncheon seemed out of character. So did just blowing it off.

Pearse stuck his head in Jess's door to tell her that he'd just received a phone call from the DA's office to let him know that Camilla Shively had been indicted for Murder One, and that she would be arrested forthwith. He had made arrangements for her to turn herself in, and he wanted Jess to go with him to collect their client and escort her to the jail, where she would be booked in and then, as soon as bail could be arranged, immediately bailed out.

That made for a particularly eventful morning, especially since Mrs. Shively wept all over Pearse until she was led away for booking. Any lesser lawyer than Pearse wouldn't have been able to manage it, but he arranged to have her bail set and then posted immediately. So Mrs. Shively, weeping still, was back in her fabulous Kalorama mansion before lunchtime. Fortunately, the still-pouring rain seemed to have discouraged the media from coming out. Only a single TV station and a few print reporters were there to witness the event.

"Whew." Pearse looked at Jess as they rode back to the office in the chauffeur-driven limousine in which they'd picked up Mrs. Shively. "We've got our work cut out for us on this one. If we end up going to trial, remind me to tell Christine to pack the jury with doddering old men."

"Do you think it will go to trial?" Jess asked. The limousine was big and luxurious, the seats absurdly plush, and the uniformed driver the touch that put the whole thing right over the top. *I could get used to this.* And then Jess realized, with a little electric thrill, that if she did her job well with Ellis Hayes, and rose through the ranks, she *would* get used to this. The limos, the mansions, the wealthy clients—all the perks of being a high-priced, successful trial lawyer—would become part of her life.

"Not if I can help it," Pearse said grimly, then discussed strategy with Jess all the way back to work.

Jess reentered her office in a thoughtful mood. Sinking into her expensive chair, she looked around with fresh eyes. Her surroundings reeked of good taste; she was now one of the elite, big-time lawyers she had always dreamed of becoming. It was unbelievable, amazing—and it had all fallen into her lap because Allison Howard had gotten married and quit.

Who quit a job like this with a phone message? Worked her tail off to get it, and then just threw it all away on a whim?

For herself, now that she had it, Jess knew they would have to pry the job from her cold, dead hands.

She was getting a feel for Allison by going over her work. She didn't think she and Allison were so very different in that regard. Allison had relished her position with Ellis Hayes.

Would she have walked away for a man?

Jess thought of Mark. If he asked her, would she give up all this to marry him?

Hell, no. Not in this life.

So maybe Mark was the wrong man. Maybe Allison had found somebody incredibly perfect for her, her very own Mr. Right.

Or maybe Allison hadn't just walked away. Jess thought of seeing Allison here in their mutual office, of the red star around the awards luncheon on Allison's appointment calendar. Of Allison's phone call to Lucy.

Something just didn't feel right.

Not your business. She could almost hear Mark saying it. And really, the last thing she wanted to do was get Allison back here trying to reclaim her position at Ellis Hayes.

But . . .

By the end of the day, despite her best intentions, Jess was deep into a background check on Allison. She was up to her eyeballs in other work, work that Pearse assigned her and that Ellis Hayes was paying her a fat six figures to do, so she had to shoehorn in her investigation of Allison. This she did by barely leaving her office, forgoing all but the most necessary breaks and staying in for lunch. By six thirty even she was impressed by how much work she'd managed to turn out.

Especially given the fact that all afternoon she'd sensed what she'd gradually come to think of as Allison's presence. Not that it really was Allison's presence, of course. First, as far as she knew Allison wasn't dead, and, second, Jess didn't believe in things like ghosts anyway. In any case, today the plant remained a plant, and she had no sightings of the former occupant of her office.

But what she did have was a feeling, this constant, pervasive, inescapable feeling, of being watched. While she was in her office, where she was indisputably (she kept looking over her shoulder to make sure) alone. As if someone was standing just behind her, silent and invisible, observing every single thing she did.

The feeling was like a weight in the air.

It was enough to give her the willies. It was enough to make goose bumps rise on her skin. It was enough to make her wish it hadn't been raining, which made the atmosphere faintly gloomy even though she had her lights on at full blaze, and her door ajar.

But the feeling persisted.

She went through all the boxes containing Allison's work files, prioritizing them, doing what she could on the spot and making note of what else needed to be done. She then accessed Allison's online records, which, since they were still stored on the firm's server, were easy enough to get to. At the time she'd left the firm, Allison had been hard at work on the Phillips case, which at that point had been right on the verge of going to trial. She'd been heading out on a weeklong business trip to the Bahamas, where Tiffany Higgs had allegedly spent a wild and wooly weekend just before her fateful encounter with Rob Phillips. No prizes for guessing what Allison had been trying to establish—whether Tiffany had a party girl past, in hopes that it would be admissible—but records from that trip were not on the computer. Probably Allison had put them on her laptop, meaning to transfer them to the office system when she got back. But then she'd never come back, although she had clearly planned to return.

Jess pulled up Allison's personnel file from Human Resources. That was a little tougher to get to, but she managed, because getting into things on the computer was one of her skills. Soon she was perusing the details of Allison's life as seen through her employment history. Allison had been twenty-eight years old and unmarried when she'd come to work at Ellis Hayes, and she'd been there three years. Her next of kin was listed as her mother, Sharon Howard, at a local phone number. When Jess impulsively called it, planning to pretend to be an old friend from college trying to get hold of Allison, instead it produced one Marty Hagman, who claimed never to have heard of Sharon or Allison Howard and didn't know why they'd be using his number, which he claimed to have had for forty years. Unlike the majority of Ellis Hayes's Ivy Leaguers, Allison had attended the University of the District of Columbia (Clarke) Law School, an urban, way un-prestigious local school, on a scholarship. She'd come into the firm just as Jess had, on a part-time basis while still a law student, and worked herself up to full time.

In fact, reading Allison's file, Jess found an unnerving number of parallels to her own life.

It was like the two of them fit a tiny, particular niche in Ellis Hayes's hiring plan: token blue-collar girls, taken on board so that the firm wouldn't be considered hopelessly elitist. Strivers who kept their noses to the grindstone, willing to arrive earlier and stay later than anyone else, workhorses who could be counted on to get the job done.

Call them the anti-divas.

Jess wasn't sure she liked the idea of that. On the other hand, if it was one of the factors that had gotten her hired, hey, she wasn't proud.

Grace called as Jess was worming her way onto Allison's Facebook page. Given the fact that Allison's privacy settings concealed almost all her information from outsiders and Jess wasn't listed as a friend, it was a little problematic, but nothing she couldn't overcome with a few judicious moves.

When Jess answered the phone, then hit the speaker button so that she could continue what she was doing while she talked, Grace greeted her with, "Have I got a gown for you."

"Oh, yeah?" That note in her sister's voice made Jess deeply suspicious.

"Galanos. Gorgeous. Your size, too."

"Is it suitable?"

"It's a dream."

"What color?"

"Come see."

Taking an educated guess regarding Allison, Jess went to the University of the District of Columbia Law School Alumni

Association page and joined it. As she had suspected might be the case, Allison was part of its network. Yee-haw. She was in.

"Bring it home tonight for me to look at, why don't you?" she said to Grace.

Allison had 139 friends, most, from what Jess could tell, professional contacts. Jess started going down the list. She didn't know what she was looking for, precisely, but she was looking. A man named Greg, maybe. If Allison had married him, it seemed likely that he would be her friend.

"Well, um, I might not be coming home tonight." Grace sounded self-conscious. That note in her voice was so unlike Grace that Jess stopped paging down the rows of friends to really listen.

"What? Three nights in a row? With Mr. Divine? That sounds like deathless love."

Grace laughed. "When you see him, you'll totally get it. Will you be all right? I hear Mark's been staying over."

"Where did you hear that?"

"Where do you think?"

"Mom." Jess pegged it with a sigh. Probably somebody had driven by the apartment and seen the Suburban, and the news had flown around the family within the hour. Judy's daughters had no secrets, and they'd pretty much become resigned to it over the years.

"You know how it is. Jungle drums."

Explaining that she and Mark were not together would involve explaining why, then, he was spending the night. Some explanations, Jess decided, were just better not being made.

"Sometimes being a member of this family sucks, you know? Would the world end if everybody just minded her own business?" Her tone wasn't quite caustic, but it was close.

"Probably," Grace said. "Are you coming by the store?"

"How late are you going to be there?"

"Since it's tourist season, we're open till nine."

"I'll be there. And, oh, Gracie, thanks bunches."

"You're welcome," Grace said, and they disconnected.

Not having found a Greg, Jess moved on to Allison's wall, which relieved a worry she hadn't even realized was niggling at the back of her mind. What she had seen in her office couldn't have been Allison's ghost, because Allison was alive and well and regularly updating her Facebook page. Her most recent posting was dated that very morning, Jess was interested to see.

Allison had written: *Having so much fun. This is simply bliss, bliss, bliss, bliss, bliss, bliss, bliss. I may never come home! Love and kisses to all.*

There were more in that vein, six in total since Allison had left for the Bahamas, four of them since she'd wed and embarked on her honeymoon.

She sounded happy.

Jess debated a moment, then sent Allison a message through Facebook: *I'm your replacement, and I have an urgent question about one of your cases. Pls call.* If Allison wouldn't answer her phone . . .

Then Jess had an epiphany. Maybe she could get in touch with Tiffany the same way. Of course, first she had to get to Tiffany's Facebook page. Having had access to reams of information about the alleged victim during the course of Rob Phillips's trial, Jess tried to remember as much about Tiffany as she could. After a couple of busts, she hit pay dirt with Tiffany's high school graduating class's network.

Once again, she was in. She sent Tiffany a message—*I found something of yours I'd like to return*—then went to her wall. The most recent post made her eyebrows twitch together.

"There is such a thing as overdoing it."

Jess was so absorbed that Mark's voice made her jump. Looking up, she found him standing just inside her doorway, frowning at her. Since she'd left her door ajar in an effort to combat the whole it-feels-like-somebody's-watching-me creepiness factor, it wasn't surprising that she hadn't heard him enter.

"Did you want something?" She glanced back down at Tiffany's post, reading it again. There was no mistake. An uneasy prickle crept across the nape of her neck.

"Yeah. To get out of here."

Jess's attention was once again all on Tiffany's wall. "I'm in the middle of something."

"It's quarter after seven. Your boss has gone. There's nobody left to impress."

"Bite me." Frowning, she glanced up at him. But whether she was on the outs with him or not, Mark was too good a resource to dismiss. "Come here and look at this."

"You know, the rest of us mortals get our kicks doing something besides working." But he came over to where she sat behind her big mahogany desk in her cushy leather chair, and obediently leaned over to read the posting Jess pointed out to him.

Tiffany had written, *Getting away like this is simply bliss. I'm so glad I did it! Love and kisses.*

Mark looked at her. "So?"

Jess called up Allison's wall, then, as Mark looked at where she pointed, she read the latest posting aloud: "'Having so much fun. This is simply bliss, bliss, bliss, bliss, bliss, bliss, bliss. I may never come home! Love and kisses to all.' That's Allison." Then she went back to Tiffany's wall and read her posting aloud: "'Getting away like this is simply bliss. I'm so glad I did it! Love and kisses.'"

"So?" Mark said again.

"Don't you notice anything?"

"Besides the fact that you're cyber-stalking Tiffany Higgs, which I'm pretty sure is some kind of big ethical no-no?"

Jess dismissed that with an impatient

grimace. "The similarity in the messages. Allison says 'simply bliss' and 'love and kisses.' So does Tiffany. The exact same phraseology. What do you think about that?"

CHAPTER TWENTY-ONE

Mark straightened away from the computer. "Jesus Christ, Jess, you need to get a life."

"Don't tell me you think that's a coincidence."

"What do you think it is?"

"A mistake. The same person wrote both these posts, and they were careless about using the same phraseology because they never expected anyone to read both walls."

"Or else they're common phrases that a lot of young women who probably watch the same TV shows and listen to the same music and surf the same web sites use."

"'Simply bliss' and 'Love and kisses'? I don't think so." Jess tapped Allison's calendar with her finger. "And look at this. This is Allison Howard's appointment calendar. See this star she drew around Shelter House's award luncheon in her honor? Do you think she would just take off and forget all about it?"

"Next you'll be asking me if there was a second shooter on the grassy knoll and if I think Neil Armstrong really walked on the moon." His voice was dry.

Jess gave him a withering look and stood up.

"We're still stuck with each other, right?" She asked. Mark's response was a curt nod. "Then let's go."

"Hallelujah."

Mark had been wrong about one thing. On the way out of the building, they ran into Hayley, who was also just leaving for the day. Instantaneously sizing each other up as fellow workaholics, the two women exchanged polite waves. Mark, on the other hand, was treated to a great big smile. Jess hadn't known Hayley had it in her.

"I think she likes you," Jess informed

Mark. Determined not to let Hayley's unabashed appreciation of Mark bother her—or at least determined not to let it show—Jess pointed out the obvious. By that time, they were in the parking garage with the Suburban in sight. Most of the vehicles were gone, and the acres of vast, echoing concrete were unexpectedly intimidating.

Sometimes having a Secret Service agent with her felt good.

"What can I say? She has good taste." He beeped the doors open and, just as he had before, came around to the passenger side to open the door for Jess. Her mouth twisted a little as she climbed in, but this time she made no comment as he got in a moment later and started the engine.

"So what do you want to eat?" he asked as the Suburban nosed out onto 3rd Street and joined the crush of traffic. The rain had stopped, but the sky was still leaden and puddles lay everywhere.

"We can eat later. First we're going to Crystal City."

"What? Why?"

Jess knew he was going to object, but

that was just too bad. "That's where Tiffany Higgs lives. With her mother."

Mark looked at her. "Oh, no. Not happening. We are not going to see Tiffany
Higgs. First of all, like I've said before, she
is not your problem. Second of all, Collins
will shit bricks, I guarantee it. And third,
I'm starving here."

"The trial's over. There's no ethical issue involved."

"Forget it. I am not driving out to Crystal
City."

"Fine. Pull over then, and I'll get a taxi. I
don't need you."

"The hell you don't. What is it about
bang, bang, you're dead that you don't
get?"

"Mark. I am going out to Crystal City.
You can come with me or not, your choice,
but I'm going. Right now."

"Damn it, Jess—" But something, either
the look on her face or her hand curling
around the door handle ready to open the
door so she could jump out the next time
he stopped for a red light, persuaded him.
"Fine. If you're bound and determined to
go, I'll take you." Neither of them said anything else as he negotiated the city streets,

until finally he asked, "What exactly do you think you're uncovering here, anyway?"

"I don't know," Jess said as he pulled onto the freeway. "It's just . . . I think there's something wrong. I've thought that ever since Tiffany recanted on the stand. You never met Tiffany, never spoke to her. I did. She had just a high school education. I doubt if she's ever read a book. By no stretch of the imagination is she the brightest bulb in the chandelier. I'm almost positive she wouldn't *say* 'simply bliss.' And for her to use two of the same phrases as Allison: what are the chances?"

Mark seemed to be thinking that over. A semi rattled by on Jess's side, so close that she could have stuck her arm out the window and touched it with no problem, causing her to shoot it a startled glance. The gray waters of the Potomac below caught her eye, and she realized they were already on the bridge. Mark was driving fast, but no faster than the traffic around them.

"And if you give me some smart-ass answer about Neil Armstrong and the grassy knoll, this conversation is ended right here," she warned.

"Maybe it's a little weird," he allowed with a flickering smile.

Jess waxed triumphant. "See?"

"So we're going to Crystal City so you can check up on Tiffany Higgs."

"Yes." Actually, that pretty much summed it up. They were across the bridge now, and she got a glimpse of the tall control towers of National Airport in the distance to her left. A blue minivan loaded down with kids and luggage cut too close in front of them, streaking across two lanes of traffic for the exit, causing Mark to brake. Up ahead, a sign announced Crystal City. Mark pulled into the far right lane.

"After that, can we eat?"

"Yes."

The Suburban curled down the exit ramp and stopped at the stoplight.

"So give me the address." He sounded resigned.

Jess did, and Mark plugged it into his GPS. A few minutes later they were negotiating the streets of a 1950s era subdivision crowded with small houses in small yards. Some had aluminum siding, some had weathered shingles, a few were brick. The GPS ordered them to stop in front of a small brick ranch with peeling white trim and a crabgrass yard that badly needed cutting.

An old blue Toyota Corolla was parked in the driveway. The curtains had not yet been drawn for the night, and Jess could see the flicker of a television through the big picture window that fronted the street. A few doors down, a woman lugged a metal trash can to the curb. Across the street, some kids played basketball in front of a one-car garage. For a moment Jess simply sat where she was looking at the house. It would be too much to hope for that Tiffany would magically appear, making a trip to the door unnecessary, but hope she did.

"So what exactly are you going to say to Ms. Higgs if she's here? 'I hacked into your Facebook page and your vocabulary has me worried'?"

That hit a nerve. Jess actually had no idea. "You know, you're the federal agent here. Shouldn't you be just the tiniest bit concerned that something isn't right?"

"Last time I checked, no crime had been committed that either of us know of. Anyway, I'm not a cop."

"Nice attitude," Jess said and got out of the SUV.

Obviously feeling that she was in no physical danger, Mark stayed put. Which she knew he wouldn't have done if he hadn't still been harboring ill feelings about her anti-relationship stance. But she wasn't changing her mind, and if Mark in a snit was the price she had to pay, then so be it.

Even over the sounds of the kids playing, Jess heard the gentle whirr as the car window rolled down and then the cessation of engine noise that meant he'd turned the vehicle off. He could see, and hear, everything that went on, and she knew that if anything he didn't like went down he'd be all over the situation like a bad rash. She took some solace from knowing that at least he wasn't going to be sitting there in air-conditioned comfort while she got all sweaty and hot. As she trudged through the wet grass to the small porch, then rang the doorbell, she could feel his eyes on her back. The steamy heat made her wish she'd thought to shed her jacket, but too late now. Through the window, she could see the TV. What she thought was an episode of *Law & Order* was playing.

The door opened without warning, and Jess found herself looking at Tiffany's sister. The one who had called her "bitch." Jess couldn't for the life of her remember her name, if she had ever known it.

The sister was wearing cutoffs and a tank top, with her long blond hair in a ponytail and her feet bare. Like Tiffany, she was pretty and fragile-looking, with big blue eyes. Those eyes collided with Jess's, and it was obvious she recognized her. Her face tightened, her eyes grew small and hard, and she stiffened.

"What do *you* want?" she asked.

"Is Tiffany here?"

"You're kidding me, right? That fucking trial is *over*, and the last person she ever wants to see again is the other side's snotty bitch lawyer. So piss off!"

"Wait!" Jess put her palm against the door to hold it open, because it was clear sweet sister was getting ready to slam it in her face. Inspiration struck. "She has some money coming to her, so if I could just talk to her . . ."

If Tiffany came to the door, she'd pull a twenty out of her purse and claim that's what Tiffany had dropped. She might even get brownie points for being such an honest person that she drove all the way out to Crystal City just to return Tiffany's money to her.

"Oh, yeah?" The sister hesitated, and it was clear the promise of money resonated. "She's on vacation. They got her out of here so that she wouldn't have to talk to any reporters or anybody like that after the trial. How much money are we talking about?"

Saying twenty dollars would get the door slammed in her face, Jess was pretty sure.

"That's something I can only divulge to Tiffany. *Who* got her out of here?"

The sister shrugged. "Whoever. You can leave the money with me. I'll make sure she gets it."

"I can't do that. I have to give it to her. Have you, personally, talked to Tiffany since she's been on vacation?"

"She's not taking calls. Anyway, why do you care if I've talked to Tiff?" Her eyes narrowed. "You're lying, aren't you? I can see it in your face. There isn't any money. You're just out here snooping around. Get the hell off our property before I call the police."

Jess decided to go for honesty. "Look, I'm worried about your sister—"

She barely had time to pull her hand out of harm's way before the door slammed in her face. A moment later, for good measure, the curtains were drawn across the picture window.

"I'm going to leave my card," Jess called through the door. "If you get worried about your sister yourself, call me. I'm on her side this time, I swear."

When that got no response, she gave up, tucked one of her business cards on top of the doorknob, and retreated.

"That went well," Mark observed as she got in beside him, earning himself a dirty look. Hot and disgruntled, she shucked her jacket before putting on her seat belt. The small smile that curled his lips as they drove away didn't make her any happier. He had enjoyed that, she knew.

"Tiffany's supposedly on vacation," Jess reported, resting back against the seat and enjoying the full rush of the air-conditioning on her overheated skin. "'They'—and you tell me who 'they' are—got her away to avoid reporters after the trial."

"I heard." The imperfectly suppressed note of amusement in his voice made her lips thin. "Liar, liar, pants on fire."

"What, about the money?" She shot him a glinting look. "It was twenty dollars. She dropped it."

"Uh-huh." They were silent for a few minutes as Jess luxuriated in the air-conditioning and he drove. They were already back across the bridge when he said, "Has it ever occurred to you that maybe your people got Tiffany out of here?"

"My people? You mean Ellis Hayes?"

"If she was influenced to change her story on the stand, whoever did the influencing might very well have wanted to put her someplace where nobody can talk to her for a while. Loose lips sink ships and all that. And either Ellis Hayes or Senator Phillips seem like the most obvious candidates both to do the influencing and the removing."

Jess thought about that. "They do, don't they?" she said after a moment. "But . . . I was there, Mark. I'm willing to swear that Tiffany recanting was as much a surprise to everybody on the team as it was to me.

Nobody, not Pearse, not Christine, nobody, knew it was going to happen."

He shrugged. "If you're right about that, then you're left with Senator Phillips."

"The Phillips trial is the thing they have in common." Jess was thinking out loud. She flicked a glance at Mark. "Allison and Tiffany. At least as far as I know. Allison was working on the Phillips trial. Tiffany was the alleged victim and star witness. Now both of them are gone."

"I can see why they might first somehow coerce Tiffany and then get her out of the way so she doesn't talk to anyone after they persuaded her to recant. But I'll be damned if I can see why either Ellis Hayes or Senator Phillips would want to get Allison Howard out of the way."

"I don't know, either," Jess admitted.

"Maybe somebody parked Tiffany with Allison. Maybe Allison is babysitting, as you like to call it, just like I am. Maybe they're together, and that's why their Facebook posts sound the same."

"Allison's supposed to be on her honeymoon."

"Maybe that's just a cover story for what she's really doing."

Jess turned that over in her mind. "I suppose that's possible."

"Anything's possible, and none of it has anything to do with you."

"You think I ought to leave it alone, don't you?"

"We've already established how much you love your job. Go poking around in matters that don't concern you, and you could lose it. Take my word for it, Ellis Hayes is run by a bunch of tight-asses who wouldn't think twice about firing you if they think you're pissing on them." He sighed. "Why don't you let me see if I can get somebody to look into it? It's not in the Secret Service's purview, but I know people. They'll keep it on the down-low."

"Would you? Thank you. It's just—I have a bad feeling. I just need to know that Tiffany and Allison are alive and well somewhere." Knowing that he really would carry through on his offer even though he'd only made it to pacify her, she smiled at him, a slow, sweet smile that he didn't return. Instead his face tightened and he looked away.

"So what do you want to eat? I could do with a pulled pork sandwich, myself."

Jess realized that they had reached Foggy Bottom.

"Not Pearl's." Jess rejected it instantly.

"Not pizza," he countered.

"Take-out Chinese?"

"No. How about—"

"Oh, my God, I forgot about Grace!" Jess interrupted as her appointment with her sister flashed into her mind. A quick glance at the clock in the dashboard told her that it was already almost nine. Jess whipped out her phone and started punching in numbers.

Mark groaned. "I'm starving here."

Jess had to smile at his tone, which was almost plaintive.

"So are you coming, or what?" Grace answered without preamble.

"I completely forgot. I am so sorry. I can be there in fifteen minutes."

"Lucky for you I'm still putting up displays for our fall sale."

Jess took that to mean that Grace would wait. She cast a significant look at Mark that directed him to drive to Grace's store and said, "I owe you big-time" to her sister.

"Don't worry, I'll collect," Grace assured her, which Jess knew was probably true. Then they disconnected.

Some fifteen minutes later they pulled up in front of Past Perfect.

CHAPTER TWENTY-TWO

Grace's shop was located on Thomas Jefferson Street, not far from Washington Harbor, which was a tourist mecca because of the sheer number of shops, offices, and condominiums located within its architect-designed wings. Besides Past Perfect's proximity to such a proven draw for locals and tourists alike, the building in which it was housed had charms of its own. It had been built in the 1800s of red brick in the federal style, and it had two doorways, one leading to the shop, which was on the ground floor, and one leading up to the apartments over it. It was within a couple of blocks of the Potomac and the waterfront in Georgetown, one of the toni-est areas of D.C. A number of the very wealthy socialites who were regular fixtures at White House dinner parties and were part of the Washington political and social elite lived in the vicinity. Since it was a point of pride with them not to be seen in the same outfit twice, and since most of them were, in their own way, rather thrifty at heart, especially now that the recession had hung on so long that it seemed to have become a fact of life, their clothes found their way into Grace's shop for dis-creet resale. A nice little bonus for the la-dies, and a nice little profit for Grace.

It was a business model that worked for everybody, and in the three months since it had been open, Past Perfect had be-come an unqualified success.

A sign on the door said Closed, but that, Jess knew, did not pertain to her. Pushing through the heavy wooden door with Mark at her heels, setting off the tin-kling bell that announced arriving custom-ers, Jess was greeted by some elusive, very expensive-smelling scent. The walls were a deep rose pink, the woodwork white, the floors a light hardwood. The look was that of a high-end boutique. Clothing hung against the walls in neat rows according to size. More clothing hung from circular racks in the center of the floor. Outfits complete with accessories were modeled by white cardboard cutouts, which Grace felt were more up-to-date than the traditional mannequins. Grace herself was on a stepladder at the rear of the three large, shotgun-style rooms, near the checkout station. She was draping a scarf around the neck of a soft blue fall jacket that was part of a display of jackets hung high up on the wall. The dress she herself was wearing was a short, summer-bright print that packed enough punch to make even Jess, never the most fashion forward of the sisters, take notice. At twenty-two years old, Grace was lovely enough to turn heads. Five feet seven, with a beautiful face, a knockout body, long blond hair, and slender, shapely legs, Grace had had males coming after her in packs since kindergarten. She was, Jess had thought more than once over the past few months, basically the female equivalent of Mark. Until Past Perfect had opened, Grace had been attending college part time and working at their mother's day care center, but fashion had always been her first love. Jess was glad that she'd had the money to help her get the shop started.

"You look tired," Grace greeted her as she came down off the ladder. She gave Mark a long, level look. Jess had to smile at the way her little sister seemed prepared to take on the big, tough, fourteen-years-her-senior federal agent on her behalf. "Okay, I guess you're not a low-life bastard any more if my sister has forgiven you. But depending on how you treat her, that could change."

"I'll keep that in mind," Mark responded dryly.

"Leave him alone," Jess ordered, feeling guilty about Grace's false assumptions and Mark's false position and the whole messed-up situation in general. But if Grace could not be told the truth about why Mark was back in her life—and she couldn't be, Jess would never put her in that kind of danger—then the fiction that the two of them had kinda-sorta made up had to be maintained. "Where's the dress?"

"Gown. In the—" Grace broke off as a

man emerged from the storage room in the back, his arms loaded with boxes. "Oh, Ron, this is my sister Jessica Ford. And Mark Ryan. He's a Secret Service agent, so watch yourself. Ron Garza, guys."

All Jess saw around the trio of very large boxes was short black hair and muscular forearms. Then the boxes were dropped practically at Grace's feet, and Jess was left looking at a muscle-bound hunk with soulful cocoa eyes and a Hawaiian Tropic–caliber tan. He wasn't quite as tall as Mark, but he was bulked up in a way that made it obvious he did some bodybuilding. Jess saw at once why Grace had spent the last three nights away from home.

"Nice to meet you." Ron's smile revealed blindingly white teeth. He had the slightest of accents. "You are the oldest sister, right? You look very young to be a lawyer, as Grace tells me you are."

Jess smiled in acknowledgment—the fact that she looked about eighteen was not only old news, it was one of the irritants of her life—as they shook hands all around.

"If you would unpack those sweaters

and put them on the shelves while I do this, I would be so grateful, Ronnie," Grace practically cooed. Jess knew that tone: Grace was in love. Not that it was an unusual state for her. Grace was always falling in love. She fell, languished in the throes for a few weeks, then got over it. It was sort of like measles, Jess thought. Grace caught it, suffered, was cured. Poor Ronnie didn't know it, but unless her sister's MO had changed, his place in her life was destined to have the shelf life of a mosquito bite.

"Of course," Ronnie said gallantly. Mark, who was acquainted with Grace's love 'em and leave 'em ethos, flicked Jess a satiric look.

Then Grace whisked Jess off. Jess only hoped that Mark wound up helping Ronnie shelve sweaters in her absence. As revenge for the way he had enjoyed her encounter with Tiffany's sister, it would be pretty sweet.

"That guy is way hot," Jess said as Grace dragged her behind the counter to the hall where the fitting rooms were located. "Where'd you find him?"

"He's my martial arts instructor, and he's practically straight off the plane from Argentina. You would not believe how good he is in bed." Grace gave an illustrative little shiver, pushed Jess into the largest of the dressing rooms, which was also painted rose pink, with a big three-way mirror in one corner, then pointed at a deep red dress hanging beside the mirror. "There it is. I even got you some shoes and things to go with it. How'd you end up back with Mark?"

"It's red," Jess said, both because the dress was and because she needed time to think of a good answer.

"It's garnet. Trust me, it's a great color for you." When Jess just stood there looking at the dress, Grace clucked impatiently and started tugging Jess's black T-shirt over her head. "So let's have it: what's up with you and Mark?"

"We're just sort of dating." Even to her own ears, that sounded lame. When her sister's hands went for the button at her waistband, Jess swatted her sister's hands away and unfastened her own pants.

"Dating? Dating is going out to dinner on

Saturday night. You're sleeping with him again, sister. Don't lie to me, I can tell."

What could she do? Backed into a corner, Jess lied. "We're trying to see if we can make it work, okay?"By this time she was down to her bra and panties.

"Oh, my God, Jess, what happened?" Grace was looking at the bruise on her rib cage, Jess realized.

"I told you. I got mugged. In our front yard, so when you do go home, be careful. It's fine, really. It's not even sore anymore." Seeking to change the subject, she asked, "So does Mom know about Ronnie—uh, Ron?"

Even as Jess spoke Grace whisked the dress over her head.

"No. And don't you dare tell. You know how she is. She keeps telling me I'm too easy, and no man's going to buy the cow if the milk is free, and all that. Like she practices what she preaches."

Jess's answer was muffled by the dress. Which was probably a good thing. Bottom line was, where Grace was concerned the milk might have been free more often than it probably should have been, but plenty of men still seemed eager to buy the cow. And as for their mother, well, Grace hadn't fallen too far from the tree.

The cool slither of the silk felt wonderful against Jess's skin as Grace tugged it into place. When it was all the way on, Jess looked critically at herself in the mirror while Grace zipped up the back. Besides the color, which was more eye-catching than she might have liked, there really wasn't anything to object to, she decided. The dress was a slim, almost tight, fitted column, with two-inch-wide straps over each shoulder and a square neckline that was low enough to be summery without revealing the slightest hint of cleavage. A discreet slit in the front rose no higher than the top of her knee. Bands of the same silk, horizontally pleated, outlined the neckline and belted the waist. Other than that, the dress was perfectly plain. It relied for its effect on the natural luster of the fabric and the cut, which even clueless Jess could tell had been designed by a master expressly to hug a woman's body. It made her look taller than she was, curvier than she was, and at the same time wonderfully elegant.

She had to admit it. She looked good.

"I knew it. It's perfect." Grace dropped a pair of shoes on the floor in front of her. "Slide those on."

"Those" were sparkly pumps with built-in platforms and heels so high that Jess was taller than Grace when she put them on, but only because her sister had kicked off her own shoes.

"It's beautiful."

"It's still a little long." Frowning, Grace gave Jess a thorough once-over through the mirror. "That's an easy fix, though. I'll just tack up the hem."

"How much is it?" Jess fingered the heavy silk with some awe. She was still getting used to the idea that she made good money, good enough to the point where she didn't have to count her pennies any more. Walmart and Target had been her clothing stores of choice for so long that adjusting to spending what it took to keep up with the Mary Jane Cateses and Hayley Marcianoes of the legal world required a real effort. But the kind of success she wanted required looking the part, too.

"Three thousand dollars retail. At Past Perfect, six hundred, and somebody will snap it up and think they got a bargain. For you, nothing, primarily because you're just going to be borrowing it. Also because you're my silent partner. And my sister."

"I knew this shop was a good idea."

Grace grinned at her, then handed her a pair of earrings: dangling diamond drops as big as raisins. Jess's eyes popped as she looked at them.

"Wow."

"They're CZ. Cubic zirconia. What did you think?" Grace said. "Nobody brings in real diamonds. But wear them at night, with this gown, and I guarantee you nobody can tell." She watched critically while Jess put on the earrings. "*Look* at yourself. You look gorgeous. I think I'm going to go for a second career as a stylist."

"I like it," Jess admitted. "I'm not going to be able to sit down, but I like it."

"You're not supposed to sit down. A gown like that is made for you to swan around and be seen in." She tucked Jess's hair behind her ears, then nodded. "Wear your hair like that to show off the earrings. Do a soft eye and a bold mouth."

Jess nodded solemnly, but Grace gave

her a skeptical look. As far as makeup was concerned, Jess tended to flick her lashes with mascara and dab on some lipgloss and call it done, which Grace had been decrying for years.

Grace picked up something from the bench behind them—a silver clutch purse with a jeweled clasp, Jess saw—and handed it to her.

"I put the right makeup in here. *Wear* the eye shadow, *wear* the lipstick. Powder your nose. How wrong can you go?"

Jess met Grace's eyes through the mirror. Grace sighed.

"I've got to hem it anyway, so I'll drop the dress off *and* do your makeup. What time do you think? About five?"

"Six," Jess said. "I have to work until at least five thirty, and then I have to get home. But you don't have to do that. I can do my own makeup perfectly well. *And* I can stop by and pick up the dress."

"We'll talk." That was sister-code for an argument to be deferred until later. "Here, let me mark this hem."

When they emerged from the dressing room some ten minutes later, it was to discover that Mark and Ronnie had bonded, while unpacking and shelving the sweaters together, over the fact that neither of them had eaten yet. Related by Ronnie, that information conjured up a mental image that made Jess giggle inwardly. She grinned at Mark, who gave her a hard look in return. But some of the semihostile vibes she'd been picking up from him earlier seemed to have faded. He was, instead, in an almost thoughtful mood as he followed her out into the once-again pouring rain. The four of them ended up having dinner together at Bourbon Steak House a couple of blocks from the shop. While Jess and Grace exchanged family gossip the men, from what snippets Jess overheard, talked mainly martial arts and action movies. When they parted ways, Mark remarked that Ron seemed to be a pretty good guy.

"Too bad he has no idea that where boyfriends are concerned, your sister has the approximate attention span of a gnat. This time next month, she'll barely remember his name."

Even though Jess had thought pretty

much the same thing earlier, she bristled. "Talk about my sister and die."

"Face it, she has issues. Just like you do. You both—all, Maddie and Sarah included—have totally fucked-up attitudes about men."

"That is not true." Jess was outraged.

They had reached her apartment by that time. Damp and disgusted, Jess unlocked the door and Mark followed her in. The routine seemed automatic by now: Mark did a walk through, flipping on lights, conducting a quick search. Not that Jess really expected an intruder anymore. She was just about ready to chalk up the attack on her to a real, honest-to-God mugger, wrong place at the wrong time, typical D.C., nothing more sinister than that. Probably, she reluctantly acknowledged to herself, because that would be the easiest thing to believe.

"Yes, it is. And you know it, too," he called back over his shoulder.

"Thank you, Dr. Phil," Jess replied with heavy sarcasm, and before the exchange could deteriorate into a real quarrel, or alternatively maybe heat to the kind of unfortunate situation that had occurred between them the previous night, she stalked off to her bedroom to get out of her wet clothes. Firmly closing the door, she did just that, popped a couple of Advil, then took a shower and went to bed.

He'd hit the nail on the head, Mark realized sourly as he stripped down to his boxers and sacked out on the couch. It had been watching Grace in action that had opened his eyes to the big picture. Jess was scrambling away from him like a quarterback dodging a blitz because she and her sisters had experienced nothing but broken relationships their entire lives. Maddie was about to become an unwed teenage mother, Grace attracted and discarded men like he changed his socks, Sarah's marriage was perpetually on the rocks, and Jess just avoided the whole problem by avoiding relationships completely. So it wasn't just Jess. The whole quartet of sisters was emotionally fucked up. As soon as he got the all clear, he was going to run screaming for the nearest exit before he got any more enmeshed with the whole emotionally fucked-up family.

Not that his family didn't have its own problems.

Females in general were a minefield, but his daughter at least had the excuse of being a teenager. His ex-wife, Heather, had called him earlier in the day to inform him that Taylor was going to a Lady Gaga concert this coming weekend with the boy he had chased out of his house the other night, and would be spending the weekend with her for that reason. Not to ask his permission, or even his opinion, mind you, but to tell him that this was going to happen. Since he really hadn't wanted Taylor and Jess joining forces against him, which was what would have happened if he'd been babysitting the one while the other had spent the weekend with them, he hadn't objected. Not that objecting generally did him any good, because Heather's invariable reply to any claim of custodial interference was, "Take me to court," which she knew perfectly well he wasn't about to do. He'd compromised by telling her again about finding that particular boy climbing in his window, and he'd warned her that he suspected their daughter was flirting with the idea of indulging in S-E-X.

Heather's reply? "Oh, lighten up. Of course she is. She's fifteen."

After which she had disconnected.

Taylor had called him later to ask if she could charge two hundred dollars to the credit card he had given her for emergencies. For what? An outfit for the concert.

What could he have done? After a series of parental warnings covering everything from personal safety at concerts to the dangers of boys, he'd said yes.

"Thanks, Dad," she'd squealed, ignoring everything else he'd said and reacting solely to the bottom line, after which she'd taken off, presumably to shop.

Remembering, he felt both good and bad. Good to know that he and his daughter were once again on friendly terms, although when he reflected that getting back in Taylor's good graces had cost him two hundred dollars, a little of the edge was taken off his attack of the warm and fuzzies. Bad to know that his daughter was growing up fast, and by trying to slow her down a little he was basically fighting an incoming tide.

Fortunately, he had other things to think about besides personal relationships.

Things like murder, which it was his job to both ferret out and prevent.

With that aim in mind, he checked his e-mail. There was a message from the office, just as he had hoped. He opened it.

"Hey, buddy. The medical examiner is going to be coming back with an official ruling of suicide next week, and at this point we're satisfied with that. Just wanted to give you a heads-up." It was from Keith Woolridge, an old friend who was overseeing the Service's under-the-radar investigation into Leonard Cowan's death. The official investigation, carried out under the auspices of the medical examiner's office, was for public consumption. Nice to know that they dovetailed so neatly.

In fact, if he hadn't made that completely unauthorized call to Rothenberg that morning, he'd probably have been heaving a sigh of relief and mentally packing his bags about now.

As it was, he called Rothenberg.

Who greeted him with a surly, "Don't you ever sleep? It's almost midnight."

"This morning you told me that Cowan's death wasn't looking like suicide. Your thinking changed on that?"

"This afternoon I was ordered not to talk to you. And since it's a hard, cold world out there job-wise, I'm going to have to honor that."

"Shit," Mark said. "Come on, Randy. This is important."

"What I told you this morning still stands. Not looking like suicide from this end. But you didn't hear it from me."

"Thanks," Mark said even as Rothenberg hung up on him. For a long while after that, he lay there frowning up into the darkness over his head.

By the time Lucy was able to coax Jaden out of the Laundromat where she'd taken refuge, it was after midnight. Lucy had almost had a heart attack when she'd emerged from the Quik-Stop that morning to find Jaden gone. Sweating bullets, racing up and down both sides of the block, trying to stay under the eaves to avoid getting wet as buckets of rain had begun to fall, Lucy had searched every open store and looked in every possible hiding place while hideous visions of her friend being nabbed by the cops, grabbed by the killer,

or snatched by some other random sicko
had played out in her brain. Her terror had
been such that she'd been on the verge of
stopping the next passing cop car herself
and to hell with the consequences when a
woman waiting at the bus stop near the
corner had called out to her.

"Hey, you hunting for a girl with black
hair?"

Lucy had looked toward the voice, spotted the woman sitting in the Plexiglas-
sided shelter, and run over, ducking her
head against the rain. The woman had
looked like a bag lady. She'd worn a ker-
chief around iron gray hair, a man's white
shirt, and a long floral skirt that had just
skimmed her tennis shoes. Plastic grocery
bags bulging with stuff had crowded around
her feet. With so many people rushing
along the sidewalk trying to get in out of
the rain and so many vehicles cruising the
street, Lucy wouldn't even have noticed
her if she hadn't spoken up.

Stepping under the roof that had been
just wide enough to keep a four-by-six-foot
area containing the bench dry, Lucy had
looked warily at her. "Yeah, maybe."

"She went in that Laundromat over there." The woman had pointed. "Went like her tail was on fire, too."

Lucy had seen the Laundromat sign stenciled on a glass storefront on the block perpendicular to the one she had been searching. With a mutter of thanks, she'd braved the rain and darted toward it. Jaden had been in there, all right, huddled on a bench in the very back, where she'd been all but hidden by the rows of washers and dryers. A middle-aged woman had been doing laundry a row over while two little kids had played near her. Another, younger woman had folded clothes on a table up near the front. The thump-thump of clothes tumbling in the dryers had been loud enough to block even the sounds of the kids' game. The scent of detergent and fabric softener sheets had been strong in the air.

"What happened to you?" Lucy had demanded, exasperated, as she'd plopped down beside Jaden.

"It was him, Lucy. It really was, this time. I saw him. I saw him driving past." Jaden's voice had been a terrified whisper. She'd been trembling all over, and her eyes had kept darting fearfully toward the door.

"Oh, Jaden." Lucy had still held the coffee and doughnut, which fortunately the Quik-Stop clerk had put in a plastic bag for her, which had kept the rain off of it. The coffee had been protected by a plastic lid. When Jaden hadn't taken the coffee, Lucy had sat it on the bench between them and broken off a piece of doughnut, which she'd offered to Jaden, who'd shaken her head, before eating it herself. Mother Mary, it had been good, so sweet and chocolatey that she'd just wanted to cram the whole thing in her mouth.

"It was him. I swear it was. I saw him plain as day. He saw me, too. I know he did. Our eyes locked. Oh my God, what are we going to do?"

What were the chances that Miss Howard's killer would have been driving down the very street where Jaden had happened to be standing outside a convenience store? After one moment in which her heart had practically stopped, that was the question Lucy had asked herself, had gotten her blood pumping again. Jaden had seen a guy who'd borne a vague resemblance to the killer and panicked, just like the cop in College Park had caused her to panic.

But nothing Lucy had been able to say had convinced Jaden that she might have been mistaken. As a consequence, Jaden had spent the day in the Laundromat, huddled on the bench, refusing to leave. Worried that her friend had been on the verge of really losing it, Lucy had done her best to look after her. She'd made a few forays forth, timed to coincide with breaks in the rain, hunting down Jaden's ex-stepdad's apartment only to discover he'd moved, buying a chili cheese dog from a stand in nearby DuPont Circle for them to split (not that Jaden ate more than a bite), and checking out bus schedules. With the flyers hanging all over the metro, traveling on the subway had just gotten too risky. Their best bet, Lucy had decided, was the bus.

Based on the route map, and her own knowledge of various sections of the city, Lucy decided they were going across the river to Alexandria, Virginia, where she had once stayed in a foster home. She knew the area, knew there were lots of fast-food places and strip malls and parks and also a community college branch, which meant it shouldn't be too hard to find a place where they could get some sleep. After that, they should probably forget California for the time being and just focus on getting as far away from D.C. as they could. Much as she hated to do it, hitchhiking was looking like the answer. Maybe they'd look for a family or an older couple at a McDonald's, somebody who looked safe, and say they were college students trying to get home on the cheap or something. Wherever they ended up had to be better than here. They could maybe rent a room, get jobs, pretend to be eighteen until they really were eighteen and the system couldn't touch them.

The problem was, to do all that they needed money. And ID's. The money was the kicker; you needed money to get the IDs, but she wasn't going to worry about how to get more money until she got Jaden out of the Laundromat and on that bus to Alexandria.

Jaden agreed with every proposal Lucy ran past her, but she steadfastly refused to leave the Laundromat until it closed at 1:00 a.m. and she was left with no choice. Shooed out into the pouring rain, armed only with plastic garbage bags that they'd found on a shelf and now held over their heads to keep from getting soaked, they dashed for the bus shelter. Streetlights glowed valiantly on the corners, but the rain made the streets unusually dark. No one was around, probably due to the rain. Almost all the shops were dark. Splashing through puddles that had formed on the sidewalks, her eyes on the bus stop, which was presently deserted but where the next bus should be pulling in at any moment, Lucy was a stride ahead of Jaden. A long black car parked at the curb at the front of the line of parked cars at the meters only attracted her notice as she ran past it because it seemed to be too close to the intersection, not in a designated parking place at all. She was just thinking that the driver would be lucky not to be towed during the night when, behind her, Jaden gave a sharp cry.

"Jaden?" Frowning, clutching the garbage bag tight around her head and shoulders, ears full of the drumming of rain against the flimsy plastic, Lucy turned to see what was up. She barely got a glimpse of her friend sprawled motionless on the wet pavement while the rain beat mercilessly down on her before a shadow—a man—lunged at her out of the dark.

With a sense of shock, Lucy felt a crippling jolt hit her in the center of her chest.

"Ahh!" Her cry was as sharp and truncated as Jaden's had been. Then the world fell away into nothingness and she crumpled to the ground.

Like Jaden, Lucy was unaware of what was happening as her limp body was scooped up and deposited in the trunk of the long black car.

CHAPTER TWENTY-THREE

"On the good news front, murder charges against our client Roger Whitney have been dismissed." Sitting at the head of the oval table in conference room 6A, Pearse drummed his fingers against the polished wood surface. Beyond him, gray clouds so low it looked like they were right on top of the city leaked rain on the busy street below. It was nearing the end of their morning conference, and those present— Pearse, Andrew, Hayley, and Jess—had cups of coffee in various stages of consumption in front of them alongside their yellow legal pads. Lenore had left doughnuts on the credenza at the rear of the room, but those were long gone. Andrew, in particular, was a fan of doughnuts. Pearse seemed relaxed, cheerful even, his mood brightening what otherwise would have been a gloomy day. "Kathleen Keeler, the victim's wife, is pleading guilty. Andrew, you're taking depositions in the Shively case today, Hayley, you're due in court at ten for a hearing on Carlucci. Jess, you've got those background checks on the witnesses in the Jameson case. Trial date on that's October first, so chop-chop. And we're all going to meet up here at—"

There was a quick tap on the door, and a worried-looking Lenore stuck her head in.

"Excuse me, but I have the Humane Society on the phone." She started out directing her words to Pearse, but then her gaze slid around the table. "Does anybody have any idea how to get in touch with Allison? They've picked up her cat. Apparently it's microchipped, and since she's not answering the phone, we're the backup number to call. I tried calling her, too. Nothing."

"I haven't heard a word from her since that e-mail saying she was quitting." Pearse looked inquiringly at the rest of them.

"Me, neither." Andrew shrugged.

"Well, she wouldn't be getting in touch with *me*," Hayley said.

"We all know that, Miss Congeniality."

"Shut up, Andrew. That whole Passion in Paradise thing was a crock anyway. She'll be back here with her tail between her legs before Christmas, just you watch."

"Me-ow." Andrew was grinning.

Jess's expression must have revealed the concern she was feeling, because Pearse said to her, "Don't worry, even if Allison does come back your job's safe." Then he shook his head at Lenore. "I don't know what to tell you. If you can't reach her by phone, try sending her an e-mail. That's the best I can do."

"I'm worried about the *cat*," Jess clarified as alarm bells went off in her mind. For a moment she was tempted to tell them her concerns about Allison, but then she thought better of it. After all, what did she really have to impart? Besides Allison's phone call to Lucy's cell, the missed luncheon, and the similarity of Allison's Facebook postings to Tiffany's, the rest— seeing, or thinking she saw, Allison in her office, the sense of being watched she had when she was in there—wasn't anything in her best interests to reveal if she wanted to continue to be taken seriously. Moreover, if she brought Tiffany into it, Pearse might very well order her to leave off anything to do with Tiffany.

"I am, too." Lenore gave Jess an approving look. "They told me the cat got turned in yesterday, and I'm pretty sure they only hold them for three days."

"Then . . . ?" Andrew finished his question by raising his eyebrows and slicing his hand across his throat.

Lenore nodded unhappily, while Hayley said to him, "How old are you, ten?"

"Call Paloma DeLong at Shelter House," Jess suggested. "She told me she watched Allison's cat during her last business trip. Paloma was worried about the cat, actually, because she didn't know who was watching it after that."

"Good idea." Looking pleased, Lenore withdrew.

"Okay, people, we're done here, so get to work. We got hours to bill, remember. And don't forget to be in the lobby at seven." Pearse looked pointedly at Andrew. "In black tie."

Andrew grinned.

"I'm impressed by the way you've jumped into the job with both feet," Pearse told Jess quietly as they were leaving. "And I'm even more impressed that you've already started in on the pro bono work. I knew you'd be an asset to the team."

"Thank you." Despite a niggling sense of disquiet concerning Allison's cat, Jess felt a little glow. Then Pearse was talking to Andrew, and Hayley was giving Jess a look like she had overheard and sucked on a lemon at the same time, and Mark was coming down the hall, summoning her with a beckoning finger.

She narrowed her eyes at him—armed neutrality was the best term to describe the state of their relationship so far this morning—but nevertheless moved to his side.

"I've got some business that will take me out of the building until late this afternoon." His voice was low, meant for her ears alone. Jess was conscious of Hayley's sidelong glance as she passed them. Mark lifted a hand to Pearse, who was behind Jess, still talking to Andrew, the silent message being, *Hang on a minute,*

I've got something to say to you. Then his attention was once again focused on her. "Don't go heading out anywhere alone."

"Well, there goes my plan to go exploring the darkest, most deserted alley I can find."

"Smart-ass," he said with a sudden, flickering grin, and left her.

Whether it was because of the news about Allison's cat or not, Allison's presence felt particularly strong when Jess returned to her office. Turning on the light, opening the blinds and leaving the door ajar did not help appreciably. The sense of being watched was almost unnerving, but short of asking for a new office—or an exorcism—there didn't seem to be anything Jess could do about it. Except, maybe, find Allison. Hopefully a message about her cat would move her to respond. If it didn't . . . well, that was something to think about later. For now, if she wanted to keep her job, she had work to do.

Jess plunged into the background checks, which helped them gauge the credibility of various witnesses and, thus, the relative strength of both their own case and the prosecution's as well. *Jameson* involved an Episcopal bishop and his church bookkeeper wife who had been accused of embezzling over a million dollars from their building fund. Their pockets were apparently deep enough to allow them to hire Ellis Hayes for the defense, and the goal was to keep Mrs. Episcopal Bishop from going to jail. Regardless of the evidence, the case should have been fairly easy to plea bargain out, because, absent a murder charge, white, upper-middle-class women were almost never sent to jail. Unless, of course, she was truly innocent and insisted on proving it by going to trial, which always involved a degree of risk, or the prosecutors had a bee in their bonnets about this case for some reason.

The landline, which was strictly for business, rang only occasionally, when a caller made it through to Lenore and her assistants and was directed on to Jess. But when her cell phone rang, she had to scramble to answer it herself, because it was still in her purse.

"Miss Ford?" The voice, which was a woman's, was hesitant, almost tremulous. Jess didn't recognize it, but the caller ID gave her the name: Mona Isaacs. It rang a bell, but before Jess could place it the caller herself explained who she was. "I'm Tiffany Higgs's mother. You left your card when you were out here yesterday. Tracy—my other daughter—said you said we should call you, that you're on Tiffany's side now."

Immediately Jess pictured her: short and heavy-set, round face, small features, a cap of slick black hair.

"What can I do for you, Mrs. Isaacs?"

Mrs. Isaacs took a deep breath. "That prosecutor, Sandra Johnson. The one that was so nice to Tiffany through everything. She called the house this morning and said that they're going to be charging Tiffany with perjury for changing her testimony during that damned trial. She said Tiffany ought to get a lawyer. Tiffany—she didn't take the money she was offered to drop the charges against Rob Phillips. She should've took it, I knew it, I told her. But she said he raped her, he was meaning to kill her, and she had to tell. The thing is, though, she don't have a lot of money now to pay a lawyer."

"Wait a minute: Tiffany was offered money not to go forward against Rob Phillips?"

"Yes."

"Who made that offer?"

"I don't know. I only know what she told me. Two hundred grand, they offered her. But she didn't take it, and then she ended up having to back down anyway, and she got no money for it, so that was a shame. Now they're going to put *her* on trial, which just isn't right." She sounded on the verge of tears. "And I can't get ahold of her, and you left your card, and calling you was all I could think to do. Will you help us?"

This had to bring into play all kinds of conflict-of-interest problems. If she agreed, Jess had an instant mental picture of Pearse's head exploding.

"The situation is a little difficult because of our representation of Rob Phillips. I can't serve as your permanent counsel. But I can advise you until you get one, and I can find someone else to represent you," she said, and Mrs. Isaacs said, "Oh, thank you. Thank God. Thank God."

Jess waited a minute while the woman composed herself. "For now I'm Tiffany's lawyer of record, which means anything you tell me is protected. I can't tell anybody anything you say, understand? But if I'm going to help Tiffany, I need to know the truth: why did she recant on the stand?"

Heavy silence was her answer. Then Mrs. Isaacs started talking in a hushed voice, as if she was afraid someone would overhear.

"She got threatened. She went out to lunch that last day and she got threatened. She told me later this man came up to her and said that if she didn't say she'd been lying about the rape her kid would disappear and never be seen again. Then he showed her some pictures of Trevor, her little baby, my grandbaby, playing outside on the swings, that he'd taken. She said she knew he meant it then, and she was scared to death."

Jess had a sudden flashback to the man she'd seen grabbing Tiffany outside the metro station, and her heart sank.

"I didn't know Tiffany had a little boy."

"He's two. Tiff never married his dad, and Trevor lives with him and his parents. But Tiffany sees him, we see him. She loves him, and she said she was lying up there on the witness stand to keep him safe."

"Oh, my God." Jess felt sick to her stomach. "Have you told anybody else? Has Tiffany?"

"Tiffany told me not to. She was afraid. That's why she went away."

Disquiet slid like a cold finger down Jess's spine. "Mrs. Isaacs, where is Tiffany?"

"I-I don't know. She came home with me, after the trial, but there were all these reporters and TV cameras around the house, so she wouldn't stay. She sent me an e-mail later saying that she was going out of town until everything died down. But she didn't say where, and when I try to call her I just get her voice mail." Mrs. Isaac's voice shook at the end.

Jess was getting a real bad feeling about Tiffany.

Don't jump to conclusions. It's only been a few days.

Jess said, "When I was talking to Tracy, she said something like somebody—what she said was *'they'*—got Tiffany out of here."

"Well—we wondered where she got the money to go. She didn't have much, you know? So Tracy thought that after, maybe somebody paid Tiffany to leave. So none of those reporters could talk to her, you see. But Tracy don't know about that man threatening Tiffany. Tiff was so scared, she only told me. She was so scared, she might have found the money to go on her own."

"I'll deal with Sandra Johnson," Jess promised. "You keep trying to get in touch with Tiffany. Let me know if you succeed."

"Don't tell Mrs. Johnson what I told you." Mrs. Isaacs sounded panicked. "Tiff'll kill me for sure. And if something happened to Trevor, that would be worse than anything."

"At some point, we may need to tell her. I want you to understand that. But we don't need to do it yet, not until we find Tiffany, and I can't do it at all without your permission, so you don't have to worry about that." Jess took a deep breath. "There's just one more thing: did Tiffany know another lawyer in this office named Allison Howard?"

"Not that I know of," Mrs. Isaacs answered. "I know I've never heard that name."

"Okay. Well, if you'll do your best to contact Tiffany, I'll handle everything else."

"Thank you," Mrs. Isaacs said, to which Jess replied, "You're welcome," and disconnected.

Then she sat staring into nothingness for a long moment while mentally running through the conversation and its ramifications.

Her first impulse was to head straight to Pearse and lay all this out for him. Once the team knew what had happened . . .

What? Double jeopardy precluded Rob Phillips being prosecuted a second time. Even if prosecutors found some way around that, Tiffany now would be absolutely not credible as a witness, having recanted once. And without Tiffany's testimony, there was no case. However, whoever had tried to bribe Tiffany would be subject to prosecution, as would whoever had threatened her son. Tampering with a witness was a felony. If they could find out who did it. If there was enough evidence to build a case.

Rob Phillips was Ellis Hayes's client. Ellis Hayes's loyalty would be to him.

Has it ever occurred to you that

maybe your people got Tiffany out of here?

She could almost hear Mark saying it. As she thought about it, the sound of her pulse was suddenly loud in her ears. Not fast, but loud, and deliberate. As if her body was working hard to stay calm.

Something's wrong: she'd known it from the moment Tiffany had recanted. Now she knew a little bit about what that something was. But there was more. She was convinced of it. Too many loose ends were left, too many connections needed to be explained. Until she knew where this was going, she couldn't tell Pearse, or anyone else on the team, or at Ellis Hayes.

The gladiators might turn on her.

Mark was who she needed, but Mark wasn't there. And spilling the whole story to someone else wasn't something she was ready to do.

In the meantime, the first order of business was to find Tiffany.

Jess pictured Tiffany as she had last seen her. At the time, she'd thought she'd been able to read fear in Tiffany's body language. Now she was more certain of it than ever.

But who had the man been?

She tried to remember what she'd seen: a tall, dark-haired man in a suit. What precise shade had his hair been? She had only seen him at night, when the light had been too uncertain to be sure. His height? Tiffany was about Maddie's height: five-six. Jess pictured Tiffany and the man together again. Therefore, the man was around six-one. Broad-shouldered, substantial, so probably one hundred ninety to two hundred pounds. His face—Jess tried to call it to mind. Complexion fair rather than swarthy. Lean cheeks, narrow jaw. Thin mouth. Clean-shaven. Straight, dark eyebrows. Eyes looking away from her, looking down at Tiffany, so she hadn't ever really gotten a look at them. She tried to focus more intensely, to form a precise mental image of the face, but she couldn't. She'd been too far away.

Would she recognize the man if she saw him again? She thought so. Maybe. Oh, get real: who knew?

Abandoning the background checks for the time being, Jess went into her computer, meaning to check Tiffany's Facebook page to see if she'd posted anything new. Maybe there was something there, or something on other social media sites, that would help in tracking her down.

Jess was just glancing over her shoulder for the umpteenth time that morning in response to that now familiar feeling of being watched when a quick knock sounded on her door. Startled, Jess almost jumped but managed to control the impulse in time. Instead, she calmly (she hoped) looked a question at Lenore, who stood in her open doorway.

"Mrs. DeLong just called. She said she tried to call you on your cell phone, but it was busy. She wants you to call her as soon as possible."

Ignoring her pounding heart, projecting what she hoped was a facade of unflappable calm, Jess nodded. "I'll call her right now. Thanks, Lenore."

Lenore left, and Jess picked up her cell phone once more.

When Jess reached her, Paloma sounded harassed. "I'm at the Humane Society trying to pick up Allison's cat, but they won't release it to me. I told them the owner is out of town, but they said in that case the cat can only be picked up by the listed emergency contact, and that's Ellis Hayes."

"Who at Ellis Hayes?"

"They said Allison listed her employer Ellis Hayes as the emergency contact. So I guess that means anyone who can show an Ellis Hayes ID." She had a brief conversation with someone on her end that Jess could only partly overhear. Then she spoke to Jess again. "Yes, that's right. And you should know, I have to be at the airport at four, so . . ." Her voice trailed off, but Jess understood: the matter was urgent.

"What's the address?"

Paloma told her.

Jess checked the time. It was just after one. "You're there now?"

"Yes."

"Don't go heading out anywhere alone"—she could almost hear Mark saying it.

So she would call him. If babysitting was his new pastime, then he could just come back and babysit. Because she was going to get that cat.

"I'm on my way."

Saying good-bye to Paloma, she next

called Mark. And got his voice mail. She left him a message, then made up her mind.

She could be there and back within the hour. It was broad daylight on a busy Friday afternoon. Taking the metro should be perfectly safe, even if there was someone out there wanting to kill her, which she was becoming less and less convinced was the case.

Of course, she was worried about the cat because it was a cat, and she liked cats. But also, for some strange reason, she felt an obligation to Allison. Probably because she couldn't shake the sensation that the other woman was there in the office that had once been hers, too.

If Allison's cat had turned up at the Humane Society, then there was a problem. Either the arrangements that Allison had made for its care after Paloma's tenure had ended had gone badly awry, or something else had happened.

Something not good.

The Humane Society was on Georgia Avenue in Northwest. When Jess got off the metro at the nearest stop, she was greeted by the smell of hot, fresh asphalt. A work crew with a big white mixer truck was patching potholes, she was relieved to see as she hit street level, which meant there were at least a few city workers around to whom she could turn if she needed help. The grinding noise the truck made was almost comforting, because even as she walked away from it she still knew it was there. Still, she felt a little jumpy as she hurried up the street. Over and above concern about any possible risk to herself, thoughts of Allison, Tiffany, and the runaway girls churned relentlessly through her brain. Allison and Tiffany she could connect through the Phillips case, and possibly their Facebook postings. Allison and the runaway girls she could connect because of Allison's call to Lucy's phone, although it was always possible that Allison had called the wrong number and thus that connection didn't mean anything. Other than that, and the fact that all four of them were either out of contact or outright missing, she could come to no conclusions. All she knew was that something just felt wrong.

Did seeing Allison in her/their office mean that Allison was dead?

Jess went cold all over at the thought.

Face it: that's what she feared.

And if Allison was dead, and there was a connection with Tiffany, did that mean Tiffany was dead, too?

Jess's heart started to thump. But speculation did no good, and she was in a neighborhood where she needed to keep her wits about her, so she did her best to focus on the here and now.

Run-down brick tenements lined one side of the block. The other side was home to an abandoned warehouse and an assortment of shops, about a third of which were boarded up. This neighborhood was in the process of being reclaimed, but so far not much reclamation had happened: it was just rough. In such an environment projecting confidence was the key, so Jess walked tall among the residents of the blighted area who happened to be about. The sky was still overcast, but it had stopped raining sometime earlier, and it looked, in fact, to be clearing. It was so muggy that Jess felt like she was breathing in fog. By the time she reached the gray cinderblock building that housed the Humane Society, she was damp with sweat.

The air-conditioning as she pushed through the door felt wonderful.

Paloma was inside.

She had been sitting, but she stood up immediately when Jess entered. Dressed in a short-sleeved, black-and-white print dress with her hair swirled up into that high top-knot that gave her several inches, Paloma was looking worried, but her expression cleared as she saw Jess.

"Thank goodness," she said. "I was planning to leave straight from work, and I still have to go back there to get my suitcase. I was afraid I would run out of time."

"Vacation?" Jess inquired as they approached the counter together.

"My niece's wedding. It's tomorrow, and I'm home again on Sunday."

"How exciting. Oh, I filed a motion to dismiss that lawsuit Jax Johnson filed against the center. I don't think it's anything you need to worry about anymore."

"I really appreciate . . ." Paloma began, then broke off as a uniformed clerk came to help them. Clearly, she'd been dealing with Paloma and was aware of Jess's purpose.

"You're from—" she consulted the computer printout lying on the counter. "Ellis Hayes?"

"Yes." While Jess was showing ID and paying the charges, the clerk spoke into an intercom. A few moments later another clerk came out carrying a black cat in her arms. Its long coat was dull and dirty, and it was pitifully thin.

"Oh, poor Clementine," Paloma exclaimed, and the cat swished its tail and looked at her with big golden eyes.

"Mee-eee-eee-eee." It was the most pathetic-sounding meow Jess had ever heard.

"She didn't look like this when I last saw her." Paloma reached for the cat.

"Looks like she's been running loose for at least a couple of weeks." The clerk didn't hand the cat over. "Do you have a carrier?"

Paloma and Jess looked at each other. Paloma shook her head.

"No," Jess said.

It was fortunate, since the clerk refused to allow the cat to leave except in a carrier, that they were able to buy one complete with a litter box, a packet of food and litter, and a water bottle affixed to the grate at the front of the carrier. It was a kitten starter kit, the clerk said.

"I've left at least half a dozen voice mails and text messages for Allison," Paloma said as they were walking out of the building. "In the last one, I told her that we were picking up Clementine from the Humane Society. I gave her your cell phone number to call, since I'm going to be out of town and I assume you'll have her cat. I hope that's all right."

Jess blinked in surprise. She hadn't planned on taking charge of the cat. She had assumed she would help liberate it, and then it would be Paloma's responsibility.

But she was holding the carrier, and she could feel the cat's weight through the handle. The cat—Clementine—was being very still. Jess felt a sudden sense of responsibility toward her.

"That's fine," Jess said. They were on the building's steps by that time, and Jess had a quick, unpleasant vision of herself trying to take the metro with a cat. She didn't know the rules on that—she'd never traveled with a pet—but she had a sneaking suspicion that only service animals were allowed on the trains. Then she thought of something. "Oh, by the way, do you know if your missing girls—Lucy and Jaden—ever used Facebook?"

"All our girls are required to delete their pages when they're admitted. We don't allow social media use. It's too difficult to supervise."

Which explained why Jess hadn't been able to find them. She was a little disappointed, probably because, she admitted to herself, she'd been hoping to find *bliss* and *love and kisses* on there somewhere.

Ten minutes later, Jess, plus cat, was in a taxi heading for her office. She'd thought about conveying the cat home to her apartment, but it was clear across town, and, anyway, if there did happen to be a killer out there lying in wait for her, going to her apartment alone was probably the last thing she ought to have done. Mark would say so, in any case, she knew.

Actually, Mark was probably going to have a whole lot to say when she saw him again.

The sixth floor was jam-packed with people when Jess reached it. Everyone was rushing around like mad. Lenore waved to her but didn't stop as Jess carted the carrier back toward her office and Lenore, carrying an armful of files, raced toward Pearse's. Jess reached her office without having to explain anything to anybody, which was a relief.

Closing her door for the first time in days, she set the carrier down on the floor and crouched in front of it.

"Hello, Clementine," she said.

Clementine crouched on the floor of the carrier. Big golden eyes met Jess's, and she felt a tug on her heartstrings. She didn't know about giving the cat the run of her office—it didn't seem like the professional thing to do, and, anyway, what if the cat got out into the hall?—but she could at least pour out some food and fix the litter box so the cat could be comfortable until they headed for home in a couple of hours.

Jess opened the crate door cautiously. Clementine stood up, stretched, and stepped out, very calmly, as if she thought that was what she was supposed to do. For a moment the two of them simply looked at each other. Then Jess stroked her, grimacing a little as she felt the too-prominent backbone, the roughness of what once had probably been a luxurious coat. Clementine arched her back approvingly. Her tail gave a gentle swish.

"You're a nice cat," Jess told her, gratified. "I'll do my best to get your owner back for you."

Then she got busy setting up the litter box, and food dish, and making sure the water bottle worked. Finally all was ready, and she stood up and looked around for the cat. At first she didn't see her.

"Kitty, kitty," Jess called, walking around her desk, because that was just about the only place that was hidden from her view where the cat could go.

Sure enough, Clementine was back there. Sitting on the carpet just a few feet behind Jess's big leather chair, she was staring fixedly at the plant. Or rather, Jess thought, looking at the unblinking golden eyes and following their gaze, at a spot directly in front of the plant.

Something about the cat's posture, her stillness and fixed regard, sent a chill down Jess's spine. It was as if the cat saw something that Jess didn't see, something that wasn't there.

Allison?

At the thought, Jess's pulse began to race.

"Clementine?" Her voice was very soft.

Clementine didn't move. She didn't look around or acknowledge Jess in any way. Instead, staring hard at that same spot, she started to purr.

CHAPTER TWENTY-FOUR

A knock on the door made Jess jump. Before she could answer, Lenore pushed through it.

"Jess, Pearse needs you to get together every case you can in which extradition from Brazil was denied for humanitarian reasons."

From Lenore's manner, Jess knew the request was urgent. She looked a question.

"Robert Flores was arrested in Brazil about an hour ago. Apparently he's been hiding out in São Paulo. They're trying to fly him out of there tonight, and we're trying to stop them. He has advanced prostate cancer, and Pearse thinks we can use it to get a stay until we can come up with something else."

Jess's eyes widened. Robert Flores was widely referred to in the press as the fugitive financier. He'd been in hiding for, if Jess's memory served her correctly, five years. The amount of money he was suspected of misappropriating was in the neighborhood of a billion dollars. That, and his subsequent flight to avoid prosecution, had made him so famous that Jess had instantly recognized the name.

"We represent Robert Flores?"

"Is he rich? Is he famous? Is he in trouble?"

They were rhetorical questions, but Jess nodded anyway.

"Then we represent him."

Their conversation seemed to have broken Clementine's trance. The cat turned and jumped gracefully onto Jess's desk.

"A cat." Momentarily distracted, Lenore looked at Clementine in surprise.

"It's Allison's. The Humane Society call, remember? I picked her up, and then I didn't have time to take her home, so I brought her here. I'll take her home with me tonight." She frowned at Lenore. "Pearse is flying to Brazil?"

Lenore shook her head. "We have a partner firm in Brazil. Pearse is working through them for now. He needs those cases by six at the latest. Hayley has already gone home to get ready for the party and Andrew is still taking depositions. I was so glad to see you come in, I can't tell you."

"Tell Pearse I'll have them ready." Jess spotted the proverbial silver lining. "This gets me out of Mr. Dunn's party, right?"

"Death, disability, and dismissal get people out of that party. Nothing else. Why do you think Pearse wants that information no later than six? You know Mr. GQ: that leaves him plenty of time to get dressed."

"Leaves *him* enough time, maybe." It was an alarmed mutter.

"If you'd been here longer, you wouldn't have been surprised." Lenore gave Jess a wry smile. "This kind of thing always happens. I've learned. I brought my dress to work with me this morning, and the women's locker room next door to the gym in the basement has great showers and a full-length mirror."

Jess thought fast. "All right, I can do this."

Lenore gave her a smile and a thumbs-up and withdrew. Jess looked at Clementine, who was washing herself, thought about putting her in the carrier, then thought, *Screw it* and let her stay out. The feeling of being watched was now strong enough to make the hairs on the back of Jess's neck prickle: too busy to do anything else, she ignored it while she put in a quick call to Grace. A few minutes later, she was so engrossed in pulling up cases that she had forgotten everything else.

When Mark walked in, he stopped dead just inside the door to glare at her.

"Damn it, you scared the hell out of me." He sounded equal parts angry and relieved to see her. She gave him an abstracted smile. It was, she saw at a glance, twenty till six and she was still knee-deep in cases that she was frantically reading through to see if they fit the bill. "You leave me a message saying you need me to drive you somewhere and then you turn your phone off? I figured, knowing you, you'd taken off without me and gotten into trouble. I broke land-speed records getting back here."

"Shut the door." This time she barely

looked up. "It was just the ringer, and I didn't turn it off until like an hour and a half ago, way after I needed your services. Anyway, I forgot I turned it off. I needed to get some work done, as you can see."

"There's a cat on your desk." He sounded surprised. Clementine's head was up and she was looking at him, Jess saw as her head came up again, too, but the cat showed no indication that she meant to get up from the ball she had curled herself into for a nap.

"That's why I said *'shut the door.'*"

He complied. "So where did you need to go that was so important?"

"Humane Society. And, actually, I did take off without you." She knew as she said it that he wasn't going to be happy about it, but then keeping him happy wasn't really her concern, was it? Seeing him stiffen before her eyes dropped back to her computer screen, she airily waved a dismissive hand. "As you can see, I survived. Look, do you mind saving the lecture for later? I have to get this done."

"What, do you think I'm just hanging around Ellis Hayes because I like lawyers? What part of somebody out there might be

serious about making you dead isn't getting through to you?"

"Well, if so, they missed their chance this
afternoon." Glancing up at him, she saw
that he was still looking majorly annoyed.
To avoid the rest of the homily, she changed
the subject to something he needed to
know anyway: "Guess what? I found out
why Tiffany recanted on the stand. Somebody got to her, threatened her kid."

Mark frowned. "I didn't even know she
had a kid. How'd you find that out?"

"Her mother called. Apparently the DA's
planning to charge Tiffany with perjury.
When I agreed to act as Tiffany's lawyer,
the mother told me the whole thing. It's
bad, too."

"You agreed to act as Tiffany Higgs's
lawyer?"

"Yep. Temporarily, anyway."

"I bet *that's* going to go over real big
around here."

"It was the only way to get the mother to
talk to me. And I told you about the threat
because I'm going to need your help finding Tiffany, but it can't go any further. Anyway, Tiffany's going to need me, always
assuming she's alive and well, which I'm

beginning to seriously doubt. But I can't talk about Tiffany now. I've got to get this done. Go away."

She made a shooing motion at him.

"If you want to get to your apartment and back by seven, you're out of time. We got to go. Or are you skipping the party?"

He sounded so hopeful that Jess would have grinned if at least three-quarters of her mind hadn't been focused on the case she was skimming through.

"Apparently no party skipping's allowed." Jess glanced up from the computer again. "I'm going to have to get dressed here. Grace is bringing everything I need. If you're going back to the apartment to change, I need you to do me a huge favor. Take Clementine—the cat—with you and make sure she gets settled in. Food, litter, everything you need is already in the carrier."

"You put yourself in danger to go to the Humane Society to get a cat?" Disbelief tinged his voice. "Why?"

"It's Allison Howard's cat. The Humane Society was holding it." Her gaze had already dropped back to the file she was reading. She could feel his eyes on her. "I'll explain later. Just please do it and let me finish this. I have to get this to Pearse by six."

"You want me to deal with this cat."

She looked up again. "Please."

"You planning to stay in this building until I get back?"

"Yes. I promise. Mark—"

"Okay, fine. Come on, kitty."

Reading frantically, Jess nevertheless smiled to herself as, without protest, Clementine let him pick her up and put her in the carrier. Remembering that Mark lived with his daughter's cat (Taylor's mother was allergic, which left the honors to Mark), Jess was slightly less impressed than she might have been. Still, she felt that Clementine was in good hands when he left with her.

By three minutes till six, Jess had forgotten all about Clementine and Mark and everything else in the rush to finish. She'd found half a dozen solid cases the Brazilian lawyer could cite to establish precedent for a humanitarian denial of extradition. Having compiled them into a file complete with index, she hit the Send button at 5:59. One minute later, at 6:00 precisely, she received an e-mail from Pearse acknowledging that he had received it.

Victory.

Feeling like the *Rocky* theme song ought to had been playing in the background somewhere, Jess twirled giddily around in her chair.

"What are you doing?" Grace asked.

Feeling foolish, Jess planted her feet and stopped her spin so that she faced her sister. Grace wore a sleeveless yellow sheath that made her look like a sunbeam, or, alternatively, a blonder, younger, way more beautiful Jackie O. A white plastic garment bag was draped over her arm, and the black quilted bag Jess thought of as Grace's tool kit hung, along with her elegant Chanel purse, from one shoulder.

"Finishing up," Jess answered and got to her feet. "Ready?"

"Oh, yeah." Grim as a soldier marching into battle, Grace followed Jess to the women's locker room in the basement.

By the time Grace was done working her magic, even Jess was impressed.

"You clean up good," Grace told her through the mirror, eyeing her handiwork with pride.

"Woo-hoo," Lenore agreed from the other side of the room. Lenore's billowy

white ballgown accentuated her curvy figure while at the same time making Lenore
look a little like Glenda the Good from the
Wizard of Oz, in the prettiest possible way.
In contrast, Jess's slim red (sorry, Grace,
garnet) column made her look both elegant
and sophisticated, she thought. Grace's
"soft eye, bold mouth" had translated into
a smudge of taupe eye shadow and a sug-
gestion of eyeliner, along with deep red
lips that Grace by some alchemy had
made look fuller and sexier than Jess had
had any inkling was possible with her own
rather ordinary mouth.

"We got to go, girl," Lenore told her.
Glancing up at the big round clock on the
wall, Jess saw that it lacked only a few
minutes of seven. Grace handed Jess her
purse, and then the three of them left the
locker room and took the elevator for
the lobby.

"Thanks, Gracie," Jess said softly when
the elevator stopped and Lenore stepped
out, leaving her and Grace momentarily
alone.

"Get out there and knock 'em dead."
Grinning at Jess, Grace gave her a little
nudge that sent her out into the lobby. It

was already crowded and noisy as everybody gathered to wait for the limos. Jess hardly recognized her coworkers, glamorous tonight in evening wear.

Taking a deep breath, cautious because of the height of her heels on the slick marble floor, Jess walked toward Andrew, whom she could see standing near one of the wide double doors at the front of the lobby, while Grace veered off with a wave, heading toward the revolving door at the side. Andrew was looking dapper in a black tux, she saw, and thought that Pearse would be relieved at his attire. Andrew had obviously seen them step off the elevator and at that moment was busy tracking Grace with appreciative eyes.

Jess smiled wryly. *So much for my femme fatale pretensions.*

"Who's that?" Andrew asked as she reached him. Jess saw that the whole gang was there, Pearse, Andrew, and Hayley, lovely in a slinky black gown that made Jess glad Grace had insisted she wear some other color, and newly arrived Lenore, flushed and adorable in her fairy godmother dress as she smiled at Pearse, who, with his black hair brushed back from his face and his obviously custom-made black tux, was looking, as Lenore had put it earlier, very much like Mr. GQ.

"My sister." Jess turned to watch Grace disappear through the revolving door. She looked back to find that Pearse was watching Grace, too, while Lenore looked up at him with an expression that told Jess exactly where her heart lay and Hayley glared after Grace.

"Maybe you can introduce me one of these days," Andrew said.

Jess's smile was noncommittal. "Maybe." Actually, the last thing on earth she wanted was to have Grace engage in one of her speed romances with somebody she worked with. Andrew didn't know it, but Grace would chew him up and spit him out.

"Glad to see you wore a penguin suit this time." Christine drifted over to them to look Andrew up and down. She was wearing a forest green evening kimono that sparkled with sequins, and with her red hair she reminded Jess irresistibly of a Christmas tree. "At least you're not dumb enough to make the same mistake twice."

"Not me," Andrew agreed. Then, when

Christine glanced away, he winked and pressed the knot on his bow tie. It lit up with flashing multicolored lights. Jess gaped at it, appalled. But by the time Christine glanced back around, it looked like just an ordinary black tie again. Jess didn't think Pearse could have seen, either, because he was partly turned away, talking with the Queen of Torts.

"Idiot," Hayley growled at him, and Andrew grinned and said something back. Jess missed whatever it was, because just then Mark stepped off the elevator, looking so outrageously handsome in his black tux that Jess's breath caught.

Nobody looked quite like Mark.

She wasn't the only one who noticed. Female heads turned to track his progress as he walked out into the lobby. Jess saw Cates, resplendent in a one-shouldered silver gown that molded every curve, waving at him. Jess's eyes narrowed; her muscles tensed; her teeth clenched. He lifted a hand in response, and Jess felt a spurt of what she hated to admit even to herself felt very much like jealousy.

A moment later he spotted Jess and came straight to her side.

"You look beautiful," he bent his head to whisper in her ear. It was so much what she needed to hear that she smiled at him. *So do you* bubbled to her lips, but she didn't say it. *Over,* she reminded herself, *we're over.*

"How's Clementine?" she asked instead, low-voiced.

"Scratching on your couch, last I saw of her."

Then the cars arrived, and the chance for private conversation was lost. They all were loaded up and driven away in groups of eight or ten, in a long procession of stately limos that crossed the Key Bridge into Virginia, where Mr. Dunn's estate stood high on the bluffs overlooking the banks of the Potomac.

The estate was called Frog Hill, taking its name from the hundreds of tiny green tree frogs that bred in the dozen or so ornate bronze fountains that graced flower gardens ablaze with late summer blooms. As darkness fell, the frogs sang their high-pitched songs from the branches of the tall elms and oaks and walnuts that crowded the grounds. A beautiful white stone mansion with a black slate, mansard-style roof dominated the hundred plus acres, which tonight, were alive with lights and music and guests. The front of the house looked out over a sheer drop of eighty feet or more to the black waters of the river below. Stone terraces led down from the back of the house toward a flat lawn with tennis courts and an enormous swimming pool, and it was on these terraces that the guests congregated. A widower, Mr. Dunn actually spent little time at the estate, preferring his lavish apartment in town. But it was kept fully staffed and ready for him at all times.

"Heard Pearse put you on his team full-time." Christine stopped beside Jess at the canape table under one of the huge, open-sided tents intended to provide shelter in case it rained again. Nearby, several dozen couples swayed to the dreamy music of a live band. Among the dancers Jess spotted Diane Babbage, a national news anchor, Kenny Adkins, an iconic country-western singer, and Crew Owen, a former football great whose ex-wife had just been found heinously murdered. There was also Andrew, with a woman she didn't recognize. The rest of the team was nowhere in sight. Apparently oblivious to the notables around them, Christine was focused on the food. Her plate was already loaded with cold shrimp and Swedish meatballs and squares of cheese, to which she added three tiny puff pastries from the tray in front of her as she spoke. Jess's own plate held one of the puff pastries and a couple of chocolate-dipped strawberries, none of which she felt particularly like eating at the moment. She'd only retreated to the buffet, which was set up near the pool and was already growing crowded, because she'd spotted Rob Phillips on the terrace above. He was there with his parents as honored guests along with perhaps five hundred other prominent people Jess assumed were clients. Besides the celebrities dancing just yards away, tonight's guest list included several movie stars, a large number of senators and congressmen, two Supreme Court Justices (that she'd seen so far), and half the cabinet. Security was present in droves, discreetly costumed in formal wear like the guests but unmistakable nonetheless. As Jess's first impulse had been to march right up to the Phillips contingent and demand to know what they knew about Tiffany, she had slapped herself with her own gag order and headed in the opposite direction. Before she started accusing anybody of anything, she had to work this out so she knew what she was talking about. At this point, it was still remotely possible that Tiffany had simply taken a vacation to escape the stress of the trial. And that Allison was on her honeymoon.

"Yes, he did," Jess agreed, picking up what looked like a tiny quiche and adding it to her plate. The spicy aroma of the food combined with the strings of Japanese lanterns lighting the tent and the live music to create an exotic atmosphere that was pure bohemian paradise. "I'm thrilled."

"Good call on his part, if you ask me. Pearse is a smart man." Christine looked beyond Jess and nodded knowingly. "Ambitious, too."

Jess turned to look and saw that Pearse was dancing with a woman she didn't know.

"Ambitious?" Jess picked up on the undercurrent in Christine's voice. The couple was outside the tent near the far end of the outrageously opulent pool, swaying in the shadows in front of the thirty-foot-high cascading waterfall that poured down into it in an effort, Jess thought, to make the whole thing look like a naturally occurring grotto. As the pool was huge and lagoon shaped and its lush landscaping gave the feel of a tropical island, she had to admit the effect was pretty impressive.

"You don't know who that is? Margo Knight."

"The ketchup heiress?" Even Jess had heard of her. Both her parents had died in a plane crash a couple of years previously, and Ms. Knight was now said to be worth something in the neighborhood of half a billion dollars. In her early thirties, she was dark haired, slim, and glamorous in a gold Grecian-style gown. Arms wrapped around Pearse's neck, snuggling close as they danced, she was laughing up into his face with the air of a woman who has seen something she wants. Jess didn't have to look far to find Lenore, standing with a knot of Ellis Hayes people not far away, sipping a drink and watching the pair disconsolately over the rim of it.

"Pearse is looking for a political career, and big money's always a help. That woman's been sniffing around him for a while, and I'd say he's interested."

Poor Lenore was what flitted through Jess's mind, but she didn't say it.

"One of those strawberries for me?" Mark appeared behind her, his own plate in his hand. Although he hadn't stayed glued to her side, he'd been keeping her in sight since they'd arrived. Even as she had followed Pearse's order to circulate, she'd been aware of Mark out of the corner of her eye. So far they hadn't had any time for private conversation, but Jess was pretty sure she was going to hear about her solo trip to the Humane Society in greater detail later. She was more interested in where he'd been all day, and what he thought the next step should be in the search for Tiffany.

"Get your own." Smiling, she pulled her plate away from his poaching fingers, then introduced him to Christine.

"You ever testify as an expert witness?" Christine was sizing him up. "I'm thinking we could sway a lot of female jurors with you on the stand."

Mark looked surprised. Then he grinned. "What did you have in mind?"

Jess left them to their discussion as she moved further along the buffet. Hayley was there at the end of the line in front of the carved meats.

"Tell me something: is there a *reason* the hunky Secret Service agent follows you everywhere you go?" Hayley asked as Jess paused to eye the whole roasted pig with a combination of fascination and revulsion.

"Sure. He thinks I'm hot," Jess answered with a tranquil smile and moved on, not having any interest in carved meat anyway. Hayley's expression was priceless, and Jess congratulated herself on scoring a hit.

CHAPTER TWENTY-FIVE

"Enjoying the party, Ms. Ford?" Recognizing the voice speaking behind her, Jess almost lost her grip on her plate. Mr. Dunn! Surprised he remembered her name, she turned with a nervous smile to find him looking her over. With approval? She hoped. At least, thanks to Grace, she was well dressed. She stood a little straighter.

"Very much."

"Glad to hear it. We go to a lot of trouble to make them memorable. In these hard times especially, letting our clients know how much we appreciate them is vital."

"Everyone seems to be having a good time."

"It's the champagne." Unexpectedly, his blue eyes twinkled at her. Set beneath bushy brows that were as white as what was left of his hair, they suddenly looked surprisingly young. Although his face was lined and weathered, and he was stooped now with age, his shoulders were still broad and he still stood well over six feet tall. Once, she thought, he must have been quite an attractive man. "Moët and Chandon, don't you know. Drink enough of it, and you'll have a good time wherever you are. We go through something like a hundred cases per party. Our clients know what the best is, and they not only enjoy it—especially when it's free, like the champagne—they expect it. Which is why they choose Ellis Hayes, of course."

"Of course." Jess's eyes touched on Tony Mancini, the handsome star of a long-running TV drama set in D.C., as he danced past with an unknown but gorgeous blonde. "I have to tell you, since coming to work here I've grown increasingly impressed with our roster of clients."

Mr. Dunn nodded. "Our clients are our

lifeblood. From the days of John Ellis—he was the Ellis in Ellis Hayes, and my maternal grandfather, by the way—we've put everything we have into building our relationships with those who come to us for help. We fight like pit bulls and go the extra mile for every one of our clients. 'Going to war when the outcome is life or death' isn't only our slogan. It's our mantra. We go to war, and by God we win. That's why we attract the clients we do. It's taken decades to build up our reputation to this point, and I must say it is one of the things in my life of which I am most proud. That, and the quality of the associates we take on, of course."

He smiled gallantly at her, and Jess smiled back.

"Mr. Dunn, how are you?" Joining them—actually, slithering in between them so that one shoulder was turned to Jess—Hayley beamed a dazzling smile at Mr. Dunn. The soft glow of the lanterns played up her smooth skin and the dark shine of her hair. She looked lovely, exotic. "What a wonderful party. You've certainly outdone yourself this time."

"Why, thank you, Ms. Marciano. I actually

can't take the credit, however. My assistant takes care of the details, and our caterers are excellent."

"But yours is the great mind behind it, as we all know. Would you mind if I steal Mr. Dunn away?" She flicked a sideways look at Jess before smiling at Mr. Dunn again and continuing before Jess could answer. "That is, if you'd care to dance?"

Mr. Dunn looked surprised, but pleased. "I'd be honored." He glanced at Jess. "Ms. Ford . . ."

"Please go ahead." Jess didn't need the brief flicker of triumph in Hayley's eyes to realize that, in the other's woman's mind at least, she'd been outmaneuvered. Hayley rammed her victory home by thrusting her plate at Jess—"Would you mind? Thanks."—before leading Mr. Dunn off to the dance floor.

"Woman's in it to win it." Andrew's description of Hayley ran through Jess's mind as she set Hayley's plate down on a nearby busing trolley with a rueful grimace. Hayley clearly felt the two of them were in some sort of competition. Jess wasn't sure what the prize was—dibs on the next

promotion?—but her reaction was both instant and instinctive: *bring it on.*

"Well, if it isn't our favorite little lawyer." An arm wrapping around her shoulders and giving her a hug wrung a smile from Jess, who had recognized the speaker—Senator Phillips—as soon as the first honeyed syllable had left his mouth, before she'd even looked around to see who'd been grabbing her. "How you doin', sweetheart?"

"Just fine, thank you, how about you, Senator?" Part of the job was being charming to the clients, and as Jess kept the smile pinned to her lips while nodding a greeting to Mrs. Phillips and Rob, who were with the senator, she thought she ought to at least get brownie points for trying.

"We're doin' real good."

Mrs. Phillips smiled at her and took her husband's arm. "Look, dear, there are the Mulligans. We really ought to go over and say hello."

"You take care," the senator said, and Mrs. Phillips smiled again as they moved off.

Instead of following, Rob stepped so

close that he brushed against her, which gave Jess a bad case of the creepy-crawlies and caused her to instinctively step away.

"Want to dance?"

Jess lost the smile. "Thanks. No."

His hand slid around her bare arm just above her elbow, his fingers lightly caressing her skin. Jess almost jumped, and she jerked her arm free of his grip. Her plate tilted alarmingly. Having now lost her appetite, she set her plate down on the cart, too.

"Come on. It'll be fun."

"Sprained ankle," she said, knowing he knew she was lying and not caring.

"You know, Jessie, now that you're not my lawyer anymore, I was thinking we could go to dinner sometime. What would you say to, oh, La Maison?"

It was the most expensive restaurant in this very expensive town, with a waiting list a mile long.

Don't offend the client. Jess could almost hear Pearse saying it.

"Not in this lifetime," she told him sweetly. "Excuse me, I see someone beckoning to me."

She walked away, because in that moment she couldn't bear to breathe the same air as Rob Phillips. Without even knowing that that was where she meant to go, she headed straight for Mark.

"Honey, your face is all flushed," Christine greeted her as Jess reached Mark's side. That was the first time Jess realized Mark was still talking to Christine, and that Andrew was there in the group with Mark, along with the woman Andrew had been dancing with and a several others she didn't know.

"That happens sometimes when I eat strawberries," she lied again, carefully keeping it light, aware of Mark frowning at her in concern.

"Me, I'm allergic to snakes." Andrew made a comical face. "One even gets close to me, and I faint dead away."

The blonde he'd been dancing with giggled. "That sounds like you're afraid, not allergic."

"Yeah, but I like to think of it as allergic. More manly."

"Dance?" Mark asked quietly as the blonde giggled again, and when Jess nodded he took her hand and pulled her out onto the floor.

"So what's up?" His voice was low.

She had just turned into his arms. Even with her high heels, her eyes were on the approximate level of his chin. The solid strength of his body was absurdly comforting. Looking up into his hard, handsome face, she felt the knot that her stomach had twisted itself into start to loosen. As they moved to the music, she took a deep breath and let it out. She was beginning to relax again. His hand was warm and firm around hers. She could feel the imprint of his other hand in the small of her back.

Just being with Mark felt good.

"Rob Phillips asked me to dinner."

"And you said?"

"Not in this life." A sideways glance told her that Rob was watching her still. A shiver slid down her spine. "I should have been more diplomatic, I know, but that guy gives me the creeps."

"To hell with being diplomatic." Mark's gaze followed hers. She could feel the sudden tension in his body as he spotted Rob. His arm tightening around her waist was the only other warning she got before he bent his head and kissed her. Caught unaware, Jess kept her eyes wide open while his lips slanted over hers and he licked into her mouth even as they continued to dance. He deepened the kiss, and her pulse fluttered with excitement. Her eyes closed and her head reeled and she forgot everything except the hungry insistence of his kiss. Pulse racing, she responded to the heat and urgency of his mouth with an instant, instinctive passion, pressing her body against his, kissing him back, sliding the hand that had been resting on his shoulder around his neck to cling to the strong column of his neck. He tasted of coffee, and champagne, and his kiss sent fire shooting clear down to her toes.

He broke the kiss, lifted his head.

Her eyes opened. A little dazed, she had to blink a couple of times before the chiseled planes of his face came into focus. He was looking down at her, his eyes heavy-lidded and hot as they met her gaze. His mouth had a sensuous curve to it that made her want to kiss him again.

That is, until she remembered where they were.

Their surroundings burst on her in a flash of disbelief. The dance floor was shadowy, but not so dark that they couldn't have been seen perfectly well by anyone who'd been interested. Couples swayed all around them: Jess couldn't see Mr. Dunn and Hayley, but she was pretty sure they were still out there somewhere, and the idea that Mr. Dunn might have witnessed that kiss made her shudder. More potential observers crowded the buffet line, sipped drinks in corners, strolled in and out of the tent.

Oh, my God. How unprofessional can you get?

"What was that?" she hissed at him, careful to keep her voice low lest she be overheard. Her hand slid from his neck to his shoulder. Despite the pressure of his arm around her, she managed to peel herself off his chest. Once again they were only dancing, but she could still feel the heat of that kiss like a tangible thing.

"I was making a point."

"A point?"

"Phillips was looking at you. I wanted the little turd to know that you were taken, that you belong to somebody. If he's got any sense, he'll leave you alone now." Mark's tone was grim.

Jess's initial reaction to that came in a swirl of emotion: a tiny, atavistic thrill at his protectiveness, a hope that maybe Mark was right and seeing that kiss would discourage Rob from ever so much as thinking of her again, and a rousing sense that the sentiments Mark had just expressed needed immediate challenging.

"First of all, I am not *taken* and I don't *belong* to anyone. How chauvinistic can you get?"

Mark smiled faintly. "My bad."

"Second of all, this is a *business* party. Being seen kissing you is not the image I want to project."

"My bad again."

"And third, you can't just kiss me whenever you feel like it. We're *over*, remember?"

"Are we?" He wasn't smiling now. They had danced to the far edge of the crowd, and Jess welcomed the faint breeze that whispered across her overheated skin. Mark was holding her close again, so close she could feel the firmness of his chest against her breasts, the hard muscles in his thighs brushing her own. "Are you sure about that?"

The question made her catch her breath. There were two answers: the one whispered by her heart, and the one in her head, the one she knew she had to give.

"Yes." Her tone was fierce.

"I panicked, you know. That day with MJ. I just flat out panicked because things had happened so fast with you and me. It was just an impulse, a stupid damned impulse, and I regretted it the minute it was done."

Her heart pounded. She could feel her pulse drumming against her eardrums. She was panicking, too, she realized. She wanted him so much, but . . .

"Look, I forgive you—mostly—for kissing Cates. I even respect you again. I appreciate your help in keeping me alive. But none of that changes anything."

He looked impatient. "Jess—"

"I can't have this conversation now." She interrupted whatever he had been going to say by pulling out of his arms. Glancing around, she registered once again the number of eyes around to see, the number of ears to overhear. "Excuse me, would you please? I'm going to the restroom."

Without waiting for his response, she hurried off.

The ladies' restroom was located in another, smaller tent behind the big one she'd left. Jess stayed in there a long time. When she came out, she was feeling calmer. She wasn't up to talking to Mark anymore at the moment, and she was relieved to discover that he wasn't, as she had feared, waiting right outside when she finally emerged.

Pearse was still with Margo Knight over by the waterfall, but they were talking instead of dancing now, probably so the heiress could enjoy the cigarette she was smoking. Jess needed to talk to Pearse—it was better that he heard from her rather than some other source that she had temporarily agreed to represent Tiffany. Besides, she also needed to stay out of that tent for awhile. Maybe this wasn't the best time to approach Pearse, but it had to be done. Anyway, she was definitely on team Lenore. If she could break up Pearse's tête-à-tête with Ms. Moneybags, she figured she should do it.

Keeping a wary eye out for Mark, she walked along the edge of the pool toward the engrossed twosome. Tall potted palms partially blocked her view. Lounge chairs in her way made her path erratic. The roar of the ersatz waterfall was loud enough to preclude her from hearing anything the couple was saying, but she saw that Pearse was laughing and vicariously felt Lenore's pain. She was maybe fifteen feet from her goal when her eye was caught by a passing guest and she stopped abruptly, transfixed, head swiveling as she followed his progress. A tall man in a tux, partially turned away from her. Black hair, fair complexion, narrow jaw . . .

The lights went off. The sudden total darkness alarmed her, and she froze until the lights came back on again and she understood that they were being deliberately flickered as a signal for something, much as they would signal the beginning of the second act. The dance music had stopped. Another band began to play from somewhere above her, presumably the upper terrace. Loud and upbeat, the song was "Margaritaville."

"Everybody, come on up to the upper terrace. Mr. Dunn has an announcement to make," a male voice boomed over the sound system.

Jess barely heard. Rooted in place, she was busy looking for the man she had just

seen in the tide of guests who were starting to head in droves for the upper terrace.
There he was, over by the tent, moving toward the path like the rest. As if he felt her
gaze on him, he turned and looked straight
at her.

Who . . . ?

The lights went off again.

This time, as the velvety black night
descended, as the band built to a cre-
scendo, as the pool area emptied of its
guests, something hit Jess hard in the side.
Too stunned even to cry out, she found
herself flying off her feet, hurtling through
space, crashing down into the churning
maelstrom where the waterfall cascaded
into the pool. In her nostrils was the too-
sweet smell of cheap cologne.

Since her sister had drowned, she'd had
a secret, morbid fear of being in the water.
She never went swimming, never paddled
in the surf, never waded.

But she was falling in.

No!

She screamed, but it was too late.

Cold and dark, the water closed over
her head, swallowing her cry, shooting up
her nose, making her choke and clamp her

lips together as she struggled frantically to save herself. Something had her, held her, pulled her down. She was blinded and deafened by the water, sensory deprived, unable to see what it was. All she knew was that she was being forced further and further under, propelled toward the bottom, helpless to get away. Fighting against it with all her strength, she struggled to hold her breath. Her heart pounded as though it would burst. Her unprepared lungs ached for air.

Horror rushed through her veins as she faced the truth: it was her worst nightmare come to life.

Oh, my God, I'm going to drown.

CHAPTER TWENTY-SIX

Water filled her nose, her ears, burned her eyes, churned against her face. It was like being caught in a washing machine, except instead of being tumbled around she was sinking like an anchor through the turbulence despite her struggle to win free of it. Desperately Jess held her breath, knowing she would die if she didn't. Her pulse pounded like a jackhammer against her eardrums. She felt like her lungs were going to explode. Something had her around the waist—*somebody* had her around the waist. A person, a man, was forcing her to the bottom. She couldn't see him. It was too dark, pitch black there beneath the water, for her to see so much as her own flailing limbs. But she knew he was there. Felt him. Sensed him. His arm locked her to him. Fiercely she fought, although the water resistance meant that her kicks and blows had no real power. She grabbed his arm, tried to pull it off her, tried to squirm free, to no avail.

Panic had her screaming inside her head.

Is this some kind of sick joke? Somebody's idea of a prank? Throw her into the pool and . . .

He's trying to kill me.

She knew it with an icy certainty that chilled her soul.

He forced her down, dragged her to the bottom, shoved her against a hard surface. She could feel the harsh texture of the concrete against the backs of her legs, against her flailing arms. He was on top of her then, shoving her away from him, shoving her against the bottom of the pool. Suddenly something caught, yanked, held her. The pressure holding her down shifted from the man on top to something beneath, something sucking at her like a giant vacuum cleaner, something that snapped her down against the concrete and kept her there while she struggled like a butterfly on a pin, unable to break free.

Terror closed like a fist around her heart, her lungs, squeezing them, compressing them until they pulsated with fear.

Help, she screamed silently.

The man was gone. She was alone. She knew it, knew that whatever now held her in its grip wasn't human. It was swallowing her alive, forcing her inside it, and no matter how hard she pushed against the concrete and clawed for the surface she could not wrench herself free.

A drain. It's a drain. I'm caught in a drain.

The horror of it galvanized her. She battled against the suction, kicking and clawing and fighting with everything she had to escape, holding her breath, fighting a desperate, urgent need to breathe.

It was her dress. The skirt of it, caught by the drain's suction, had already been swallowed as far as the slit would allow. Realizing that, she yanked at the wet silk, pulling with all her strength. She couldn't get free.

Far away, in the world above the water, the lights came on again. She could see the white froth where the waterfall hit, see the blue curved edge of the pool, see the blackness of the sky high overhead, as if through a filmy lens.

Get out of the dress.

The zipper was in the back. Caught as she was against the concrete, she couldn't reach it. Straining for it, then ripping at the neckline, the straps, the slit, she made no headway. The silk was too strong. The drain held her fast.

Somebody help me.

Her lungs burned for air. She thrashed like a hooked fish. Water crammed into her nasal passages, pushed toward her throat. She could taste it, taste the chlorine.

Courtney.

Her sister, three years old. Drowning. Big blue eyes, brown curly hair turned black and slick because it was wet. Looking at her with wide-eyed fear before the wave swept her away.

Oh, God, Courtney, did it hurt?

She had asked her sister that a million times in her dreams. Now she had the answer at last: it hurt dreadfully. The pain of

needing air and being denied it was indescribable. It shredded her insides like red-
hot claws. Her body twisted in agony. She
had to breathe.

Please God, please . . .

Heaving, kicking, battling against the
suction for all she was worth, she prayed
for her life. Her lungs felt like they were collapsing, no oxygen left at all, sticky membrane adhering to sticky membrane. Her
heart beat so hard that she could feel it
slamming against her ribs. Every cell in
her body cried out for air.

**It takes less than two minutes to
drown.**

She'd read that somewhere.

How long has it been?

Even as the question slipped through
her brain, her thoughts grew fuzzy. Her
vision started to blur. Her struggles weak-
ened. She had to, had to, had to, fill her
lungs . . .

The man was back, grabbing her around
the waist again, but she no longer had the
strength to fight him off. Anyway, it was
too late. Her limbs floated rather than
flailed. The struggle suddenly seemed re-
mote, the world increasingly far away. She

couldn't resist the need to fill her lungs with something, anything, to gasp and suck in whatever was there, for more than a second or two longer.

The pain was too intense, the compulsion to breathe too great.

Filling her lungs became this ferocious, driving need.

She saw it now: how easy it would be just to let go and let the water claim her.

Unable to fight it any longer, she gave up and inhaled.

Not air, water. Horrible, horrible water. Gushing into her mouth. Coughing, choking, struggling against it as it poured down her throat, burst through to her lungs. Not easy at all. Hard, so hard.

I don't want to drown.

All of a sudden she shot upward. Barely conscious now, Jess registered it with dreamy surprise. The suction had released. The same force that had pulled her down was carrying her up.

Too late . . .

Then she must have blacked out, because the next thing she knew she was lying on her side beside the pool, choking and gasping and spewing out water and finally sucking in air. Blessed air.

"Breathe, damn you," she heard a harsh voice gasp. "Breathe."

She breathed, coughing and sputtering but *breathing.* Her surroundings were blurry, but she saw that a man was on his hands and knees beside her, trim and fit in black pants and a white shirt, hair soaked, water streaming off him so that she knew he'd been in the pool, too. She felt a little frisson of fear until he moved so that the weird pale light hit him just right and she could make out the broad strokes of a handsome, familiar face.

"Mark." It was a croak.

"Jesus, Jess, what are you trying to do to me here?" He was coughing, hoarse, but indubitably there.

Immediately she relaxed and gulped in more air, and wheezed and gasped and breathed some more, greedily, as if she could never get enough, while a crowd began to gather around and Mark wrapped her in his coat, which was dry. That was when she understood that she was clad only in her soaking wet, flesh-colored bra and panties, and that Mark had shed his coat to jump in after her, and that the reason everything was still blurry was because she must have lost her contacts in the water.

"My God, what happened?"

"How did she fall in?"

". . . that little girl lawyer from the Phillips trial . . ."

"Probably too many mai tais."

"Who found her? Oh, that guy? Who is he?"

". . . tell Mr. Dunn . . ."

"Look out, here come the EMTs."

"Jess? Is it Jess?"

The jumble of voices she was overhearing was too intertwined to make out more than a few random phrases, but that last voice belonged to Lenore, Jess was almost sure. Just as Jess looked up to see that Lenore, and Hayley, and then Andrew and Pearse were standing over her looking down in concern, the EMTs arrived. Jess tried to sit up then, tried to tell everyone that she was fine, but her voice was low and ragged and easy to disregard, and she was so weak that she found that sitting up was not an option after all. Instead she was scooped up and deposited on a gurney, then silenced by an oxygen mask that they kept clamping over her face and she kept pushing aside to try to insist, in a raspy, weak voice, that, except for being shaken up, she was fine. Her objections were overruled by everyone from Mark to Pearse to Mr. Dunn, who insisted she go to the hospital to be checked out.

"Really, I'm all right," she tried to say one last time as they trundled her away toward the waiting ambulance, but the words turned into a spasm of coughing and she got the oxygen mask treatment again and gave up.

Mark rode in the ambulance with her. Knowing he was there made all the difference. Without the strain of having to worry about her safety, or keep up a brave front for her colleagues, she was able to close her eyes and be as weak and trembly as she actually felt. She could suck in the healing oxygen, secure in the knowledge that she was safe, and there was only Mark to see.

In the emergency room, when the doctor had finished examining her and she and Mark were finally left alone in one of the little curtained cubicles, she lay back against the raised head of the bed, feeling limp and exhausted but so glad to be alive. Her head swam, her throat was sore, and a clip on her finger monitored her oxygen levels, but the doctor had said he didn't think she had suffered any lasting damage. They were just waiting on the results of a couple of tests, to be sure.

It wasn't an accident.

There was no chance. Someone had deliberately tried to kill her. As she faced the incontrovertible truth of it, fear formed a hard knot in her chest.

"Mark. I didn't just fall in." It was the first chance she'd had to tell him what she had been bursting to tell him since she'd gotten her wits together. Her voice was croaky and hoarse. Her throat felt raw. Jess shivered as she remembered swallowing so much water, remembered the chemical tang of chlorine, remembered the horror of it rushing into her lungs. They'd taken her wet underthings when she had arrived and dried her hair and wrapped her in warmed blankets, so that now she was swaddled like a baby in blue thermal cotton. But suddenly she felt freezing cold again.

"What?" He was sitting in a chair just a few feet away, his head tipped back against the smooth green wall. Nobody had thought to offer him a blanket, so his clothes had more or less dried on him. Due to the absence of contact lenses, her vision was still blurry, but she could see that his white shirt was still damp enough to cling to his broad shoulders and wide chest, and his black bow tie hung open from the unbuttoned collar of his shirt. But he had to be feeling cold, too, and clammy in the air-conditioning. She would have passed him a blanket if she'd had the energy to move. But she didn't.

"Somebody pushed me in, or tackled me or something. A man. He forced me all the way to the bottom of the pool and held me there until my dress got stuck in the drain."

Mark didn't ask if she was sure. His hands curled around the ends of the chair's wooden arms. Then he abruptly got to his feet and came to stand beside the bed. His face changed, hardening and tightening, and his eyes turned from their usual clear ocean blue to an opaque shade of denim as they slid over her.

"That means the attack in front of my apartment probably wasn't just random either." Her voice was very small as she followed her thoughts to their logical conclusion. "I think"—she remembered the cologne—"it was the same man."

For a moment they simply stared at each other.

"To hell with this. We're getting you out of D.C. If I'd been a minute or two later, you'd be dead now." Mark sounded angry, violent even.

To hear it put so bluntly made Jess's stomach clench. It was true, she knew. At the thought of how close she'd come to dying her heart beat faster.

All my life, since Courtney, my worst fear has been that I would drown.

Okay, deep breath. It didn't happen.

"That won't help." Keeping her voice steady required an effort, but she managed it. "If this is some government assassin type trying to kill me, no place is far away enough, and you know that as well as I do. If it's not, the way to stop him is to catch him. I think I saw him, Mark." The memory of a tall, black-haired man with a long face and a narrow jaw swam through her mind. Distance and darkness had kept his features indistinct to a certain degree, but she was convinced she had seen him before. Her pulse raced as she searched for the elusive link—and then a pair of memories came together in her mind and she knew when and where. "I think he might have been the same man I saw with Tiffany that night after the trial ended. You know, when I got out of the Suburban to talk to her."

"I remember." A hint of wryness touched his expression. Then his eyes hardened again. "How sure are you of that?"

Jess hesitated, mentally comparing what she could remember of the two images. "Not one hundred percent. I'd say it's a possibility. A good possibility."

"Think you could describe him to somebody? I know a forensic artist who does really good work."

"You mean have somebody sketch him? That's a good idea." Jess hesitated. "I didn't really see him close up either time. I can't quite picture his nose, or his mouth, or even his eyes. What's in my mind is just kind of a general face. You know, the shape, long, angular, with a narrow jaw, and the coloring, and the position of the features."

"It can't hurt to try." He managed a small smile for her. "Okay. Tell me what happened. I saw you come out of the ladies' room, but then the lights started blinking and I lost you."

"I wanted to tell Pearse that I was going to be representing Tiffany. He was over by the pool, and I was walking toward him when I looked around and saw this man— *the* man. He saw me, too. Then the lights went out and . . . he tackled me. Or somebody did. *Boom*, and I was in the pool."

"You never got a look at him while he was pulling you under the water? Not so much as a glimpse?"

"No. It was dark. And—once I was in the water, I was so scared." As soon as she said it she started to shake inside. Then she realized that she wouldn't have confessed that to anyone but him. And what part of *over* did that have anything to do with?

Her breath blew out in a little sigh.

Mark didn't say anything. Instead his lips thinned and his eyes narrowed. He walked over and picked up his phone from a little pile of shoulder holster, wallet, and keys that lay atop his folded coat on a cart near the bed. Jess assumed he'd had the presence of mind to shed those things before leaping into the pool after her. She wondered about his shoes, but she guessed he'd kicked them off, too, and then put them back on again to go to the hospital.

"What are you doing?" she asked as he punched in a number.

"What does it look like? Making some calls."

"To whom?"

"First, Hasbrough. Second, MPD. I want to make sure there's a priority on this, and some kind of coordination so that the left hand knows what the right hand is doing. After that, some guys I know. Twice in the last week somebody's come after you. This needs to stop now. Third time just might be the charm."

Jess looked at him in sudden alarm as the ramifications of putting her situation out for public consumption hit her.

"Oh, my God, Mark, no. Stop. Wait. I don't mind Hasbrough, but you can't call the police. I can't cause some big stink about being attacked at Mr. Dunn's party.

The police will question everybody—not just the people who work at Ellis Hayes but the guests . . . the clients." Jess almost shuddered at the thought. "It'll be this huge thing. If Mr. Dunn thinks I come with all these problems, I'll get fired. Or maybe not fired but . . . pushed aside. Eased out. I might as well kiss my career good-bye."

"It's better than being dead."

"Mark—" But she broke off and listened as the call went through and he spoke to Hasbrough, describing what had happened, taking Hasbrough through the different possibilities, suggesting that if it hadn't been an attempt to silence Jess about what had really happened to Annette Cooper, then it might have had something to do with the Phillips trial that had just ended. When he disconnected, Mark looked slightly less grim.

"We're going to get this guy, whoever he is," he told Jess. "Keeping you alive has just become job one. Hasbrough promised to pull out all the stops. We got the uber-cops working this thing now, baby."

"Then we don't need to involve the police."

Mark looked at her hard. "Your career is really that important to you, isn't it?"

Jess knew the answer without a shadow of a doubt. "Yes."

"Christ." He shook his head. "Okay, we don't involve the police. They probably wouldn't be a lot of help at this point anyway. And you're right, they'd stir up a lot of shit. I don't want this guy going to ground before we catch him."

Jess sighed with relief. As terrifying as it was to know that someone was trying to kill her, she had every faith that Mark and his associates would do whatever it took to both keep her safe and find and stop whoever it was. When that happened, she wanted to have her career intact. Then something occurred to her that she'd been too shaken to wonder about before.

"How did you know I was in the pool?"

"Pure damn luck." He looked grim again. Jess's expression urged him to continue. "You were over there by the restroom one minute and then I didn't see you. I came looking for you, and then the lights started going on and off and they made that announcement asking everybody to go to the upper terrace and it was like a tidal wave of people all heading in the same direction. I almost went up the path with everybody else, thinking you'd gone that way. But something made me take one last look around first, and I saw your shoe, one of those sparkly high heels you were wearing. It was in the pool, floating on top of the water, the sequins or whatever catching the light. Then I looked down, into the water, and saw this dark shape, and I knew it was you, and I dove in."

"Thank God you did. I would have drowned."

"Yeah."

"So how did you manage to get me loose? The drain—"

"I ripped the hell out of that damned dress."

The most fleeting of smiles touched Jess's mouth. "Grace will—"

Before she could complete the thought, she was interrupted by a way-too-familiar sound from just beyond the curtain. It made her stiffen with dismay.

CHAPTER TWENTY-SEVEN

"Did you . . . ," Jess began, looking at Mark as her mother's voice reached her ears for the second time.

He was saved from having to reply by Judy's sudden eruption into the room, followed by Maddie's. Judy wore an orange T-shirt and green floral cropped pants—mismatched and obviously hastily pulled on—with white slides. Her heels clacked on the smooth hard floor as she made a beeline for the bed. Maddie was in a sundress and flip-flops, her hair in a ponytail, her stomach sticking out to there.

"Oh my goodness, Jess, when Mark

called and told us what had happened, I about had a heart attack. My poor little girl!" Judy swooped on her, wrapping her in the tightest of hugs. Over her shoulder, Jess glared accusingly at the traitor, who'd risen to his feet at her mother's entrance. He responded with an apologetic half smile and a slight shrug.

"We brought you some clothes." Maddie held up the plastic grocery bag she was carrying. "Mark said you needed some. How did you manage to fall into a pool?"

"Just clumsy, I guess." Jess suffered her mother's hug and smiled at her sister before shooting Mark another killing glare. At least he hadn't told them that it hadn't been an accident. Of course, when he'd talked to them—it must have been while the doctor had been examining her—she hadn't yet told him the full story.

"Of all the horrible things to happen. I can't believe it." Jess saw the pain shining in her mother's eyes and felt her heart contract. Of course, as Courtney's mother, her suffering would have been even worse than Jess's. For all these years afterward, Judy had kept going, putting the tragedy behind her, taking care of her remaining daughters and living her life as best she could—but in that instant Jess saw that the terrible well of grief was still there.

"I'm okay, Mom." Contrite at her perfunctory response to the previous hug, she held out her arms to her mother, and this time, when Judy enfolded her, Jess hugged her tightly back. For a moment the two of them, the only two who could, shared the memory, the sorrow, the love they both still felt for she who was lost. Then Judy straightened with a sniff and a smile and a pat on Jess's shoulder before turning to look at Mark. "Thank you from the bottom of my heart for being there to fish her out."

"My pleasure," Mark responded as Judy hugged him, too, while Maddie, to whom the tragedy was only a distant, though moving, family story, rolled her eyes and dropped the plastic bag on the bed beside Jess.

Maddie said, "What I don't understand is what happened to your dress. Grace said it was the most gorgeous thing ever."

"It got caught in a drain. If Mark hadn't—"

"I had to park three lots over." Sarah pushed through the curtain before Jess could finish. She was perfectly adequately dressed in white shorts and a tee, but her hair was all bouncing fat ringlets, as if she'd just pulled curlers out of it, and her face was bare of makeup. Obviously when the call had come in she'd been ready for bed. Her eyes went straight to Jess, moved over her as if in swift evaluation, and her face re-formed into its usual placid lines. She said to Jess, "Just so you know, there are all kinds of people out in the waiting room on your behalf. In long dresses and tuxes, yet."

"Oh, no," Jess moaned.

"I heard them asking for you at the desk. The nurses aren't letting anybody but family back."

Jess was horror-stricken. "I've ruined the party."

The doctor came into the room. He looked briefly surprised to see so many people in the small space, but the news was good: Jess was free to go.

"You're coming home with us for the night," Judy said to Jess when the doctor left, in a tone that brooked no opposition. "If Grace is sleeping elsewhere—and, yes, I know about her new boyfriend, girls—I don't think you should spend the night alone."

"There's Mark, Mom," Sarah reminded her in a low but perfectly audible undertone.

"Do you think they're sleeping together again? So soon?" was Judy's equally low-voiced but audible rejoinder. She then looked at Mark. "Are you sleeping . . . ?"

Before Judy could finish the embarrassing question, Jess jumped in. "I'm coming home with you, Mom, don't worry."

Another unannounced, unexpected visitor made her stiffen and clutch the blankets closer.

"Had to pull rank to get back here, but I just wanted to see how you were doing for myself," Mr. Dunn boomed, standing in the opening of the now parted curtain. He was still in his tux. His age was all too evident beneath the harsh emergency room lights, but he still looked every inch the rich, influential man he was. His blue eyes were bright as they met Jess's. "You certainly gave us a fright, young woman."

If she could have, Jess would have crawled under the bed. "I'm so sorry to have spoiled the party, Mr. Dunn."

As he came toward the bed to take her hand and pat it consolingly, Jess spotted her team—Pearse, Andrew and Hayley, plus Lenore and Christine—hovering in the hall behind him. She gave them a little wave and Andrew lit up his tie at her, which made Jess smile. She suddenly felt like a real, accepted part of the team, and it boosted her spirits. Then they came in, too, and Jess spent the next few minutes making introductions and reassuring everyone that she was fine, perfectly fine.

She said it so much that she almost believed it herself.

It was quite some time before she was finally able to get dressed and leave the hospital.

In the world of spooks, there were good guys and there were bad guys. Sometimes they were interchangeable. Usually, Mark liked to think he was one of the good guys. But now the lines were blurring, and he was going to do whatever the hell he had to do to keep Jess safe.

Which was why he had left Jess cocooned in the bosom of her family with a couple of undercover agents, sent over by

Hasbrough, on stakeout duty outside and why he was breaking into an apartment in Congress Heights in the middle of the night.

He'd spent most of the day off the grid, working with some people he knew to ID that partial picture they had of the perp who'd attacked Jess. He'd left one Service guy running the partial through all kinds of databases in hopes of a hit, which so far hadn't materialized. He'd also taken a copy to the forensic artist he'd spoken about, who just happened to be an old friend of his. Okay, so her name was Mallory, and they'd been lovers, and it hadn't been that long ago, maybe a year, which was probably going to make Jess see pea green if she learned of it, which, if he could prevent it, wasn't going to happen. Why borrow trouble? He and Mallory had parted friends, and she was willing to do him a favor by trying to re-create a face using measurements and norms and whatever. How she did it he didn't know exactly, but he did know she was good at her job. And she'd promised to have something for him—a sketch of a face—in a couple of days. When she did, he'd take Jess to her and see what the two of them could come up with, and how it compared. The only really distinguishing feature they'd been able to pull off the partial was a round scar on the guy's right hand. They'd run that through all the databases, too. So far, nothing.

The DNA was going to take a little longer, ten days to two weeks, maybe. And that was the timetable Mark got by calling in every favor anybody in the lab had ever owed him. Most cases languished for months, he was informed. There was simply too much stuff coming in, more every day, some of it on the most horrific cases imaginable, and *everybody* needed results tomorrow.

Tonight's attack had cranked up the urgency meter. There was no longer any doubt: somebody wanted Jess dead.

His emotions, as he'd realized that it had been her under the water of that pool, had been something he didn't care to think about just at present. Right now, what he had to be was a pro on a job. The personal he could deal with later.

As Mark had expected, there was a trip

wire just inside the door of the apartment, which was pitch black. He identified the spider-silk-thin gleam of silver via a quick sweep of his flashlight, then sidestepped it. See, that was the trouble with cheap apartments where bad guys liked to hide out: you had to provide your own security. Which the smart ones did, in a rudimentary, but effective, fashion. From experience, Mark knew that the trip wire was attached to a weapon that would have blown a hole through his chest if he'd been unwary enough to touch it. Fortunately, he wasn't that unwary.

Rusty, though, he was forced to admit. Which was why the only warning he got was a soft snick that he recognized just a split second too late as a knife blade being extended before somebody leaped on him out of the dark, knocking his Glock out of his hand, going for the kill.

The fight was short, violent, and very nearly lethal. It would have been lethal if he hadn't ended up the victor, pinning his quarry to the cheap-feeling wall to wall carpeting and holding the guy's own knife to his throat.

"Getting old, Gooch," he said amiably to the man lying spent and panting beneath him.

"What the fuck do you want, Ryan?"

"Believe it or not, I got a job I want to offer you."

There was a moment of silence.

"You ever hear of something called a phone?"

"I didn't realize you were taking calls."

"You for real about the job? When I saw you come creeping across my living room, I figured you were moonlighting as a hit man."

"If I was moonlighting, you'd be dead."

"True that."

"So you interested?"

"You want to get off me, we'll talk."

"You planning to jump me again if I let you up?"

"Where's the paycheck in that?"

Good point. Mark got up, cautiously, keeping the knife, picking up his Glock and the flashlight. Of course, Gooch probably had a dozen other weapons near at hand. Sometimes you just had to trust that the other guy wasn't going to let paranoia, or vengeance, or something like that out-weigh monetary considerations.

Once on his feet, Mark asked, "You mind if I turn on a light?"

"Hell, yeah, I mind. Whoever got me sprung from the clink didn't do it out of the goodness of their heart. I know where a lot of bodies are buried—literally, I do—and I figure they got me out before I could use that to make a deal. Now that I'm out, smart thing to do is kill me. I can see I'm not wrong: you found me. You had to get my location from somebody. Which means somebody is interested enough in me to know where I am. Which is why I'm in the process of packing up and moving on. An-other hour, and you would have missed me. Turn on a light, and anybody coming knows I'm home. And that ain't good. Might precipitate something I'd just as soon gave me the go-by. So you want to cut to the chase with your offer? Cause I got places I need to be."

See, the thing was, Dustin Yamaguchi—Gooch, for short—was one of those spook bad guys. He hadn't always been—he and Mark had worked together when Mark had been a newbie Secret Service agent and Gooch had been on one of his first missions for the CIA, many years before—but about ten years ago Gooch had gone over to the dark side. Until finally he'd ended up out of the spook business altogether, killing people for money. But Gooch knew a great many other spook bad guys. Which was where Mark's job offer came in.

"I want you to use your contacts, check around, try to find somebody for me."

Gooch was wary. "Who?"

"I don't know who, precisely. If I did, why would I need you? But somebody deep inside is maybe trying to kill a friend of mine, and I want to find out if that is indeed the case, along with who it is, and who ordered it."

"What friend?"

"Remember that lady lawyer I brought to see you?"

"The cute little chickie? Sure." Gooch sounded interested. "She your girlfriend? Didn't really seem like your type."

Mark wasn't going there, especially not with somebody like Gooch, who was a horndog from way back. "She's my responsibility. My screwup is the reason why she's being targeted. You know how it is: you break it, you fix it."

"You want me to whack whoever this is when I find them?"

"I'm not completely sure there's any-body there to find. I want you to nose around, listen to the word on the wind. If there is somebody trying to kill her, I want to know who it is before anything else gets done. Then you and I will talk again."

"What's your time frame? And how much green we talking about?"

That brought them to the details. By the time Mark left, carefully skirting the trip wire once again, he and Gooch had a deal.

Not that he didn't trust Hasbrough, who had agreed that protecting Jess was the Service's responsibility and had vowed to pull out all the stops to find this guy. But Mark wasn't naive: he'd worked in the field too long.

Which was why when it came to Hasbrough—or anybody else who he thought was supposed to be on his side, for that matter—his motto was trust, but verify.

In his experience, people tended to live longer that way.

I don't want to die.

After hours spent entombed in a car trunk, Lucy sent that out into the universe with just about every too-fast heartbeat.

The only reason she and Jaden were still alive was that the car had run out of gas. At least, the engine had finally stopped after sputtering a few times, and Lucy had thought an empty gas tank had probably been the reason. Or maybe the engine had simply conked out. Whatever, Lucy had known they were supposed to have been dead. She'd been conscious enough to be aware when the car had come to a halt at last, had been petrified with fear as she'd listened to the car door opening and slamming closed again, followed by footsteps on a hard surface.

He's coming. Panic had sent her scrambling as far back into her dark prison as she'd been able to get. But the footsteps had walked on by.

A moment later she'd heard the rumble of what had sounded like a garage door closing. She had guessed it had been clos-

ing, because, just before the car had
stopped moving, she had heard that same
rumble, which had probably been the door
opening.

Where is he? What's he doing?

Now, all these hours later, she still remembered the sharp terror of her thoughts.

She'd lain there, cramped and shaking,
in total, complete darkness, waiting for
whoever had taken them to pop open the
trunk. The engine had still been running,
so the guy couldn't have gone far. No matter what he had done next, no matter if
he'd had a gun or whatever, she'd been
planning on going to jump out of there like
a kangaroo on springs and run or fight or
do whatever she'd had to do to save herself. Jaden hadn't been moving, although
Lucy had tried to rouse her again just like
she had tried to rouse her umpteen times
before, so Lucy had waited alone, sweating, terrified, crouched, getting ready to
make her move, so that her legs had
bunched under her, although the cramped
space had made that difficult.

Jump for your life. It had sounded like
some kind of stupid game show, and she
would have laughed hysterically at the idea

if she hadn't been pretty near hysterical, period.

But nobody had come, nothing had happened, and finally her legs had cramped and she'd lain down to stretch them out as best she'd been able, and then she'd been too tired to get back up. For a long time she'd stayed curled up in a ball just listening to her own heart pounding, listening to the purr of the running engine, growing increasingly short of air in the suffocating heat, then getting sick and dizzy, wanting to sleep. She would have slept if she hadn't been too afraid to close her eyes, but fear had kept them open, kept her conscious, until, finally, she had figured it out. She and Jaden were locked in the trunk of a car. They were probably in an enclosed space such as a garage. The engine was still running. Her head swam, and she felt like barfing up her toenails before passing out.

Carbon monoxide.

In a blinding burst of enlightenment, it came to her that that was what it had to be. He was going to kill them by using carbon monoxide, without ever opening the trunk. She wasn't going to get a chance to run, or fight, or anything else, because she and Jaden were both going to be dead before the man came back.

Please don't let me die.

Galvanized by a fresh burst of terror, she lost it then, screaming her head off and kicking at the seam where the trunk closed and pounding on the metal roof over her head until exhaustion or fumes or something overcame her and she collapsed into a sobbing, trembling ball, clutching at the unconscious but still breathing Jaden and praying like there was actually a God up there and He cared enough to help.

Please please please please please . . .

Two things happened almost simultaneously: Jaden woke up, and the engine coughed once, twice, three times, then died.

No sound. No vibrations. Nothing. Nada.

Her first thought was that the guy had come back and turned off the car.

But she hadn't heard anything. No rumble of a garage door opening. No footsteps. Nothing. And nobody came.

Please. God. Please.

She lay there, dizzy and sick and so scared that she was shaking, feeling stupid as she muttered another prayer to a god she was pretty sure didn't even exist. But hey, the first one seemed to have worked. Or something.

After a while, Lucy realized that the fumes must have dissipated, because she was feeling better.

They were still trapped in the trunk of the car. They had been in there a long time now; she didn't know how long exactly, because being locked in a closed, dark space that was hotter than an oven and smelled sickeningly of gasoline and motor oil—and she didn't even want to think what else—probably made it feel like it was forever when it hadn't been. But it had been hours, at least. Maybe as much as a day.

The man hadn't yet come back. Because he thought they were dead in there, she supposed, so what was the rush?

If we don't get out of here, we're still going to die.

"I'm thirsty," Jaden whispered. It was the first thing she'd said for a long time. Weak and sick, she lay curled on her side at the far edge of the space, out of Lucy's way. They were both sweating and achy and miserable and scared out of their minds.

The difference was, Jaden had given up, while Lucy wasn't going down without a fight.

"Yeah, me, too. Try not to think about it."

Legs folded beneath her, Lucy was bent into a pretzel as she used a screwdriver they'd found to pry at the seam where the trunk closed. She'd been doing it for a while. In the pitch black, it was difficult to tell if she was making any progress, but she thought she'd at least bent the metal some. The carpet was scrunched beneath her legs in an uncomfortable wave, because they'd torn it up trying to get to the well where the spare tire was kept. They'd found the tire, which had been useless to them, and a jack, which had also proved useless because they hadn't been able to figure out how to work it in the dark, and the screwdriver. So far it had proven pretty useless, too.

The head-on clink of metal on metal made Lucy think she'd hit the latch. If they could just somehow break it . . .

"Hold this," she told Jaden, reaching for her friend's hand and curling it around the screwdriver's hard plastic handle. "Whatever you do, don't let it move."

"Why?" Jaden's voice was apathetic. Lucy put some bite into her own voice to try to put some fight back into Jaden.

"Just do it."

Jaden moaned, but she wriggled forward until she was in a better position to do as Lucy asked. Lucy kept her own hand in place until Jaden's grip was strong and steady enough to do the job. Then Lucy wormed around until her back was wedged against the back of the trunk.

Please, God. Please.

Bringing her knee up as high as she could, she slammed the sole of her boot against the end of the screwdriver handle with all her might.

Miracle of miracles, the trunk sprang open with a metallic clank. A light blinked on.

The trunk light, of course, Lucy realized even as she cringed and threw up a hand to ward off what felt like a dazzling brightness.

Jaden blinked at her. Her face was a shiny, sweaty white and her hair stuck out all over the place. Lucy thought she looked like a day-old corpse. For a moment neither of them moved. Lucy's heart pounded like a *Riverdancer*'s feet. Her stomach turned inside out.

Is anybody out there?

The darkness beyond the trunk was degrees less black than the trunk itself had been, like a dark night compared to the inside of a cave. Except for the rasp of their own breathing, the silence was absolute. Cool air poured in. Not fresh, exactly, but cool. The feel of it on Lucy's damp skin was phenomenal.

Lucy was almost sure they were alone.

"Lucy, you did it! You did it!" Jaden's whisper was filled with awe.

"*We* did it."

Tremulous with fear and excitement, they scrambled awkwardly out of the trunk. Lucy's knees threatened to give way. For a moment after she hit the ground the world seemed to tilt. If she hadn't grabbed the back of the car, she would have crumpled to the pavement. Jaden did collapse, her legs buckling beneath her.

"Jaden. Come on." Lucy crouched beside her, putting an arm around her, but Jaden was already pushing up onto her hands and knees.

"I'm coming." Moving slowly, Jaden

made it, first onto her hands and knees, then to her feet. Lucy had already determined that they were, as she had suspected, in a garage. The big black car they had escaped from was the only vehicle in it, although it was easily a two-car garage with space left over. There were two overhead garage doors, Lucy saw as they headed toward the one directly in front of them. She let go of Jaden, reached it, pulled up on the handle hard.

It was locked. So was the other one. So was the person-sized door set into the side wall. Locked from the outside, with the kind of locks that need a key. Flipping a switch she found on one wall led to exactly nothing: no door opening, no light coming on. There was no inside button that Lucy could find to operate the doors.

Leaving Jaden sitting cross-legged in the middle of the floor, Lucy worked her way around the walls, looking for any possible way out. It was a metal building with a concrete floor. No windows. A pole building, Lucy had heard similar structures called.

They were trapped inside it.

Lucy was just facing the horrible truth of that when the trunk light went out.

"Lucy," Jaden whispered. "Listen."

That's when Lucy heard it, too: the faint crunch of footsteps on gravel approaching the garage.

Her first terrified thought was. He's *back.*

"It's him, isn't it?" Jaden's voice shook.

They both knew who Jaden meant: Miss Howard's killer. Lucy didn't bother to answer.

Who else could it be?

CHAPTER TWENTY-EIGHT

It was 2:00 a.m., and Jess wanted to go home to her apartment. She was tired, scared, and traumatized from her recent near-death experience. Her throat was sore, she ached all over, and she needed sleep.

The thing was, at Ellis Hayes, Saturday was a work day. Oh, not an official one. But still, everybody showed up. And she had things she needed to do. Not all of which involved her job.

A knock on the kitchen door made Maddie and Sarah, who were sitting around the kitchen table talking to Jess, jump.

Jess didn't jump because she was expecting it. Judy had gone up to bed some twenty minutes before, pleading exhaustion, and Jess had immediately texted Mark, who, she presumed, was still somewhere nearby. Having remembered from the last time how unpleasant it was to get up early and go home in borrowed clothes only to get dressed again to go to work, Jess had no desire to repeat the experience. Besides, she was worried about Allison's cat. And to tell the truth, she hated the idea of Mark keeping watch outside the house in the Suburban all because of her, which she assumed was what he was doing. He had to be nearly as exhausted as she was.

"Who on earth . . . ?" Sarah asked as Maddie, having no clue there was any reason not to, went to the door.

"Ask who it is first," Jess told Maddie sharply before she could open it.

Sarah frowned at her, but Maddie did as she was told.

"Mark," came the answer, just as Jess had expected. Still, given recent events, it was wise to be careful.

Maddie opened the door.

"Hey." Mark stepped inside the kitchen. Jess met his gaze. She could see properly again because she was wearing a spare pair of glasses she kept at her mother's house. A glance told her that he'd lost the tux and was wearing a black tee and jeans instead. With his hair ruffled and stubble darkening his jaw, he looked handsome and tough and tired all at the same time. She smiled at him, and he smiled back, the small exchange feeling disturbingly intimate.

Over, she reminded herself, but she was so glad to see him that she didn't even care.

"What are you doing here?" Maddie closed the door again.

"He came to get me." Standing up, Jess answered before Mark could. "I didn't want to upset Mom, but I'm going home to my apartment. I have to go in to work tomorrow."

"What?" Mark looked at her like she'd lost her mind.

"You don't mean it," Sarah said.

"It's Saturday," Maddie protested.

"In case it's slipped your mind, just a few hours ago you nearly died," Mark said, to which her sisters nodded vigorous agreement.

The nearly identical sentiments, although expressed in different terms, seemed to unite the speakers. All three frowned at Jess.

"I'll go in late," she promised Mark as she moved around the table toward him. She was wearing an old pair of her own knee-length khaki shorts and a green tee that could have been anybody's, plus a pair of Maddie's flip-flops. The opposite of hot, but she realized she was perfectly comfortable with Mark seeing her like that. "But I'm going in." He looked like he meant to object with more force, but she forestalled him by speaking over her shoulder to her sisters. "Tell Mom I'll come by on Sunday, would you?" At their concerned expressions she frowned impatiently. "And you can both stop looking at me like I'm going to keel over at any minute. I had a bad experience, true, but I survived and I'm fine. And I'll feel better sleeping in my own bed."

Remembering that to their minds "sleeping in my own bed" presumably meant sleeping with Mark, Jess suddenly felt self-conscious. Something of what she was thinking must have shown in her face, because both sisters' expressions changed noticeably.

"Oh, I get it," Maddie said, while Sarah murmured, "Uh-huh," while looking Mark up and down. Sarah added a twinkling, "Welcome back" to him while Maddie piped up with, "I bet Taylor's excited. She said the best thing about you being with Jess was it kept you too busy to stick your nose into her life."

"Good to know." Mark's response was dry.

Sighing inwardly, Jess decided the best thing to do was just let them think what they would for the time being.

"See you Sunday, Maddie. If you're not here, I'll call you, Sarah," Jess said on her way out the door, because presumably Sarah would have reunited with her sons and been back in her own house by then. Or maybe the boys and Sarah would be staying with her mother. Given the state of Sarah's marriage, it was hard to tell.

Outside, the world smelled like damp grass. A streetlamp in the alley kept the night from being utterly dark. Jess supposed there must have been a heavy cloud cover overhead to keep her from seeing any hint of a star or the moon. The humidity curled around her like smoke. For once the heat felt good.

"So where is Taylor this weekend?" Jess asked as they went down the back steps.

"She stayed with her mother. There's a concert, and she has a date." Mark's tone as he said that last was so sour that Jess had to smile. "Next weekend she's going on a class trip. I practically have to beg to get any time with her anymore, and then all we do is fight."

"You're a good father to her. She'll appreciate that when she's older."

"I'll believe it when it happens. You realize that your sister is going to tell my daughter we're back together."

"Probably."

"Something to straighten out later, I guess." His tone changed. "You're serious about going in to work tomorrow, aren't you? You know that after what happened everybody's going to expect you to stay home, right? Especially since it's Saturday?"

Mark was close behind her when they stepped into the shadows that darkened the area near the rickety privacy fence that separated her mother's backyard from her neighbors'. His hand rested protectively on the small of her back as she went through the gate and toward the Suburban, which she could now see parked in the alley behind the house. Another car waited not too far away, pulled over against the row of garbage cans that lined the other side of the alley. The car was seemingly deserted, but still Jess eyed it nervously. If Mark hadn't been right behind her, she would have turned and hightailed it back to the house.

"I've officially been on Pearse's team for less than a week," she said. Mark came around to open the door for her. Given the other parked car, at which she cast another worried glance, although she didn't point it out since he had presumably noticed it too, she discovered she was glad. She had to wait until he'd gotten in himself before she continued. "Somebody's trying to kill me: yes, I get that. And I know I don't have to go in. The thing is, I can't just lie in bed with the covers pulled up over my head until you tell me it's safe to come out. There's Tiffany, for one thing. And Allison.

And that lawsuit against Shelter House. And even if I didn't have anything else going on, I really, really want to do my best at this job. Anyway, there are some things I want to check out that I can only access at the office, like Allison's computer files. So I'm going in to work. I'll get brownie points for showing up under difficult circumstances, and I'll get a chance to do some digging around on my own."

"What you need to do is hole up in your apartment until we figure this thing out." Mark pulled off down the alley. "We'll get it done, and we'll be as quick as we can, I promise."

"I know you will, and I appreciate it. But I'm still going in to work tomorrow." A glance in the sideview mirror revealed that the parked car was pulling in behind them. Its headlights came on even as she watched.

"You are the stubbornest—"

"There's a car following us," she interrupted, her eyes wide with alarm as she tracked its progress through the mirror. "It was parked across the alley when we came out."

"It's backup." He barely even bothered to glance in the rearview mirror. "I had to run an errand, so they sent somebody over to keep an eye on your mother's house while I was gone. I told you, Hasbrough's committed to protecting you. Besides me, there'll be people around constantly until whoever this is is stopped."

"Discreetly," Jess stipulated. "And, see, that means I'll be perfectly safe wherever I am."

"Absolutely discreetly. But, for the record, screwups happen. I just don't want you to be on the wrong side of one."

He sounded so grim that Jess changed the subject. "What kind of errand did you have to run?"

"Grab some clean clothes, check the house, you know."

"Oh." Watching the car following them turn off and head for the Beltway, Jess briefly lost track of the conversation.

When she finally looked at him again, she was frowning. "My question is, can we trust Hasbrough? And whoever he sends out for backup?"

"Oh, ye of little faith."

His tone was light. But she knew from the sudden tightening of his hands on the wheel that she'd hit the nail on the head.

The real answer was, maybe, probably, who the hell knew?

They were in Foggy Bottom by that time, and traffic had picked up. A surprising number of people were out and about, and Jess remembered the colleges in the vicinity; it was Friday night, and the bars and restaurants were still open for people who actually had a life. Letting her head rest back against the seat, she slanted a look at Mark. "What happens to my Secret Service protection if it turns out that this isn't some kind of government hit squad thing at all? What if somebody is trying to kill me because of something to do with Allison, or Tiffany, or even those two missing girls? I told you Rob Phillips was there tonight, and his parents were, too. I keep thinking that it all has to be tied into that, because as far as I can tell, what Allison, and Tiffany"—then she saw it—"and I have in common is that trial."

"How about we worry about that if it happens?" He was pulling into the way-too-convenient-because-it-was-illegal spot near her apartment, and Jess sighed again. She was suddenly too tired even to remonstrate.

"Fine."

They walked in near silence up to her apartment. Jess's eyes were so heavy that she barely even spared a look for the shadow behind the magnolia. She missed the lock the first time she tried to put the key in it. When she frowned and blinked at it myopically, Mark took the key from her, inserted it, opened the door, then stood back for her to precede him. As she flipped on the light, an unfamiliar sound greeted her.

"Mee-eee-eee-eee."

Having clearly been napping on the couch, Clementine stood up, stretched gracefully, jumped down, and came toward them. Jess bent to pick her up, while Mark did his customary walk through.

"You're very pretty, Clementine." Jess noticed the white patch under her chin for the first time. Held in her arms, the cat began to purr. She was way too thin, but that would soon be remedied now that she once again had access to regular food. Looking down into the big golden eyes that regarded her unblinkingly, Jess thought of Allison: if what she feared was true, Clementine had no home to return to. But maybe she was wrong. Maybe she was wrong about all of it.

For the first time ever, Jess actually hoped that a government assassin was trying to kill her. Because if it turned out that the attacks had something to do with the Phillips trial, she was afraid that Allison at least, and probably Tiffany, too, and maybe even those girls, if they were all connected, were already dead.

Jess shivered at the thought.

"All clear." Mark walked back into the room, and Jess put Clementine down. The cat went over to him, weaving around his legs.

"She likes you," Jess said, and Mark bent down to pat the cat.

"I fed her earlier," he pointed out. Jess grinned, then yawned so suddenly that her jaw cracked.

As she clapped an embarrassed hand over her mouth, it was Mark's turn to grin. It hit Jess then that having Mark there in the apartment with her made it feel like they were home. Together. As if he belonged there.

Oh, no.

She looked at him in dismay.

"Go to bed," Mark told her. His voice was perfectly even. His eyes were impossible to read. But she knew him, knew he could read her like a book.

She turned and walked out of the room, took the world's quickest shower, and went to bed.

Alone.

Of course she dreamed of drowning. She should have expected it, but her head had been so full of so many things that worrying about having the kind of nightmare she hadn't had for years had been the furthest thing from her mind.

When she woke up, tears were streaming down her face.

"Damn it." It was the fiercest of whispers, uttered as she flopped onto her back and dashed her fingers across her wet cheeks. Taking a deep, shaky breath, she stared blindly up into the dark. Her heart pounded. Her pulse raced. The memories swirled thick and fast through her head, and with another muttered curse she sat up and flipped on the bedside lamp to chase them away. Something leaped off the foot of the bed to land on the floor with a thump, startling her. Alarmed, Jess couldn't imagine what on earth it could have been until she remembered: Clementine. The cat had obviously been sleeping on her bed, and *she* had startled the cat.

"It's okay, Clementine." The bedside clock read 5:23 a.m. Jess almost groaned. Standing up, meaning to head to the bathroom to wash her face before trying to go back to sleep, Jess spoke to the animal soothingly.

"Mee-eee-eee-eee." The cat looked at her over her shoulder before waving her plumy tail and padding away.

"Jess?" Mark was coming down the hallway.

Of course she had awakened Mark. Under conditions like these—when he considered himself on duty—he was the lightest of light sleepers. Under more normal circumstances, like when they'd lived together before, he'd slept like the dead. Listening to such a gorgeous man snore like a chain saw had been one of life's little revelations.

"I'm fine," she called, hoping to head him off. No such luck. He reached her room about the time the words left her mouth. Wearing only his boxers—tonight's were blue—he stopped in the doorway to stare at her, all broad shoulders and long, hard-muscled legs. She was suddenly acutely conscious of her tousled hair, which she'd been too tired to put up for sleep, and her bare legs beneath the oversized T-shirt that was all she was wearing. It was purple with Sweet Thing scrawled across the front in pink script and ended at approximately midthigh.

Her glasses were on the nightstand. She glanced at them, thought about putting them on, then remembered what he'd said about them before.

Bad idea.

"The cat woke me up," she offered, putting up her chin. The thing was, he knew her too well to miss the fact that she'd been crying.

But he didn't challenge her about it. Instead he simply stood there, all six feet two inches of bronzed, muscular, near-naked, yummy man, looking her over without saying a word. She could see the five o'clock shadow darkening his cheeks and chin, the faint shadows beneath his eyes, the gleam of bright blue surveying her from head to toe.

And her heart, damned traitorous organ, beat faster.

"Mark . . ." Even from that distance and without her glasses, she knew what his expression meant: he wanted to take her to bed.

Just the thought made her body tighten and quake. She could feel the sudden sizzle of sexual tension arcing between them, and she did her best to close her mind to it. The idea of sex with Mark might have made her go weak at the knees, but with them things were way more complicated than that.

"Everything's fine," she repeated. "You should go back to sleep."

His mouth firmed. He leaned a shoulder against the doorjamb, folded his arms across his chest. *Uh-oh*, Jess thought. She knew that particular stance: it usually meant he was spoiling for a fight.

"This is stupid," he said. "You love me. And you know it."

Jess sucked in air. His words hit her like a punch to the stomach. She'd been expecting a fight, not that.

"I . . ." She lost her train of thought because he was coming toward her. Panic curled through her stomach. She would have retreated if there'd been any place to go, but immediately behind her was the bed. When he stopped in front of her, so close she could have reached out and placed her hands flat on his wide chest, she looked up at him almost piteously. Her pulse raced. Her breathing quickened. She could feel the heat rising in her veins.

"See, the thing is, I love you, too." Instead of being passionate, his voice was flat. "I knew it when I was pulling you out of that pool. If I'd been too late, if you'd been dead . . ."

His voice trailed off, but his expression said the rest.

Jess closed her eyes. *I love you.* How often over the last few months had she longed to hear him say that? She felt the bedazzlement inherent in those words clear down to her toes.

"I can't do this." Keeping her eyes tightly closed in an effort to keep her defenses in place, she shook her head as the panic spread. There was nothing personal in her rejection at all, which she would have explained to him if he would have just backed all the way across the room again and given her enough space to get her thoughts in order. It was an act of self-preservation, pure and simple.

"Sure you can."

The next thing she knew his fingers were tilting up her chin. She could feel him studying her face, but she kept her eyes stubbornly closed.

"You've been crying." His knuckles brushed her still damp cheeks. "Why?"

Her eyes flew open. "I had a nightmare," she said.

"I'm not surprised."

Of course he knew about the nightmares that had been a near nightly ordeal for years when she'd been young, about Courtney, about her whole life, because she'd told him. He was the only person she'd ever told, and suddenly it hit her what a big deal that was.

He knew her. He said he loved her.

"Mark." Even she didn't know what she wanted to say. Just his name, that was all. But she had a terrible feeling that her unthinking heart blazed at him through her eyes.

His hands slipped to her waist. He bent his head and kissed her, the slightest of soft kisses. At the feel of his warm lips against hers, her heart leaped. Her breathing got all uneven. Her senses went haywire. She reached out instinctively, meaning, she thought, to push him away. Instead her hands, with a mind of their own, flattened against his chest. Which, she realized, they'd yearned to do all along. Then they went further still, sliding up over the warm, firm expanse of his chest, over his broad shoulders to lock behind his neck, almost of their own volition. As if she didn't really have any say in the matter at all.

He lifted his head to look down at her. His eyes were hot and dark.

"I love you," he told her again, his voice now slightly husky. "But say the word, and I'm back on the couch. I'll be damned if I'm going to seduce you into this."

Her heart slammed against her chest. Her body pulsed with longing. Her throat closed up so that even if she'd wanted to, she couldn't have answered.

But now at least she knew what she wanted.

Once again she let her body do the talking for her, rising up on her tiptoes, closing her eyes, and fitting her mouth to his.

CHAPTER TWENTY-NINE

"Okay, I want to hear you say it when you're not naked." Mark gave her a level look as she straightened up from pouring more food into Clementine's bowl, for which the cat thanked her by digging in hungrily.

Mark didn't have to specify further. She knew what he wanted, what he meant.

Dressed for work, they were in the kitchen grabbing coffee before heading out the door. It was almost ten thirty, already so late that Jess knew she was going to feel embarrassed when she made it to Ellis Hayes's sixth floor. Of course, her colleagues would think she'd passed the hours since they'd seen her last recovering from her ordeal. No way could they know she'd spent at least three of the last five having wild, thrilling, mind-blowing sex with Mark.

She should have been feeling scared about going back out into the world, where someone had twice tried to kill her, she supposed. But she didn't. Somewhat to her own surprise she felt cool, composed, and determined. *We're going to find you*, was her mental message to the man who'd dragged her under the water. As for the fear factor, to combat it she had her brains, the pocket-sized canister of pepper spray she'd swiped from the drawer of Grace's nightstand, and a hunky, lethal, armed Secret Service agent for an escort.

"I love you," she told Mark. Of course she'd said it before, multiple times. Each time she'd come, to be precise. As in, *I love you, I love you, I love you, Mark.*

Now, remembering each occasion with his eyes on her in the unforgiving kitchen light, she could feel herself blush. Saying the words in the cold light of day like this made her feel exposed, vulnerable, raw, afraid—until she looked into his eyes.

They were warm and steady and reassuring—and they made her instantly hot.

God, am I a slut for him or what?

He knew what she was thinking; she could tell by the satisfied curl of his mouth.

"There you go. See what you can do if you try?"

She made a face at him, and he laughed and pulled her close and kissed her. For a moment, under the influence of that warm, firm mouth, all Jess's good intentions hung in the balance. Her body flamed, her mind went blank, and she plastered herself against him and kissed him back. Still, there it was, the fear. It was cold and hard and real, like a tiny rock in a comfortable shoe. Her attraction to him was so strong that it was almost impossible to deny, but the thought of making herself vulnerable again made her go cold all over.

She pulled away, looked up at him.

"I'm not going to like this, am I?" His tone was resigned.

"Just to be clear, we are not back together."

"What? You just said you love me."

"That doesn't mean we're in a relation-ship."

"Want to tell me what this is, then?"

Okay, he had her there. "It's a . . . I don't know what it is, exactly. But I know what it isn't. It isn't an engagement. We're not get-ting married. I don't even want us to be locked into any kind of commitment."

He studied her. "In other words, we're both free to do exactly what we want."

"Yes."

"Suppose what we want is to be to-gether? Not necessarily permanently, but for now. We could take things one day at a time, see where it goes. No strings."

That made so much sense to Jess that she could feel herself brighten.

"You're okay with that?" she asked with some suspicion. She knew Mark, a tradi-tionalist to his core.

"Thrilled to bits." His voice was dry.

"Then great." Smiling at him, feeling as if a weight had been lifted, she reached up to kiss him. The kiss got hot fast, and if it hadn't been for Clementine twining herself around their legs, it probably would have been at least another hour before they left.

But Jess jumped at the unaccustomed contact and the spell was broken.

"Later," Mark promised as she dragged him out the door.

And just like that, a hundred erotic images chased each other through her head, and her body quickened with anticipation while her blood turned to steam.

But she really needed to get to work, so her inner slut was going to have to wait.

As she had expected, the sixth floor—indeed, the whole building—was as busy when she got there as it was on any weekday. In broad daylight, with so many people around and so much bustle and activity going on, Jess felt pretty secure in assuming she was perfectly safe. Which was a good thing, because having Mark dog her every footstep was sure to give rise to the kind of speculation she most wanted to avoid. In fact, having Mark dog her every footstep was not going to work for her, and so she told him. They agreed that just having him in the building was protection enough, and he left her at the elevator bank with no more than a warning not to leave the building without him. Knowing that she was liable to turn crimson if questioned by her colleagues about why she was so late, Jess hurried straight to her office as soon as she got off the elevator with no more than a brief wave for Lenore, who was on the phone at her desk. The rest of the team was presumably working hard somewhere out of sight, which she was thankful for. With any luck, given the fact that there were no 8:30 a.m. team meetings on Saturday, maybe nobody besides Lenore would know she was just getting in.

The first thing she meant to do was check with Pearse to see if he needed help with anything else having to do with Flores. Then she was way behind on the background checks for Jameson. And . . .

Frowning as she went over her to-do list, Jess opened the door to her office and walked inside while still deep in thought.

And in the gloom that existed before she turned on the light, she caught just a glimpse, the merest hint, of something. A shadow, maybe. Or a shimmering shape that she didn't even really see before she hit the switch and the light came on and it was gone.

She stopped dead. Her heart lurched.

For a moment she stared fixedly at the place where whatever she had seen had been, which was, of course, in front of the plant and the window. She looked at the plant, the window, the absolutely ordinary, empty section of carpet in front of both and the wall on either side.

Nothing was there. Of course nothing was there.

Her heart pounded like she'd been running.

Allison.

Maybe it was a stupid thought, proving how credulous and superstitious she really was, but she was increasingly convinced that Allison, or whatever spiritual spark remained of Allison, was there in that office.

Which meant Allison was dead.

Jess took a deep breath and closed the door.

"I'm going to find you," Jess said aloud. "Dead, alive, whatever, I'm going to find you, I promise."

She said it as if she were making a vow.

Then, feeling vaguely foolish, she sat down at her desk and got to work. Only she didn't make the call to Pearse about

Flores, and she didn't start cross-checking information on the Jameson witnesses. The sense of urgency she felt about finding Allison was too strong.

It was almost as if there were a voice in her ear whispering, *Do it now.*

What she did first was check her voice mail and e-mail for any response from either Allison or Tiffany—nada—and look at their Facebook pages for new postings, which neither had made. Then, deciding to start at the beginning, which as far as she knew was with Allison, Jess methodically began to put together a profile of her predecessor. Drawing on all her computer expertise—which was quite considerable, and one of the reasons she'd been originally offered a job at Ellis Hayes—Jess started delving into Allison's life. She was a whizz at bypassing access codes and divining passwords—the one Allison used most was easy; Jess had guessed *Clementine* on almost the first try—and worming her way into various data systems. Working diligently, she amassed Allison's phone records, her banking records, her credit card records, and her various membership accounts (YMCA, Weight Watchers

Online, library, Book-of-the-Month Club, Sam's Club, grocery club, that kind of thing). She did a background check. What turned up on Allison surprised her: she'd been a former foster child with parents who'd been long gone by the time she was ten, which made the "Hey, Mom" phone call to Lucy's phone even more of a mystery. Jess did a credit check, and even pulled Allison's motor vehicle records and tax returns from the IRS files to confirm that her only income source was her work at Ellis Hayes and she didn't moonlight as something that could have gotten her into trouble. Finally Jess combed the Ellis Hayes computer system for what Allison had been working on just before she'd left for that business trip—the Phillips trial, as expected—and even pulled up her browsing history: a lot of eBay. When Jess was done, she had so much material that just contemplating the sheer volume of it was daunting.

Start with the most recent activity and work backward.

Allison had left on the business trip from which she had never returned in July. The first thing to do, then, was see if there had been any transactions recorded on any of her accounts in August.

Bank records indicated that Allison's rent, utilities, and car payment had all been paid the first week in August, when she'd presumably been on her honeymoon. Jess would have taken that as a positive sign, except the payments had been set up as automatic withdrawals that would have happened without any need for current authorization from Allison.

There had been some texting activity on her cell phone, but no actual outgoing calls.

No credit card charges were posted to any of her accounts in August except, again, for automatic payments.

Looking at the picture presented by the data, Jess started to feel cold all over. Before, all she'd had had been a bad feeling about Allison and a maybe-it-didn't-even-really-happen sighting of Allison in her/their office. Now she had concrete evidence that something had happened. How could Allison survive without accessing her bank account or using any of her credit cards?

There was likewise no activity on any of the membership accounts, except one. Allison's Quik-Stop preferred customer card showed daily transactions for the month of August up until two days ago.

That made Jess sit up and take notice.

Frowning, she looked at the data. The transactions were not purchases. They indicated the redemption of complimentary good-customer rewards, which were recorded by a swipe of a preferred customer card at the time of the transaction. Exactly what the reward was wasn't part of the record, which showed only that it was redeemed and the card was swiped. Which meant that an individual had been present to present the card. Most of the redemption activity had occurred at a single Quik-Stop in College Park. But the latest, and last, transaction had been recorded on Thursday morning at a Quik-Stop on M Street. Jess double-checked the address: it was near DuPont Circle, which was nearby.

Her heart started to beat faster. What the data meant Jess didn't know, but there the transactions were with no possibility of mistake. Printing out the address of the Quik-Stop, then a picture of Allison that she got from the copy of her driver's license, which was on file with the Department of Motor Vehicles, Jess called Mark.

"I'm coming down," she said when he answered. "I've got something to show you."

She disconnected before he could reply.

"We're going out," she told him without preamble when she walked into his office. He was seated behind his desk with his jacket off doing something on his computer. Seeing Mark pecking away at a keyboard struck her as vaguely amusing, so she smiled. Besides his shoulder holster provided a nice counterpoint to his red tie as it nestled against one of those typical businessman/Secret Service agent white shirts that he rocked the crap out of. He looked handsome and competent and just a little out of place behind a desk, as if he more properly belonged out on the sun-drenched sidewalk she could see through his tinted windows. His office was more modern than hers—metal desk, no plant— and not as luxurious, but it was about the same size. Looking up from what he was doing as she entered and closed the door behind her, he lifted his eyebrows at her questioningly.

"Somebody's been using Allison's preferred customer card at a Quik-Stop on M Street," she burst out, waving the picture of Allison at him. "I want to show this to the people working there and see if they recognize her. It's the only activity I can find on any of her accounts this entire month. So grab your jacket and come on."

"I don't suppose you want to give the information to me and let me pass it on to the *professionals* to investigate?" Clearly he knew the answer to that, because he was already on his feet reaching for his jacket. Pulling it on, looking hot as usual in his charcoal suit, he came toward her to drop a quick, hard kiss on her mouth. Momentarily dazzled—being back on with Mark even in the provisional capacity they had agreed to was something she hadn't totally gotten her head around yet, but it definitely felt good—she had to blink a couple of times to refocus.

"And take the chance that they'll maybe get to it in a week or two *if* they don't get sidetracked? No way."

"I didn't think so."

Mark opened the door for her, and she stayed a brisk step ahead of him as they walked down the hall toward the elevator that serviced the underground garage.

She was wearing black ballet flats with snug black pants, a white tee, and a short gray blazer—the flats made it her version of business-casual Saturday—with her purse slung over her shoulder. There were a number of people about, some interns whose status she knew because they were wearing laminated badges with the word INTERN in big black letters, a few law-yer types, half a dozen or so blue-uniformed security guards. There were so many wandering that particular area because, Jess saw as they passed it, the security staff office took up an entire section at the rear of the first floor. Just being reminded that all those guards worked in the building was reassuring.

When she and Mark were in the Suburban on the way to M Street Jess gave him a quick rundown on everything she had discovered so far.

"Could be her new husband's picking up the tab," Mark suggested as an explanation for the lack of financial activity on any of Allison's accounts.

"She hasn't even used a credit card. Or made a phone call," Jess argued.

"Maybe something was going on in her life that made her decide to deliberately disappear."

That was a possibility Jess hadn't considered. Frowning, she mulled it over and came to the conclusion that, regardless of her gut feeling to the contrary, it wasn't a theory she could entirely discount.

"Maybe. But she would still have to have money, wouldn't she?" Jess said at last, reasoning it through. "If that's the case, there should be some fairly substantial withdrawals in the weeks and months leading up to the time she left."

"You would think," Mark agreed. "Unless for some reason she had to leave in a hurry."

Then they were pulling into a parking spot near the Quik-Stop. Jess took a quick look around as they got out into the steamy afternoon heat. Lots of pedestrians, lots of traffic, lots of noise. A bus, putting out tons of smelly exhaust, loading passengers on the other side of the intersection. A Chase bank branch, a Tom's deli, a Chinese take-out place, a Laundromat. And, on the corner, glass walls covered with advertisements looking out onto both streets, the Quik-Stop.

Neither the clerks nor the manager remembered Allison. Producing her picture netted nothing but a few shrugs and a lot of head shaking. As for her preferred customer transactions, well, they had a lot of preferred customers. It was impossible to remember every one.

Jess's one hope was the security camera mounted so that it monitored the cash register. If Allison had been there, the swipe of her customer card would have happened at the register. The camera should have recorded her.

The manager wasn't talking about the camera. At least, he wasn't until Mark flashed his badge and went all Secret Service on him. Then he was suddenly cooperative.

"It's a seven-day loop," the manager, who turned out to be a forty-year-old former car salesman named Bobby Lutz, told them as he took them back into his private office, which was tiny, shared space with boxes of snack-sized potato chips apparently waiting to be shelved. From the intermittent flushes that could clearly be heard, it also shared a wall with the store restroom. "Every week the memory gets recycled, and everything from the previous week gets recorded over."

"When does the week start?" Mark asked as Lutz reached up on a shelf to turn on a black-and-white monitor. On a shelf below it sat a computer hard drive, and the cables running between the two indicated they were attached.

"Sunday night, six p.m. I hit reset before I go home." He hit a button on the hard drive, and suddenly blurry images started appearing on the monitor. Jess stared, but they were moving so fast that it was impossible to really see anything. "You're looking for Thursday, right? What time?"

He was, Jess realized as she consulted her printout, fast-forwarding through the pictures, which weren't actually video but a series of stills.

"Six forty-three a.m."

"Hmm."

"This is low-end equipment. The camera takes a picture like every thirty seconds." He flashed forward some more. "Okay, here's Thursday morning. Let's see . . ."

Flashing forward a little more slowly now, he stopped the reel with a quick stab of a button.

"There you go," he said.

Jess looked at the picture on the screen. The time was stamped on it, in white letters high in the left corner: 6:43:15. For a moment she stared at it, disappointed. Whoever was nibbling the doughnut while the clerk swiped her card certainly wasn't Allison.

"Next one," Mark said, and Lutz obediently advanced the tape: 6:43:45.

This time the customer was turning away from the register. She was holding coffee in one hand, the doughnut in the other, and Jess could clearly see her face—and her frizzy red hair.

"That's Lucy," she said, surprised.

CHAPTER THIRTY

"There's a connection between them. See there?" Jess was so wired with excitement that she could hardly sit still as they headed back to Ellis Hayes with a copy of the video tucked safely into the console between them. Mark had already told her of his intention to turn the DVD over to a guy he knew to see what else—such as, possibly, a glimpse of Allison—turned up.

"Allison Howard knew Lucy Peel through Shelter House." Mark's voice was thoughtful as he pulled into the underground garage. "Lucy's missing. Allison is missing. Maybe they're together. Maybe they've

got some kind of thing going on, and that's
why Allison decided to disappear. It wouldn't
be the first time an adult mentor took off
with a kid."

"That's sick." Jess glared at him.

He shrugged. "If you're going to investigate, you've got to cover all the bases."

In her heart Jess was sure Allison had
not absconded with Lucy, but, as Mark
said, it was smart to cover all the bases.
So when she got back to her office—which
took a little while, because this time she
ran into Andrew and had to field his inqui-
ries into her well-being—she went back
into the computer to check Allison's bank
accounts for a pattern of withdrawals that
would support the theory that Allison had
simply chosen to disappear.

What she found surprised her.

Looking for the last week during which
she knew Allison had been alive, Jess
found that Allison had spent it in Nassau.
Then Jess checked the Bahamas for a
bank account in Allison's name, reasoning
that Allison might have moved some money
offshore if she'd been planning to disappear. Sure enough, she hit pay dirt. Allison
had opened an account in the First Bank

of the Bahamas on the very day she'd arrived on the island. Five hundred dollars had been the initial deposit amount. But four days later, a wire transfer had upped the balance considerably: to *three million dollars.*

Jess's eyes popped at the amount. Knowing Allison's background as she now did, and her work history and salary as well, it seemed inconceivable that Allison could have legally obtained that amount of money. But there it was.

Jess trolled through the account data and discovered that the entire amount had been withdrawn by a wire transfer the following week.

On a Monday, to be precise. Allison's other financial transactions had ceased a day and a half before, on the previous Saturday night.

Of course, three million dollars was more than enough to go into hiding on.

"What did you get involved in?" Jess demanded aloud of the presence in her office, which she was starting to think might not be any more than a figment of her imagination after all. Because if Allison wasn't dead, if she had simply taken that truly enormous amount of money and run, then she wasn't a ghost and thus could not be haunting their mutual space.

Of course, that amount of money could also get somebody killed.

Frowning thoughtfully, Jess looked through the files Allison had been working on at the time of her disappearance. Standard stuff that as far as she could tell was all about the Phillips case.

Then Jess had a thought. Allison almost certainly had her own laptop. What if the files Jess was looking for were too sensitive to be kept on the company computer network, which, in a pinch, just about anybody with a modicum of tech savvy could access? What if she'd kept the personal stuff, the important stuff, on her private computer?

Jess didn't have Allison's computer, but she did have a way in. Because Allison had downloaded files onto the company computer network from a personal computer Jess suspected had to have been her laptop, Jess could follow the trail back and remotely link with that computer. All she needed was Allison's password.

Clementine.

Bingo. She was in.

The first thing she did was a little tricky, but then, she was good: she remotely turned on the laptop's camera. Now whatever the computer saw, she could see, too.

Unfortunately, all the computer was seeing was a whole lot of black.

The computer wasn't destroyed, the camera was operational, and she was now seeing what it saw. That was the good news.

The bad news was, it was seeing precisely nothing.

Disappointed, Jess started calling up Allison's files. Half an hour or so later, she sat back in her seat, sighing with discouragement. Allison's computer files contained nothing of interest at all. Some recipes, a *Wall Street Journal* subscription, hundreds of pictures, most of which seemed to be of Clementine. Information related to the Phillips trial, all pretty much identical to that which was in the files Jess had already seen on the company computer. It added up to not much. Certainly none of it explained where three million dollars had come from.

Jess frowned thoughtfully at the tiny

black square on the upper-right-hand corner of her screen, which showed her what Allison's computer was looking at: still nothing.

"Where are you?" she asked it aloud.

Fiddling around, checking various settings just as something to do while she turned the various things she knew and suspected over in her mind, trying to see how they fit together, she noticed something: the amount of space remaining on Allison's hard drive was surprisingly small, considering the number and sizes of the files she'd seen.

Staring at the number, considering the discrepancy, Jess almost smiled. Of course, Allison had hidden the most important, and sensitive, of her files. It only made sense.

But what a lot of people failed to realize about computers was the fact that nothing was ever really gone. You could delete, you could scrub, you could smash that puppy up with a sledgehammer and throw it in a river, and somebody, somewhere, could still retrieve the files.

Somebody like her.

Working remotely through the link with

her office computer, Jess downloaded a program onto Allison's laptop that allowed her to restore lost files. Then she activated it.

A blink of an eye later, there they were.

Four files, each labeled with a name: Shelly Smithers, Ellen Hunter, Cassandra Maheu, Tasha Gupta.

Opening them one at a time, first skimming and then reading every word, Jess started to feel sick to her stomach.

The first, Shelly Smithers, was from eight years ago. There was a photo, clearly a school picture, showing a pretty blonde with long, straight hair. Fifteen years old, the daughter of a mechanic and a nurse, she was found raped and strangled in a woods near Redfern Academy, an exclusive private prep school in New Jersey. Her killer was never found.

Ellen Hunter was eighteen. Her picture showed that she, too, was a pretty blonde. A senior in high school, the daughter of a single mother who was a nurse, six years ago she was found raped and strangled in a garage on the outskirts of Bar Harbor. Her killer was never found.

Four years ago, nineteen-year-old Cassandra Maheu, another pretty blonde, was found raped and strangled just off the Lake Trail in Palm Beach. Her killer was never found.

Twenty-two-year-old Tasha Gupta, pretty and blond like the others, was found raped and strangled in a New Haven, Connecticut, park. That was two years ago. Her killer was never found.

Looking at the pictures, reading the files, Jess already had an inkling of what she was seeing: four different, heinous crimes. One perpetrator. A serial rapist/killer at work. The girls were too similar in appearance, the crimes too similar in execution, to lead to any other conclusion.

But there was more. Another file. Its contents tied the four crimes together. One exhibit was a virtual map that marked with a red star the place each body was found, and labeled it with the victim's name and the date of her death. The map also marked a location near each body by surrounding it with a translucent blue square. The first blue square was labeled Redfern Academy, along with the year in which Shelly Smithers was killed. The second encompassed a house in Bar Harbor, along with a period of two weeks that included the date Ellen Hunter was killed. The third square surrounded an exclusive hotel in Palm Beach, along with a three-day span in which Cassandra Maheu was killed. The fourth was set down on top of Yale University, along with dates that included the date of Tasha Gupta's death.

Besides the dates, which clearly indicated when another person had been in those nearby spots, something else was written in the blue squares, too: a name.

Rob Phillips.

According to the map, he had been present at all four locations at times spanning the dates when the four girls had been killed.

More evidence had been compiled: a sighting of a car matching one Rob had been known to own leaving the scene of Ellen Hunter's murder; bite marks on Cassandra Maheu that matched Rob's dental records; the fact that Shelly Smithers was known to have been an acquaintance of Rob's and he'd been considered a "person of interest" by the local police at the time; and a physical description by an eyewitness of a man seen with Tasha Gupta the day before she'd been found dead. The description matched Rob Phillips to a T.

The killings were in four widely separated locations. By themselves, the details wouldn't add up to much, certainly not enough to allow local police departments to solve the crime. But put them together, and the evidence they provided was damning.

Jess was willing to bet anything she possessed that Rob Phillips had committed all four crimes.

Tiffany looked enough like the other victims to fit right in. If Tiffany's recantation had been false, if she'd been telling the truth about what had happened to her, then Rob was following his pattern of attacking a woman approximately every two years. Would he have ended up killing Tiffany, too? *Had* he ended up killing her?

But the man Jess had seen her with outside the metro had definitely not been Rob.

Jess didn't realize she'd quit breathing until a tiny beep made her jump and sharply inhale at the same time.

The beep came from her computer. It was an alert, cluing her in to the fact that the tiny square in the right-hand corner of her screen had just come to life.

Jess's pulse began to race.

Someone was there. A small face was looking back at her. Jess frowned at it. Her first thought was a disappointed, *not Allison*. Enlarging the square with the click of a button, her eyes widened. Her heart thumped. Her stomach clenched.

She was looking right into the narrow, dark eyes of the man she was almost sure had tried to kill her in Mr. Dunn's pool. The man she'd seen with Tiffany outside the metro.

Shoving the wheeled chair back from her desk in a panic, Jess almost jumped up and rushed from the room. Then she remembered that what she was looking at was an image captured by a camera. The bad guy was where Allison's laptop was, not right there in her office with her. And while she could see him, he couldn't see her.

Jess let out a breath, picked up her cell phone, and dialed Mark.

But whether the bad guy was physically there or not, even watching him through a camera lens was unnerving. When Mark answered, she found herself almost whispering.

"I've found something. I accessed Alli-

son's computer and turned on her web-
cam, and I can see the guy who tried to kill
me on it. Oh, God, he's looking right at me.
Come up here *now*. You've got to see this."

"Sit tight." Mark's answer was short and
terse. "I'm on my way."

Mark had no sooner disconnected than
the image vanished. The now enlarged
square went black again. Jess frowned at
it in consternation, to no avail. Her attacker
was gone.

Or maybe the connection had been lost.
Jess tried activating the camera again, just
on the off-chance. She really, really wanted
Mark to see . . .

She was so busy trying to restore the
connection that in the first seconds after
she heard her office door open she didn't
even look up.

"I lost him," she said distractedly to Mark.
"He was here, but he's gone."

A closing door and a couple of quick
footsteps preceded by perhaps a fraction
of a heartbeat the sure knowledge that
something was wrong.

"Mark . . ." Jess glanced up to find her
attacker standing just a few feet in front of
her desk.

Horror shot cold as ice through her veins. Eyes popping, heart jumping, she leaped to her feet and opened her mouth to scream, only to have him fire something at her before the sound could emerge.

A stun gun. She realized it even as the probes hit her in the center of the chest.

Her breathing stopped. For a split second she felt like she'd been kicked by a mule.

Then she crumpled bonelessly to the floor as the world went black.

At first, when the lights went out and the elevator stopped, Mark wasn't too worried. He and three others—a man and two women, lawyer types all—were inside it, facing forward as elevator passengers tended to do. As they stopped with a jolt and were plunged unexpectedly into Stygian darkness, one of the women (he thought it was one of the women, although it was impossible to be sure) gasped, and the man said, "What the hell?"

An emergency light came on, glowing pale from the button panel.

"We're stuck in the elevator," the shorter

of the two women, a white-haired, matronly type, announced in a tone of disbelief.

"Will it fall?" The other woman, maybe fortyish, had short auburn hair and a frightened expression. Like the other two, she wore a suit and clutched a briefcase.

"No." Reaching past the white-haired woman, who stood in front of him, Mark leaned forward and pressed the emergency button. He had to press it twice before anyone answered.

"Is there an emergency?" The security guard who answered was female, with a sweet voice.

"Elevator five has stopped, with four people trapped inside," he told her.

"Oh, dear," was the response. "Just stay calm. I'll get somebody right on it."

But by then Mark was beginning to feel anxious.

I accessed Allison's computer, and I can see the guy who tried to kill me on it.

Mark's blood ran cold as he remembered Jess's words.

"Do you think we're going to be in here long?" The other man had edged around to the front and was pressing the floor buttons with desperate jabs.

"I don't think you should do that," the auburn-haired woman said nervously. "If they jam—"

"We're already stuck," the man replied.

"We should just stay calm like we were told and await rescue," the white-haired woman said.

Meanwhile, Mark had tuned them all out. Having begun to feel as jumpy as a cat on hot bricks, he was on his cell phone, calling the backup agent, a newbie, whose name he couldn't recall right off the top of his head, who'd pulled stakeout duty in front of the building for the afternoon.

"I'm trapped in an elevator," he told his counterpart, trying hard to stay calm. "You need to get in here stat and get up to the subject's office on the sixth floor. And I mean as fast as you can possibly move. Secure the subject and stay with her until I can get there, then call me and let me know she's safe. And send somebody to get me out of this damned elevator *now.*"

"Yes, sir," came the reply.

"Are you some kind of cop?" the auburn-haired woman asked as he disconnected, regarding him with a fascinated eye.

"Secret Service," he answered, terse rather than polite, and she started to tell him some convoluted story about her nephew in the FBI.

The last thing he felt like doing was talking. His internal radar was giving him fits. Jess summoned him with urgent news, the elevator taking him to her stopped. Maybe a coincidence, but in his experience bad things going down didn't come much more obvious than that.

He had to restrain himself from tearing into the door with both hands. If he hadn't been pretty sure they were between floors, that's just what he would have done.

A few minutes later, just in time to keep him from totally losing his mind, the lights came back on and the elevator started up again with a lurch.

He was just bolting through the open doors on six when his cell phone rang. He answered it on the run.

"Ryan."

"Sir, the subject's not here," the newbie said.

This was, Lucy calculated as she sat on the hard concrete floor with her back up against the hot metal wall, the second full day of their captivity. They'd spent this one locked in this hellish garage. Last night, when they'd escaped from the trunk to hear someone walking up to the overhead doors, they'd practically died of terror on the spot, sure it had been their captor coming to finish the job of murdering them. Staying quiet as mice, they'd prayed that whoever it had been would go away. And whoever it had been had gone away. They'd listened as the footsteps had turned back the way they had come, only moving more quickly, as if the walker had been called away. At the time they'd been almost giddy with relief. But as the hours had ticked away and they had faced the horrible truth that *there really was no way out of this damned garage*, the true scope of their predicament had become increasingly clear. It had dawned on them only gradually, as the sun had risen and the heat inside the metal building had increased to a nearly unbearable level. The fact that they had no food and very little water had also started to assume larger

and larger significance. No electricity, either, which meant they had no lights and
no air-conditioning. Lucy was so hungry
that she was sick with it, but the thirst
was the worst thing. She craved water.
Her throat burned, her tongue felt thick,
and her mouth was so dry that she couldn't
even swallow anymore.

If it hadn't been for the half-full bottle of
water they'd found in the car's front seat
after smashing a window in hopes of finding a garage door opener or cell phone or
OnStar system or something—to no
avail—Lucy guessed they already would
have died of thirst by now. Or been close
to it, anyway.

"He's going to come back and kill us,
isn't he?" Jaden sat slumped beside her,
her head resting on her raised knees. Her
voice was a hoarse whisper. Thin before,
she was skeletal now. Her cheekbones
were so sharp that they seemed about to
poke through her pale skin.

"We're ready for him." Lucy said that
with more confidence than she felt. They'd
wedged the trunk back down so that
it wouldn't be apparent at first glance that
they'd broken out of it. They'd kicked the

glass from the broken window under the car. She was armed with a shovel she'd discovered in a corner, along with a couple of bags of mulch, a wheelbarrow, and a rake. Jaden was armed with the rake. If— when—the killer came back, they meant to hide in a corner near the door, concealed as much as possible behind the wheelbarrow and the mulch, which they'd moved into position, then slip out and run for their lives before he noticed them. If that didn't work, they were going to fight him off with the shovel and the rake.

Lucy *really* hoped it didn't come to that.

"If he doesn't hurry up, we're going to be dead anyway." Jaden's glance at the nearly empty water bottle sitting on the concrete between them said it all. After another twenty-four hours, they'd be unconscious or dead, Lucy was pretty sure.

"We could try banging on the walls again." As their desperation had increased, they'd given up on the whole quiet-as-a-mouse thing and tried screaming, banging on the metal walls with the shovel and rake, honking the horn—useless, because the car battery was dead—prying at the doors, digging away at the concrete.

None of it had worked. They'd just ended up exhausted and *thirsty*.

It was getting dark inside the garage now, not the pitch dark of night but a creeping gray that told Lucy twilight had fallen. Expecting the heat in the garage to ease seemed reasonable, but so far it hadn't happened. Probably because with all the metal and the concrete, the place was a natural oven.

"Why don't you try going to sleep in the car?" Lucy suggested to Jaden and licked her dry lips. Not that it helped much, because she was fresh out of saliva. "I'll keep watch."

Jaden shook her head. "I think we ought to—"

She broke off. Her head came up. Her eyes widened. Lucy heard it too: the purr of an engine, the rumble of tires on gravel.

He—somebody—was coming.

They scrambled into position, behind the wheelbarrow, behind the mulch, just as the garage door nearest them started to rise with a nerve-jangling rattle. No light came on inside the garage. Lucy's take on it was that the building was too makeshift to have one.

"Wait until the car's all the way inside, then run," Lucy whispered. Jaden nodded.

Lucy's heart began to thud. Jaden was breathing so hard that she sounded like she was wheezing. Just in case, Lucy's fingers curled around the shovel's wooden shaft. It was about five feet long, with a sturdy metal scoop. A great weapon—if he didn't have a gun.

Like the car they'd been locked in, this one was big and black, although it looked to be a lot newer. The sound of its engine made Lucy shiver. The thought of the carbon monoxide it emitted caused her to glance longingly out the opening door. It was all she could do to keep herself from bursting from their hiding place and running toward the gravel driveway and shadowy strip of grass and sliver of woods she glimpsed beyond it. Jaden made an abortive movement as if to do exactly that.

"Wait," Lucy cautioned, her voice the merest breath of sound, warning herself as much as Jaden as the blaze of headlights revealed by the opening garage door sliced through the gloom.

As the car nosed into the garage, Lucy

shivered. Fear tasted as sour as vinegar in her mouth.

They waited until the car was all the way inside. Then they would have run for it, but they couldn't.

Another big black car pulled up behind the first. Another set of headlight beams sliced past them. This car stopped just outside the garage, on the gravel, and a man got out. It was too dark to see anything much about him except that he was tall and wore a suit and carried a gun.

Sick with horror, Lucy grabbed Jaden's arm. She shook her head at her. Jaden's eyes gleamed wildly at her through the gathering dusk.

Footsteps on the concrete brought Lucy's attention back to the car that had pulled into the garage. Its headlights and engine were off now, and the driver was coming around toward the trunk. He gestured to the man with the gun, who walked toward him.

Heart pounding, Lucy held her breath. The man with the gun would have to pass within just a few feet of their hiding spot. Dizzy with fright, she ducked her head, afraid to look, afraid he would feel the weight of her gaze or see the pale gleam of her face. Beside her, Jaden did the same thing. Lucy could feel her friend's arm shaking as it pressed against her.

Cringing, she listened to footsteps on the gravel, and then, with rising terror, to the softer tread of footsteps on concrete. He was almost even with them now.

The *ping* of a trunk release had her looking sharply back at the car inside the garage. The driver was behind it now. He lifted the trunk—

"Back off, you bastard!" a woman screamed, lunging up from the depths of the trunk, spraying something for all she was worth in the man's face. Lucy saw at a glance that she was small and blond and young and big-eyed with terror.

"Ahhh!" He fell back, shrieking, his hands clapping over his face as she leaped from the trunk, spray still spewing from the small black canister in her hand. Even from a distance Lucy caught a whiff of the acrid scent of pepper spray. "I'll kill you, you bitch!"

The woman stumbled as her feet hit the concrete, then she gathered herself to run—

"Stop right there," the man with the gun yelled. His hand came up, the gun aiming at the woman, who screamed like a banshee as she swung her spray toward him.

Spray versus gun: Lucy knew how that was going to end. Faced with watching a woman who was as much a victim as they were die before her eyes, she did the only thing she could. She sprang out from her hiding place and swung at the head of the man with the gun, like his head was a baseball and her shovel was a bat.

He must have heard the whistle of it coming, because he turned to look at the last moment, just enough to keep her from taking off his head. But the blow knocked him sideways, and sent his gun sailing.

It was enough.

"Run," Lucy cried, throwing her shovel aside. As it landed with a clatter, she turned and darted out the garage door, with Jaden and the unknown woman just steps behind her.

CHAPTER THIRTY-ONE

Heart pounding like a jackhammer, Jess bolted into the woods after Lucy and Jaden. She was dizzy and sick at her stomach and her legs felt like wet string, but she ran like her life depended on it, because she knew it did. Casting a single terrified glance over her shoulder before the slope she was plunging down blocked the garage from her sight, she saw the man she'd fought off with pepper spray burst from the garage. He had attacked her in her office and tried to drown her, and she was almost sure he was the assailant who had grabbed her in front of her apartment. The too-sweet smell of his cologne lingered in her memory: it had been the same every time. But she didn't even know who he was, and as for the second man, she hadn't gotten more than a glimpse of him. As she looked back at her pursuer, his hand snapped up and she saw he had a gun. It was pointing straight at her. She ducked, bending almost double as she crashed through the undergrowth. The sound of a bullet smacking into a tree just slightly ahead of her made every tiny hair on her body stand on end. One of the girls screamed.

"Be quiet," she called to them in an urgent undertone. "Any sound we make helps them track us."

After that there were no more screams, but there was nothing they could do about the sounds that marked their frantic passage. Full night had not yet fallen, but it was as dark as night under the trees. The ground was slippery with leaves, and brambles tore at Jess's clothes. Insects whirred, and the smell of damp earth was strong. A few leaps ahead, Lucy and Jaden were scarcely more than shadows fleeing through the dark.

Behind them came the unmistakable sounds of pursuit.

Jess's heart leaped as another bullet sang past her, so close she could feel the wind of its flight against her cheek. Up ahead, there was a thunk as it hit something solid—and a cry as one of the girls went down.

Oh, no. Jess's blood turned to ice in her veins.

"Jaden!" Lucy cried, turning back. Reaching the girl's side in two great bounds, she was relieved to find that she was moving, groaning, rolling onto her side.

"Are you hit?" Jess crouched beside her, casting fearful glances back all the while. The men were coming, she could hear them, they had to move . . .

"My leg," Jaden groaned, and Jess saw she was clutching it just above her knee. Putting her hand where Jaden's rested, she felt the warm ooze of blood.

"We've got to keep going," Lucy said urgently, wrapping an arm around Jaden's waist. She looked across the injured girl at Jess. "That one guy's a murderer. He killed Miss Howard—Allison Howard. If he catches us, he's going to kill us, too."

"How do you know he killed Allison Howard?" Jess wrapped her arm around Jaden's waist, too, and between the two of them, she and Lucy managed to haul Jaden to her feet.

"We saw him. He saw us, too. That's why he's after us." Three abreast now, they ran awkwardly on.

"Oh, my God. I knew she was dead."

"Who are you, anyway?" Lucy asked.

"My name's Jess. I know who you and Jaden are. I'm a lawyer. I've been looking for you."

They wove through the densely packed trees and smashed through tangles of vines and stumbled over roots and fallen branches at a lurching run. Another bullet sang past, smacking into a tree to Jess's left. Jaden gave a frightened little cry, and Jess felt cold sweat break over her in waves.

"Do you have any idea where we are?" Jess asked desperately as she tried to come up with a plan, some avenue of escape, that might save them. If she hadn't happened to have had Grace's pepper spray in her pocket—and Lucy hadn't hit that second man with the shovel—Jess had little doubt that she would have been dead now. Clearly they meant for Lucy and Jaden to be dead, too. She could still hear the men coming after them, although they seemed to be moving more slowly and methodically now. Stalking them, Jess thought, and shivered as another bullet, this one thankfully wide of the mark, hit something with a sharp *crack*.

"No clue," Lucy gasped.

"You guys should leave me," Jaden's voice shook. "Stick me under a bush where they won't find me and run. Without me, maybe you can get away."

"Like that's gonna happen," Lucy scoffed as, bent almost double, they barreled on through the trees.

"The driveway." Jess remembered it. Her breathing was labored now. Jaden wasn't heavy, but she was tall, and holding onto her was awkward. Sheer terror gave Jess added strength. "If we could figure out where it is and try to go parallel to it, it should lead out to a road."

"Look up ahead," Lucy said. Jess looked. She could see a glimmer of a lighter kind of darkness through the trees. Horror clutched at her heart as she realized they were running out of woods. A gun exploded behind them. The bullet whistled maybe a foot to the right. Cowering, they lowered their heads and sprinted. Bursting out of the woods, they found themselves on a C-shaped curve of grassy land that jutted out all on its own. It was a promontory overlooking the Potomac, Jess saw with a rush of panic as they ran out almost to the edge in hopes of finding a way down, far enough to see that all three sides were sheer drop-offs of close to a hundred feet. The sky was dark now with a shifting layer of thunderheads, and the rising moon was just visible above the horizon. Down below, the water was inky black. The promise of a storm hung in the air.

"What do we do now?" Lucy cried as it became obvious to them all that they had reached a dead end. The rush of the river below was loud enough to partly muffle her words.

"Go back," Jess said.

But it was too late. Even as they whirled, meaning to plunge once again into the cover of the trees, the man who'd attacked her emerged from the woods. They froze. Looking at him, knowing they were trapped, knowing there was nowhere left for them to go, Jess's heart practically leaped out of her chest.

She let go of Jaden.

"Stay behind me, girls," she ordered, and moved in front of them.

"Gotcha." Walking toward them, the man waved his gun almost playfully at them. Just looking at the tall, black-haired man with his long face and narrow jaw sent fear shivering along Jess's nerve endings. Heart pounding like a trip-hammer, she took a deep breath, meaning to yell at the girls to run for the woods and do the same herself, on the theory that he couldn't shoot all three of them and if they stayed where they were they were, almost certainly dead anyway.

But the emergence of another man from the woods shocked her into immobility.

"Mr. Dunn," she gasped when he got close enough for her to be sure of his identity. For a moment she thought, given who he was, this had to be a rescue. Then she saw the gun in his hand and realized with a sense of shock that it was he whom Lucy had hit in the garage. From both men's satisfied expressions, she realized something else, too: they hadn't been stalked, they'd been herded through the woods. Once they'd escaped from the garage, here on this promontory was exactly where their pursuers had wanted them to end up. How easy would it be to pitch them, or their bodies, if they resisted, over the cliff?

Jess felt surging nausea at the thought.

"Hello, Ms. Ford." Mr. Dunn's tone was genial. His gun gave the lie to it. Unlike his friend, who held his gun almost negligently, Mr. Dunn pointed his weapon directly at her. They both stood no more than three feet away. "I'm sorry it's come to this. I liked you, you know."

Facing what she realized was almost certain death, knowing that the lives of the two teens hung in the balance as well, Jess went with the only plan she had left: stall for time. The one thing she could be certain of was that Mark would be moving heaven and earth to find her. She even knew, or thought she knew, where she was: Frog Hill. But how, could Mark possibly figure that out?

"You should've kept your nose out of other people's business," the other man said to Jess. Behind her, she heard a soft rustle. A glance over her shoulder told her that Jaden had sunk to the ground. Lucy crouched beside her, wrapping what looked like a tank top around her bleeding leg. Jess's skin prickled as cold sweat broke out along her hairline. If Jaden was sitting, making a break for it became out of the question. "If you hadn't seen me that night when you went chasing after Tiffany Higgs, none of this had to happen. Or maybe it did. You probably would've gone looking into what happened to Allison no matter what. I've been watching you, you know. And listening, too. Good thing I planted a bug in Allison's office when she started causing trouble, or I wouldn't have known what you got into today in time to stop you from telling Ryan about it."

"Who are you?" Jess felt goose bumps chase each other up and down her arms as she looked at him. One hand slid into her jacket pocket. She didn't know how much pepper spray she had left, but the canister was still there. "I don't even know you."

"I know you don't. Since you saw me with Tiffany Higgs, I've gone to a lot of trouble to stay out of your way. I figured you'd recognize me if you saw me again, and if you kept working at Ellis Hayes you were gonna see me sooner or later. What could I do? I had to get rid of you. God knows, I've been trying."

Mr. Dunn said, "Jessica Ford, meet Ed Lally, Ellis Hayes's director of security."

Jess's stomach turned inside out as she realized that the man who'd been trying to kill her had been in the building all the time.

"You killed Miss Howard," Lucy spoke up. The girl had courage, Jess had to give her that. Although maybe calling attention to herself at such a time was a little foolhardy. "We saw you."

Lally inclined his head at Lucy and Jaden. Jess's throat was suddenly tight with fear as he lifted his gun and took careful aim at Lucy, mouthing *"Bang."* She heard the girl suck in air, and with a quick sidestep she moved between them. Lally lowered the gun a fraction. Jess felt her knees sag.

"I saw you too, Red. I have to give you credit, you were hard to find. If I hadn't been keeping a watch on Allison's accounts to see if the cops had started looking for her, I don't think I ever would have caught up to you, although I was searching. But when I saw somebody kept getting free doughnuts, I had a feeling it had to be you. And I was right."

Jess looked at Mr. Dunn. Maybe there was another way to get them off this cliff alive. If she could talk them into a more populated area, she would. "Allison had compiled an extremely damning dossier on Rob Phillips. I'm assuming she put it together during preparations for his trial. It concerns the murders of four young women, and it's vitally important that the authorities get it. If you'll take me to a computer, I can access it for you."

Mr. Dunn laughed. "Nice try, Ms. Ford. But I don't need you to access it for me. I know all about it. It seems Ms. Howard was playing devil's advocate, trying to see what prosecutors might dig up on Phillips in preparation for his trial. And did she come up with some stuff! I was pretty impressed with her work when I saw it, I don't mind telling you. Prosecutors never did find any of it. Nobody ever has. The problem was what Ms. Howard did with the information once she put it together. What do you *think* she did, Ms. Ford? Tell somebody in the firm about it, maybe? Keep

quiet and see if the prosecutors put it together? No, she decided to use it to enrich
herself. She took that information and used
it to blackmail one of our clients. She sent
a copy of everything she'd put together to
Senator Phillips, along with a demand to be
paid three million dollars to keep her mouth
shut. You see how reprehensible that was?
Senator Phillips came straight to me and
told me about the information and that he
was being blackmailed. Of course, at the
time we didn't have the slightest inkling
who was doing it. But we managed to trace
it back to Ms. Howard. I hope I don't have
to tell you that I was outraged. What she
did was one of the worst breaches of legal
ethics I've ever heard of in my life. It was a
complete violation of attorney/client privilege. It was sleazy, Ms. Ford, and under-
handed and low, and totally unworthy of
our distinguished firm. Senator Phillips left
it in my hands to deal with, so I did. We
paid Ms. Howard the money she wanted to
shut her up, and then I asked Mr. Lally
here to rid us of the stain on our reputation." He looked at Lally. "You did a good
job, too. You killed her, and you did it in
such a way that nobody except these three

people here have even realized she's dead. Then you got our money back for us." He looked back at Jess. "It was an honor killing, Ms. Ford, plain and simple. I'm proud of it, not ashamed."

Jess's mind boggled. "But Rob Phillips—"

"Is our client," Mr. Dunn said firmly.

Jess stared at him in disbelief. A spurt of anger took the edge off her fear. "If we're talking about breaching legal ethics, how does threatening Tiffany Higgs's son to get her to recant a rape allegation you knew was true fit with that?"

"Senator Phillips was unhappy with us because of what Ms. Howard did, and rightly so. What it took to make him happy was to get his son acquitted, so we did what we had to do to make that happen. We owed him that. We did threaten Ms. Higgs's son, yes, but only because she wouldn't take a payoff. But we were going to see that she got a nice sum of money, too."

"Except then she threatened to go to the media about what we'd made her do," Lally said. "I don't mind telling you, that made me a little upset."

"So you killed her." Jess's voice was soft. A cold, hard knot had formed in her chest, and she kept darting quick little glances around to see if she could come up with a way out. So far, nothing had occurred to her. Except her pepper spray.

She didn't like her odds.

"You do what you got to do." The way Lally said it made it a confirmation.

"So Allison's dead, Tiffany's dead, but Rob Phillips is not only alive but free and able to go on his merry way?"

Mr. Dunn said, "We owe our loyalty to our clients."

Jess thought of her team, and her stomach twisted into a pretzel. "I can't believe Pearse was a party to this."

"He's not high level enough. No, Ms. Ford, when it comes to Ellis Hayes, the buck stops here. It was only me, with Mr. Lally's—or, as Ms. Howard knew him, Greg Abernathy's—able assistance."

Suddenly Jess thought she saw something moving in the trees. Her throat constricted. Her blood seemed to freeze. Her imagination, or . . . ?

"Drop your weapons! Federal agents!"

The roar belonged to Mark. What seemed like a battalion of agents rushed from the woods. "Drop your weapons!"

As quick as that, a hand closed around Jess's arm and she was yanked almost off her feet. Lally pulled her in front of him, imprisoning her with an arm locked around her waist. With a gasp of horror, she felt the hard jab of a gun against her temple. Terror quickened her breathing, made her heart race.

"Back off, Ryan," he yelled. "Or I'll kill her."

Jess saw Mark then. Flanked by other agents in firing stance, he was maybe twenty feet away, with his gun aimed at Lally.

"Drop it, Lally," Mark ordered again.

Lally laughed and started backing toward the cliff edge, dragging Jess with him. Suddenly she saw his only possible way out: a leap into the Potomac's dark waters. Would he take her with him? Her legs turned to jelly at the thought.

Lucy and Jaden had already been surrounded by agents. They were on the ground, looking at her with horror. Mark was advancing steadily, keeping pace with Lally's progress, but not getting any closer. His gun was aimed at Lally's head. But Jess knew him. With Lally's gun at her temple, he wouldn't take the chance unless he had absolutely no other option.

She risked a quick glance to the side. Out of her peripheral vision she saw that the cliff edge was maybe a yard away. He *was* going over the edge. Jess's heart pounded. Her breathing came fast and shallow. Her pulse rate shot sky high.

"Let her go, Lally." Mark's voice had gone soft and dangerous.

Suddenly Lally shoved her violently away from him. Tumbling to the ground, Jess caught just a blur of movement behind her. She thought he was going over the edge in a low, fast dive—and then the night shattered around her as gunfire exploded all over the place.

Jess screamed and flattened herself on the grass.

Seconds later Mark dropped to his knees beside her. Scrambling up, she cast herself against him.

"Jesus Christ, you took ten years off my

life tonight. Are you all right?" He held her away from him, looking her over with fear shining from his eyes.

"I'm fine." Clutching the lapels of his suit jacket, she let her forehead drop to rest against his chest, and this time his arms came tight around her. Dark shapes hustled all around. Jess smelled gunpowder, and something else that she reluctantly identified as blood. The girls, she saw, were surrounded by agents, and Jaden's leg was being looked at.

Two bodies were sprawled on the ground.

"What happened?" She was surprised to find she was trembling.

"Lally tried to go over the cliff. Dunn shot him. We shot Dunn. It's all over."

"Oh, my God." For a moment all Jess could do was breathe. Then she lifted her head to look at him. "How did you find us?"

"Biggest damned piece of luck in the world. I had all the security camera tapes around that Quik-Stop pulled, and the one watching the ATM across the street caught a man throwing two unconscious girls into the trunk of a car. Got the car's license plate number from the tape, tracked the car down through its GPS system. When its current location came through, I started believing in miracles."

Jess smiled at him and slid her arms around his neck. "See, *me*, I believed in you."

Then she kissed him.

CHAPTER THIRTY-TWO

By Monday, life had pretty much settled down again. Mark and Jess were still together, still happily taking things one day at a time. Since Grace had broken up with Ron and moved back into the apartment, Mark and Jess were living in his house in Dale City, along with Clementine, who was now officially Jess's cat, and Zoey, Taylor's cat. The two cats were not nearly as friendly as Jess would have liked, but they would, Jess felt, one day learn to get along.

Lucy had been taken in by Judy, who was so grateful for the shovel blow that had rescued Jess that she vowed she already loved the girl like a daughter. Jaden had been reunited with her brother, Jax, and both girls had had their sentences reduced to time served, through the services of a very good lawyer.

Ellis Hayes had acquired a new managing partner: one Thomas Boone.

The bodies of Allison and Tiffany had been discovered buried in a flower garden at Frog Hill. The new graves had been hidden beneath lots of mulch.

An investigation was scheduled to be launched into abuse at Shelter House, triggered by complaints by Lucy and Jaden, which were reinforced by statements given by the other girls.

And Leonard Cowan's death had officially been ruled a suicide.

So all was well—hunky-dory, actually—in Jess's world. Except for one thing.

The murders committed by Rob Phillips, which Allison had uncovered, could not, Jess felt, just be forgotten about. But that presented a dilemma, which was why she brought the matter up in her team's regular 8:30 a.m. meeting.

"Can't do shit," Andrew opined cheerfully.

"You are so crude," Hayley told him. "And so wrong." Then she looked at Jess. "I'm with you. I think we have to do something about this."

Jess looked at Pearse, who shook his head.

"You still don't get it, either of you. We're Phillips's lawyers. We're the only ones who know what he's done. The prosecutors didn't find this information. Only Allison did, and now we know it, too. But we can't tell anyone. To do so would be unethical. Whoever broke attorney/client privilege in that fashion could be disbarred. We're like the confessional, bound to keep secret whatever is revealed to us. Because our loyalty is, and must be, to our clients."

Jess and Hayley exchanged glances. The sad thing was, they knew Pearse was right. The horrible thing was, that meant their lips had to be forever sealed.

Except that Jess had already told Mark. Which, as he was still kind-of, sort-of consulting for Ellis Hayes, didn't really count as going outside the firm. She didn't think.

Feeling horrible about the whole thing, Jess went to her office and got to work.

And resolutely ignored the presence she could still feel in the room.

Probably she would get used to it.

If not, there was always exorcism to fall back on.

CHAPTER THIRTY-THREE

One week later, Rob Phillips jogged along the C&O Towpath in Georgetown. It was near dusk, and the path was largely deserted. Dustin Yamaguchi watched him from a comfortable distance. And readied the high-powered rifle that was one of the primary tools of his trade. When the angle was precisely right, he pulled the trigger. Phillips dropped in midstride. There wasn't even a *bang*.

Then Gooch packed up his rifle and left.

See, the thing is, you do bad things

to people, it's gonna come back and bite you in the ass. Some people call it karma; others, justice.